PATRIOTS

Book One

Cover Design by Mary Graw & Alaina Garren
Cover Illustrations by Caroline Rabic

www.patriotsthenovel.com

ISBN 9781549891809 (KDP pbk)
ISBN 9780692963937 (IS pbk)

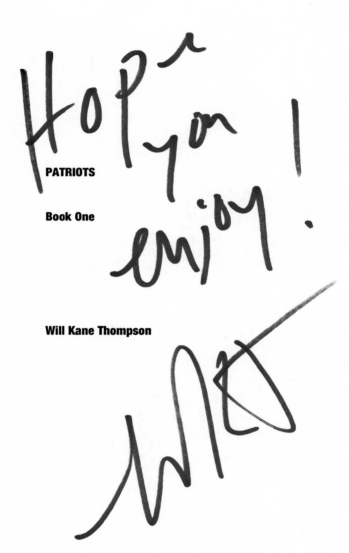

PATRIOTS

Book One

Will Kane Thompson

To all you patriots out there …

… you know, the *real* ones.

Friday

October, 21ˢᵗ

2:16 AM

Skin was the thing that owned us tonight. Demanded the full attention of our eyes. Rushed that merciless yearning to our groins. Young skin. Perfect skin. Skin warmed daily by the sun even in fall. Skin smooth and firm over muscles and the lowest of body fat worked out daily in the gym or at beach volleyball or ocean kayaking or on long campus runs. Guys in tank tops or with their shirts yanked off and tucked into the backs of their pants. Girls in crop tops and spaghetti strings and breasts moving freely to the beats under sheer tops. The strobe lights tantalizing us by beating these fleeting images of it into our brains and in the dark spots in between still the glow bracelets and occasional streaks of neon body paint highlighting it. Skin moist with dancing, but who cared? Sweat that didn't smell. The intense music carrying us on and forward to more and more and more.

The party was the best of the year, so far. People would be talking about it for weeks to come. Right here and now in this moment dancing together it felt like the culmination of so much we'd so longed for and so often fought for. It was what we needed now with all the problems of this semester. What college should have been, not what it was when we got here. It was all the things we weren't supposed to think about growing up and college was supposed to finally give to us. Like under the super-strict eyes of my parents who never wanted to even admit that sex existed and my stupid school that preached we should just wait for marriage. God, I *needed* this. This is what I came here hoping for. To be with these people who were like me, who got it, who wanted the same things. This. This was Freedom. Freedom from parents and rules and the things we were supposed to be doing, the way we were supposed to be living our lives. Freedom from the trespass of the outside world trying to come onto our campus with problems that weren't ours, but that so many of us were succumbing to and obsessing over. Freedom from that outside world that seemed to be going slowly, but lately more and more quickly, mad. Freedom to reach over and touch the skin of the one dancing near us even though they were a stranger before just now.

How crazy was it that something without mind or soul could drive us so wild and control us so? The way a shoulder curved around and into a bicep. The hint of a nipple under fabric. The smooth or jagged ravines that cut through the perfect set of abs. The sly little curves of a flirtatious smile. These were just lines, just shapes, just colors and even at that just the slightest variations from that which we found gross. How could they control our emotions and desires and every thought? The small of a girl's back or a boy's just before it traces down below the low-sitting pants or skirt and into the barely-hidden valley of their ass. And around the front, those happy trail, vertical or curvy-v-shaped muscles that drew your eyes down and down below the waistline to that sacred place: the place you'd only get to see if you were special. If you made it tonight.

And the pressure of that. In the weeks that we'd be talking about this party—who did you get, fuck, pull down the pants of to follow the path of those happy trail muscles and smalls of backs to secret gardens to spend some quality time there and work all your tricks?—that would be the topic of conversation, despite all the problems, and our answers, real, or embellished, or completely imaginary, would be the cards we could play in the most political game of all: popularity. So the pressure was on. And nothing was more important than the skin.

We'd have to be careful, of course. There were dangers there, even in the most pure- and innocent-looking of us. But we had protection, didn't we? And, anyway, that was for later. For now, we should enjoy this moment. All of us here dancing together. The DJ was on top of his game and worth every dollar they must have paid him. Surely, there were still others outside dying to get in. But we were here. We'd made it. And with the strobes and the beat and all of us moving together with them in this party packed wall-to-wall with this sea of college students we looked out over it felt—and maybe it was all the booze or the drugs—but it felt as if we were one. We—many of us strangers before, but now intimate, half-naked together—were dancing together as one.

The bookbag was an annoyance. What drunk asshole left his bookbag in the middle of the dance floor? We kept dancing despite it. I think I kicked it once—angry at it. The beats and the strobes continued on, but then one was different. One beat was more of a pop. To most, distant and unnoticeable; but to some, very loud; and to a few, quieting. Like suddenly and with pain we'd lost our hearing to a ringing. And with the pop one of the flashes of the strobes seemed different. Different color, different intensity. Suddenly confusion seemed all around, but just right here, just near the strange pop and flash. Was it the drugs? What was happening? Some students were lying on the floor now. Why the fuck? Like a big hole in the center of the dancing mass. And there was a smell in the air different from the cotton candy smell you'd expect from a fog machine. And pains suddenly noticeable all over. Pains I'd never felt before. And confusion and some people suddenly rushing around us and no longer as one.

And then I saw her at my feet. I think I slipped on her blood. She was choking and as she choked blood came out from a deep hole in the right side of her throat and more from around her collarbone and the whole right side of her face, half-hidden under the hand she held it with, was a bright red and seemed to have these, like, bubbles of clear flesh on it. I knelt down to her even though it hurt so bad to do so. Why was I in so much pain? Why was it so hard to catch my breath after the pop and had it felt like some huge guy had slammed into me at full speed when no one had? Why did the skin of the whole right side of my body seem to singe with a million little stings of pain as I reached out to touch her arm? I wanted to help her. I don't know why I thought touching her arm would do that. But as I touched it, it jolted, and there, underneath where her hand had been holding it, sticking out of her cheekbone was what seemed like a piece of metal. Did something explode? One of the huge speakers or something? What the fuck just happened? What did I take? I thought it was just Molly. Jesus, was it laced with something? I feel faint now. I need to rest here a minute. Oh. My head's on this girl's tummy now. When did that happen? She's breathing up and down. Her skin is so soft. It's pleasant here.

Later, we'd learn nine of us died right now. Two more, of the sixteen critically injured, would be dying soon. One of those two would be me. In a few more hours.

In less than half that time, I'd wake up in a hospital and it'd all be explained to me. I hadn't really felt it—not like I would have thought—but a jagged piece of metal had ripped through my liver and something smaller, maybe a nail, through my spleen. I was bleeding more within than without. They needed to put me under and operate immediately. My parents weren't there. I was alone and I never wanted them so badly in my life. My life. She told me she wasn't going to lie to me, the doctor. She said things were serious. That my chances were bad. What?! What was she saying?! I was 18 years old! I just got here! Death wasn't ... *What*?! No. I wasn't going to *die*. God wouldn't do that. She said she'd tell the anesthesiologist to wait a few more minutes if I wanted to call my parents to ... to *what*? Call my mom, my dad? Wake them up to tell them ... what? That this could be *goodbye*? *No*. That couldn't be how this would end. God, You wouldn't? ... You *wouldn't*. I'd ask for the anesthesia and to get on with it. I'd have faith. I'd know I'd see my mom again, my dad. Everyone that mattered. I'd *know* it. I *had* to know it. Because if that wasn't true ... then why did any of it matter?

But I didn't know all of that yet.

For now, a guy above me is yelling with all the air he's got, his voice squealing, unmanly. "Cut the music! Cut the music!" But it didn't cut. The music wasn't stopping, nor the pulse of the strobes. And most of us were still dancing. Especially the further and further out I looked. Legs moving all around me to the beat. Still dancing. Still as one.

They must not have heard, must not have seen.

They didn't even notice.

3 Days Earlier

Tuesday

October, 18th

9:46 AM

Campus was a paradise. But lately some seemed intent on ruining that. Florida South Coast University was an oasis surrounded on most sides by thousands of square miles of the parks and preserves that make up what's left of the Everglades, and on its southwestern border by Chokoloskee Bay, the Ten Thousand Islands, and the Gulf. The university was formed when its conglomerate of wealthy donors purchased Plantation Island and much of the bayfront land adjacent it in the 40s, later acquiring Chokoloskee Island and eventually snagging back Lumber and Rabbit Keys from the hands of those intent on preserving them for the national park, and changing the names of these two to Sand Tiger Key in the 60s to fit with the school's new mascot.

A lot of colleges out there didn't take much pride in a beautiful campus, but FSCU was different. The grounds crews worked tirelessly to keep the greens manicured, the palms trimmed, the schedule of blooming flowers staggered throughout the year, despite campus being beaten up every so often throughout its history by hurricanes. The architecture was rooted in the Spanish Renaissance of Old Florida, but with plenty of modern, environmentally conscious design too. Courtyards and fountains and bench setups and nooks and crannies with statues from art students were numerous for reading or contemplating the great questions of existence or playing Frisbee golf. Miami was an hour and a half drive east, but despite all their big plans students actually went there very seldom. Naples was a 45-minute drive northwest, but it might as well have been three times that for how little most students wanted to go there or, more importantly, for how much they hated it when anyone from there or any of the little towns or patches of suburbia or camping grounds dotted throughout these woods and wetlands came and infested their private world. This was their world and they didn't want any outsiders—old people, rednecks, biker gang losers, or children—coming in and messing it up. But now, some of their own were messing it up.

At the heart of their oasis lay the vast lawn of The Campus Commons, and this was where the mess started. The Commons were the entryway between campus proper and the small, very small, town that serviced it with bars and bookstores and coffee houses. About half of FSCU's 29,000 students lived "off campus" in and around the town, which meant they'd trek their way through The Commons several times a day to get where they needed to go. And, for many, this morning was business as usual.

The sun beat down on a hive of students pushing their way to class, to food, to practice or home for more sleep after dreaded 8 AM lectures. But clogging the main arteries of these sidewalk thoroughfares was a bit of mayhem caused by two distinct groups that set up camp, some literally, on either side of the chokepoint of passing students to solicit or soapbox stump or just put in their required service hours.

The latter, on one side, were mostly fraternity and sorority kids whom, after a few particularly egregious incidents, the Administration decided to force to do so many good deeds a year. And there were also a few true believers mixed in with them. Student Dems and Reps, the handful of Federalist Society members and whatnot. They all had their different Get Out The Vote tables, banners, fliers and clipboards. Up until last week, the GOTVers were trying to get every student they could (or at least those of their kind) to register before the deadline. Now there was vote-by-mail and early voting info and reminders of the date and polling places and petitions for and against online voting and fliers and stickers and buttons for every conceivable subcategory of identity politics. But, of course, the biggest issue of all was the war. And there was no forgetting that—it was being yelled at them from bullhorns across the sidewalk.

Here, on the other side, were the Occupy Campusers. They'd been there about three weeks now. But compared to the Occupy Wall Street movement that happened when these kids were still in middle school, this was pretty lighthearted. Their tents were set up and spray-painted with every symbol from peace to anarchy. Their protest signs and banners and face paint and t-shirts covered the gauntlet of political minefields too. But even so, all but the most hardcore of them would still go to class, walk back to their apartments for a shower and change of clothes or a good night's sleep—and it wasn't like there weren't plenty of soda bottles mixed with booze or one-hitters or sneak-a-tokes disguised as pens or highlighters or cigarettes snuck and toked.

And it was among these tents that the well-padded belly of a University Police Officer meandered through with a face of slight disgust above it taking in another day of the filth a liberal university president's leeway had wrought on this fine lawn. His eyes scanned the students for any of those illegal soda bottles or marijuana paraphernalia or other illicits. But then they were yanked to the site of one of the tents, which was moving in a certain rhythmic fashion. He walked over. His ears confirmed his suspicions with faint sounds of grunts and breaths that could only be from one thing. He paused and listened to the sounds for a little while. Then he pulled his ridiculously large flashlight out of its holster, gave the side of the tent a few good whacks, and with the cockiness of needing to do little more than this, cleared his thick throat.

A voice from inside the tent shot back, "What the fuck?!"

"Campus Police!" he said with all his authority.

After some more grunting and shuffling the long arched zipper of the tent unzipped halfway, and out of the hole popped a head of shaggy, dirty blond hair. This was Tristan.

Tristan looked up at the cop and knew him as soon as his eyes adjusted to the sun behind the douchebag's head. It was "Sergeant Chubs," the guy who was always showing up at parties and taking his sweet time talking with the pretty girls before they could rush away at the sight of his entrance. Chubs deluded himself into thinking the young girls liked him, blind to the fact that they were clearly being as nice as they could be so as not to get arrested for underage drinking. Then, when he'd had his fill or whatever, Chubs would suddenly announce that the party was over and for everyone to go home. The nickname was for the obvious reason and for the chubbies some thought they saw him get when talking to these girls.

"Morning Officer," Tristan said with a voice that gave precisely two shits.

"The University gave you people permission to voice your freedoms of speech out here, not … engage in public," he made a lewd gesture with the length of his flashlight through a couple of circled fat fingers. Tristan had to close his eyes for a second in disgust for this man's still-stuck-in-middle-school loserdom. It was clear to everyone who had met the fool that he had grown up miserably friendless and was now using his badge, his uniform, and his dripping-with-psychological-maladies choice of a campus cop post to get back what he could of a sense of worth that never matured from the needs of a 5th grader.

But Tristan knew what he had to do, the game he should play right now—you had to choose your battles.

"Sorry, Officer. Just getting in some morning pushups. Keeping up my physique," and gave a sly, *we're friends, right?*, smile, which he hated every millisecond of having to produce.

Chubs grunted an "uh-huh," re-holstered his flashlight and continued on his wandering beat.

Tristan sneered at the back of him, then took a moment to look around at his friends and fellow protestors. He was proud of them. More and more people were starting to get it. But there was still so much to do—and so many seemingly insurmountable obstacles in their way. And, then too, far more concerning, so many people who still didn't get it—who needed to be shaken awake.

But first, Tristan needed to finish what he started. His messy head re-submerged into the tent. The arch re-zipped shut. There was some giggling inside. And then the tent resumed its rhythmic movement.

9:57 AM

Even the sun was becoming unbearable, even this early in the day, because they'd been at it so long. But still, Ryan shouted,

"Again!"

And his dead-tired, but loyal platoon of twenty-three ROTC students, weighted down with overstuffed backpacks, attacked the steps of the track stadium bleachers once more with what little was left to give of their quads, calves, hamstrings, glutes, and hearts.

Ryan ran with them, of course, always. These were his cadets and he knew how much they probably hated him right now. But he needed them to be ready. And he needed himself to be ready. The war was clearly coming; there was no questioning that anymore for Ryan. He had had a man-to-man with FSCU's Professor of Military Leadership, Lieutenant Colonel Bill Golding, who after two tours in Iraq, one in Afghanistan and some key advisor placements in some of our lesser-known or discussed "operations" of late, still very much had his ear to the reserved talks going on amongst the bureaucrats of the US Military. The drumbeats to war were not just political and pundit pounding—they were being beaten out far from civilian earshot in ships being repositioned, munitions being stockpiled, logistics taking shape. "The seeds of this war are all planted." Professor Golding had said. "Like a million little bombs just waiting to be lit."

The war was coming and Ryan and his cadets would be graduating right into the shit of it. A year and a half from commencement on The Commons, Ryan knew he would be leading a platoon of 40 men—and not a platoon that in three more minutes would hit the gym lockers, pull off their sweaty IPFUs (Army-green "ARMY" t-shirts and the super-short "silkies" that Tracy always wanted Ryan to wear to bed, clean ones, of course, which, when feeling frisky, Ryan sometimes obliged) and turn back into the lazy days of college life—but men who didn't know if they would ever make it home, but if they did, knew for certain they would never be the innocent youth they once were again.

They reached the top and bent over for air. If only they had water there too.

Ryan looked over his crew, proud of them. Then he stepped over to look out at the handful of students on the track field who were tossing a football, maybe waiting to start a game of pickup. He knew his crew would rather be out there. He would too.

He checked his watch. Not 10:00 yet. "Come on guys, one more." And started toward the steps.

He could hear the thoughts behind him. No one moved.

"Ryan, come on bro. Enough's enough, huh?"

Are you fucking kidding me?! That was Scotty. His fucking Platoon Sergeant. Ryan was fucking Platoon Leader and this asshole just whipped out his dick and took a piss on Chain of Command like it was nothing! *Like we were those cubicle-bound fucks down there tossing a football!*

Ryan stepped over and got in Scotty's face. He was about to lose his shit, but he felt it coming and checked himself. Ryan knew he had serious anger issues. ROTC Command knew, and it's why Ryan, as a senior, wasn't higher up in the Battalion Command. And he knew where Scotty and half his guys' minds were: they were also his fraternity brothers and had shit to do for the party Thursday. It was a huge deal for everyone in the House. A year ago they had been put on probation by the University for some alleged hazing and underage drinking incidents. The hazing evidence couldn't be substantiated though—the Fraternity's national headquarters had hired a big Florida law firm for the proceedings and that helped a lot. So they weren't suspended, only on probation, and told they couldn't have any events with alcohol for a year. Probation ended this week and Thursday was going to be their comeback party. On top of that, the following weekend would be filled with Halloween madness, probably at least three days of partying for that, and most people were racking their brains to plan multiple costumes for the different events. There was a lot going on, a lot on their minds. Ryan knew Scotty had to drive over to Miami today to pick up the inflatable waterslide that was going out one of the back, second-floor windows of the House. He calmed himself down and decided to address his cadets rather than his asshole "friend"/"brother"/Platoon Sergeant.

Still working for air himself, "You guys know shit's about to get real for us." There were three girls in the platoon, but everyone just said "guys," the girls too, even though they'd had that conclusionless discussion on whether that was a gender-neutral term. "Yeah, we've got parties to plan or what-the-fuck-ever, but all that's about to end real soon. Real fucking soon. Even for you freshmen. This war gets going, it's not ending for a long fuckin' time. This is the big one. The one that stirs everything up. You graduate in three more years, yeah? That's probably just about the time some insurgency that could give a Goddamn about the 'Rules of War' we get in class is gonna be fucking us over with IEDs and suicide kids. The least we can do, the abso-fucking-lute *least*, is be in the best shape of our lives, right? I'm goin' again. You can come or not."

And Ryan headed back down the steps. One by one, his platoon followed. Even Scotty, who was proud of his boy for holding back that deadly temper of his.

But, as Ryan descended the steps, his anger grew. Why did he have to tell them this? How was this fucking news to them? *Goddamnit*, they needed to *wake the hell up*!

9:59 AM

Kristi placed the flowers on the altar table next to the framed photo of the 13-year-old girl who was smiling big in her braces. She looked back to Luke to see if he approved. He seemed to. He handed her a candle from the bag and took out the second one for himself. They each placed a candle near the photo and Luke struck a match and lit them both.

"I think it's nice," said Kristi.

Luke gave a smile so subtle and so imprisoned with pain that probably she only saw it because, by now, she knew his face so well.

It had been hard lately for Kristi with Luke. It had seemed to her that after they decided to get married, he started backing away. But she'd also had to admit to herself that maybe she was the one backing away and that he was only responding to that. Luke's relationships with the Lord and the Church were more strict than hers. More old school. More like her father's. She had started to fear whether this was really what God wanted: for them to be together. But it wasn't just that. Luke really was different lately. Not the man she first met and fell in love with.

But this was nice. Being here with him for his sister's anniversary. He had held her hand when they left the store with the candles. He was opening up again, letting her in.

Luke went to his bookbag and brought out his Bible. It was peaceful being in the empty church. Just the two of them and this special moment.

He opened his nearly falling-apart Bible, notes stuffed in different pages, his firm block handwriting in many of the margins. She'd bought him a new one, but he didn't use it. She could tell he was ready to begin. She bowed her head. He spoke:

"'Precious in the sight of the Lord is the death of His saints.'"

Kristi couldn't help but look up. The quote he'd found was so lovely and his voice so tender, she needed to see his face along with it.

"'Happy are those whose way is blameless, who walk in the law of the Lord. Happy are those who keep His decrees, who seek Him with their whole heart.'"

His voice cracked. She'd never heard that. He took a pause and then—she couldn't be certain she heard it; it was as subtle as the smile before—but when he continued she thought she heard a hint of anger.

"'Who also do no wrong, but walk in His ways.'"

He closed his eyes, but she couldn't do the same. She needed to see this side of him she'd never seen. She remained there with him, silent, until he opened his eyes and looked up. And his eyes were glossy, then so were hers. They stayed like that for some time. She, watching him, having longed for more of his depths. He, eyes unmoved from his sister and all they had lost.

10:01 AM

"Again!"

Ryan shouted and again they ascended the steps. But this time Ryan noticed the backpack of a freshman, which wasn't even an army pack, but a Jansport, but worse was how lightly it bounced as he ran. Ryan reached over and grabbed the pack, nearly yanking the kid backwards down the steps and stopping the whole platoon halfway up the bleachers as he did.

"What the fuck is this, Freshman?!"

The pack was light as hell. Ryan unzipped it and pulled out a hoodie and a beach towel. He looked at the kid in disbelief.

"Fifty pounds! Fifty fucking pounds, Freshman!"

The kid looked so scared of him Ryan had to turn his attention to the rest of his cadre.

"Goddammit, you guys, when the hell are you going to get it?! You think this—" he threw out his arms at the idyllic campus before them, the guys leisurely tossing the football "—is how the people planning to kill us are training? You think this is how the poor fucks you'll be leading into battle one day will train in their boot camps after they're picked up at some Walmart in Texas and told how great it's gonna be? What would happen at Fort Bragg if some dickwad stuffed his fifty-pound pack with a hoodie and a beach towel?

"Have you been watching these ISIS fucks? Not to mention what's left of al-Qaeda's fucking fan club resurging around the globe?"

"Come on, Ry," said Bret, a junior and a fuckup, "our pansy-ass leaders ain't gonna do fuck-all with this war talk. And you kidding us with al-Qaeda still? They're over there in their caves jerking each other off because they can't see any tits and ass under all those damn clothes they make their bitches wear. Fucking Osama, when they capped his ass, was mid-stroke, masturbating to old-school porn videos!"

Some in the group laughed as Bret started jerking an impressively large air-dick as he continued with, "Ooooh, I'm Osama. I'm a Muslim fanatic, but damn, these infidel tits looks so gooooood. Ahhhh!" He ended in mock ecstasy as now most of the platoon was laughing.

But not Scotty, who knew that comment hit home on Ryan hard. He looked at Ryan and took a couple steps up the bleachers to position himself incase Ryan attacked.

But Ryan thought about duty, the platoon, the Code of Honor, and controlled his rage again. He turned away from Masturbating Osama to help check his emotions—but then he saw the thing that pushed him over the edge.

The Freshman was laughing too.

"You think this is funny, Freshman?" Ryan asked, charging the kid.

"Ryan, I'm sorry man."

"You're 'sorry man?' *Sorry man!* Is that what you're gonna tell your buddy in some fucking desert when he takes two in the chest because you weren't willing to do the simplest fucking thing your country asks of you?!"

Scotty yanked him back from the half-inch that remained between Ryan's face and the kid's, who looked as if he could almost cry. And now Scotty got in Ryan's face, but with a whisper.

"Calm the fuck down. The kid made a mistake. We'll put it in his fucking file, but right now, get your fucking issues in check."

Ryan looked out and took a deep breath. Scotty was wrong. It wasn't his anger. It was his duty. But he could see in the faces of his peers and friends this wasn't a battle he was going to win.

"Platoon dismissed," he said and started back down the steps toward the gym.

The rest of the crew started down too. Scotty put his hand on Freshman's back as they walked. "He just wants to help you, little man. And he's been through some shit you don't know about, okay?"

The Freshman nodded and they both looked at Ryan walking off ahead of them.

"He'll never forgive life for not letting him be the one to cap Osama," Scotty said. "He's wanted that since he was five."

10:07 AM

Luke had stood there for maybe a minute staring at his sister and Kristi had given him his time. She wasn't really sure what else he planned to do, but as his face seemed to show his thoughts coming back from wherever it was in his memories, his soul, he had gone to just now, she could see that he hadn't really planned anything else. His eyes did that thing where they sort of noticed her, but didn't acknowledge it. He was coming back to reality and feeling a bit uncomfortable with it, she thought.

She bowed her head again to give him his privacy, but it was too late. He sort of nodded to himself and walked toward the candles like he was about to blow them out.

"Wait," Kristi said. He stopped and looked at her. Kristi struggled for her words, but found them. "Talk to her. She's watching, I know. Grateful. Thankful for you." She smiled and could feel his resistance. "I can leave if you want to be alone."

She started toward the altar steps, but to her surprise was stopped by:

"No," Luke said holding out his hand for her to come back. She came back and took his hand in both of hers, so happy for it. And he looked again to his big sister.

It took a little. His lips trying out some false starts before he found the words he wanted to voice. But he finally found some.

"I miss you, Sis."

He squeezed her hands tighter.

"Thank you. Again. For … always being there for me. You were the best …."

He stopped himself. Kristi could tell he wanted his words to be better. He kept searching. Then,

"Without you it … life wouldn't have had its good moments."

That line hit Kristi with an aching for him, his childhood.

"Ten years today we lost you. And I can't believe it. Ten years this world hasn't had you to bring it joy … You were too good for this world—" repeating something he'd heard too many times, but still it brought comfort "—so God had to take you back."

The first tear fell from his eyes, but with it other, unexpected emotions seemed to be battling behind the contours of his face: for a half-second anger, for another back to immense sadness, and for another nausea. His hand yanked away from hers and he went to the first row of cushioned chairs to sit as if he had to, as if he might hit the floor otherwise, and buried his contorted face in his hands.

She rushed over to sit by him and hold him. She didn't know what to do. She kissed the back of his bent shoulders. He was really crying now. The tear before was the first she'd ever seen from him and now this. It was so strange: she was grateful for the emotion from him, finally, grateful to be let in, but scared and heartbroken for him. What was happening?

Then, Kristi could barely make out the words, clearly not meant for her ears: "I'm so sorry I failed you."

Kristi's stomach dropped in anguish for him. She had feared before with some of the things he said about his sister that somehow he blamed himself for her death and this was confirmation of it.

"No, babe. No. You were just a child. There was nothing you could do. The doctors couldn't even—"

"*No*."

And it was the harshest he'd ever spoken to her. He twisted up and looked at her with, she hated to think it, but it really did seem like hatred.

"*I know* how she died."

The tone was so possessive, and rightly so, of course. This was his life, his memory, his sister, his pain. Kristi hadn't been there. But still, the tone of his voice just had this power of its own that forced her away, out of his head, his memories, his inner life—expelling her from what was his and his alone.

But then, as if some part of his brain reminded him of everything Kristi had done for him and was grateful for her, his voice seemed to shed some of that anger, but only some.

"God told me. He told me why. And I will *never* forgive them."

Kristi reached over and took his hands again. He accepted her hands holding his. And they sat there for a while, slowly regaining their normal breaths, trying to calm the unstabilized beatings in their chests, and Kristi desperate to understand what she knew he was not likely to ever tell her.

10:16 AM

Tristan was finally done enjoying his post-orgasm sleepy high and thinking about getting his day started. And anyway, it was getting hot in the tent. He reached up and unzipped the door the whole way and let in the breeze and the world around them.

Kyle startled out of his sleepiness with, "Uhm, still naked, thanks. You too."

Tristan looked down at himself. "Oh." He cupped off the condom and tossed it in the corner, found his balled up shorts and pulled them on, then climbed out of the tent and stood up to a full tall-as-he-could-stretch stretch to welcome and enjoy the day.

His various tats shown in the sun, especially the big one Kyle hated above his heart (more, even, it seemed to Tristan, than the scars so near Kyle's own), and almost some of his lesser-seen tats below the curvy-v-shaped muscles of his lower stomach as his waist slimmed even more than usual in the stretch and his shorts began to fall. But he relaxed his body and dropped his arms to grab them up in time.

"No. Uh-uh. Not yet. Get back here." Kyle, naked in the tent, had his arm lifted up to Tristan, his eyes squinting against the sun. "Get back here, pleeeeeeaaassse."

Tristan had to laugh a little. He got down on all fours and crawled back into the tent and kissed Kyle's lips. "What?"

"Just a little bit longer. Then, I promise, you can go be Mr. Protest Man."

Kyle was so freaking adorable right now, Tristan decided to give him this. He flipped around and into Kyle's snuggle, lying on his side and looking out as Kyle, ironically for their sizes, big-spooned him, his arm wrapping gently around Tristan's stomach, his hand holding Tristan's chest, feeling his heartbeat.

Tristan was glad he'd found Kyle. He liked this one. A lot. And he felt really happy this morning looking out at the tent roofs and signs and passing legs of his fellow "radicals." He could hear one of his friends on the bullhorn off in the distance. She must have been turned the opposite direction because Tristan could only make out a few words here and there about the war and, more dreaded by some, the draft. It brought him some peace. People were finally starting to get it.

Tristan had "gotten it" for years now. High school had been the most frustrating for him. He couldn't understand how his generation could be so … impotent. How kids his own age could talk about all the shit going down in the world and like all the posts about it and say they cared so much, but actually *do* so little. How could they just go about their lives like democracy was real, like a few sporadic posts or tweets or protests would make any difference, like God, the eyes of the world, or the Social Network cared about them and every little bullshit thing in their lives, like the people really in charge didn't even exist? College had gotten a little better, until he realized it, too, was all just talk and clubs and nothing with consequence, impact. Still no one was actually *doing* anything. He kind of hated his own generation for this. At first, he'd had this sort of nostalgia for the generation that was young in the 60s and 70s, but then, the more he read about them, the more he felt maybe he'd over-idealized them. A lot of people on the "Radical Left" back then seemed like outright fools to Tristan as he read about them now, but still, at least they had *done* something. Action. Some of them, at least. Even if it was blowing up empty buildings. Talk and talk and talk of acceptance and people's feelings and subtle unseen prejudices behind things never meant that way and bull-fucking-shit "trigger warnings" before class discussions about anything that might shake your perfectly safe little bed-and-blankets-you've-wrapped-yourself-up-in-to-fend-off-the-dangers-of-the-world world—those were his peers. Some were fighters, yes, and they were fighting, but they weren't choosing the right fights. Their macro-responses to micro-aggressions only played into the hands of our true masters. Get us to spend our time and energy and focus arguing about which of we slaves got picked to work in the house, rather than even contemplating the idea that we should rise up against them, skip the demanding of our freedom, and rather, by force, *take* it. The big shit, the stuff that really mattered, no one wanted to touch that.

So he was grateful in some opposite-reaction-than-you'd-expect way for all the shit that had been going down lately in the broader world far beyond the protected and secluded Eden of campus. Talk of reinstating the draft had been the biggest thing that slapped them in the face and had at least started to get their attention. That was why there were so many "Hell No, We Won't Go!" signs and banners and shirts resurrected from the 60s amongst the OCers.

This particular firestorm had ignited when a group of former generals and one former member of the Joint Chiefs took to an OpEd in the New York Times and stated unequivocally that America's fighting forces were worn the fuck out. Everyone knew it was, what?, less than half of one percent of the population who fought our wars? If you followed the news at all, you'd been hearing your whole life about the numerous tours in Iraq and Afghanistan, the enormous prevalence of PTSD, the poor excuse for care many were getting at the army and vet hospitals, etc., etc., etc. But the generals drove this point succinctly and compassionately home. America's supply of the poor and/or the blindly patriotic youth willing to take up arms for its War of the Month was dwindling. And then the generals brought home the final and most damning point—it was also because many vets now knew they'd been lied to. Trust. Faith. Shattered. The government had given far too many differing reasons for risking their lives, shedding their blood, shattering their emotional stability; tried to change its own history too soon, too often, and the pawns were no longer willing to play the king's game.

That—and that all the TV-know-it-alls kept saying that the perfect storm was brewing over there—that this time it wasn't going to be just one or two Middle Eastern countries, but the whole damned place, borderless, Middle East, Northern Africa, spilling over sporadically onto the streets of Paris, the tubes of London, and any hometown in America now armed with post-9/11 dollars with which they purchased police tanks and espresso machines. We were going to need more men.

… Or, make that: more teenagers with guns, Tristan thought. But that didn't matter. Tristan knew the draft propaganda was just a ruse for something else. Something more conspiratorial and corporate. But he was glad for the ruse and anything that helped force his fellow youth at long last into in the fray. Whatever it takes, he thought.

But someone else had grabbed the bullhorn now and his voice carried better and Tristan could hear him spouting some bullshit consent-manufactured crap about how the youth vote needed to go Democratic— thoughtless continuation of the Democratic vs. Republican falsehoods of their parents' generation and so many before. Tristan's happiness for the morning started to wane. Yes, he was glad his generation, some of them at least, were starting to fight back. But even those were still so fucking blind. There was still so much this knotted feeling in Tristan's stomach ached for them to see. They were still so damned far from knowing the Truth.

■ ■ ■

10:23 AM

Tracy's firm legs drove her cute-as-hell sandals to smack against the brick of the sidewalk with a strong slapping sound as she walked like a girl on a mission toward the heart of The Commons. And she had dressed the part too. Her highest-riding daisy dukes and a white tank top she stole from Ryan and had to tie up in the back that said, "Support Our Troops" across her breasts. Very patriotic. She carried a plastic drugstore bag in each hand filled with every magic marker the place had had left.

This summer, Tracy had read with a building religious fervor the book everyone was talking about—the female CEO's blockbuster call to action: Make Moves. She loved every word of that book. And sitting on the back patio of her parents' house in Ohio as she read, she finally realized what she needed to do: she needed to *not* be her mother. Mom's mission in life, like many of Tracy's sorority sisters it started seeming to her, had been to get everything she needed from a man. Despite all the progress made in how women viewed themselves and were viewed by others, Florida was still "The South," at least in this part of it, and it made Tracy want to vomit to think of how many of her "sisters" happily sat around in groups together, watching TV, drinking wine, and folding their boyfriends' boxers. (If Ryan ever asked her to do his laundry, she'd squat down and take a piss in the basket.) Tracy knew now she would go out into this world and take what she wanted her damn self. She'd spent August and September developing the details of her overarching career strategy, last week figured out an excellent first step toward her goals, and just this morning had a brainstorm on how to get that first step in gear. It was time for Tracy Reynolds to make moves.

10:24 AM

Ryan stood with his eyes closed under the hot water of one of the showerheads washing away the morning, letting his muscles relax, trying to bring himself back to "College Ryan," the one people wanted.

As he opened his eyes he caught a glimpse of Freshman walking out of the showers, towel wrapped tightly around his waist, another thrown around his shoulders. Ryan felt like shit about earlier—the kid's face had looked like a middle schooler's when Ryan was tearing him down. He turned off the water, toweled off and walked out.

A couple of locker rows down he found the kid and walked over to him.

"Hey," Ryan said.

"Hey—ah—yes, Sir," Freshman said, trying to pull his boxers on under his towel, awkward to start with, but more awkward now. Ryan tried not to notice.

"Listen ... I'm an asshole. I'm sorry about going off on you out there."

"No, Sir. I was in the wrong. I'm just ... there's so much to get used to here and ..."

"I get it." They shared a look. "And ROTC's over, so cut the 'Sir'."

The kid smiled a bit at the silliness of all that in this place with regular students around.

"Listen," Ryan continued, "we're having this party Thursday night. 'Sig Chi O: Back in Business.' A bunch of the ROTC guys are brothers too, so you'll know people. I'll tell the guys out front to let you in. Get you laid or something to make up for today."

Freshman smiled big. "Thanks, man."

"No worries. See you Thursday." Ryan slapped some lockers and headed back to his own. That felt good.

10:25 AM

Tracy dumped out the magic markers all over the GOTV table her sorority sisters were manning. The plan was simple, now that she'd figured it all out. Tracy was going to be the next Megyn Kelly—the beautiful, brazen, badass host on Fox News. She wanted her own TV show and she had the looks, the brains and the gift of strong opinions on any subject to get her there. Her path to fame: YouTube. She'd start her own show online and once she made a name for herself move up to the big screen of TV. Before launching her YouTube show she needed to shore up her popularity, her "platform," they called it, she'd learned, and start building content. Fortunately, the perfect opportunity had presented itself. Her sorority's Community Service Chair had opened up and Tracy was going to win it. This would provide plenty of opportunity to get out into the community, film what she was doing, and provide commentary on the various situations people faced. It would also get her name out there amongst the fraternity and sorority crowd, who, of course, had a long history of going on to do big things. And her campaign to win the Chair started today, with her brilliant idea.

Florida cut off voting registration last week. So there wasn't a specific thing for the GOTVers to do now, other than remind people to vote. And how do you remind college students to do something? *Tattoo it on their freaking bodies!* The plan was irresistible.

The hot sorority girls would walk up to all the passing guys and the hot frat guys would walk up to all the passing girls and say, "Remember to vote!" and then write, "Tuesday, Nov. 8th" on the top of their hands, or across their forearms, tummy, thigh, forehead—wherever the person wanted it. Who doesn't want a hottie coming up and touching them? And it would make such great video. She told her sisters to whip out their phones and film the action. This was going to be a big hit. Everyone would see her great idea in action, which would snag her the vote for the chair and the rest would be history. But first, to get everyone properly motivated, after she explained the details, she slid her big purse off her shoulder, plopped it down on the table and pulled out a bottle of Goose.

"Shots, girls! We're doing this." And everyone laughed. *Why the hell not?*

10:43 AM

Ryan was heading over to The Commons before his 11:00 AM class. Tracy had texted and wanted him to come by and see her big idea in action. It was the wrong way from class and he'd be cutting it close, but it was a huge lecture hall and he could sneak in a little late.

10:44 AM

Tristan couldn't take it anymore. Bullhorn Boy and some girl who clearly sounded like a member of the student Federalist Society at best, or one of the many moronic youth, who somehow had the opinions of 90-year-old-misogynistic-jingoistic-racist-"Real Americans," voting for maybe the worst piece of shit we've ever had running for president at worst, were now locked in an all-out yelling match digging each other deeper down into the bowels of blinded partisanship, and then the girl said it. That fucking line. Tristan knew the rest was coming when he heard the word "kept." That fucking word repeated so many times in the same gospel-certain phrase, that brilliantly simple brainwashing phrase disseminated to The People for repetition in the heisted presidency of their childhood: "George W. Bush kept us safe!" she said. A child repeating something her parents, her TV, had repeatedly said. No questioning. No thought. Just swallowed the talking point whole. And Tristan's poor mind felt, as it often did in times like these, like it had just slammed full-speed into a wall of immovable stupidity. That this guy who had been president for eight fucking months when it happened and had been warned repeatedly during that time by the CIA, the NSC and others, again and again in increasingly dire ways, until finally the blatant, simple words even he could understand shoved in his face as the title of his Fucking Presidential Daily Brief, "Bin Laden Determined to Strike in US," that the guy and his administration who would keep saying over and over again that awestruck line of "no one could have ever imagined that they would take planes and fly them into buildings," when that was exactly the fucking scenario imagined by multiple branches of government and numerous experts leading up to the attack from the Pentagon, which had multiple exercises preparing for what to do when it was hit with a hijacked airplane purposefully flown into it, to NORAD, the FBI, the FAA and others, some who even specifically mentioned the Twin Towers as targets for such an attack, and even at least one and probably more "exercises" going on *the very fucking morning* of the attack, with "fake" hijackings and "simulated" airplanes slamming into key government buildings, the *very fucking morning* that the guy who sat there for seven fucking minutes reading *My Pet Goat* with that "Gee, what the fuck should I do now?" look on his face after they told him the second plane had hit and we were clearly under fucking attack, while Cheney, the real president, was rushed to a secure bunker to actually run things, and then the idiot, while the only planes we were allowing to fly were flying the Saudis and bin Laden's family out of the US, stood up on the still-burning mountain of rubble with a bullhorn of his own in his hands to proclaim the crowning moment of his presidency, and God, Tristan could go on and on and on ... that that *idiot* had *"protected"* us was a crowning achievement for the master manipulators who can get the herded masses to believe *anything*. It was upside-down world. It was *1984* doublespeak and football stadiums upon football stadiums full of chanting Americans in unison had swallowed it whole and then regurgitated it for their children to drink down the predigested slush. Nothing could be further from the Truth.

Tristan pulled off Kyle's arm, grabbed his shirt and headed out toward the front lines.

.   .   .

Ryan found Tracy and walked up to her. He liked it when she wore his shirts. She spotted him coming and looked him up and down in his little khaki shorts and button-down. She looped her finger around his belt to bring him in the final few inches and said, close to his ear and sexy, "I thought you'd be wearing your silkies."

He half-laughed, "They're all sweaty, babe," and gave her a kiss. "What'd you want to show me?"

.   .   .

Tristan grabbed the bullhorn out of the kid's hand, put it to his mouth, and turning it back and forth between Federalist Girl and the now Bullhornless Guy, shouted,

"Open up your fucking eyes!"

.   .   .

"Great, your boyfriend's here," said Tracy. "I'm sure this will be pleasant." Ryan looked at Tristan with a bit of annoyance.

.   .   .

Tristan had noticed a hot girl writing on a mesmerized dork's arm when he walked up. He grabbed the kid's arm pulling him out of his horny dream state, and held it up, showing its half-done tat—"Nov. S"—and continued, "It

PATRIOTS: BOOK ONE | 35

doesn't fucking matter who you vote for, they're all owned by the same people!"

. . .

"Can't you go kick his ass, please?" Tracy said. "He's ruining my thing."

. . .

Tristan dropped the kid's arm as Sergeant Chubs started making his unhurried way over to the building commotion.

Standing in the middle of the two groups, right in the way of the poor "normal" students just trying to get to class or wherever, Tristan threw his free hand at the GOTVers and proclaimed,

"Democracy is dead! The Oligarchy rules!

"Can't you see that? Can't you see who really runs this world?"

He pointed his horn at the kid he took it from, "Yeah, give us some marijuana or some gay marriage," then back at Federalist Girl, "or some prayer in public schools or, better yet, tell us that you keep us *safe*! But it's all just to get what they really want, what they've always wanted. To regain the reins of serfdom! To concentrate money and power in the hands of the few and *nothing*, nothing in the history of the world ever made them more money than *war*! They've led us into killing ourselves a thousand times for their gain and now they're doing it all again! And we just happily play their game pretending it's for our own good. When are we going to see what's been done to us and stand up as one and say, 'No more!'?"

A dozen or so of his friends on the OC side hollered, whooped and cheered for him—preach it, brother.

But then his eyes caught a sign by one of the right-leaning tables, a poster of the Twin Towers under the words, "Never Forget." And a wholly different kind of emotion swelled within him. But he wouldn't let that emotion escape. He willed it back into his depths because he wouldn't let that girl see it—that Federalist Girl with her ear-piercing southern twang who had just been talking about 9/11 like she knew a damned thing, like she was there, and there was nothing a New Yorker, even a little kid at the time like Tristan, hated more than some Southern American, who watched the horror of that day from their Goddamned TV in the safety of their fucking living room, talking about what that day was like, what it was about, when there, on the Brooklyn Promenade, Tristan had pulled away from his teacher's protective hug to look back and the Towers just after the first of them had fallen, and that horrible cloud of ash was replacing it, before he was pulled away again and his eyes covered by the darkness of a teacher's arm that said, no, no, *no*, this is too much for you to see. No one knew what happened to their city, to their families, to his best friend Ryan that day. No one knew but them.

He aimed his rage back at her big head of hair and said,

"And you! You stand there and praise that puppet of the true traitors who committed the greatest treason of our lifetimes—and you say he was our *savior*. How could you be so fucking stupid?!"

"That's it you piece of shit!" said one of the guys at the Federalist table who started toward Tristan, followed by a friend, and Tristan saw them and he knew he could easily knock both these overweight blobs into a pile of their own fat on the ground, but his eyes also felt pulled again to the poster of the Twin Towers and he couldn't hold back, he had to say it. He pointed to the poster and said,

"The Oligarchy! The War Profiteers! The Masters of War! That's who did 9/11! Bin Laden was just their fucking patsy! Their Oswald! That's what we should 'Never Forget!'"

He paused. Looked around at the impact of his words on peoples' faces. Then added, "But instead we're just going to let them do it again."

Tristan lowered the bullhorn and tensed his muscles, readying his body for a fight as the two brutes neared him, but he didn't need to, as, irony of ironies, Officer Chubs stepped in between them, loudly stated, "That's enough from the Nut House!" and grabbed the bullhorn from Tristan's hands.

Tristan turned to walk away, feeling that was enough for him too—for now. But then, he caught sight of Kyle's face. But Kyle was probably the only student not looking at him right now. He was staring at something else. Tristan followed Kyle's stare past a blur of all the other eyes still watching him to the one pair that mattered. Ryan's.

Fuck.

Tristan hadn't known Ryan was there. And he could see it in Ryan's eyes. Not just the rage—but, more importantly, more painfully, the betrayal.

Tristan had never said anything to Ryan in all these years about that, the conspiracy behind 9/11. Not to him, not in front of him, not knowing he, or even a friend of his, was anywhere within earshot. It was too personal, too emotional, too close to Ryan's soul. It was probably the last thing in their long and how-the-fuck-could-these-two-ever-be-friends friendship that Tristan was still in the closet about to Ryan, and now here, on this otherwise perfect morning on The Campus Commons, the Truth was out.

They stood there. Motionless. Staring at each other. Until Ryan turned and walked away. And it was a turning—the way his face, his eyes looked as they turned—that hurt Tristan more than had all the brutes on the GOTV side who wanted to kick his ass right now come over and done it. The coldness in Ryan's last look at him made him want nothing more than to put it all back inside. To take back everything he'd said … even, maybe, everything he'd thought. Ryan was too important. *Goddamnit, Tristan, what have you done now?*

■ ■ ■

10:57 AM

Ryan walked off to class without a word to Tracy. *What the fuck was wrong with Tristan? God, that kid's been crazy forever, but now?! What the fuck was he even saying? An "oligarchy?" He lost his fucking mind!* And, yes, it hurt. It hurt like hell. How could Tristan, who knew *everything* Ryan had been through, who knew …

No. No, Ryan thought. *I'm not going to do it.*

Done. No more, Tristan. I don't know who the hell you are anymore.

That happened in life. It was real fucking shitty, but it happened. You could be so close once. As kids, you could never want to spend a day without each other. That person could know you better than you knew yourself sometimes—could call you out on shit you didn't ever even notice about yourself. The two of you could have whole conversations with just the tiny lines squinting a certain way around your eyes, the way the corners of a smile turned into a barely-held-back laugh at a joke only the two of you knew. This handful of people who made their way that deeply into your soul, they could turn the most mundane shit into a memory you will never want to let go of as long as you live. But then they change.

And that's it. There's nothing you can do about it. *Tristan was important to me when I was a kid,* Ryan thought. *Keep the memories, put them in a box in the back of your mind, and move on. Ryan Sheridan and Tristan Harris are finished. He's no longer a part of my life.*

Fucking done.

. . .

Tristan had walked right by Kyle without even noticing him standing there. Kyle had come out of the tent and walked over in time to see most of it. Tristan's little rant. And then that head-on collision of Tristan finally looking over to catch Ryan's eyes staring back at him. Kyle had noticed Ryan there almost as soon as he walked up and wanted to walk over, grab Tristan from behind and stop him before he went to that place Kyle knew he was going, but he was too late, or too scared, or for whatever reason too unable to do what deep down he knew he should have. And he knew everything that must have been going through Tristan's mind in that horrible moment and much of what must have been in Ryan's. And he felt so badly for Tristan—and for Ryan too, even.

God, Kyle hated all this. Why did campus have to be this way? Why couldn't they have just had a normal college experience? Wasn't there enough to worry about with grades and tough professors and careers to be figured out and built and sex and relationships and how hard it was just to find someone to love, and who was God, and what did he/she want, and what the hell were we all doing here on this rock in space—wasn't that enough?

But he'd picked Tristan, hadn't he? The bad boy in the middle of all this. He loved him. He really did. Despite—or, admittedly, maybe because of—all his badboyness. So he was going to have to hold on for the ride.

Things between Tristan and Ryan were surely about to get ugly. Kyle felt bad for Tristan, bad for Ryan too, *the little shit* (well, they were both little shits, he guessed). And bad for himself. It should have been simpler, all this. But it wasn't.

.   .   .

Yep, Tracy thought as Ryan just wordlessly walked away, her man was pretty worthless. She'd have to do it all herself. She grabbed a marker, walked into the seemingly never-ending flow of on-comers and grabbed the first male arm she saw.

"Remember to vote," and she'd only gotten "No" down on the guy's arm when he said, "I'm not a citizen." She looked up to see the guy's *Pakistani-or-whatever* face and could only muster an "urrrrgh!" as she threw his arm away.

■ ■ ■

2:38 PM

Luke crossed the street between town and campus and stepped onto one of the crisscrossing sidewalks of The Commons on his way to his 3:00 class, replaying the morning in his head and upset with himself for how he'd acted in front of Kristi, the weakness and emotion he had let her see, probably he was wrong to have let her come, should have done it by himself, just he and his sister.

Noise was entering his mind. Right, the protestors, he thought. He should have walked the long way around. Images started pulling his thoughts away from where he wanted them focused. Crude signs against the war or the different candidates, some vulgar, obscene, an American flag with the words "WORLD DOMINATION" painted across it, and then, what stopped him, what he thought at first was Jesus upside-down on The Cross and for one beat his heart sent suddenly boiling blood through his chest until he realized it was not Jesus at all, but some odd combination of peace symbol with the Vitruvian Man upside-down instead—the point of it unclear to Luke, probably made up by some student who thought himself clever for it—but still, the first image had stopped him and there he stood, stuck suddenly, taking it all in.

Probably it was the passage he'd thought of for the millionth time in the church this morning while losing control of his emotions, the most damning passage, literally, of his life that he couldn't, ever, tell Kristi about because she would brush it off, find a modern-Christian-everything's-hope-and-love excuse for it—probably it was that passage that brought his mind here, right now, but looking at his fellow students, these lost souls he'd been forced to surround himself with these past few years with their signs and their chanting and their day drinking and drug smoking, he couldn't help but think of the debauchery of those weak and easily manipulated souls who at the foot of Mount Sinai danced and drank and prayed to their own golden god, the one they'd forged for themselves, made up from their own imaginations to pray to, unable to wait for Moses to return with the Word of the One True Lord. And he thought of Moses's wrath. The mass murder he ordered, "each of you kill your brother, your friend, your neighbor," the three thousand dead. And as he looked around at his fellow students the question came to him again, the question he'd asked so many countless times:

Why are they not punished, God?

He asked in the silence of his mind.

The only answer that came was the one that always came—the one Meeks had finally given him years ago after so many painful years of the question going unanswered. Pastor Meeks, from the little old church he'd finally wandered into on his own, bicycled there because his parents wouldn't take him. Meeks had given the answer: Patient Endurance. Patient Endurance until, finally, the Revelation.

College life had been especially difficult for Luke to accept. Where he grew up in North Carolina, it seemed that young people, at least those around him, still had a respect for The Lord, a reverence for Him. And surely there were many who had the right morals in Florida too or Luke would never have chosen to come here, but this campus was such a melting pot of so many different cultures—American and foreign—that relativism clearly ruled in morality and few sinners ever gave half a thought to repentance. It had been digging at his soul since he first moved here that the sinful natures of those around him partied on with impunity while he and his sister had been sentenced to suffer so harshly.

But he was a sinner too. He knew it as he stared at this one girl in particular, judging her, the girl clearly drunk in the middle of the day, clearly showing off her skin for all to see and lust over, laughing unashamed with the two or three guys currently flirting with her, her large breasts half exposed under the thin straps of a white tank top, but worst of all, what she was doing to Luke as he stared. He could feel it against his will in his groin, in his slowly growing penis, the lust, the sin, the Devil working through her to manipulate him there.

He pulled his eyes away and continued on to class sick of the corruption these people brought to his soul, more mad at himself than anyone.

6:23 PM

Tristan was walking back to the dorms after his day of classes, feet scraping the sidewalk a bit, skateboard strapped to his bookbag, having worked himself into a numbed, zombie-like state to keep all the sickening emotions building within him about Ryan—the potential loss of him, the pain between them—as far out to sea as he could force them.

Nearing his dorm complex, maybe it was the emotionally vulnerable place he'd worked himself into throughout the day, but for the first time, really, he felt like a bit of a loser for still living there. It was his senior year, but he chose, one last time, to remain there. He liked it there. He had his reasons, even if no one else quite got them. The dorms were actually nice, if small. They were the newest on campus, the Honors Dorms, and as part of Tristan's scholarship he got to live there for free. He'd also worked things out quite nicely for himself by scaring off his first- and second-try roommates so badly with all his crazy theories and his uncontrollable sex drive that Student Housing had given up trying to place anyone else with him. He also liked the "tiny living" aspect of it. No space meant the fewest possible possessions. And then there was the continuous new crop of freshmen every year and Tristan knew enough about himself by now to know he always preferred younger guys. That's where he'd first spotted Kyle last year when Kyle was a freshman and moved in several floors below. Then they'd taken that amazing class on the Gulf together and it was on.

But Tristan's thoughts were pulled out of his funk by a girl's voice.

"Who's the babe with the tats? Give him to me *now*!"

Tristan looked up to see his friend Jasmine coming at him from across the courtyard in front of his dorms and had to laugh a bit. She must have been visiting a friend because she definitely did not live here.

"Hey gorgeous," Tristan said as she kissed him on the cheek.

"What's wrong babe? You look pouty. Sexy pouty, but pouty."

Tristan liked Jasmine since the day he met her freshman year at a coffee house in town after Tristan sat down to eat the first and last bagel he'd ever again order outside of New York City. It was an everything bagel and after his first bite this stunning girl leaned over and whispered with mock sexiness dripping from her voice, "How's that bagel? Is it *everything* you want it to be?" They both laughed and have been friends ever since.

"Nothing," Tristan said. "Just a bad day."

"Well then, I've got news to cheer you up!" Jasmine said. "Did you hear the boys of Sig Chi O are having a comeback party?"

"I guess," Tristan said, totally unsure how that was suppose to help.

"Well, in honor of the University yet again bending over and taking one for the Fraternity Team, I've decided to throw my own, 'No Way Bro!!!' (she said in Mock Frat Guy) Anti-Frat-Party party." And she handed him a postcard flier for a party really called *No Way Bro!!!* "Fresh off the presses. I just decided this morning. And look—" she went digging for something in her purse.

Tristan thought it was brilliant. Jasmine had an incredible five-bedroom apartment (she'd asked him more than once to be one of her roomies). It was huge with a tremendous living room, but best of all, it was just across the street and up a little ways from Ryan's fraternity house with a huge balcony that you could see the frat from. How perfect—how Jasmine—to have a sort of "protest party" across the street from them.

She found what she was looking for, producing her phone and pulling up the images she wanted. "I'm making t-shirts! Tank tops, actually." She showed him a pic of a shirt and zoomed in on the writing. "The writing's like one of those old eye charts, you know, the words on top are big, but they keep getting smaller. So this one says," and she read her words aloud to him as she showed him:

PLEASE DON'T RAPE ME!
Even though I drank so much
I passed out on your couch
with my legs wide open
and my tits falling out—
I just want to be respected
for my brain!
Thanks!

Tristan's eyes went wide. "Woah."

"I know, right! If we're going to mock the boys, lets mock the stupid girls too. Oh, and you'll like this one." She slapped his arm as she showed and read:

NO HOMO BRO!
But please paddle my ass,
get naked with me all the time
and maybe just a little
"bro job"
I won't tell!

"And then around the back over the top of your ass, it says:"

... okay, stick it in.

Tristan laughed, "Yes. Definitely wearing one."

"Yay!" She kissed his cheek. "I'm still working on the rest. Definitely need one on hazing and one totally focused on those paddles of theirs, but I'm on it."

"You're amazing. Can't wait." She was amazing and he was certain her party would end up as one of the year's best. Knowing her, she'd probably get as many people, if not more, than the frat. Tristan needed this.

"Yay! Okay," she said. "See you Thursday!"

9:37 PM

Tristan and Kyle opened the door they weren't supposed to with its signs about "ALARM WILL SOUND" and "EMERGENCY ONLY," only they always opened it and alarms never sounded, as they stepped out onto the roof of their dorm and walked across the silver, rubber-like tar, holding hands even, to their spot. Even then they knew it, even the first time they came up here together, even Tristan when he came up here by himself in the years before meeting Kyle, or with another boy, they knew somewhere in the recesses of their minds, in places they didn't like their thoughts to go—to the future and away from this place, to old age and looking back on youth—they knew that this view over campus was where their minds would go in nostalgia to a time when life seemed "perfect," when the world of opportunity lay before them, but when *right here, right now*, rightfully deserved the complete domination and absorption of their thoughts because it was, relative to so much else, truly perfect. Campus looked so peaceful at night. The tower of Ponce de León Hall, the original campus building that sat as the focal center of The Commons, rose above the rest of campus, lit at night in a warm, welcoming light. Everyone knew that tower and had their own affinity for it in this privileged club of people who got to call this place home, if only just for a little while. Catching a glimpse of Ponce Tower here and there centered you, let you know you were here, where you were supposed to be. Off to the west the breeze blew in off the Gulf, which you couldn't see over the pines and palms, but still you knew it was right there. In the east, just before the line of dark trees that went to the horizon, was their massive football stadium, lit just enough to remind you of its presence. They'd had sex here many times on the soft silver tar, Kyle could even make out some elbow and knee indentations, and just as often they'd laid quietly afterward looking up at the stars, the moon, thoughts of what life was and what it would be. Tristan took Kyle in his arms and held him from behind as he often did here, kissed the top of Kyle's head, took a whiff of his hair and there they stood as they had many, though not enough, times before. Kyle held Tristan's arms holding him and it felt as good as it always did even though he knew, with what happened today, problems were coming.

.　　.　　.

Luke stood in the hot shower needing the water to cleanse more than just his skin, needing it to wash away his tensions and even his sin, but, of course, it couldn't.

.　　.　　.

Kristi sat on Luke's made bed reading for class, but found it hard for her mind to concentrate on the chapter on Behavioral and Cognitive Neuroscience when it wanted to think about the young man behind the bathroom door taking a shower—not sexually, of course—she just so desperately wanted to know what was going on in his mind lately, in his heart and soul. Yes, she still wanted to marry him, but she did have to admit that, yes, there were those fears growing somewhere within her about Luke. God, he was always such a good guy, but lately … lately she worried his inner demons were gaining ground on him.

She closed her book for class and pulled the workbook for their first premarital counseling session tomorrow morning from her bookbag and flipped to page where she'd written some thoughts about Luke's emotional similarities with her brother and Dad when it came to certain issues about how men knew they were supposed to behave, and even with her mom's clamming up when it came to discussing anything too emotional. Kristi took the workbook seriously, even more so than she would have anyway, as this was all a real-life example of something she would actually be dealing with one day from the other side of the room. Kristi was majoring in Psychology in order to become a Christian Counselor. She was still debating whether she would take out more loans to go on to grad school—though there were a few very good master's programs at the top Christian colleges and she had done her homework on them. But to be a Christian Counselor you didn't always need a master's. At any rate, the material was especially interesting to her and she set to work in the margins of the page making notes on how she wanted to approach Luke about what happened this morning, words she wanted to make sure she used.

.   .   .

Tracy was not about to lay around all night with Ryan sulking about his annoying gay best friend being a little bitch and saying stupid things as he always did. She was going to cheer him up and have some fun doing it. She opened his shorts drawer, pulled out a fresh pair of silkies and held them up. "Will you put these on for me?"

Ryan looked up from his engineering homework and found a smile for her. "What is it with you and those things?"

She just stared at him with a mischievous smile until he finally stood up and started taking off his clothes.

Tracy had had a boyfriend in high school who had a sneaker fetish. It took him forever to come out of the closet to her about it, but once he finally did, the sex got really, really good. At first it was just that he wanted them both to wear sneakers while they had sex. Then he wanted to hold a shoe to his face sometimes, his nose stuffed inside, smelling it. Then he started putting his cock inside one for a few good rubs before putting it inside her—his cock, of course, not the shoe. Tracy had told him to hold it on that one and that he wasn't allowed to do that unless he got a brand-new shoe that he kept clean and for this purpose only, so he did. Tracy definitely thought the whole thing extremely weird and definitely in need of some kind of "what-do-these-shoes-really-mean-to-you?" therapy, but also, a lot of fun, because the way it drove him crazy drove her crazy too.

She thought maybe she was developing her own fetish for these little green silkies and her boy's well-established package at first just outlined beneath the fabric, but then aching to bust free of it. Or maybe she just wanted to have a fetish, liked the idea of it. Ryan looked good standing there naked, but even better after he slipped on the little tight shorts. Tracy stepped toward him.

.   .   .

Kyle wanted to speak up more. Not in any sort of political way like Tristan, but in a personal one. He hated that about himself, how much he kept inside. He knew he was gay in the 5th grade, but couldn't begin to muster the courage to tell his parents till freshman year of high school. And there were so many things he wanted to say to the boy who held him now from behind and had just kissed the top of his head and now snuggled his nose into his hair, but couldn't. Or, at least, just hadn't. He wanted to tell him, despite how he knew Tristan would be mocking him internally, that he'd been thinking more and more, wondering was probably the better word, about God. Kyle did believe in some force out there, some benevolent being, but he wasn't sure if Tristan did, or if he did, would he discuss it— really, truly talk about it. He thought about his mom and how strong a person she was—all she had been through moving to Lebanon for his dad, but then, even worse, moving back to The States after she'd fallen in love with life there despite the hardships. She was so quiet, but so strong. When she spoke, it mattered. Her words carried weight because everyone in the family knew how much she thought about them before speaking. Kyle wanted to be more like that.

Tristan liked this moment with this boy of his. It was nice. But his eyes kept glancing toward Ponce Tower and what he knew lay beneath it—The Commons, the movement, the conflicts. But it was the conflicts, plural, so many of them, that were starting to bug Tristan about himself. That's what he'd been thinking about today, that what he'd said in front of Ryan wasn't the half of it, not even the tip. Probably it was senior year and thinking of graduating and what next that had Tristan taking some big steps back lately and looking at his life like campus now from above. There were so many conflicts, so many issues, so many battles Tristan wanted to fight, but as Professor Mc had said a hundred times from grave experience: you have to choose your battles. Tristan knew what he saw when he stepped back to look at himself: just a playboy still sowing his wild oats, yelling through a hundred stupid bullhorns, actual or a Tweet thread or a YouTube video or an outburst in class, in a hundred different directions at a hundred different causes, but getting nothing done. He knew that everything he said he hated about his generation was really what he hated about himself. He'd learned what he'd needed to learn. He knew what he believed. Now it was time to *do*. It was time to matter.

.   .   .

Luke closed his eyes in the shower and leaned his forehead against the wall and maybe it was the warmth or the feel of the water over his body, but his mind started thinking about that girl from The Commons again, her breasts, her smile. He opened his eyes, driving the image from his mind, hating it, and shut off the water.

.   .   .

Kristi heard the water stop and tried to finalize what she'd been thinking she wanted to say, but then, for an instant, she realized maybe she should get up and go into the living room to give him his privacy, would he think to put on a shirt or something before opening the door?, but it was too late, he opened it and there he stood in nothing but his towel. Kristi looked away, though she did like his body; he took nice care of it. "Your body is your temple," he'd said when she commented once on his exercising.

"Sorry," he said, quickly finding a shirt on his chair.

"No," she said, "I can step out." and started getting up off the bed.

He finished throwing the shirt on as she stood. "It's okay, I'll change in here," motioning to the bathroom.

"No," Kristi said, then stopped herself, wanting to say the thing she'd been wanting to say. She turned back around to him and put her hand on his arm. "I just wanted to say, that was brave of you this morning." Brave was a word she'd wanted to emphasize. "To allow yourself to feel those emotions. That's healthy, you know, to share them. And I want to be that person for you. I think that's what God wants for husband and wife. That you can tell me these things." She was looking straight into his eyes and she could tell he was grateful for what she was saying. She desperately wanted to know what he'd meant about knowing why his sister died and who was it that he'd never forgive and why, but she knew it wasn't the time to push for all that.

Luke looked at Kristi, grateful to her and for her. He'd really never had much of this in his life—someone who really cared about what was going on deep within his dark places. His sister was the last—the only one, really— before Kristi. He felt so truly blessed by God bringing her into his life. He put his hands on the sides of her head, and with some of that real, true emotion that she wanted finally coming through, said, "Thank you." And then he kissed her.

Kristi felt a chill up her spine, she was so pleasantly surprised with his response. With the way he'd been lately she feared he'd close up again, shut her out. But God, he really was a good guy, wasn't he? And his kiss felt so nice right now.

.   .   .

Tracy reached her hand underneath Ryan's shorts to grab and massage his dick. Once it was hard she grabbed it at its base and started rubbing its head on the smooth inside of the silkies. She knew how much he liked that.

Once, after a lot more foreplay, he'd blown his load just from that, right through the fabric of the shorts—it was hot. He closed his eyes and she could see the tensions disappearing from his face. He stepped back to his bed and sat down as his hands pulled off her shorts and panties. He looked at her body and was about to pull his shorts off too, but she said, "Uh-ah," and pulled his cock out from under the leg of the shorts and straddled him, inserted his aching dick within her, and began to slowly ride him. He lifted her bra over her left breast, licked, nibbled its nipple like she liked. Just enough pressure between his teeth. That line on which we teeter between pain and ecstasy.

. . .

Kyle turned around in Tristan's arms and brought his own around behind Tristan's back and buried his head against Tristan's chest. "Are you going to be okay? About Ryan?"

Tristan took a thoughtful breath, then, "Yeah. I guess it is about time he and I finally confronted this."

Kyle didn't believe what Tristan believed about 9/11, or most of the conspiracies. But he knew how strongly Tristan felt about them and most especially about 9/11. And he knew how long these thoughts had been churning like an acid inside Tristan, eating away at his gut that he couldn't tell his best friend what really happened that day that meant so much to them both, that changed everything in their young worlds.

"Just be careful, you know? He's hurt you before."

And Kyle looked up at Tristan with those beautiful Persian eyes of his and Tristan melted a bit for his concern. He bent down and kissed Kyle's lips—at first just the simple firm pressure square in the center, then taking just Kyle's upper lip in his, then just his lower and sucking it just a little longer, then a swipe of the tip of his tongue between Kyle's lips and across his front teeth, then a second pass and Kyle's mouth had opened just a little more and their tongues touched and played with each other and tasted so good.

.   .   .

Things had gotten strange again, but just like the time before, Kristi decided to just let him continue. She knew he was a man and needed his release. The kissing had gotten heavier and heavier and Luke seemed to be losing control of himself. They were now lying on the bed, Kristi still fully clothed and Luke in his t-shirt and towel, kissing her madly and rubbing his erection up and down under the towel over her fully clothed thigh. It was weird, very weird—but she knew he needed it. She kissed him back and waited for him to be done.

.   .   .

No. Fuck. Ryan could feel it starting to happen, his cock losing a bit of its strength, and he knew, by now, once it started, it was over. He'd been having problems this year. Too much on his mind and probably, he guessed, less and less interest in Tracy. But Goddammit, now he'd have to deal with that look she gave him and her fucking questions. And there it was—she started to realize it too.

"Babe?" she said. *Jesus Christ.* "Is it the shorts?" She stood up off of him and began to pull them down. "We can take them off."

"It's not the shorts. Just—"

He looked at her and she at him and he had to look away. "It's just— there's a lot lately, you know?" She should have fucking known, he shouldn't have had to fucking say, but then that was fucking Tracy, wasn't it? *Jesus, it's so much easier to be a girl with just a hole you need filled.*

He knew that was harsh, but right now he didn't care.

.   .   .

Tristan finally pulled back a bit from Kyle's mouth. Their lips were getting tired. He rubbed his nose on Kyle's, then kissed Kyle's closed eyelid, then his forehead, then returned his nose to a nested spot in Kyle's hair and breathed in deep.

After a little while, Kyle said, "You want to go to the beach tomorrow?"

"I've got my paper to write."

Kyle made a little disappointed noise as he snuggled back into Tristan's chest.

Tristan gave the top of Kyle's head a little kiss. "Well. Come by the library after your class. Maybe if I get enough done in the morning."

"Okay," Kyle said, his voice muffled and sleepy against Tristan's left pec.

.   .   .

Luke was climaxing. Kristi could see it in his face and in the sudden stop of his rubbing. She tried to smile in case he opened his eyes, but it wasn't really a smile, and thankfully he didn't.

But when he did open his eyes, it was like he was trying to reorient himself to where he was.

Then he looked right at her and again she tried to smile, again it didn't really work, but what smirk she found quickly faded anyway as she could see the fear overtaking Luke's face.

"Luke, it's okay," she said.

But he'd launched into a barely audible, but then louder and louder, deluge of, "No, no, no, no, no, no, no."

"Baby, it's okay," she repeated.

He had lifted himself up now and looked down at the wet spot on his towel. "Oh, God!" He grabbed her hand and yanked her harshly down with him to the floor, almost pulling her arm out of its socket and at an awkward angle.

"Babe!" she said, meaning that hurt, but not wanting to say it.

And there on the floor he pulled her head with his straight to the ground, foreheads against carpet, and tears flowing from his eyes as the words began to seethe from his clinched mouth like steam finally forcing its way through some crack that finally burst open in some awful near-exploding thing, "Please, please, please, *please* forgive us! God, we are so sorry for our sins, for the immorality of our souls, for the grossness of our act before You, for the waste of Your Blessed Seed of Life!"

He went on and on in harsh whispers she couldn't always understand. And Kristi finally lifted her head to watch him losing his own in pain and fear just as she felt each of these awful demons growing within herself.

Wednesday
October, 19th

8:57 AM

It was hot in the bed when Ryan woke up, Tracy's right leg still bent around his left. She loved that, sleeping with their legs all intertwined, she facedown, her arm over his chest. He hated it. So many times he'd wake up with an arm in that strange combination of being both numb and sore and trying to pull it out like dead weight from under her shoulders or ribcage. Other girlfriends had liked to cuddle in the beginning, but then retreat to their separate sides. Ryan got that, he missed that, but not Tracy, all night with the touching, the dead-weight arms, the sweaty spots he felt right now in the places their legs still touched. But lying there, hot and uncomfortable, he had to admit it wasn't the physical stuff at all. Mom had been right. She didn't like Tracy from the beginning. He should have listened to her. Ryan knew he'd have to be the one to end it. For reasons he didn't understand, she seemed perfectly content. He should do it soon and get it over with, he thought. Why drag it all out?

Houston would take it the hardest. Ryan's dog. He loved the cuddling. His head now asleep on Tracy's other thigh.

Ryan pulled his leg out from under hers and turned away, images of things around his room playing on his thoughts: his ΣΧΩ letters on the wall, an ROTC uniform on his desk chair, some pictures here and there of parties, boating, The Great Gulf Floatopia of ridiculous drunkenness, "brothers." He was struck by the sad irony of it all: to be surrounded by so many people and yet be so alone.

And then his eyes fell on a framed photo on his cheap bookshelves of two young boys, boogie boards tossed to the sand, two arms around each other's shoulders, and the other two thrown to the sky in victory from a day spent conquering the waves, and the long-lost smiles on their faces so unaware of all the pain that was yet to come.

Ryan shot up from bed, grabbed a towel, slammed the picture down on its face and then the door behind him into his bathroom.

9:01 AM

Kristi and Luke sat on the tropically flowered loveseat with their workbooks before them, Luke's on the coffee table, Kristi's on her lap, "The Marriage Jesus Wants You To Have," waiting for Pastor Todd and Mrs. Connie. The community was just like those that dominated much of Florida, all new, one-story homes, terracotta roofs, arched front windows, vaulted ceilings, tiled floors. There was barely enough unprotected land left near campus for a place like this, but somehow they'd squeezed it in. They were sitting in the back pool area covered with one of those giant Florida screened-in-backyard structures. The pool was small, just enough to wade around in, but it was all very pleasant, the morning air refreshing, the birds, as always, chirping.

Of course, they hadn't discussed last night, and Kristi knew they likely never would. She'd gone home after he calmed down and he'd picked her up this morning to drive here, not a word about it in the car.

Luke thought the house was a little too nice for a pastor, though he knew the homes here were inexpensive. Still, Meeks, his pastor from home, had lived in a very old, very small house the church had owned from the beginning. But Todd was no Meeks, not even half the man.

Todd, in his late 40s, Luke guessed, had revolutionized the campus evangelical church into a "mini-mega" as Todd liked to call it. The new building had just been completed when Luke first got to campus and it was a big success. Todd had raised several million in bank loans to purchase the property of an old bookstore with a large parking area across the street from one corner of Campus Commons and built the new facility there, very modern and youth-oriented with Youth Center attached, complete with game room, pool tables and all. Luke served on Todd's Youth Council so he knew a fair amount about the inner workings of the church and Todd's main focus on "getting the youth in" and the "battle" or sometimes "war" he was fighting "for the hearts and minds of the young." The band on the stage seemed to grow every semester and the music got louder. Todd hired a new Youth Pastor, a guy in his early 30s who had the same "in" haircut that a lot of the college guys were starting to get and wore his jeans in the same way. Jeans and t-shirts on the church stage, or altar, rather, and the things that came out of this pastor's mouth sometimes while he was speaking for the Lord, Meeks might have torched the place. But it was working. The new building continued to fill more and more. Todd's formula, proven over and over throughout the country, was picked up at the various pastor conferences he attended. His most recent, in Atlanta, had featured a keynote speaker who was a Hollywood film producer of some good family movies, discussing the tricks of the trade for getting them into their seats and keeping them there. The church now bought a series of videos from his company, nearly one every Sunday, which they showed on the flat screens during the service. They were expensive, the videos, but again, they worked. Flashy and well produced. MTV for Christians. But none of the showmanship was as important to Luke as the message and that was where his true fears lay. He was deeply worried about the liberalizing effect the focus on youth outreach seemed to have on the True Message of God. Meeks had warned in private conversation with his favorite young pupil, "You know that sayin'—the greatest trick the Devil ever pulled was in convincin' the world he doesn't exist?"

"Yes, Sir," young Luke had said.

"Well, he's done far worse than that, Son. His greatest trick of all has been when he's convinced the world he was God."

Luke knew from Meeks that the deadliest blow to the church, when it came, would come from within.

Kristi smiled at him and put a hand on his knee, anxious to get started. Todd was always running late lately.

9:03 AM

Damnit. Slamming the picture down only made its memories ricochet around Ryan's mind. The trips their families used to take together in the good times. Their dads day-drinking cheap beers on the beach. Their moms taking long walks. The two of them, Ryan and Tristan, glued to their boogie boards; how could they not turn back after sliding sand-filled-shorts up the beach to ride just one more wave?

No, that must have been later. The boogie boarding. Back then they would have been too young. That's when they'd just dig those big holes together in the sand. The ones that would fill with water. They'd stand in them and somehow that was enough. Just playing in a hole in the sand filled with water. That was enough, back then.

The water on his skin now in the shower. The memories of those beach days long ago. Their first Great Gulf Floatopia, freshman year.

Tristan had spotted Ryan from his raft and yelled over. You couldn't count all the rafts or blowup sharks or mermaids (or even a gigantic rubber ducky once) on the water during this annual festival celebrating nothing much other than itself. It was so massive Campus Police basically gave up trying to stop the public, underage binging and just stood on the shore and said let us know when you're drowning.

Ryan had just met Tracy a couple weeks before. He'd gotten a little raft for the two of them, one of the last ones in the store. It was for little girls, pink with yellow flowers, but *whatareyougonnado*?

Tristan's and his friends' was like its own island in comparison. He was on it with a bunch of new people Ryan hadn't met. Tracy was so excited to meet Tristan and Ryan was tipsy from the sun-drenched day-drinking and so he rolled over on his stomach and started paddling with his arms toward Tristan and Tristan did the same (with the help of a couple new friends) and finally their rafts collided and they grabbed each other and laughed just because it was all so ridiculous. This was all you needed. Just some boogie boards and the endlessly coming waves, just some sand, some buckets, and the day to dig away a hole together that you could call your castle and fight to protect it.

Out there on their rafts together, Tracy asking Tristan what Ryan was like as a kid. Tristan played along. Talked him up. "Did he tell you he was captain of our high school lax team?"

"No!" She'd play-slapped him.

"Yep. All the girls wanted him. A couple of the guys on the team too, I hear." Tristan was drunk and taking another drink.

The way Tristan looked at Ryan just then, Tracy laughed the loudest Ryan had yet heard her—a real laugh, unconcerned for how it looked.

Ryan kicked Tristan, Tristan grabbed his foot to—who knows?—and they both fell in the water.

Tristan even answered all her questions about his tats that day, which Ryan knew he didn't like doing. He just did it for him. He liked people looking at his body as a work of art, for sure. But he usually didn't like to be honest about the meaning behind all the tats. But he was open with her that day. He told the truth. Even about the one on his heart. And all the pain behind it.

Tracy said how much fun she was having and how she loved hearing about them as kids and wanted to hear more.

As they were paddling back to shore toward the end of that day, both on their bellies, working together, she said, "Let's just go ahead and make this official. Boyfriend-Girlfriend."

"Yeah. I'd like that," Ryan said. "A lot, actually."

Ryan heard the bathroom door open and close, some movement, then the shower curtain pulled back and in came Tracy. There was no such thing as alone time with her, not even the solitude of the shower.

"I see you're still mad at your boyfriend." She must have woken when he slammed down the picture. He didn't say anything just started finishing up to get out of there. She was pouring some of her essential oils into her hands, then started to rub them on his back and shoulders. "So babe, your party tomorrow … this is going to be my first big event after I announce I'm running for Chair."

He didn't say anything.

"It's important to me, you know, that we present our best face."

He turned around, letting the water wash the oils off his back and threw a hand back there to help speed the process. "I'll do what I can," he said, opened the curtain and got out. He was glad today was his full day of classes. He couldn't wait to distract his mind from all the other shit in his life. He wanted the sanctuary of civil engineering's agreed upon simplicity, where answers were knowable and the processes for finding them laid out for you in long-established equations.

9:07 AM

The morning air had that crisp pine-and-palm-scented Florida smell, Tristan thought, mixed now with occasional whiffs of the Costa Rican beans of his black coffee as he walked back from town to campus. His ritual walk was long and out of the way, some might say, but the long way around to get the details you wanted and see the sights you liked seemed like the good way to go to Tristan. Yes, there was plenty of coffee on campus, but not this coffee from this little walkup window Tristan loved at the little café run by the heavyset woman from Massachusetts whose mission in life seemed to be finding the right combinations of cinnamons and honeys and whatnots to delight the senses and who made the morning muffin Tristan wanted to start every day of his life with that was falling apart with carrot and coconut shavings and nuts and raisins and apple chunks and oats and brans. And besides, Tristan was a New Yorker at heart; walking was what his legs were made to do. He found it sad that that wasn't true for most Americans.

He walked back through The Commons, saw his tent was fine, knew it would be, and part of him felt he should be with his friends again today, but he knew he had to get this paper done. He walked through the grand open archway under Ponce Tower that brought you through the building and into another lawn beyond, but a very different one, smaller and meant to have the same atmosphere as the great building which lay beyond it, Cullier Library, little signs all around reminded students and visitors that voices on this lawn were to be kept to a library whisper, it was the Quiet Lawn, they called it, for reading. Tristan's favorite bench was open and he snagged his spot to eat his muffin, enjoy his coffee, and prepare for the thoughts of the day.

Tristan only knew a handful of people his age who loved physical books and the great libraries that held them as much as he. But if you were one of those people Tristan automatically had a greater respect for you, even if you otherwise believed stupid things. The New York Public Library on Bryant Park was one of the few places left in the changing (and not for the better) Manhattan that Tristan still loved to frequent. When he was touring different colleges he was so thoroughly disheartened by some of their libraries— books mostly gone, fluorescent lights, a celebration of nothing, just storage and places to sit, but why would you want to? Tristan thought you could tell a lot about a school from its library—its respect for the quiet solitude of learning and the written word.

FSCU's was one of the most elegant he'd seen. Three of the buildings on this quiet little courtyard had porticos wrapped around them, lending this space a cloistered effect. Students often, sometimes Tristan, would lean against a column to do their work in the shade. The library not only held onto its books, but cherished them. Never had it succumbed to those rows of desktop computers from his parents' generation—those had been banished to lesser buildings. And up the grand staircase to the second floor you entered the Great Hall of Reading, some 250 feet wide of long tables lined with low lamps, and corners and alcoves of comfortable leather (or, at least, leather-like) sofa chairs (that, yes, some students napped on between classes) and all kept quiet and focused under the great arched ceiling with its Sistine Chapel-esque mural of Ponce de Leon's search for the Fountain of Youth.

What a place to think.

He thought about a book he'd read, *The Shallows: What the Internet is Doing to Our Brains*. Much of Tristan's research was done online, but he would print the good articles out and read every word, underline good points and important facts and pause to think about them. He wanted to fight with everything he could becoming a mere skimmer of dissipated shallow thought and remain the "deep reader" he had fallen in love with becoming—to remain a member, with great pride in it, and in the face of the great war upon it, of what the book called, "The Reading Class."

Knowledge. Reason. Wisdom. These were the foundation of our defense. Like another book had said: *American Fascists: The Christian Right and the War on America*. It said the thing they really hate the most, these fascists, is Secular Humanism. Tristan was happy to read that—because that meant him. What else was there than that—when we were honest with ourselves—than us and the search for Truth? He looked at this place and smiled at the thought: Secular Humanism was his religion and the building before him its cathedral.

And it was time to go to church, wasn't it? Time to focus with a religious intensity. A zealotry.

There was something to admire about the Fascists: their unrelenting focus.

It could all seem like such a mess sometimes. His life. Everything that led him to be who he was. That led him to be sitting on this bench this morning in Florida of all places, still, after all this time, after all these freaking years, thinking about Ryan, worried about Ryan *and what he thinks of me, fucking Ryan.*

The mess of The Commons and the mess that little bit of Truth he'd let seep out in front of Ryan would surely soon add to their lives, all of it was nothing compared to the mess Tristan felt warring within his mind. That perfect storm the seed from his father and egg from his mother and all that happened since created.

The mess of his mom having devoted her life again and again to the liberal causes and the politicians who use them only to end up time and time again that broken woman whose pain he felt as he squatted by the glass doors to the back deck and listened to her tears as she sat wrapped in a blanket out there in the dark smoking a joint after W. won his second term and she'd given her everything to stopping him and the next song on her Pink Floyd album played and it was the one about beating your heart against some mad brother's wall and the words of that song right then were her.

And that Dad was that wall. In so many ways. Dad, the quiet corporate conservative, who, in his devotion, only found the further corruption of his … soul. (Secular Humanists needed a better word for that.) The layers upon layers of things Dad had hidden within him.

Mess.

And all the things he'd read in this cathedral and others like it and in the quiet of his room—his dorm now, his bedroom at home—and all the things he'd heard and seen.

Mess.

What he needed, Tristan, was to impose some clarity.

So he was grateful for the paper Professor Mc had encouraged him to write. The words he was now about to finally start putting to paper.

There were so many enemies to fight. With this paper Tristan was finally beginning to focus his energy upon one enemy. One. The key to them all.

And the one Fate had clearly most well positioned him to fight. The wall he could finally break down for his mom.

Or just bust a few bricks through. So that she, so that so many others, could begin to peek through it and begin to understand.

To focus on this one issue. To put the words to paper and find clarity in them. To know thy enemy.

The last bite of his muffin looked back at him.

A perfect little mess.

Ingredients most people wouldn't throw in together. So many they seemed to be always on the brink of falling apart, but somehow they still held each other as one. For they were, messy as they might seem to some, just right for each other. Picked after a life spent tasting so many variations of each—do you toast the coconut shavings or leave them raw?, what family of apple and from what state, what grocer?, did the answer change based on the season?, only the purest you could find of each ingredient you chose, nothing synthetic, nothing processed—by a woman who loved their nuances. By a woman who knew and loved the whole their mess would combine to make.

That's what Tristan needed to do now.

He popped the last bite in his mouth, crushed up the white paper bag it was in, grabbed his bookbag and coffee and went to the compost, recycling and incineration bins to throw the waste away.

He swallowed the sweetness of his perfect little mess and walked up the steps to his sanctuary.

9:08 AM

Pastor Todd's bombastic voice shot at them from the sliding door even before he'd gotten more than a few inches of it open. "Well, if it isn't the happy couple!"

"I finally pulled him away from that cellphone attached to his ear," said Mrs. Connie following him out.

"'Much to do, much to do, and little time in which to do it.' As they say." Todd sat his large self down on one of the two sofa chairs just as flower-upholstered as the love seat they faced and placed his huge, held-together-by-two-rubber-bands-there-were-so-many-folded-pages-of-notes-sticking-out-of-it Bible down on the glass coffee table with a thump as Connie sat in the chair next to him with a workbook similar to their counselees, but it was the Teachers' Edition, with the answers. Each also held a coffee.

"Well we should jump right in since we're running a bit late, but Todd an I do just like to start all these counseling sessions off by saying how wonderful we think it is that the church can offer this fellowship to young people thinking of engaging upon the greatest commitments of their lives, really," said Connie with a big smile on her face for all involved.

Kristi was excited to get into this and see what she would learn about Luke. This workbook was such a blessing to her. The questions it so blatantly asked with its blank lines staring back at you waiting patiently, nonjudgmentally for an answer. Questions Kristi hadn't found the nerve to come right out and ask Luke and now all that was left to do was for him to open the workbook sitting on the table just a foot away from her left knee and open his heart along with it, and bare out the truth of what he'd written there to and for and about her and their relationship and his innermost feelings, with their wonderful pastor and his amazing wife there to witness and help guide them through. She'd been looking forward to this for months.

"Well, I couldn't say it better than my bride! That's right—the greatest commitment of your lives. Isn't that something? Well, second only to your commitment to Jesus Himself, we should say," said Todd, correcting her a bit.

"Oh, of course!" said Connie.

"And, actually, the best way to look at it is probably: Jesus, Church, Family. I think that's the right order, wouldn't you say, dear?"

"Absolutely."

"So there's a lot we want to get into in these sessions," Todd continued, "but mainly it's all about what it means to commit to each other in a *Christian* marriage," he said, placing a hand on his Bible, then pulling it back, "as opposed to a *pagan* one. What it means to be a Christian Husband and a Christian Wife."

Luke listened to Todd's words with the weight of the action he might or might not take here balanced upon them. He was here because Kristi wanted to be here, but Luke was becoming more and more convinced in the past several months that Todd was not the man to marry them. He wanted to ask old Meeks out of semi-retirement for the purpose and have the ceremony back in North Carolina, in the old church, but he would hear Todd out. He'd noticed in many of the more private meetings with Todd that there were two Todds emerging before his eyes of late—the Todd who spoke from that stage with the loud band behind him welcoming in all the flock who would come through the open front doors, and the Todd who spoke in private to those he knew had been baptized through the real trials and tribulations of the Bible, its harsher truths. Luke listened carefully to see if his theory was true and, if so, which Todd would they get here, which would officiate their vows before God. If the answers weren't the right ones, Luke was fully prepared to stand up and leave this peaceful setting behind him in a fearful state of confusion and explain himself to Kristi later.

"Now what does that really mean, a Christian Husband, a Christian Wife?" Todd looked to Connie and she nodded knowingly of the difficulties there. "It means we're gonna have to talk about some tough things before we can give our approval to this marriage. And we need you to agree, right now, you don't even think about sending out announcements until you have that approval. Agreed?"

Luke didn't nod, but he didn't need to. Todd had only looked at Kristi on this, assuming Luke's obedience. Kristi nodded, though she didn't like the way he said the word "approval." She knew, of course, he'd have to approve … but still.

"So we'll talk about some tough things: the *birds* and the *bees*, marital *purity*, what to expect the wedding night, all of that."

Kristi's stomach squirmed a bit thinking about last night and the times before. Was that sex? Would they need to disclose that? They couldn't lie, if asked.

Todd looked to Luke. "And I mean it. We'll break up into groups— man-to-man, woman-to-woman—and we'll open up those closed doors. Pornography! A big problem," he said, nodding back and forth between the two of them. "You wouldn't believe the problems we've seen, the addiction there, the gateway drug that is to worse things, the marriages just in *shambles* because of it. Those are *Satan's* sites, I believe."

Good, Luke thought—the first he'd heard Todd talk like this in a long time.

"And I know it's *controversial*," he said giving a half-hearted one-handed quote sign to the room, "but we're gonna talk about the roles of men and women too. How different they are. Who has the Biblical responsibility for the headship, leadership of the household, and who is the 'helper,' as The Lord said, given to him?"

Kristi didn't like the way Todd just looked at her. He seemed different here than the Todd she'd grown to love and respect so—the one she looked up to at Church on Sundays, welcoming in the new diverse crowds and with them, she'd thought, a newer, more understanding, more welcoming, more Jesus-like Christianity. They were a bit unsettling to her, Todd's face and tone of voice now. And she was surprised too at the way Mrs. Connie's smile seemed to defer to him now. She usually seemed so ... "her own woman." He wasn't *really* saying that was he? He wasn't really going to tell her that Luke was to be in charge of her spiritually and day-to-day? Not Todd?

Luke was glad to hear Todd edging toward Biblical Truth here and relaxed more comfortably into his half of the loveseat.

"A Christian Marriage," Todd said with concluding authority, "following the Bible."

"Well—" Kristi said wishing she hadn't. Everyone looked at her.

"Yes, Kristi? This is an open environment. What were you going to say?" Todd leaned back in his chair with his coffee and assumed his exceedingly pleasant, you-can-tell-me-anything face.

Kristi wasn't prepared to do this. She was prepared with the first session's homework assignment (though now she wished she had read ahead after telling herself not to, to see if the workbook too went down this path). She was prepared with the page she'd filled in on what she loved about Luke and why she wanted to spend the rest of her life with him. She was anxious to say some of these things to him and to have him say some in return! But ... *okay, Kristi,* she thought to herself, *if there was ever a time to be honest ...*

"Isn't it the case ..." Kristi said.

Luke prepared himself for what he knew was coming. Kristi's liberal views. They'd have to face it right here in this room, the very civil war within the church itself.

Kristi'd stopped herself to find the words she wanted. She found them. "Don't we need to look at the Old Testament with New Testament eyes?"

Connie gave Kristi a sorrowful smile as if to say *you poor thing*.

Luke's blood began to boil.

Todd asked, pleasantly sounding enough, "What do you mean by that, dear?"

Kristi was so nervous now, it was like her stomach had dropped and there was this big hollow spot there preparing itself to be smacked and filled in with a wave of pain, but still she wanted to come forward, into that wave, she knew she must be truthful with herself, before her God and let come what would come. Of course, she was thinking about the argument Luke and she had had the one time she brought that poor, sweet Kyle to her Bible Study. Yes, he was homosexual, but a child of the Lord's nonetheless, and she knew Luke was thinking about that too. But it was all that, the old Leviticus stuff wrapped up into this view of marriage, the Old and the New.

"I mean," she said, "if we followed everything Leviticus and Deuteronomy and the others say about marriage, wouldn't Mrs. Connie and I basically be your slaves?"

The room went dead.

"All I'm saying is, there were the old ways and now, there are the new ways … since Jesus came. Shouldn't we be viewing the Old Testament in light of His Love, with His view of—"

Luke's hand slammed across the table, grabbing Todd's Bible, knocking Mrs. Connie's coffee over onto the glass with the force of bringing the mammoth book up into Kristi's face as he forced what his soul wanted to scream into the highest acceptable volume for the company present:

"I think we should *read* it, and *follow* it."

Todd and Connie's eyes went back and forth between Luke and Kristi's. Luke's eyes did not deviate in the slightest from Kristi's as hers went from the Bible he held in her face to look back at his angry eyes with a bit of pity for him, actually, and then down to herself with a bit of pity for them both.

9:13 AM

"Sergeant Cooper!"

Scotty turned too quickly on the steps and stumbled down a couple.

He looked up to see the peak of the beret, the Military Intelligence Battalion flash, all squarely aligned above the left eye. The finger's width from the headband to the eyebrow. The crisp uniform. The shoulder chords. Insignia. Brass buttons. He must have had an event.

Scotty almost squirmed in his sweaty gym clothes feeling filthy in comparison. He just needed to run into the Armory for two seconds, but of course Golding would appear from nowhere.

"Profess— Lieutenant Colonel Golding." Scotty saluted. He might have been "Professor" if Golding were in his civilian sweats coming from the gym too.

"I take it B Company, First Platoon, had some insubordination yesterday?"

Shit. Did he mean the Freshman or Scotty?

"Something about a bookbag."

Phew. "Yes, Sir. Sergeant Sheridan and I handled it."

Jesus, Ryan already got his report in.

"My read is Sergeant Sheridan attempted to handle it. You challenged that."

Goddamnit, sometimes Ryan took this shit too seriously.

"The kid—" *Shit.* Scotty's mind was so not in this right now. "Private Chester's been having a rough time. You push someone like that too hard—they might not stick with this."

Golding nodded.

What did the nod mean? What was he thinking the way he was looking at me?

"But Sergeant Sheridan is Platoon Leader, is he not?"

"Yes, Sir."

"Chain of Command, all that."

"Yes, Sir."

"All this … it isn't just fun and games, I hope."

"No, Sir."

"Glad to hear it."

Golding turned and headed off to whatever trim ceremony was waiting patiently for him.

Scotty hated the second-guessing he was left there with. The constant Goddamned second-guessing of his life.

9:14 AM

He should have walked a different path, he knew that. But he was aware of why he'd taken this route to class. His subconscious had brought him this way, through The Commons and the Great Divide that had been established there.

To come to the spot again where Tristan had said it and he had heard it. Where Tristan had so abruptly declared that the world as Ryan knew it was a lie.

Where the divisions between us—though less so this morning, students still sleepy, still setting up, more alike than not—were laid out so clearly, so simply.

When the times came to think, when quiet overtook, Ryan often thought about the many divisions in his life. There were so many great divides, it felt like his life was constantly being split in two.

Two Ryans. Always.

The biggest of all, of course: Ryan before and after the world changed.

But there were others. Too many others. College Ryan and ROTC Ryan. Those were only the most recent two in a long list.

He passed now the spot on The Commons and kept on his way, but his mind stayed there. The Ryan who loved Tristan. And the Ryan who hated him.

Their lives Before. So similar. Always at each other's side. And then After. Tristan moving on with his life. Ryan moving away. The irony in that. That Tristan stayed in the city and moved on, while Ryan moved away, only to remain stuck.

Tristan stayed in that cushy life Ryan soon came to realize to be "upper class" compared to Brockport where they moved. The two Ryans. Having known that cushy life. The expensive New York City elementary school. The nice house. And then Brockport. The despair of his family there.

There it was again. That feeling that someone, God Himself maybe, was sliding a great knife down the middle of him, slicing him in half.

And of course, he thought of his mom. Ryan with his mom, and Ryan without her. Trying to protect her ... trying to move on from her.

He needed to talk to her. But class would be starting soon.

Class. He needed that too. Class and homework and ROTC and the Frat and parties and bros on boats drinking beers and a girlfriend with a million little needs and everything he could to keep at bay the quiet of his mind and the forever ripping of his soul in two he experiences there.

9:21 AM

Tristan's two favorite spots were already filled up with studiers and nappers: the couch areas at either end of the Great Hall under the cathedral-like windows. But fortunately there was an open sofa chair and coffee table in his third favorite spot, an alcove of anthropology books about mid-Hall. Tristan liked being surrounded by the anthropology books on three sides whilst he looked out at the rows of students studying, or pretending to, along the width of the Great Hall laid out before him. He liked both thinking like an anthropologist, questioning the practices and primitive beliefs of his own generation, and thinking about all the "aboriginal" and "native" peoples in those books who have, or at least had, no use for the bullshit we fill our lives with. Some of the books were about the Native Americans who once lived on this land, who first built up Chekoloskee Island, a drop in the bucket of blood we spilt and the peoples we genocided in order to take this land for ourselves. Tristan liked thinking about them, how they once lived out their lives here in this very place.

And there was one other ingredient present that Tristan liked to have in a perfect library spot—some pleasing eye candy. Sitting at a table nearby was a totally adorable little freshman or sophomore, probably freshman, complete even with ginger hair and some freckles. Tristan was smitten. *Ha.* He liked that word. A word his grandma had used. He snagged the chair, unzipped his bookbag and began to set up shop. Sex in the library was legend and legion. One was always spotting a used condom on the floor of the stacks or hearing accidently (or perhaps purposefully?) escaped strained sounds of pleasure and looking up from one's work to smile at others who'd heard it too and wished they were doing the same. Sex in the library was the ultimate for Tristan—for his love of books and boys; he felt like Old Socrates himself "corrupting the youth" as they sought wisdom—so he was always on the lookout for opportunities, and besides, the tension-filled energy of that helped one to stay awake in the otherwise quiet of study.

First things first, Tristan turned off his phone. Not even simply silenced it. Off. Tristan liked no distractions save for the ones he chose to situate himself near. Once his research was complete, he'd disconnect his laptop from the wifi too. No popups, notifications, online temptations for wandering thoughts, no multitasking, a.k.a. half-assing, but the full focus of his faculties on the words of his paper.

Mc was a tough customer. But he was also, quite ironically, turning out to be Tristan's favorite professor. Even though he wasn't a professor, really. Well, meaning, he didn't have a Ph.D. But what Jay McTiernan had was a 33-year career in the CIA and FSCU's PoliSci department hired him on just this year to teach a couple courses on international terrorism and national security policy. Tristan had signed right up, not about to miss a chance to meet an insider of that dirtiest and most legitimized of American crime syndicates, and was smacked in the face immediately on his first paper with the worst grade, by far, Tristan had ever received in the grade-inflated academia he'd attended his whole life, and next to his D+ a note from Mc, "You're an internet Nut Job already! Come see me ASAP!" and in the little office/former closet PoliSci had found for Mc, Mc had told Tristan point-blunt, "I'm not gonna treat you like any of these other professors, I'm gonna treat you exactly like I would an employee of mine at The Company, got it?" and Tristan had gotten it, liked it, and accepted the challenge. Half of Mc's class dropped after the unfathomable grades of the first paper. No professor or teacher had ever treated them so harshly, they wouldn't dare, the evaluations would be negative, adjuncts wouldn't be invited back, tenure-tracks would derail, and Administrations would crack down on those nasty old professors who dared to demand that their students learn. After all, their precious customers must be coddled, entertained and told constantly of their greatness or they might take their business elsewhere. But Tristan could give a shit about GPA. He knew Mc had something to teach him.

But now, to write his paper, the one closest to some of Tristan's innermost demons and most metastasized fears, and to write it for this man who took no bullshit, only solid evidence, and on the topic, too, that Tristan knew would take a stab at Mc's gut, or a least serve a shot across the bow to secrets Mc had sworn by fear of blood to protect, his paper about the owners of so many, including Mc's former employer and "family"—the War Profiteers.

Tristan knew he was walking into dangerous territory with this paper and Mc. His evidence would have to be incontrovertible and his argument clear, free from any flourishes of style, serial metaphors, very Strunk & White. Drinking and smoking pot with a small circle of friends, Tristan could talk for hours, if they'd listen, contribute, stoke him on, about the evidence, knowing admittedly, just under the surface, that in this atmosphere "evidence" could be punched a bit, pushed through holes a clearer analysis wouldn't let it fit through. Not lying, just shorthand. People were high, after all; there was no interest in footnotes. But the blank page, with Mc waiting to attack any words he put upon it with his pen, that was where clearer analysis made it harder to begin. To find the things that couldn't so easily be thrown back in his face. All this was so hard because of all the covering. All the mythmaking.

But far more than that was the problem here that Mc wasn't an ivory-towered man of thought, but a man very much connected to the action. The more right Tristan's accusations were, the more in danger he could be placing himself: an A+ from Mc and he could be a marked man. Mc liked him, but Mc wouldn't want him piecing together some of these dots and adding them to "The Great Lunatic Conversation of the Crazies," as Mc had christened the internet. Sure, this was just a paper for a class. But there really was no telling what a man like Mc might do if he'd thought you'd connected certain dots in a certain way that might expose certain things The Company he's kept might rather stay kept very very quiet, very very hidden amongst the many many dots, some real, many not. Mc was a nice guy with a hearty laugh. But people got suicided for things like this. And by men who can otherwise laugh heartily in public.

And also ... these were emotionally precarious arguments Tristan was treading out onto the thin ice of. The argument to Mc here was in some ways a trial run for the argument Tristan wasn't sure he'd ever have the guts and emotional fortitude to make to his own father about how he's made his rather cushy living all these years. The one, of course, from which Tristan had benefited his whole life—a devil so close to home he walks its comfy halls.

Somewhere in the senses we don't quite understand we have, Tristan felt something and looked up to catch the ginger boy staring at him then quickly look back to his books to hide his sins. Tristan smiled. The game had begun.

9:47 AM

It wasn't working. Class. It wasn't pulling his thoughts into a unified focus. "The elegance of an equation," as another professor had said. A series of complications and twists, yes, but that by the laws of the universe as we've come to understand them, each knotted-up mess, no matter how impossible it seemed at first, could be smoothed out and solved for itself until in the end all that was left was one simple, clear, verifiable, repeatable answer.

Rather, in Ryan's mind, it was like the equation of his own life kept growing and branching out into other directions, and who could know for certain if solving any one part of it would ever lead back to solving the whole?

Branching. Dividing. Constantly. New divisions to be formed down every path.

Grandpa would have said this is the problem right here. Sitting in these classrooms. Losing your mind in thought. Surrounded by others doing the same. Listening to a man like this who'd spent his life doing the same. You gotta get off your butt and *do*, Grandpa would say. Stop thinking about the theory of the problem, get your hands on it and make it work.

Grandpa had worked for Kodak all his life. Not as an engineer, but as a tradesman. Until his trade was no longer of use. They'd wanted him to learn something new, stay with the company after all those years. But, as he said, he was an old dog, no new tricks left. And, as it turned out, the company couldn't stay with him anyway. The plant closing. The beginning of their downfall there. The shells of buildings that once meant livelihood, purpose, dedication. The shells of people who once had the same.

Ryan realized he'd gone down another branch of his equation. Maybe one that wouldn't lead to any answers.

But it was all Ryan. All of this. All his "B"s, his mom used to call them when he was a kid. His early years living in Bedford Hills and going to school in Brooklyn. Then seven years in Brockport. His uncles and aunts and cousins who struggled there. So little work to find. Much of it hard. So many theories as to who was to blame. Then Mom's decision that he should return to that now distant elite world of his youth for high school. Her determination to make it happen no matter what. Tristan's parents taking him in. Four years living in their house, a part of their family, Tristan and he becoming more brothers, really, than friends—the brother each never had. And now here. Florida. Tristan somehow still in tow. "Paradise." And the war he knew he was going to.

Somehow it was all him. This great tangled mess of an equation that even the great man of thought down in front of the room wouldn't be able to solve because though the boards would be filled with the branches shooting off in different directions, still there would be more to the equation underneath, on the boards behind, that could not yet be seen.

Ryan knew he presented a simpler answer on the surface. An equation anyone could solve. But it was a lie.

10:34 AM

The car ride home was somehow more silent than the one there. There was a festering civil war going on within the church, and just like that of America's history, this one was often being fought between family members and was clearly going to have to be fought between Luke and Kristi should they continue with their marriage plans.

Mrs. Connie had broken the stare-down, saying why didn't they start with the more pleasant stuff, the stuff Kristi had prepared to say. That all-important workbook question, the one Kristi had been so antsy since she first read it to reveal her answers—and hear revealed his answers—to, the one that was the very reason for and foundation of all these premarital sessions in the first place, the key to it, the heart of it: "In the space provided, list the reasons you know Jesus has laid in your heart that this is the person He wants you to spend the rest of your life with."

It was weird reading out her comments about how much she loved a young man strong in his Christian convictions, right after Luke's outburst that was so strong in his convictions, yes, but not quite those she thought "Christian" by her own definition of it.

But it was worse than she could have feared when they got to Luke. Even to get him to open his workbook took some time. And when he finally did, she faced the harsh truth why. The blanks were still blank. There were some false starts. His neat writing scratched out roughly, messily for him. But most of the lines were as empty as the simultaneously widening holes in her stomach and heart. She couldn't stop staring at those empty lines. The emptiness of all they stood for. How she'd longed to hear the words that would fill them these past weeks, struggling over her own answers, writing them out on scratch paper first to get them just right before committing them to the sacred pages of this book, thought, in her foolishness she now saw, that he was doing the same, late at night struggling for a way to say it just right, to explain his love for her with the best words he could find, and now she was faced with this ugly, barren truth: nothing. Nothing.

He'd tried to fix it, like so many rough spots before, by taking her hand and telling her he wasn't good at putting thoughts like this into words, but that he'd never felt love like he did for Kristi, and before her he didn't know for sure that feelings like that could exist. And, God, did he seem to mean it. His emotions so real. That's what she was trying to remember now—what she tried to hold onto.

10:41 AM

Privilege. Ryan had gotten stuck on that branch of his equation. Two Ryans: one that knew great privilege and one that knew great hardships.

Leisure. That was Grandpa's word. The Men of Leisure. Wasting their time away. Ryan was surrounded by that now. The Youth of Leisure. But it was Tristan's word too. Leisure. On one of his philosophy kicks. The need for leisure. In order to think. Two very different words. Ryan believing the truth in both.

Maybe it was Tristan's privilege and all his leisure that led him down these tangled paths to the point where he could say what he said yesterday through that bullhorn. Where he could believe the bullshit he amplified through it to his fellow youth of leisure, privilege.

Oligarchs ruling us. Did it take a privileged little prince like Tristan to see the world as kings and pawns?

But that's what was so strange about some of Tristan's conspiracy talk. That it sounded so similar to talk the other Ryan knew. Among his cousins and aunts and uncles in the Upstate. They were but pawns in Tristan's eyes, for sure. They were the fools who could be herded into believing anything. But they, too, seemed to see the world as pawns ruled by the conspiracies of kings.

That was one of the things the two Ryans got to see. Strange similarities between these American extremes.

Crap. What was his professor saying about the homework?

10:59 AM

Tristan had been playing with the ginger boy a bit, just with the occasional knowing look and coy smile, and once he'd stood up for a big stretch and the guy-flirt move of for some reason needing to lift his shirt to scratch an itch that was not there, but, oops, look, I revealed my flexed stomach washboard and a tat or two more. Ginger took notice and liked.

But Tristan's "better angels" told him to stop. This paper was due tomorrow and, for the first time really, Tristan was in a relationship where nearly every time he thought of another guy, his mind, maybe even his heart, returned to Kyle. Even if he knew he could get away with it and Kyle would never know, for the first time in any of his eclectic and messy history of relationships since that first dance in middle school—Tristan knew, deep down, he didn't want to do it. He didn't really want anyone but Kyle. And he knew that if he ever did anything to hurt him like this, the pain he'd cause Kyle would be ... unforgivable.

So he'd gone back to his work and was finally starting to put words on the page for the actual paper he'd turn in, when in walked the douchebags.

The boys of Sigma Alpha Phi, better known by their initials standing for "Sexual Assault Please!" or from recent videos of their racist chants streaming around in infamy. A pack of five approached their prey, the beautiful girl happy to stop her studies for them. Their "library whispers" loud and obnoxious enough to pierce Tristan's earplugs, seemed to Tristan the vacuous sirens of an element of society any anthropologist worth his or her salt would see as the personification of all those cancerous forces that will one day lead this once great empire to fall as certainly as once did Rome's.

Tristan sat back in his chair knowing there was no use fighting their annoyance; all he could do was wait them out. He pulled out his earplugs like a student worthy of this anthropologist's alcove to study more closely the "whispers" of this strain of human evolution which had veered off to remain neurologically closer to our brute ancestors than to Tristan's line. It hurt Tristan that Ryan chose to join one of these clans of regression. They stood for everything Tristan despised, these people who seemed to take pleasure in showing off their stupidity when yet they were privileged enough to have overcome it with ease had they merely but opened their ears to the words of some of the decent teachers along the way in school or out; these conformists of the highest degree who wore so nearly precisely the same outfits as their "brothers" they might as well have submitted to uniforms; these historically homophobic places of refuge for the closeted male fuck; these budding grounds for the wannabees of America's Wall Street cokeheads, or billable-hour law firm robots, but who, as depressing as that was, were more likely just destined to be cubicle-fillers for the never-ending fluorescent-lit rows of nothingness they would waste their lives earning a living in. That, and of course, the army. He recalled some of his favorite Einstein quotes about, "that worst outcrop of herd life, the military system ... Heroism on command, senseless violence, and all the loathsome nonsense that goes by the name of patriotism—how passionately I hate them!" Einstein said of the man who could take pleasure in the military's ways: "He has only been given his big brain by mistake; unprotected spinal marrow was all he needed." And here was his best friend from childhood, just as intelligent as he, and yet marching along these dual paths to the destruction of humankind in plenty more ways than one.

Tristan listened again to these great wastes of tuition dollars talking now about some story that high school and college kids and idiots at bars had told a trillion boring times and would tell a trillion boring more: "I was so drunk and ..." and Tristan knew he'd been wrong years ago in middle school when he happily proclaimed he didn't have an ounce of prejudice in him. There were people Tristan hated, and here were some of them taking a shit in the middle of his sanctuary.

He couldn't help it. As he watched them, his hatred for them grew. But fortunately, his eyes fell on the ginger's face, which held the same look of disgust on it for the frat boys as his own. *Good, there's hope yet in the world.*

11:01 AM

Mom had called. She could never remember his schedule. Ryan was walking out of the building, checking his phone. After the missed call notification, a text: "Hey You. Haven't heard from you in a bit. Everything good?"

He was about to call her back on reflex, but the sun hit the screen of his phone and in the fraction of a second it took his eyes to readjust, some protective force within him moved his thumb to tap the text instead.

Ryan was strong. He'd had to be most of his life. But even he knew his limits. He couldn't add the weight of her to his shoulders just now. Maybe later today.

He wrote back: "All good. You?"

He slid his phone back in his pocket to await notification of her lie in return. Their ritual, mother and son, constantly reassuring each other everything was fine.

11:06 AM

Kyle stepped out of the Biological Sciences building and into the gorgeous day it had become. As soon as he felt the sun on his skin he knew he wanted to get to the beach today despite not wanting to be a bad influence on Tristan's paper. But they would just be a few hours, Tristan could probably use the break from whatever depths of conspiracy his mind was wandering in now, and it was going to be getting too cool soon to really enjoy the water. He walked toward the library, not even bothering to text as Tristan would never have his phone on there. But he slowed his walk, noticing up ahead a young man in front of the Religious Studies building in an Arab dishdasha and taqiyah.

The Arab dress was something of an anomaly on FSCU's campus and intrigued Kyle with thoughts of his family life and younger years in Lebanon rushing back to him, and of course, of his grandpa on his dad's side always pushing him to remember his roots and learn more about them. As he got closer Kyle took in the even stranger sight of a rather scantily clad girl standing next to the boy in the dishdasha, all smiles. The table they'd set up in front of them said, "The Truth About Islam." Ok, Kyle was intrigued, he stopped by.

"As-salamu 'alaykum, brother," said the boy in the dress.

"Asslaam alakkam," said Kyle not having heard these words from his own mouth in too long. "What are you guys selling?" he said with a bit of a laugh, but at the same time thinking that sounded a tad Tristan of him.

The girl spoke first. "We're in the Arab-American Student Association. Have you heard of us?" she said with a smile and a voice Kyle found immediately flirtatious, and, come to think of it, she had seemed to look him over in a certain "I could eat him up" way as he walked over.

"Oh, yeah. You have all the speakers come and stuff, right? I've been meaning to go to some of those."

"Well, you definitely should! You want to put down your email and we'll add you to our mailing list?"

"Yeah, sure," Kyle said putting his bookbag on the sidewalk and leaning over the form they had.

"You should join our Facebook page too. We have a lot of social event info on there."

"Sweet," Kyle said.

Finally the boy spoke up. "And our next event is about what Islam really means—for all those who think we're just terrorists."

So, there was that word, Kyle thought as he kept writing. "Cool."

"Are you a Muslim, brother?" the boy said.

Kyle finished writing and stood up. "Sort of a religious mutt, I guess. My dad's family's Muslim, Sunni, my mom's is Christian and agnostic," Kyle said with a funny smile and received a sort of okay, sort of not, look from the guy. Kyle was starting not to like him.

The guy was studying Kyle's face. "Palestinian?"

"No, Lebanese. Well, Persian by way of Lebanon. And then American. I lived in Beirut till I was 5, then the burbs in Maryland."

"Oh. My family's Egyptian. Sara's is Saudi."

"Like three generations ago," she said.

"Nice, well, send me the invites," Kyle said picking up his bag.

"Would you like to come to our Truth event? Stand up to the prejudice against us?" the guy said, holding out a flier.

Great, Kyle thought. Just what he needed in his life. But he thought of his grandpa and "Yeah," he said, "that'd be cool."

"I'm Tahir," the kid said as Kyle took the flier.

"Nice to meet you. Kyle."

"Sara," she said again with a little laugh and little more flirtation.

Tahir, clearly aggravated by her, picked up a small copy of the Koran from a stack and handed it to Kyle like a knife cutting through Sara's stare. "Maybe you'd like to read this too—speaking of getting to the truth."

"Yeah. Okay, thanks." Kyle took the little book and added it and the flier to the contents of his bookbag.

"Nice meeting you guys!" Kyle said, walking away. His grandpa would be proud of him, Kyle thought. But something about that Tahir kid rubbed Kyle like sandpaper on his balls. Like maybe he approved of hanging homos by the neck in the middle of the town square or something. Sara seemed fun, though. He kept on toward Tristan, the beach, and escape from the images of young gay men dangling from their nooses in Iran or Saudi Arabia he'd seen online that had just come back to haunt him.

11:22 AM

The frat boys had finally left and Tristan had been exchanging flirtatious glances with ginger boy for a few minutes and enjoying how flushed the ging was getting. Tristan liked his power over the kid and wanted to see if he could get his face even more flushed. His chubby had been growing inside his shorts as he thought about taking this little ginger to the bathroom and bending him over, so he decided to give the sweet young innocent a peek, and slyly slid his right leg over while holding the crotch of his shorts with his left hand to let the head of his chubby fall out for the boy, and anyone else for that matter, to see. The move had the desired effect. The kid's face was going nearly as red as his hair.

"Hey, babe," Kyle whispered, and Tristan shut his legs as Kyle bent down and gave him a little kiss. "We going to the beach?"

Now Tristan's cheeks caught some of the flush as he said, "Yeah, definitely," and stood to pack up.

As they walked out, Tristan mouthed, "Sorry" to the boy with a shrug. And the ginger watched the two of them leave, not even trying to hide the jealousy in his eyes.

11:49 AM

As they drove down College Boulevard with main campus on one side and town on their other, Tristan's thoughts were pulled for a moment to the irresponsibility of leaving campus and his paper and the OC movement and his worries about Ryan's silently growing anger at him behind for a while to go play in the water, but tossed aside such concerns as easily as he always did with the carpe diem, the spontaneity, the you-only-pass-this-way-but-once-ness of it all. Soon enough Tristan would have to be someone's employee. Spontaneity and seizing the day would be things of the distant past. His life, for those working hours anyway, would be owned by the person who paid for "his living." And there was only one year left of this, the extended vacation, the prolonging of youth before adulthood that was college. Less than eight months now, actually.

It was all a part of his perfect little mess. His desire to live fully. A desire at the heart of his and Kyle's relationship. Kyle, who had far more reason to feel this desire than Tristan. But they both had their reasons. And he had gotten in a couple good hours on the paper. And he knew he'd get the rest done tonight. He always worked best under pressure.

So he drove past The Commons and his friends and the library behind Ponce Tower in his orange Jeep, faded to a paler shade now by the years of sun, the top down, of course, the doors long ago banished to his storage shed the day he moved to Florida, his left bare foot on the door frame, toes taking in the passing breeze, and his right pressed the pedal again and they turned onto the old Ocean Boulevard and headed to Sand Tiger Key and the AC. He felt his adorable boy by his side, the wind in their hair, the freedom of their youth and these college days, and he was happy Kyle had pulled him away from everything else—if just for a little while.

Kyle, of course, had noticed the little redhead and his boyfriend showing the kid his semi-hard cock. Fucking Tristan. God, Kyle thought, why was he staying in this crazy relationship with this crazy boy and only setting himself up for all the irrevocable pain it was certainly one day going to cause his heart when the wild and crazy ride of Kyle & Tristan finally came crashing horribly, unbearably down. Kyle had had a couple other hookups here and there, but only in spite of Tristan's philandering. He didn't want anyone else: not for himself, not for Tristan. Why couldn't it just be like this always, just the two of them, Tristan driving, Kyle by his side, the road to freedom, to anywhere they wanted to go, before them?

An Earth-killing, ridiculously large pickup truck drove by them, going the other direction on the little two-lane road on this manmade landbridge that snaked through the Thousand Islands out to their key, filled with frat guys or rednecks or other dumbasses, tires larger than Tristan's already decent-sized ones, and Tristan for the trillionth time just couldn't understand how a mind could enjoy nature whilst killing it. Tristan had specifically wanted a diesel Jeep Wrangler in high school, one, because he thought guys who drove them were hot, and two, because he wanted to convert the engine into an all-American fastfood eater. He'd found a series of videos on YouTube and convinced Ryan, with his pre-engineering brain, to help him, and over summer vacation the two of them turned the Jeep into a grease-eating machine. Tristan paid for his "gas" most of the time by smoking up a high school kid who worked at a local diner and poured the leftover deep fryer grease into one of Tristan's huge jugs. He had a whole system set up in his storage shed down the road. It was a big combined "Fuck You!" to the both the oil and "food" industries. On the back tire cover he'd painted, "This Jeep Runs on the Crap You Eat," followed by a little smiley face stuffed with French fries.

But mostly, the thing was, Tristan loved his Jeep. It was his high school years, it was he and Ryan working together with tools and grease and laughing at each other, it was days at the beach and sand on the floorboards and wetsuits hung out to dry on the roll bars and so many fun road trips, some planned, others not, and the time a friend at high school prom had fucked his girlfriend in the Jeep's little backseat and left the condom hanging on the antenna as a joke to Tristan, and Ryan sitting beside him, his strong arm holding the roll bar, his foot up on the door frame just like Tristan's, their more than confortable silence. He planned to keep his Jeep the rest of his life—taking care of it, driving it on weekends, passing a joint to some high school kid thirty years from now for more grease to fill him up.

Kyle loved the image of the old blacktop road, faded gray by the sun, passing by under the doorless frame; the road framed on either side by the grass, some trees, the bay and the islands beyond. He remembered one of the opening lines to the book Tristan loved so much and had made him read, *Zen and The Art of Motorcycle Maintenance*: "Tensions disappear along old roads like these." And there was something about this old road to their beach, the foot and bicycle paths worn down to the white Florida sand all along it from carless students walking with beach towels over their shoulders and bodyboards under arms or taking their morning or evening runs or riding their bikes, so many of which had these PVC pipe attachments made by a local, which held their body-, or skim-, or wake-, or windsurf boards. Something about all those countless little pebbles that made up the road, passing by underfoot at a speed the eye couldn't possibly perceive their individuality, told, to Kyle's mind anyway, of the passing of time and life—we shall never pass this way again. That was one of the things he and Tristan shared in their times of deep conversation—the importance of the here and the now and how fragile it all was. He looked over to his boy's wild hair playing and dancing like it was drunk in the wind and reached up to run his fingers through it and massage the back of Tristan's head, despite all his flaws, he loved him so.

Kyle's head massages were the best, his nails gently scraping your scalp, and Tristan could feel his tensions disappearing with every pull and push of the skin and the tightened tissues covering his tense skull beneath.

They reached Sand Tiger Key and he pulled into the gravel parking lot of the AC—FSCU's fancy new Aquatic Center and probably every Sand Tiger's favorite part of the campus. Tristan found it ironic, or perhaps prophetic, that the Sand Tiger Shark was FSCU's mascot, as after the spill they were endangered in the Gulf. But there were some signs they were making a comeback. Tristan turned off the grease-eater and they hopped out.

12:01 PM

"There is a pain he keeps from me."

Kristi wrote the words in her journal and then paused to look at them. It hurt, writing them and seeing them there. Because now they were real. They existed outside her mind. And the truth behind them was real. And she knew she had to go on. She knew there were more hard truths she needed to face.

Her Tupperware sat unopened on the bench beside her. Students walked in competing directions all around her. It was another beautiful day in paradise. But she'd been staring blankly for some time out at the campus before her, waiting for all the competing thoughts in her mind to find some unison, to flow in one direction.

She'd been journaling off and on since maybe late middle school. She found its powers almost like that of prayer—but in some ways more focusing, because of the time she'd take with it. The world moved at such a fast pace. But pen and paper took their time. Each word mattered more this way. And each word pulled from the circling mess of thoughts in her mind and placed carefully onto the paper helped her find clarity.

Clarity. How she longed for that now.

So she continued.

"A pain behind his sister's death. More than the loss of her ~ awful as that is. What did he mean? He knew why she had to die? I've never seen a pain in his face ~ in anyone's maybe ~ quite like that. What ~ or maybe <u>who</u> ~ does he blame???

"And then there's that ~ what he keeps from me about his beliefs ~ what goes on in the depths of his mind.

"But the piece that hurts the most ~ is the <u>LOVE</u> he keeps from me."

At this a teardrop formed and fell from her eye before she could catch it. She touched her eye to hold back any more, momentarily noticing the flow of students around her, but forcing herself not to care and back to her thoughts, her insecure world, on the page.

"God, those blank spaces, those scratched-out words. How dare he show up like that and expose before everyone that he had <u>nothing</u> for me there, nothing to say of why or even <u>if</u> he loves me!!! And after I had poured my heart out into those restricted blanks, writing as small as I could to fit it all in. 'Men aren't very good at this,' Todd had agreed. I won't accept that. I won't live my life that way!"

As she wrote those words so much came rushing back to her about her parents, about parents of friends, about aunts and uncles, so many marriages she didn't admire, didn't want, that seemed almost, she hated to admit it, like prisons.

"I know it's in him," she wrote, "I've seen it in him. Deep down in his heart. That's where God places our greatest truth. That's where mine is. The part of me that cannot accept the coldness, the aloneness, he wants to leave me in."

She stopped. A rush of thought stopping her. And then she resumed.

"There's a truth I hide from him. Rooms in my heart I've not let him see. That I think his version of Christianity"—these next words hurt to write too, but, once written, also released so much pent up ... anger. It was anger, she realized—"pains Jesus to see it. To see it proclaimed in His Name."

She stared at those words for a little while. Breathing more deeply in her belly.

"There's the truth about how I feel about us, him, that I hold back. That I've been worrying he might not be the one and that maybe God gave us these premarital sessions so that I could finally see that harsh truth.

"And there's the truth of how I feel about me. That I'm not going to put up with it any more.

"I can't control what he does. But I am in charge of what I do."

She needed to tell herself that. To sit down and have a good talking to with herself about it. And it felt so good to have it there—on paper—staring back at her.

She glanced up at all she'd written today. And then she was overcome with one final thought to end today's entry:

"Jesus ~ Dear Jesus ... the truth we hide from each other."

12:19 PM

Sand Tiger Key was a special place for most FSCUers, but especially for Tristan and Kyle. They each remembered the first time they saw the other in their dorm: Tristan first spotting Kyle when he was moving in, his parents helping him, looking even younger with them in tow, and thinking to himself that he'd never had a Middle Eastern boy before, and this one, clearly a half-and-half mix of the dark-skinned man and white-skinned woman behind him, was super cute and so sweet looking, and Tristan was immediately reminded of another of his favorite books, Mary Renault's *The Persian Boy*, and thought he'd very much like to Alexander the Great this young Bagoas; and

Kyle's eyes being caught by Tristan walking out of the building one day, Tristan's hair in the sun being the first image to grab Kyle's attention, then his tanned skin under an array of not-yet-decipherable tats, barely covered by his loose-fitting tank top and tiny little short-shorts, something about the confidence of the way he took a couple steps, threw down a well-used skateboard and hopped on with such ease, he was just the bad boy Kyle's perfectly wholesome upbringing (after Damascus anyway) had always wanted. But here, at the AC, was the first time they talked. They were both so pleasantly surprised to notice that the other was in this "real world lab" and tried to play it cool, not staring or anything, knowing in this class of wetsuits and locker rooms there'd be plenty to stare at later. The class was a part of FSCU's renowned Environmental Studies program—Kyle's major; Tristan's minor, soon to be second major—and what they were studying were the long-term effects of the Deep Water Horizon Spill and subsequent "Clean Up" on the Gulf, but they were also studying each other: Kyle struggling to get his wetsuit up over his shoulders that first day on the beach, Tristan not offering to help, preferring to watch; Kyle walking out to the beach one morning before class to find Tristan standing there, wetsuit on only up to his waist, hands planted on top of his head, staring out at the rising sun and seemingly endless sea in deep thought Kyle would never dream of disturbing, he just got closer, sat in the sand and watched him, wondering who this mysterious boy was. And then finally the day they'd come back in from a snorkel to collect soil samples near one of the protected patches of what was left of the Everglades on one of the countless keys nearby Sand Tiger, and pulling off wetsuits, Kyle finally got the nerve to say his first words to this boy, "Nice tats," and Tristan smiled to himself and then to the boy that he'd gotten him to talk first.

Now, they showed their Sand Tiger cards to the stoned kid manning the counter before the turnstile gate under the shaded hut of the main entrance and stepped out into the main pool area, where in front of them a tour guide was showing off the campus crown jewel to wide-eyed high school kids and their wide-eyed parents, and beyond college kids were sunning themselves rather than studying on the lazy lounge chairs that wrapped around the leisure pool, distinct from the lap pool down to the left. Campus tours always saved the AC for last—it sealed the deal. Who needed to hear about the brilliance of a school's professors when you could look out on this island resort of half-naked bodies laying around mid-"work"-day with the beach and the Gulf beyond? Sign the loan papers, go into debt and let this four-year (oh hell, let's make it six—why leave the party early?) vacation begin!

Tristan and Kyle walked past the pools over to the boat rentals— "rentals" that required no money, of course, that was all part of the bloated line item of "Rec Fees" in the tuition bills no one wanted to spend too much time thinking about—you just dropped off your Sand Tiger card with the stoned student manning this particular counter and picked up your kayak or multi-person float bed or whatever you were borrowing. Tristan had wanted to get two windsurf boards and do a little racing around, but Kyle had something he wanted to talk about out there on the water alone and persuaded Tristan to get his favorite—one of the little Hobie Wave catamarans. Kyle loved the intimacy of the two of them on this little boat. They picked up the neon bracelets they'd need to get back in from the beach and a little key on an accordion cord to unchain their boat once they found it in the row on the sand. Security was tight around the AC because of all the randoms who were always trying to get in. Tourists and people from Naples and whatnot heard stories of an exclusive island filled with college girls sunning themselves and they were always trying to break in. So Campus Police hired students in official white "Student Police" polo shirts to guard the entrances. If you didn't have your Sand Tiger card or the right color bracelet for the day, forget it. Unless, of course, you knew a kid at the gates or bribed him or something.

They found their boat, untethered it, and dragged it out into the water, which today felt even warmer than the air. As soon as the first little wave smacked their balls with salt water, they both let go of the catamaran and fell back, fully submerging themselves in the floating quiet of a world away from everything else, everything human. Well, almost.

It felt so good. No wetsuits needed yet, though surely they would be sooner than they'd like. There was a give and take to being in the Gulf knowing what they knew. It wasn't just the billions of barrels of oil BP had released, but also the un-fully-disclosed and un-ever-fully-knowable effects of the dispersants the government had let them dump to hide the oil from The People's eyes. The People were so easily fooled, weren't they? Just get it out of sight. But the noxious mix of all the pollutants had killed off countless sea life, dolphins and whatnot carried away in the night and buried or burned by who knew what unscrupulous mercenaries subcontracting themselves to the oil companies or the governments involved. And even though the worst of the lasting effects seemed to be wreaking their havoc mostly on the northern shores, and even after the detritus and lingering chemicals they'd still found in their sands during class, the government had said it was all perfectly safe now, like the mayor in *Jaws* telling people their beaches were safe for need of the tourist dollars, and as Tristan's head reemerged from the waves and he wiped the saltwater from his eyes he heard again, as he often did in his mind, the words of Pink Floyd: "Mother, should I trust the government?"

But screw it. Everything was killing us, wasn't it? There were carcinogens everywhere humans had conquered nature. Might as well live a little before they get you.

"Let's do this," Tristan said, swimming around and pulling himself up on the Hobie.

After a moment, watching Tristan lift himself up, feeling the water on his own body, trying always to commit the images of times like these to his long-term memory, Kyle did the same.

Tristan, despite growing up in New York, was at home on the water. In high school, he lifeguarded summers at a beach on Long Island and most of his family's vacations were to beaches around the world. Tristan was a natural cutting the Hobie around in the wind, knowing just when to tack the sail, sometimes too violently, throwing one or both of them off into the water, Kyle usually just hanging on for the ride and sometimes, it seemed, for dear life, like right now, as Tristan leaned back with the wind to pull Kyle's hull up out of the water several feet into the air, and they sailed along at even faster speeds with less drag from the sea and Kyle screamed with fear-laced joy.

12:48 PM

Ryan stepped into the dark classroom, the motion of which made the lights turn on, though he wished it hadn't. He was glad, at least, he could shut the door and have a few minutes of silence before the others started coming in for his 1:00 class. He took a seat and put his head on the desk. He felt like a zombie. Trying to tell his brain not to think about Tristan, the Two Ryans, the Great Divides, rich and poor, privileged and not, peace and the coming war, only made it obsess on all of it more. His forehead felt good on the cold desk. If he stayed motionless enough, maybe the lights would turn back off. But then the fucking door opened again and, of all people, in walked fucking Bret.

This was Ryan's only ROTC class today, and why Bret was early for it he could not fathom as it was also Bret's favorite class to mock. Military Leadership 4150: Operational Cultural Awareness was a key part of the modern wave of the military's efforts to avoid some of the major cultural blunders of its recent wars. Sensitivity training for the cultures they were likely to encounter. Examples of things gone bad and very, very bad. After you kill a bunch of locals, try not to pull out your dicks and piss on the bodies while one of your buddies takes pictures to post for the world's eyes. If you arrest a bunch of Muslims, it's probably not a good idea to gather up all of their Korans and throw them in a fire. Stuff like that. Stuff that was a waste of time to have to tell someone like Ryan, but, unfortunately, just as much of a waste of time to try to teach someone like Bret, for whom cultural awareness was, at best, a joke. Bret referred to the class alternately as Towel Head History, Terrorist Religions 101, How to Talk Towel Head, Sand N----- Studies, and others Ryan gladly forgot. Once, drunk, Bret had said to some of the boys, "Why learn about 'em, when you can just kill 'em?" And later that night, as if imparting one of the great secrets of existence: "Either we kill 'em now, or Jesus will get 'em in the Rapture—what's the difference?"

Only once had Bret ever let hints of this out in class, and in response the professor, who'd served in Iraq, called him an idiot to his face and in front of everyone in the room and said the mentality of morons like him was exactly what got good men like his friends killed by locals turned against us rather than grateful for us. Bret had nothing to say to the professor, but much to say later.

"You been in a hell of a funk lately," said Bret as he sat near Ryan.

Ryan nodded, not willing to give him anything more.

Bret eyed him in a way you couldn't tell if he was thinking something over deeply or about to throw a punch at him. But then, finally said, "Some boys and I are headin' up to a little ranch I know tomorrow afternoon. Gonna do some shootin', break out some of the big guns. You should come along. Do you some good."

Ryan had heard plenty of stories from Bret about he and his boys. War games they liked to play in the woods. He'd even bragged sometimes that they'd made some of the explosive ordinances in the "Army Improvised Munitions Handbook" and fired them off. Ryan was clearly not Bret's biggest fan, but the image had entered his mind of holding a semi-automatic weapon and firing at some target, and the release even in the brief little daydream felt pretty good.

"What time you all goin'?" Ryan said.

2:23 PM

She put her groceries down on the counter and started to unpack them. She hoped she hadn't forgotten anything she'd need for tomorrow night. It seemed like it was going to be a pretty well-attended Bible Study. There was this sort of buzz in the air on campus about some parties tomorrow night, even more so than usual. That was probably why everyone said they were coming. Thursday nights were hard for Christians at FSCU. They were the biggest party nights of the week, and it seemed like the whole town got inebriated at once. So they needed the refuge.

Eggs. Milk. Brownie mix. She stopped. Her hand still on the brownie mix box. Luke called her Bible Studies, Brownie Studies. Because, he said, they tended to be more about the desserts and the gossip of what was going on in peoples' lives than …

The more important questions God puts to us.

She looked at herself. Sort of more with her mind than her eyes. Standing in the kitchen. Hand on the brownie mix. Worries there too.

She left the kitchen and went to her desk. She pulled her journal from her bag, found the next blank page, and poised her pen above it for a moment. Then wrote the words:

A Strong Woman.

She took the words in. Let them stare back at her. Let herself question them.

She heard her father making one of his comments back when she was in high school: "You're not becoming one of those feminists, I'll tell you that right now." And she saw again her mother's nonresponse.

A Strong Woman.

She just kept staring at the words.

Stuck.

Stuck, because the truth was, as she was only, finally, admitting to herself right now, she didn't really know what they meant.

Mom was a strong woman ... in the workplace. She'd gotten her degree at night and now managed a pretty large senior home. People looked up to her. She made all the final decisions. But not at home. Their home. There, Dad was in charge. And Mom ... Kristi couldn't think of a single time Mom had ever contradicted Dad to his face.

And Mrs. Connie this morning. She just let herself be run over by Todd, didn't she? *And she wasn't there for me at all when I tried to make the pretty freaking obvious point that ...*

She couldn't stand up for me.

And Kristi's mind went back again to a memory that had haunted her for years. The first time the comfort—the safety—of her Church Family back home in Winter Park, FL., was breached.

There was this high school girl. Kristi was in middle school. And the high school girl had done something. Something that was "unspeakable," at least to a middle school girl's ears because the older girls would never tell Kristi what it was. She guessed a dozen different things: pregnant?, lesbian?, just "fooling around" with a boy? ... until she realized it didn't really matter so much to her what the girl had done. What mattered was the response of all the other girls. They shunned her.

It was the opposite of everything Kristi had come to expect of her Church Family. She loved this place so much because she'd never felt so welcome anywhere. Certainly not by everyone at school, outside her group of friends. Nor even—it had been painful, but helpful, to realize—with her *Family* Family. In her actual home. In the Church Family it was like everyone was nice to you always. Like there was no such thing as cruelty in this special place.

But then this girl did something. And whatever it was, her unspeakable thing, it showed little Kristi that cruelty did very much exist there within the Church Family, just beneath its surface.

She didn't say anything to the other girls then. She was too young.

She knew now that whatever the reasons the girls may have had then, they were not the kind of women Kristi wanted to be.

She needed a new map. That was it. A new way of looking at things. A better way.

She thought of President Voorhees. FSCU's fearless leader. She was the quintessential strong woman, wasn't she? So many glass ceilings she must have had to break through in her impressive career—Kristi couldn't even imagine all she must have been through. But she was such a clearly secular woman. How could Kristi see her as a role model?

She thought of the women of the Bible. Mary Magdalene, herself. Who was she for sure? Would we ever know the truth of her? Queen Esther. Perhaps she, Kristi, was also here "for such a time as this?" What would her purpose be?

Her mind went to the workbooks she'd seen at the Christian bookstore on the *Women of the Bible*. Maybe she should do a Bible Study on them. Maybe ...

No, wait. Come on, Kristi. Use your training. Psychology. Take a good hard look at yourself.

Her question wasn't about what other people thought a strong woman should be. Her question to herself was what does being a strong woman mean to *her*?

That was it, wasn't it? That was a good goal to set for herself. To discover what being a strong woman would mean for her, in her life.

She knew some girls from class who seemed to feel you needed to be entirely free of men in your life to be a strong woman. It seemed like every time a boy in class opened his mouth to respond to them, they'd tell him to stop "mansplainin'" them.

She knew others wouldn't be able to hold onto both being a strong woman and following Christian teachings. But Kristi wasn't giving up her Christianity or her desire to marry and raise a family, and, yes, from time to time, bake some freaking brownies. She liked brownies, *gosh darnit*. *Ha.* She chuckled to herself.

So that's it, Kristi. You have to find your *path to being a strong woman.*

And that started with this. All of this in this journal. Understanding herself better.

Know yourself.

She thought about the book she'd read in high school that had been one of the early seeds for her long-term goal of becoming a Christian Therapist. She found it now on the shelf above her desk and pulled it out. *The 7 Habits of Highly Effective People.* Just holding it, she started to remember things. "Seek first to understand, then to be understood."

She went back to her journal and started drawing a Venn diagram on the page. All the things that made her up.

The first, and biggest, circle was her "Faith." Then, she surprised herself (only a little), by drawing another circle, partially within the first and partially without, labeled "Church." Yes, the two were different. She drew another for "Family." Another for "Studies/Career Goals." But as she drew she noticed that the little shape in the coalescence of all the circles—that started as a curvy diamond, then a triangle, and was now more like a trapezoid— kept getting smaller. The more she added, the smaller the piece was that was her.

That didn't make sense. She was thinking about all the pieces that make up her whole, but with each new piece, her whole was getting smaller.

They were crowding her out, all those comparatively massive circles.

And they seemed to get larger as she stared at them. And her little piece of them all, smaller.

Family. A lot of people in college talked about how nice it was to finally be free from that. A lot of people seemed to feel suffocated by their families. Or they felt they were so different from them. It was nice to get away and explore your own self more. Your own choices. But how "away" would we ever really get?

A professor had once reminded the class that at our simplest, we really are just half our mom and half our dad. It was amazing how often, when she took a good hard look at herself, she could see that that was true. But then she'd fight it. It was way too simple a view; there were so many other influencers on her life. Her brother, for one. All her experiences. These other circles.

Career. Would she always be doing this? Self-analyzing? Seeing herself in patients and them in her? Would she become too self-focused? She'd have to fight that.

Church. Faith. God, how she hated that there seemed to be more and more battles to fight there too. These were suppose to be her refuge. He safe place. Void of cruelty. But more and more they crowded upon her. Squeezing her soul into a shape she did not want it to take.

She wanted to shove out those walls of her tiny trapezoid and say, "No, this is *me*! I'm in here! I'm bigger than this!"

There was a truth that was all her own.

Maybe that was it. She flipped back a page to that last line of what she'd written earlier today. "The truth we hide from each other."

That was the step she wanted to take now in her life toward being the strong woman she wanted to be.

That was the step she hadn't had the courage to take when the other girls of her Church Family shunned the one who'd done the unspeakable thing.

That was the step Connie did not take with Todd this morning.

That was the step her mom took every day in the workplace, but never with her father.

She wanted her voice to be heard and respected.

It began with that.

"Seek first to understand, then to be understood."

To be understood.

Yes.

"You want me to put these eggs and milk away for you?" her roommate yelled from the kitchen.

"Oh. Yes. Thank you!"

Oh, God, what time was it? She had to get going.

2:47 PM

They'd worn themselves out and were lying now on the canvas between the two hulls of the Hobie, each on one side of the mast, legs from the knees down dangling in the water as they rose and fell with the gentle tide. They'd been like that maybe twenty minutes now in silence. God, comfortable silence, Kyle thought—what a wonderful thing that was. Sometimes their fingers would touch, sometimes their toes in the water; their breaths long and full, filling even their tummies like toddlers, seemed in unison.

It was this incredible feeling of oneness.

One of Kyle's favorite memories of the two of them was a time just like this. They'd come out on the water despite forecasts of a big storm coming and the manager of the AC having told the kid at the desk not to let them out. But Tristan said they'd have at least another hour of sun and made it happen anyway. They were out pretty far, further than they were probably supposed to be, when the storm clouds started rolling in. Kyle couldn't remember ever seeing a storm form so rapidly.

But Tristan didn't want to move yet. They waited as the storm approached lying there then just like now. Same sides even. Silent together. Fingers and toes.

Kyle loved getting away with his bae. Just the two of them. So far away from the rest of the world.

One. He felt that with Tristan then. He felt it now.

The storm came upon them then and they just stayed. The rain pouring over them. It felt so good.

There were moments when Kyle felt scared. But with Tristan there, he just ... he couldn't be that scared.

Finally Tristan had thrown up the sail and they rode the storm winds and waves back to shore.

It was the wildest, funnest ride they'd ever had out there.

The manager had been pissed. But the memory was worth it to Kyle a thousand times over.

Sometimes you need a storm to remind you not just how good the sun feels, but how good too can be the raindrops, the energy, the crazy skies.

Kyle did want to ask about his thing. But he didn't want to ruin the sanctity of this moment or the sanctuary of this place. Of all the things Kyle loved about the AC, his favorite was that Tristan never spoke of politics here. It was like he returned to a purer part of his soul here.

But that's also why Kyle wanted to talk about his thing here. He wanted to talk about it on the spiritual level, freed from its politics. Despite Tristan's faults, Kyle loved him and wanted to share this journey with him.

And time was passing by. The quick clouds of a clockwork Florida afternoon shower seemed to be rapidly building. Soon, they'd have to head back.

So he broke their silence.

"Hey," he said.

Tristan took in another deep breath and asked, "Hum?" in a sleepy voice.

Kyle twisted over on his side to make sure he could take in all of Tristan's reactions, even the subtlest.

"Ok. I promise you, I *don't* want to have another conversation about religion," Kyle said. And, God, he really didn't. The times they'd broached the subject Tristan had gone off on rants: Religions were nothing but fairytales given force by the Powers That Be because they saw how they could use them to manipulate the masses, "Slaves! Obey your masters!" and such; stories of men who might or might not have lived, but if they did, their lives were turned into legends in the oral retellings, turned from mere men of human deeds into superheroes. Religions were how the powerful got the masses to accept their miserable lots in life, to want nothing from life, in the hopes of finally getting it in the next. Heaven, Tristan had once said in a stinging moment, the myth of it, was perhaps the greatest evil ever bestowed upon humanity—imagine all the lives wasted because they thought this, their one and only chance at existence, was just a precursor to the next—where everything would finally be perfect.

"And fine—forget about religions. But ..." Kyle said glancing up at the clouds building above them, the power and beauty of it all, "you think there's something, right? I mean—some benevolent force that did all this, created all this, wants ... I don't know ... something good for us? You don't just think it's all ... blackness when we die, right? 'Cuz, what would be the point?"

"Well ..." Tristan said as Kyle waited nervously for his answer, "it wouldn't be blackness, right, because that would be *something*. You'd be cognizant of the dark. It's hard to contemplate it—but it's nothingness. No consciousness. You cease to exist. You don't have thoughts to know you've lost them with."

It felt like some fat hand had just plunged into Kyle's stomach, curled its fingers around his guts and started twisting them in a type of pain the external layer of our bodies can never know. He had to look away from Tristan. He'd accepted Tristan's disbelief in so many things, the world's most prominent religions, Kyle's father's faith-filled view of the goodness of America and all it still could be, all those things Tristan thought childish, but this ... he'd hoped there'd be at least a seed of some belief in something greater, something more than mere humanity, more than mere chance. Kyle could deal with a lot in his "bad boy," but to be a real, true, atheist … he didn't know if he could love someone like that, trust someone like that to hold his heart.

Tristan could see what his comment was doing to Kyle. "I … I just don't fucking know, is all. I don't think we can know. There's no evidence for it."

Something about the way Tristan said that gave Kyle hope. "I just think—I can feel it." Kyle said. "This. Benevolent force. Something that created all this. That wants good for us … But … you think that's silly, I guess."

Tristan laid his head back again and looked up. It had just started to rain. The rain felt good. After a little while he said, "I don't know why it would be benevolent. If there is some sentient force that created all this … I'd think it'd be pretty pissed off to see what we've done with it."

Kyle lay back down too. The rain started falling harder; they were getting soaked. It was like the last time, but it wasn't. This time it just felt cold and a bit scary to be out there all alone in it. And what did it mean not to believe in anything like God? What would keep you moral? What would stop you from doing something horrible?

He didn't like these thoughts. And he didn't like the rain, not this time. This time the beat of the cold drops on his skin just felt annoying.

"Come on," he said, "I want to go back."

3:59 PM

Tracy was having a pajamas and blankets day. It had been warm today, before the clouds started forming, but she needed the blankets, so she pumped the air conditioning. Her roommates were at campus, but she'd decided to skip class and the GOTV today; she wanted to regroup. People had liked her remember-to-vote-tattoo-idea and it was still going on today— she'd been getting pics on her cell—but it didn't quite meet with the excited reception she'd hoped for. Ryan had made a bitchy little comment after their shower this morning about her being a walking "like button" and it had stung. So there she sat today on the living room couch, two fluffy blankets, four throw pillows, PJs, a cup of chamomile tea, her third for the day, and a marathon of one of her favorite reality shows on TV. The only thing missing was that, despite her anger with Ryan, she wished she'd taken Houston with her on the way out to snuggle with her now. In plenty of ways, she loved his old dog more than him. But her roommates would kill her for the fur—like they probably were going to anyway for the utility bill.

She kept thinking about what he said and she knew the reason it stung so was its being packed with the ammunition of truth. But she also kept thinking it sounded like something Tristan probably said behind her back and Ryan had only finally gotten the nerve to repeat to her face now.

Then she remembered something and grabbed her phone and flipped back in time through a flurry of thumb-swiped photos to the one she was looking for. She had an unnatural ability to find anything on that phone in under 3 seconds. She opened the photo: a screenshot she'd taken of a post before demanding its author delete it and shortly thereafter deleting him as a "friend." It seemed insane to her now that she had ever friended Tristan, but when she first heard about him she was excited that her "BF's BFF," as she called him was this hottie gay guy and had every intention of making him one of her best friends too. Fail.

But she'd kept screenshots of the post and subsequent DM bitch sesh because part of her knew they contained the same ammunition as Ryan's comment this morning. She looked them over again now. Tristan's post had been in response to her post of pics from sophomore year's Floatopia. She and her sisters on their sorority's massive float. Looking like a row of models. Every sister in the shots had approved the photos before posting. No bad angles. No hint of flab in the twist of a torso. A less attractive sister on the end had been cropped out.

Tristan posted a pic of her from freshman year's Floatopia ridiculously and not-too-successfully trying to hula-hoop on Tristan's float, Ryan laying flat on his belly trying to help hold up her thighs.

She looked hideous. The way her torso bent forward and the flab fell over. Her skin not tan enough, no filter on the photo. And God, that stupid face she was making.

Her thumb had almost deleted the post on its own reflex. But she stopped to take a screenshot of it first to somehow use as her ammunition against Tristan. To tell people, "Look! Look what he did!"

She reread what he wrote with the pic now. "I like this 'Floatopia Tracy' better."

Then their argument. She'd DM'd him immediately. "How could you post a pic of me like that?! Don't you ever THINK?!!! What if I put out a pic of you like that?!" It went on and on. Five screenshots worth of back-and-forth between them.

It was the first time Tristan used that word against her. "Check your façade," he'd written. *Façade!* Boy did she let him have it in return.

"MY façade?!!! Look in the fucking mirror, dude! Like I'm sure you do 50 times a day. How much time do YOU spend in the gym to have that body? How much time do YOU spend shopping to look so perfectly like you don't care, while, like, oops, the collar of my t-shirt has just been stretched so big it shows this little tattoo on my collarbone. Gee, wonder how that happened? And, speaking of that, how many hours have you spent under the ink gun, how many thousands of dollars, how many hours drawing them in your SO SELF-CENTERED notebook to get them just right first? YOU want to tell ME about having a façade???!!!"

"Wow, is that the opposite of reality. My tats are the EXACT OPPOSITE of 'façade'. They're me trying to tell the world what I believe. Trying to put what's INSIDE on the OUTSIDE of my skin. How do you not know that after the conversation we had the day I took that pic?!"

She hit him back. "That is such a lie and you know it. You know the image your tats give off. That you're a 'BAD BOY', that you're just SO COOL, that you're TOUGH, when actually behind them you're just a scared little shit."

It went on. But their friendship didn't. They were just trying to be friends anyway, for Ryan. That was the façade. This pierced it.

But ... despite her despising him, she couldn't help it, his words still got to her. And she'd kept them, hadn't she? She put her phone down and absentmindedly reached over with her free hand to pet Houston, but it was just a pillow.

She felt alone and hurt, but she knew one thing for certain: she wasn't going to stop being who she was, and was most certainly not going to change the path she had set for herself. Look at those women on the screen and the fabulous lives they lived. If Tracy knew anything it was that she was not going to allow herself to be normal. Have some normal marriage, get some normal job, live some boring life. She had greatness in her. She *knew* it. And someday, somehow, she would make the world see it too.

4:07 PM

Tristan's cock hadn't forgotten about what it started in the library, and by now it really needed to release what his balls had been building up since. He'd wanted to fool around on the Hobie—that's why he'd thought Kyle chose it—they'd had some good, clean fun out there on the water a few times before. Once, some jet-skiers had sped by and one of the guys yelled, "Get'er done, Bro!" not realizing who was under Tristan at the time. But then Kyle'd brought up God.

So now, in the AC locker room, before hitting the showers so Kyle could clean up for his five o'clock class, Tristan was playing with Kyle as he got undressed and trying to cheer him up enough to join in the fun.

"Good God," Kyle said as Tristan, unable to take it anymore, pulled down his briefs to let his hard dick fly right out there in the middle of the locker row. But Tristan's powers had worked and Kyle was horny now too, and no one was in this row of lockers right now but them, so Kyle bent down and gave it a little playful lick, then stood back up.

"That's all he gets?"

Kyle smirked, then bent back down and took him all the way in. He was getting into it, forgetting where they were, when,

"This is a public place!"

Kyle looked up half-laughing in nervousness, but lost his laugh immediately on seeing who it was who stood there.

Tristan just pointed to his cock and said, "You wanna suck me too?"

The guy's face reddened with anger as he turned and left.

Tristan laughed, but lost his laugh, noticing Kyle's face as he stood up.

"What?" Tristan asked.

"That was Kristi's boyfriend."

Noticing this meant nothing to Tristan, he continued, "From the Bible Study I went to a couple times."

And Tristan forgot all about his now flapping penis as his entire body contorted around in uncontrollable laughter.

4:11 PM

Luke stormed out of the AC and toward his car, legs still covered in dried sand from getting caught out in the rain in his kayak. He'd wanted to shower off and clean up, but forget that now, he couldn't stomach being in that place a second longer.

He got in his car, shut the door, started the engine, and stopped for a moment, hit with a sudden strange realization: he was glad he'd seen it. Sickening as it was, this first time to see in its grossest mutations what has become of America's youth, the Sodomites set free, this Sodom & Gomorrah surrounding him, horrible as it was to be exposed to those images, he knew it was God's plan for him to see this and see it now, the Lord's reassurance that he, Luke, despite all his fears, was on the right path.

He put the car into gear and backed out. Meeks had wanted him to go to Liberty University or Bob Jones or Regent or any of the good Christian colleges, but Luke knew deep down that that selective seclusion, that burying of his head in the sand, was not the right path for him; that we should not try to escape it, but rather to face the reality of life in America now head-on.

But Meeks had prepared him enough. When he saw Luke as a boy racing through the hugely popular *Left Behind* series (having rightly steered clear of the witchery of *Harry Potter*)—Luke had even been addicted to the videogame for a while wherein good young Christians could blow away the nonbelievers—Meeks suggested some more books for him to read, among them the works of James Dobson, Jerry Falwell, Pat Robertson. Once Meeks learned that King James was a homosexual, that version of the Bible was immediately banished from the Church—"So great is the power of the Enemy's Deception," Meeks told the congregation, "that he has even infiltrated one of the most widely promoted editions of God's Holy Bible itself!" One had to be careful what one read, Meeks said, what one let through one's "eye gate." For this, he encouraged home or Christian schooling with the right books. But Luke's parents never listened.

Those boys back there corrupting their souls in sin, enjoying the pleasures of the temporal flesh only to suffer for it in eternity ... it might not be their fault, for they were raised in this filth, in the fallen state that this once great nation has become. Had they been raised in Christian schools, Christian homes that taught them the Truth, the right morals, they might have been spared their evil futures and damned destinies. Had their parents read James Dobson's *Bringing Up Boys* or *Dare to Discipline*, or other books Luke remembered seeing in the Christian bookstores like *A Parent's Guide to Preventing Homosexuality*, these poor lost souls might have avoided their unthinkable fates.

And that Kristi thought it was *okay*, all this? That she'd invited that child of Satan's into her Bible Study. This was indeed the Devil working his way into the Church through the "feel-good" liberal philosophies of Kristi's camp. He was grateful he knew, now he'd be able to help her, Kristi, to save her, before it was too late. That's what he most wanted. Look at these half-naked kids walking back down the beaten paths from the AC, that place of sun and skin worship. He wanted to save them somehow from similar destinies of damnation. So he was glad God's Hand had brought him here, to see the world as it truly was, to come face to face with its ugliest truths.

But Kristi. Kristi first. He needed to find her. And tell her. Now.

4:23 PM

Luke opened one of the absurdly large and heavy glass doors to Todd's absurdly expensive and modern and welcoming-to-all Christian Youth Center to go find Kristi where he knew she would be, the missionaries' table from 3:00 to 6:00, he knew her schedule by heart. Students on ladders were hanging yet another of the student art pieces that Todd encouraged so much, this one a gigantic painting, maybe 8 feet wide and 16 high of Christ on The Cross, but not a weak and whipped and tortured-to-submission Christ, not one of the many "bearded lady" Jesuses of the old, effeminate church many complained about in certain chat rooms, but one who looked like he just left the gym for the tenth time this week, and with his huge protein-shaked muscles was in the process of breaking free from The Cross, the wood behind his massive left arm having snapped in half under the force of his strength, a strength that appealed to the young southern men who had conceived it, painted it, and were hanging it from wires dropped from the ceiling of Todd's lobby to this place of games and bake sales and welcomeness-to-all and $8 million in debt, $8 million Luke could still not bring himself to comprehend Todd's acceptance of the debt of, the interest, the usury, to build this opulence and why?, to send what message to the new recruits, that God wants you pampered and comfortable and playing pool and drinking free, bottomless hot chocolate? As Luke climbed the steps to the "Main Hangout Area," as it was officially named, the thought emerged of the Biblical inaccuracy of Christ breaking free from The Cross like that, and with that broken Cross, the breaking of Christ's Church, how much was breaking and crumbling as we welcomed all thoughts and hung them in the lobby, painted them in bright colors, spreading a myth, a lie, for all to see and believe. And that was the same, though far worse, that Kristi had welcomed into her house with that sick Kyle whom Luke had disliked from day one with his relativist's ways, trying to paint Jesus in a liberal's light and even on more than one occasion bringing up similarities he'd noticed between Christianity and Islam to the silent, confused, sickened, affronted, angered faces of others in Kristi's Bible Study who knew not why he'd been welcomed.

This was what happened with the 'laxing of the rules, Luke thought as he scanned the Main Hangout Area for the missionaries' table, spotted it against a back wall, and headed for it, the Devil began to find cracks in the wall that he could enter, or even, when things got bad enough, large glass doors that he could walk welcomed through or smaller wooden doors into your apartment to share in the food you'd cooked and confuse you and your guests with the maybe-this's and what-about-that's of other views, until one day there you are kneeling in public, no shame at all in others seeing you, on the dirty locker room floor of the gymnasium, another boy's penis in your mouth and Satan bent over laughing uncontrollably with pleasure.

Kristi looked up from the table and gave him a slightly confused smile. "Babe. You're all messy," she said, nodding to his legs, which were caked in a Florida muddy sand mix from the knees down. Everyone looked.

Luke did too. Having forgotten his appearance. And his mind started focusing on that—what would people think?—only half-listening to what Kristi was saying now about, "Did you come to support us?" and another girl, "How sweet!" as his hand sensibly began feeling for his wallet.

There were three or four girls at the table. Cookies and candy and pamphlets. They were raising money for a missionary team the church was sending to ... an African country Luke couldn't remember right now and couldn't quite read the sign in front of him, everyone looking at him and seemingly talking all at once. Somehow so many memories of high school and middle school, of being laughed at or treated as different, as odd, as "not one of us," seemed to be lighting up the dark recesses of his mind and he was the last boy to get a date to the middle school Homecoming dance, the one who looked at the others with a hilarious fright when they talked about masturbation that one day at recess and for weeks they'd imitated his face, and the pressures of everyone looking at him now, as he laid down a ten from his wallet and said some words of hopefulness for their mission, were overtaking him in ways they had done before and that he still could neither understand nor control, and he was helpless as a middle schooler left alone at recess with only his thoughts for comfort.

Kristi could tell something was wrong and that he'd wanted to talk. She had motioned with her head and a look—did he want to step aside somewhere?—but he didn't seem to notice her hint. And then there was something behind the unreal smile he was giving the others now that brought some other sense within her to fear what he might have to say. She thought, *if it's bad, if it's another one of his fits, I'd rather he tell me later, not here where others might overhear.* It was bad enough she had to deal with his changes, his darkening moods; at least her friends hadn't noticed them yet, or at least they hadn't said. If and when they did, then she'd have to explain. Then it would be, why are you putting up with this? Or worse, why can't you help him? She wasn't ready to answer those questions yet, because she had not yet answered them for herself. So she stayed there behind the safety of that table, and as he smiled and walked away she turned to her friends and said something about how sweet he was, and they all agreed.

She thought about the words she'd written only hours before in her journal, and smiled again, to keep hidden the things she needed hidden now.

■ ■ ■

6:03 PM

Scotty did not have time for this. Everything about picking up this damn waterslide was such an annoyance and had been the bane of his existence the past two days. He'd driven all the way across the state to the outskirts of Miami yesterday, only for the morons at the party store to tell him they hadn't gotten it in yet, though they also hadn't bothered to call to let him know that beforehand. So, he'd had to rush back today to get it, because there was absolutely no way he'd have time tomorrow, and, admittedly, he'd been speeding back to campus to try to make his 6:00 study group, but was now pulled over on the side of the highway with flashing lights behind him, waiting for the cop. And Scotty hated to think it, hated to have to think about it at all, but he was pretty damn sure he knew what was about to happen.

He rolled down the window as the man got close, and yep, there it was, something in his eyes, something that changed as he realized the driver of this Porsche Cayenne was a young black man. They went through the motions, Scotty being sure to be as polite as possible, though he despised having to be, but he remembered his father's pleas to him so clearly it was like his dad was sitting right there in the car with him, though thank God he wasn't.

Dad had spoken to him several times throughout Scotty's middle and high school years about making certain he showed the greatest respect around police, should he ever encounter them. At first, it had all just seemed wrapped up in his father's great patriotism. He'd served in the army and loved this country, which was why, despite his great financial success, he still wanted his son in ROTC.

But then Michael Brown happened—and his father's plea seemed different—though maybe, Scotty feared, his father's fear had really been there all along, just buried beneath those more common words about respect for authority. After Ferguson, Baltimore, and all the rest, his dad's reminders to his son were less and less about respect, and more and more about being careful—you just never knew.

And that pained him so much to see in his dad, a man who had always been so proud of this country and "The American Way." His father had risen himself up from abject poverty, crediting, always, his biggest first steps to the army and the technical training he received there, and then joining the early tech revolution and rising through the ranks to the executive suites.

But still, there was his skin. He remembered the thing that broke his proud father when they were moving from Scotty's childhood home to an even nicer one in Florida with his dad's new company, and despite it being a great market, months went by without a bid. Scotty, as a kid then, didn't think much about it, until the thing that broke his dad happened. A friend had pulled his dad aside and told him the thing the real estate agents didn't want to say. Despite the fact that they were moving to an even nicer home, the one they were leaving was still very, very nice, upper-middle class, at least. The friend said, "You've got to get rid of all the pictures of your family." The house sold three days after his father succumbed to doing it.

"How do you make your living?"

How in the world was that question pertinent to the giving of a speeding ticket? Scotty could translate Florida Redneck. The question meant, "You a drug dealer?"

"I'm a college student," Scotty said and produced a smile for the officer that hurt inside to make.

"Will you step out of the car, please."

Un-fucking-believable. This was the second time Scotty had been asked to get out of his own fucking car by a fucking cop for no fucking reason. After the first, he'd been told the cop had no right to do that, no probable cause, but fuck right, there is no right right now when it's just you and the man with the badge and the gun. And if he argued that, if he said the words "probable cause," it would only confirm in this asshole's thick head that he must have had some "run-ins with the law."

Scotty got out, knowing full well that Ryan or any of his white fraternity bros would not have had to, knowing if his ROTC crew saw this they'd want to kick the shit out of this shithead, knowing that if his father saw this it would only make the proud American drop one more notch down in his pride for his country and even, far worse, for himself.

Scotty worried as the guy searched around his car. Had one of his bros left a baggie in the car with just enough left inside? If so, could this trip to pick up the fucking waterslide end up with Scotty going to prison for decades under some bullshit mandatory minimum sentence? What about an empty (and thus "open") beer can? Dammit, why hadn't he checked his car? *Fuck*, why did he, far more than the others, have to?!

A car drove by. Camping equipment tied to the roof. White faces looking out at him. Kids in the back. What did they see as they saw him standing there? What did Daddy say when the kids asked why the policeman was searching that man's car?

The car continued on and the road was empty again save for Scotty and the officer. And then Scotty noticed something he hadn't before—something his growing anger had not quite let him register. The officer's right hand was on his gun. Holstered, yes. And maybe this was the pose they always took. But still, as he walked around Scotty's car, there was his hand on that thing that could take his life.

YouTube memories. Philando Castile shot. His blood soaking through his white shirt. His girlfriend sitting next to him in the car filming it. The fear and pain constrained in her voice. Her daughter seated behind her pleading for her mom not to get shot too. The officer screaming, sounding so scared and confused as to why he did it. As to why Philando now lay dying for no reason. No reason.

Terence Crutcher shot down in the street for looking like a "bad dude." Michael Brown's lifeless body lying in the street. Other flashes. Black bodies. Human blood. Hands in the air.

Scotty's anger had been covering something that now overcame him. Fear. And not fear of a fucking speeding ticket. Fear for his life. *My hands are where you can see them, Sir. I'm stepping out of the car, Sir. I'm standing on the side of the road right where you said to, Sir. Please don't shoot me, Sir.*

He hated his fear. He felt cowardly in his fear.

The anger was better.

Skin. Fucking skin. That's what this was about.

He watched the deputized redneck searching through his car almost, it seemed to Scotty, hoping to find something. He thought of one of his favorite lines about the race wars he'd watched in a YouTube clip a dozen, or maybe twice that, times of the badass old queer-and-black-and-proud-and-held-down-by-no-white-man-and-no-stigma author James Baldwin saying, "And if it is true that your invention reveals you, then who is the n-----? ... I give you your problem back. You're the n-----, baby, it isn't me." And he repeated that line in his mind now, watching this man treat him like a criminal—"You're the n-----, baby, it isn't me." And it did somehow give him some release to know the truth of that. To feel the empowerment of that knowledge right now when he so needed it. To know that he was not lesser for what this man thought of his skin, but that this man was lesser for thinking it.

The cop reemerged with nothing. He asked Scotty about the mound of rolled-up plastic in the back. Scotty explained. The waterslide. Politely. While his mind raced with what it might look like? Something with drugs?

For a grow house? The officer told him to get back in his car, came back a bit later with Scotty's ticket and told him to, "Be safe."

But the translation seemed very much to say, "Stay in line, N-----."

■ ■ ■

8:43 PM

The sweet color of the whiskey in the glass; the way it held onto the walls of its container a little longer than you'd expect before rejoining its compatriots in the bottom as you gave it a little swirl; the smell from the second you uncorked the bottle with the sweet little chirp-squeak it made; the heft of the glass and the weighty fact that it was his father's drink—all brought the consistent and trustworthy comforts back to him now.

His dog, Houston (pronounced the New York way) sat with him there on the floor as he, leaning back against his bed, looked up at framed photos on his shelves, and especially, on the top shelf, the face of his father, inlaid in a majestic image of the Twin Towers with that line beneath them: Never Forget.

Ryan, of course, would and could never.

The counselors and therapists and teachers and adults in his youth had been scattered in their advice, usually proffered without request, on whether or not it was healthy for the boy to spend too much time remembering or dwelling upon the events of that day. Somehow, they'd hoped, despite the seeming impossibility of it, the incomprehensibly devastated boy, his world shattered, his father stolen from him along with his sense of safety and perhaps, the Good Protecting Hand of God, would have to move on.

So he tried to stop himself from thinking about it too much. Though he did remember the day in late middle school when it had suddenly occurred to him that the day before had been the first full day when he hadn't thought about it—him—the day or his father—even once. And how he cried and hated himself for that.

He took another sip of the work of his father's favorite distiller. Straight, the whiskey. Neat. *Don't ruin it with ice please, please don't do that,* pollute it with water. The alcohol allowed the many grips on Ryan's brain to loosen and in the more easy breaths of that freedom he allowed himself to think about the inner sanctum of memories Tristan had violated and tried to pollute yesterday.

It had been a while since he let himself think about 9/11—the events of the day, the details—in any prolonged way. Every so often, more and more seldom, maybe once a year now, maybe less, he feared, life sat him down to think about it. Usually on the anniversary. But this past one, like many others, thinking back to his childhood therapy, Ryan chose to take control of his thoughts and focus them on his father, on his love for his dad and his dad's for him, on the good times. On the little smudges.

His mom had told him about those one day, years later, when they both were focusing on the good times. Ryan's dad worked for the New York State Department of Taxation & Finance, Mediation Services in their offices in the South Tower. He'd just sort of fallen into it. It wasn't like he had some great plan to end up working there; who would? Dad never really cared so much about what he did for a job, he cared about the rest of it. He'd tell people he was just a "blue collar guy" who had worked his way up in a "white collar world"—literally, two separate elevator trips up, one express, one local, to the top floors of the towers. Just getting from the ground floor to his office was a commute in itself. Dad made good money, but as he used to tell his son, "I may be the bread winner, but Mom buys the steaks."

That's where the real money came from—Mom's real estate career—until it, like everything else, came crashing down.

Anyway, one of the anniversaries his mom had told him about the smudges. Ryan remembered that his dad loved to take him to the office and show him how cool it was to stand on top of the world, but his mom had let him in on a little secret this time, that the cleaning people only cleaned Dad's windows every few weeks or so—and that's when they'd wipe away the smudges from little Ryan's hands and forehead, where he always planted them against the glass to look down from the Heavens. Dad liked catching sight every once in a while of those little smudges and the memories they left with them of the exhilaration in his boy every time he got to come here, which, in turn, reminded the boy still inside his father's soul of what a cool thing it was to be on the 87th floor of one of the world's tallest buildings looking out over, perhaps, the world's coolest city. He didn't like it when they wiped his boy's smudges away.

Seeing that window or thinking he saw it, or straining so hard to see it, impossible as it would have been, from where the boy stood on the Brooklyn Promenade that morning staring across the river to the tip of Manhattan and the gaping, burning holes in both buildings ... the teacher had just grabbed Tristan behind him, he could hear, and soon enough would grab him too and pull him away, but not before Ryan willed the word, the single word toward those buildings, above that awful hole where he thought his dad might be, said the word meant somehow, if the world's creator gave a damn at all anymore, to bring his dad the courage to fight through to safety, the one word, the simple word, that somehow said all of this: "Dad."

As soon as his word left his mouth he was in the arms of the teacher, pulled away, and Tristan there too—there, Ryan knew, for him.

There had been some strange happenings that morning in the brownstoned private school the two attended in Brooklyn Heights, one of the best schools in the city (which was why their parents carpooled from where they lived in Bedford Hills, and took the two boys and two other kids to school every morning on their ways into work). Administrators kept coming in and whispering things to the teacher that caused the teacher's face to strain for normalcy in ways the kids had never seen. Eventually, words were overheard and spread. Someone passed Ryan a note: a plane hit the towers? It seemed like something a kid had gotten wrong in translation from adult-speak. Then it seemed like it must have been a small plane, something wrong with the pilot, maybe. But administrators returned, things seemed more strained, something was wrong. Ryan knew there was a TV in the teachers' lounge. Without permission, without asking, without letting the teacher grab hold of him, he was out the door and down the hall and pushed open the lounge door, and there on the screen he saw it for the first time— the black hole in that building that would remain in his heart as long as he lived.

Mr. Russell was in the lounge too. He was the first to notice Ryan and the first to run after him. But Ryan was a fast runner—and this was no ordinary sprint. He bolted for the building's front door, sounding an alarm when it opened after normal receiving hours, and ran as if in a dream, and as he would again and again in nightmare memories of this morning for many years to come, to the promenade overlook to see the buildings for himself, to know if this was real—in the real world—not just on TV.

Along the way he became aware that Tristan was behind him, and behind them both, Mr. Russell. Apparently, Tristan had followed him from class, stood there behind him at the lounge and followed him out the front door of the school as well, but he only remembered noticing his presence now.

And then, there, on the promenade, all huddled together in Mr. Russell's arms, there was a noise. And a woman screamed. He knew he'd never heard a scream like that before, and now, on his bedroom floor, knew he'd never heard one since. And like someone supposedly lifting a car to free a person in a crisis, little Ryan somehow found the strength to pull out of Mr. Russell's hold and he'd missed what caused the scream, but saw what it had left—the South Tower, his dad's Tower, was gone. Just one Tower stood. And smoke. And, he'd never forget, what seemed to be pieces of metal floating in the smoke, reflecting back bright shines from the sun.

"He got out," Tristan said behind him, having broken free too. "Your dad is so fast. He got out." And Tristan grabbed him. And he grabbed Tristan back. Because there was nothing left to hold him up.

9:01 PM

The problem about the Truth, of course, was not just in finding it, but in convincing others of it. Preaching to the choir is the cliché for the easy argument, but preaching to the choir of a different "Truth," that's the opposite of that cliché's ease, isn't it? How does a Jesus believer walk into a mosque and tell them they've got it all wrong? Belief was thought-ending. Question-stopping. There was a kind of oxygen necessary for thought that got sucked out of the room when certain people were present. And so to even begin the discussion, you needed to find ways to pump it back in.

This was what Tristan was thinking about looking away from the screen of his partially, very partially, perhaps 3/40th's finished paper. Mc required the paper in-hand or uploaded by 10:00 AM, just under thirteen hours from now. Tristan was ready for another all-nighter, his large coffee from his walkup window in hand. Tristan liked drugs, but only for fun, not for work on anything serious. So while many other students would hit the coke or at least the Adderall at a time like this, Tristan preferred the clearness of sobriety.

But still, his clearness was getting a bit muddied by a word. A word that crept into his consciousness and seemed to be creeping up more and more lately. A word that stopped him. Futility.

He'd been feeling that—its sickening beating down of your heart, its ripping at your insides—somewhat often in recent months. Maybe it was college life coming to a close, and the dreadful paths of monotony that seemed the only options beyond it, the lives of "quiet desperation" Thoreau mourned. Maybe it was looking back on all of his protests, on all of his "activism" in high school, on all of his mom's efforts to fight the horrendous elections of W., twice, both times the harm done to his parents' marriage, and all of this together seeming to have accomplished precisely the same as had they done nothing. All the work and energy and emotion poured into it—and no one was listening. The choirs we strove to change the minds of simply sang on, clueless and brainwashed as ever.

And the same, surely, would be the effect of his paper now. Mc, to his credit, had encouraged him like a good teacher should: focus on the facts, the evidence—that, in the end, is all you've got to convince rational minds with. That, and your persuasion for how those dots connect.

And that's what Tristan had been doing for his paper on the War Profiteers. His notes were filled with numbers and links to where he got them. He had the books in front of him.

The bravely gotten and exposed information from James Risen's work in *Pay Any Price: Greed, Power, and Endless War*. The truckloads, literally truckloads, of pallets of 100-dollar bills secreted away from the Federal Reserve's secret warehouse of cash in New Jersey in the early days of the Iraq War to be put on planes with minimal supervision and shipped to

Baghdad to ... disappear. All in, approximately 20 billion dollars. Where did it go?

His abused-and-destroyed-with-notes-and-underlines-and-tabs-and-spine-broken-in-a-dozen-places copy of Andrew Feinstein's *The Shadow World: Inside the Global Arms Trade*, in which from the breadth of history and the span of the globe we see not only the long entrenchment of the War Profiteers and their immense power, their easy corruption of government "leaders," but, especially for Tristan, how the unwinnable War on Terror had been expertly designed from Day 1 as an unbeatable business opportunity.

He had the audiobook of Amy and David Goodman's *The Exception to the Rulers: Exposing Oily Politicians, War Profiteers and the Media That Loves Them*, on his phone and had just finished listening again to Track 17 and taking notes on the Goodmans' extensive, yet not nearly exhaustive, list of companies who benefited greatly from America's wars in Iraq and Afghanistan and who also, coincidentally, had contributed heavily to Republican campaign coffers.

He had James and Molly McCartney's *America's War Machine: Vested Interests, Endless Conflict*, Suzanne Simons' *Master of War: Blackwater USA's Erik Prince and the Business of War*, Douglas Farah and Stephen Braun's *Merchant of Death: Money, Guns, Planes, and the Man Who Makes War Possible*, a half-dozen other books and dozens of articles printed out and annotated.

His notes on the $2.3 trillion Rumsfeld said his Pentagon had lost track of—Oops, we misplaced that!—the eve of 9/11, right before even such an astonishing number as that would surely be all forgotten in a matter of hours and in the months to come much, much more added to it.

The cost of one M1 Abrams Tank: $8.5 million. One tank!

Think about that. You can get a baseline Rolls-Royce Ghost for $295,000. Or deck out a Phantom for $500,000. You can get a Maybach for less than $200,000. And this hunk of metal costs $8.5 million?! How is that possible? And how many thousands of these have we bought to fight terrorists who hide in mountain caves or attack tube stations or nightclubs?

The individuals who directly profited from 9/11—foreknowledge blatant—yet the leads on them not only not followed, but covered up by those whose job it supposedly was to find the culprits.

Even back to old Ike, himself, that magnificent paradox of Dwight D. Eisenhower who sounded the great, repeated-but-never-listened-to, warning on the Military Industrial Complex and his simple, poignant reminder of the sad, despicable, and unforgivable truth that "the cost of one modern heavy bomber is this: a modern brick school in more than thirty cities [or] two fine fully equipped hospitals," that was the very playing out of Randolph Bourne's spot-on pulling back of the curtain to see the truth of the ones in charge and know, as Chomsky quoted him, and as Tristan had now quoted him for the opening salvo of the unfinished paper before him:

War is the health of the state .... It automatically sets in motion throughout society those irresistible forces for uniformity, for passionate cooperation with the Government in coercing into obedience the minority groups and individuals which lack the larger herd sense .... Other values such as artistic creation, knowledge, reason, beauty, the enhancement of life, are instantly and almost unanimously sacrificed, and the significant classes who have constituted themselves the amateur agents of the State are engaged not only in sacrificing these values for themselves but in coercing all other persons into sacrificing them.

"Who are these 'significant classes'?" Tristan asked on the page. "And for what purpose do they demand this sacrifice not only of our life, liberty, and pursuit of happiness, but of our communal fortunes?"

The answers were all so clear to Tristan and his choir, but contrary to Mc's too simple egging on, facts would not be enough. For one thing, despite all he'd found, days and days of scouring for the facts had only reminded him of the futility of thinking you could find very many of them. There were not dozens of James Risens and Andrew Feinsteins and James and Molly McCartneys and Amy Goodmans, or hundreds as there should be. And even what follow-the-money trails had begun to be sniffed out ultimately led cold, didn't they?, or got so muddied we'd lost the scent. That's what we most needed to do—to follow the money—and, as such, that's what the true culprits behind it all most knew they most needed to hide.

Surely, they drooled at the ancient wealth, the kind that could seemingly never be attained today, of those war profiteers of history, the masters of war who led their Roman legions and returned to march triumphantly to the Capitol with the pillaged hoards of wealth that in today's dollars would make Bill Gates's fortune seem pitiful in comparison. But that was their mistake, wasn't it? Parading their plunders. This must be hidden, the true reason for war. The People must think we only fight—they only sacrifice their lives—for good and noble causes. And so now, the trails run cold. And for some, perhaps, who got too far down those trails, the cold they met there was death.

But even if all the facts could be exposed, there were still the manipulators of the masses' thoughts, the mythmakers. Even with dinosaurs of evidence standing before them, The People could be convinced not to believe—or rather, to believe in something in total opposition to the facts. As some asshole once said, "The bigger the lie, the easier it is to get people to believe it."

So Tristan sat in his little dorm room surrounded by his mess of books and notes and protest posters—stopped in his tracks by the futility of his paper, by yet another wasted effort, wasted energy, wasted time. What the fuck was the point? Words on paper. Even the books that got close, the ones people risked their careers, perhaps their lives, to write—what little effect they had.

Words, words on paper for a class or for mass publication, words to be sent through the ether of the internet, to be yelled through bullhorns to passing students, even written into a documentary or a film that could be praised by all for a fleeting moment, words were not enough.

Bourne wrote his words as America was entering World War I, and yet the world has still not listened.

Eisenhower gave his grave warnings about the Military Industrial Complex at the end of his presidency, and yet the world has still not listened.

So who on Earth was going to listen to Tristan?

Words were not enough.

9:07 PM

The worst part about what Tristan said, those few lines that escaped his brain and shouted from that bullhorn, was what they could mean for Ryan's Destiny. The Destiny he'd been planning since that morning on the promenade looking across at only one Tower, not his father's, left. He knew from that moment, even as a little boy, but a little boy who within these vital minutes had seemed to mature years, that his life must now be devoted to a singular mission: Revenge. The people who did this to his father must pay, and Ryan, personally, so very personally, must play a key role in making them feel the pain of that justice.

And that's how he'd lived his life since. Despite all the therapy sessions, despite all the "carrying on," despite all the moments he'd allowed himself to let loose and enjoy, as he knew his dad would want, despite, or maybe, rather, buried beneath them all was one constant and building desire that his soul could never truly rest until fulfilling.

But he needed to be a good son to his mom too. She had suffered so much—both with Ryan and apart from him—alone, when sometimes he heard her sobs. And she feared so deeply the need for retribution she knew he harbored. She had begged him not to go right into the military, but to get a civilian education first, to take more time to mature and know for certain first, and so, in an attempt to pursue what he knew he must, while also trying so hard not to re-break his mother's fragilely-re-pieced-and-glued-with-love-and-therapy-and-determination-to-raise-her-son-without-constant-sadness-but-with-joy-for-the-good-in-life heart, he agreed to not join the military right after high school, but get a college degree first, through an ROTC program. The decision hadn't been so hard after Osama had been killed and there seemed to be relative peace for a while. Though lately he'd thought often of tossing it all aside and enlisting right now.

Even as kid, though, he'd known his revenge would not be so simple. It wasn't about just joining the military, going to whatever war they put him in, and shooting all the Muslims he could find. That was a Bret-level mentality, and he, as a New Yorker, a city that seemed the "melting pot" of the world, despised it. Over the years he'd understood the sophistication that went into planning and carrying out a horror like 9/11, and he intended to respond with at least that level of sophistication in finding the organizing powers, far behind the foot soldiers who flew the planes, and hitting them in such a powerful way as to wipe them from the face of the Earth.

So the path he'd wanted to take was more geared toward the higher echelons of the military, and, perhaps even, ultimately, Military Intelligence or

CIA. For now, he studied his engineering and Arabic and the histories of al Qaeda and ISIS and all the iterations of them and most importantly the sources of power at their helms.

But that was the most damning hidden blade of Tristan's bullshit conspiracy-nut-job assertions yesterday. That was what had been digging at him ever since he heard Tristan speak the words. For sure, he'd occasionally heard other nut-jobs mention 9/11 conspiracies, known of, but refused to watch, viral videos about it online. But the bitch of the thing about Tristan was that he was one of the smartest people Ryan had ever known. Tristan had aced the SATs and had his choice of colleges despite his mediocre GPA. Tristan only did well in classes he gave a shit about, on the rest he didn't waste his time. You never saw such a variety of grades as Tristan accumulated. So the top schools were out of the question, but still there were plenty who wanted to add his SAT scores to the incoming mix and bring up the average a bit. Which brought up again in Ryan's mind the question of why Tristan had come here, to FSCU, or rather, more accurately, followed Ryan here. But that was a Tristan conspiracy all on its own and one Ryan didn't care to rehash tonight.

The question he mulled over as he continued sipping his whiskey was whether he would ever dare to look into that dark gaping hole of 9/11 questions, himself. Consider the possibility of it. That his rage all these years, his vengeance, could possibly be directed toward the wrong enemy. Would he drink enough tonight to dare to type into Google words he'd sometimes thought of trying, but always stopped himself from? Simple words. Like "9/11 conspiracy" or "9/11 truth?"

Tristan had been wrong before. But he'd also seemed more right sometimes than any other explanation Ryan had heard for some of the more questionable of history's events. He was wrong, Tristan'd admitted, about the kick he'd gone on in late middle school when he'd discovered YouTube videos about the first moon landing being faked. He'd been on that kick for at least a month, before, to his credit, learning and then admitting the errors in the first theories he'd bought into. But still, when Tristan would go off on his rants about JFK's assassination, it sure didn't seem like Oswald could have done all that on his own, and, even more so, that he did have a history with CIA and might well have been planted there by the more corrupt branches of that organization under the duplicitous Dulles, who had a powerful hand in things even after Kennedy sacked him. So Ryan's mind went around in circles and the whiskey wasn't stopping them, but making their effect more dizzying.

He looked up at his dad's eyes.

His revenge. That's what Tristan was trying to pull away from him now with these fucking comments. The possibility of it. The one thing he had left to bring any closure to the black hole still open and burning in his heart, like the one in his father's Tower that morning, smaller now than it once was— but still open, and burning.

9:18 PM

But, despite the futility, Tristan kept writing. The paper was due. The grade was needed. Graduation and the certificate that said, "I'm smart enough! Hire me!" were needed. Because the jobs would be needed. Because that's what we as a society had chosen to submit our lives to: to sell our lives, hour-by-hour, for dollars.

But then, thankfully, he got another distraction. A friend messaged him with a link and a question: "Did you see what Fuck Face just said?"

Tristan opened the link to a video of Fuck Face, a.k.a., Candidate Kill 'em All, as Tristan had dubbed him, one of the two pitiful contenders The

People were being given to choose from for that Orwellian focal point of all their societal hopes: The American Presidency.

Fuck Face/Kill 'em All now said this: "It's their religion." And he paused for the effect and the praise.

"Nobody wants to say that; I'll say it. A President needs to have the guts and the clarity of mind to identify our enemies for what they are. It's their religion that leads them to this. My religion tells me to love my neighbor. Theirs, apparently, tells them to kill their neighbor. They call this Jihad. That means, 'Holy War!'"

"Now this is gonna be even more controversial, but I'll say it too. I won't clean it up for you. I won't dance around the issue. I'm gonna be honest. And tell you the Truth. *I agree with them*. This *is a Holy War!*"

He fought on through the applause: "Their religion tells them to kill us because of our religion. It's as plain as that. How could this be anything other than a Holy War? No one has the guts to tell you the Truth. As a candidate and as President, the *Truth* is exactly what I'm gonna give you!"

And the diverse-enough-as-they-could-find faces behind him and the massive no-diversity-required crowd before him cheered, but not just cheered, as the news reporter was now saying, but gave an incredible 30-second-long standing ovation, which the candidate, despite several attempts, could not quiet.

Tristan leaned back in his chair and thought for a moment. And what he thought was: that was a good move. Smart. Give The People what they want. Tap into the preexisting structures of their religious mythologies. Give them the passion of God's Master Plan, His Final Solution, His Beckoning of Armageddon. And give them, thereby, the freedom to do their greatest evil. For "Men never do evil so completely and cheerfully as when they do it from religious conviction," as Pascal warned to centuries of people who remembered and repeated his quote and liked the quip of it, but paid it no attention.

Yes, there was no chance of stopping the war. All that was at issue in the election was how the new war would be marketed. Candidate Kill 'em All and Candidate Measured Response. Those were our choices. Either way, we were going. Either way, it was the War Profiteers who were going to win.

It mattered absolutely nothing, there was to be no pause to consider, no reason for it, that for this group, this new wave of ISIS or ISIL or IS or Insurgents or al Qaeda or Jihadists or Boko Haram or Mujahedeen or Hezbollah or Hamas or Black September or Jewish "extremists" or Palestinian "terrorists" or al Qaeda of the Arab Peninsula or al Qaeda in the Islamic Maghreb or al Qaeda in Your Neighbor's House! or Skinheads or Klu Klux Klan or White Supremacists or Patriots or Armies of God or Liberation Fronts or IRA or Anarchists or Crusaders of the Holy Roman Empire or Native American "Savages" in the night with tomahawks who once had brought us food and gifts, or "Some worthless piece of shit (though maybe he wasn't always) who walked into that gay club and pulled out his legally bought and golf-game-and-million-dollar-donations-lobbied killing machine and ended the lives of innocent infidels in the midst of the ecstasy of their drinking and drugging and dancing and living life to its fullest, its freest, its most ready for a good fuck, because somewhere deep down inside his own colon it was he who wanted to be fucked by those he'd kill that night," or whatever they were being called or calling themselves now, religion was not actually at the heart of it. Even if religion's poison had originally allowed the cancer present in all of us to grow and overtake the good, it was now just a mask which covered the true cause, a shield which protected it, a sword which gave its hurting soul a means to release its pain. Religion was its body armor, its weaponry, its genetic warfare to start the cancerous process anew in the souls of its "collateral damage" victims. And what a powerful sword it makes. So powerful, Candidate Kill 'em All had just turned it around and offered its grip of salvation to us, The American People, to give us an outlet for our pain, to give us reasons to feel justified in the terrors we would soon commit in whatever name we prefer to call our religion, but surely, in there somewhere, a Religion of the Rightness of America.

At the heart of it, it was all very simple, actually. It was pain. Unforgivable pain. Pain and hating the people who caused it. Or who you thought caused it. Or who you were made to believe caused it. A crying child who hits his parent, and the good parent says, "No, no, don't hit. Use your words." But words are harder to come by than fists. They take a maturity we are, as a society, as a planet of societies, mostly, still so far from attaining. And so, the argument goes, our aggressors will not understand and respect our words, they only understand and respect our fists. So fists and swords and bullets and bombs are what we must use ... to end our pain.

9:23 PM

My God, Luke thought, *it really is happening.*

"This *is* a Holy War," this man had said, this man who could be President.

"This is a Holy War," Luke whispered aloud. "Thank You Jesus ... for the path you've given me ... for my salvation."

His mind began to wander to the many heavy thoughts weighing on it, but his attention was then pulled back to his laptop, as this President-to-Be,-By-God, continued, "For many decades now, in America, there has been a war being waged against Christianity. Our beliefs are oppressed. They try to take the lessons of Jesus Christ out of our schools. Try to keep God's Law out of our courthouses and legislatures. Try to spread the *myth* that this great nation was not founded as a *Christian* Nation. Here we have the war on Christian Beliefs. Best witnessed by the War on Christmas, but spreading its tentacles far beyond. And we must rise up against that war at home. We must not be afraid to be who we are, to stand for what we believe in—our *Culture*. Despite all those who are out to stop us. But over there, over there, my friends, things are far worse. Over there the war is not simply against Christian Beliefs. That war, I'm afraid, they won a long time ago. Now, over there, the war is upon the very lives of Christians themselves. There, they are seeking out Christians, drawing them out into the public square—to where they behead them."

The jumbo-screen behind him now switched to cell phone video of Christians being lined up and men entirely robed and masked in black preparing their beheading blades. The video paused before the beheadings themselves took place and across the images of those soon to die the news company that aired the video threw up the word, "BLOODBATH!"

"How, I ask you, can we, a country God has bestowed so many blessings upon, sit back and watch that—and do nothing? And how could anyone look at that and tell me this is not a Holy War?

"I invite you all now to engage in a moment of silence with me for those slain brothers and sisters in Christ. And to pray for the protection of those brave souls who remain in this Land of Terror."

Luke shut his laptop, got up from his desk, and down on his knees at his bed to do just that. He prayed for the safety of the Christians whose lives were in danger. He prayed for our country to return to Him and His Calling. But also … he prayed that Meeks was right.

Meeks, in his semi-retirement, had come upon a new, perhaps final, Calling from God. He'd taken to blogging out this message on their church's rather basic website. Luke had shown him how, one break at home. Only Meeks didn't call it blogging. He called them his Epistles, these letters, in a series he titled, "'For The Time Is Near' Rev. 22:10."

Luke knew God had been preparing him for this his whole life. As a boy, he'd first found the children's version of the *Left Behind* series, called *Left Behind: The Kids*, at their Christian bookstore, then he'd graduated to the adult series, reading all sixteen of the novels. And he and his friends put countless hours into the *Left Behind* videogames, killing all the nonbelievers, fighting off the armies of the Antichrist. But that had all been fiction. Fantasy.

But there was nothing fantastical about Meeks' Epistles. They were all grounded in the coldest and hardest facts of our sad reality. The signs were everywhere and growing. Meeks called them the "fissures"—the first cracks in the breaking of The Seven Seals.

They were all so blatantly there for us to see, but we were being fooled, Meeks said, by the clever powers of the Antichrist who had devised modern mythologies for us to believe in so we wouldn't see the Truth. As always, the favorite tools of the Antichrist were the atheists, the unbelievers, the "Secular Humanists," some were calling them now. With all their considerable powers, they were spreading the false prophecies of what was behind the mounting destruction of God's Creation, the escalating wars between His People, the spreading disease that could not be stopped. They tried to divert our attention from the Truth by telling us it was our fault. And the greatest blasphemy, Meeks pointed out, behind their message, was that human beings could change through their mere efforts the Destiny of Destruction the Lord has ordained for this world.

And of course they'd want to stop it, Meeks said. Of course they'd want to prolong their reign on this planet and hold off the day when Judgment shall come. But Judgment, Meeks said, is coming soon. Therefore, listen not to false prophecies of how mere humans can alter the course of the Lord's Grand Design. Revelations tells us why the waters will rise to disappear the islands and bring the mountains low. Revelations tells us why the rivers will be poisoned; why much of the oceans and the land will be destroyed; why the sun will be allowed to scorch the Earth; why there shall be no peace; why war, famine, pestilence shall overtake; why earthquakes, thunder and hail, storms of all kinds shall worsen; why so many must die and, most especially, those who must be slaughtered for professing the Word of The Lord. Luke thought again of those just beheaded.

Meeks continued in his memory: what fools to try to "save the planet" by driving their tiny, effeminate cars, killing jobs to save trees, whilst they kill babies to save their sinful ways! What fools to not see it is because their sinful ways can not be hidden from the Eyes of God that this planet must be destroyed! What fools to not see the Mark of the Beast in the dark patches of skin that form upon those struck with AIDS for their great immorality! What fools to not see that a horror like 9/11 must be allowed upon even God's Country when, as The Lord promised, He must take peace from the Earth. What fools to ignore the Word of God laid before them these 2,000 years soaked in the blood of His only Son!

And now, the foretold Holy War, Luke thought. The War to Babylon.

The Lord is coming, Meeks said. And He is coming soon. And Jesus comes not as the Lamb this time. Not the little baby in a manger. The God of all power who allowed himself to be crucified. That was the carrot. Now, it's time for the stick. This time, Jesus returns mounted upon his War Horse. This time, not the Lamb, but the Lion. This time, not to be crucified—but to do the crucifying. So you'd better be ready.

And then Luke thought again of poor Kristi. What she had let into her house. Meeks had said to prepare yourself like Lot was prepared for the Lord's Return to Sodom. Lot's house was pure and good. But what would the Angels of the Lord find when they knocked on Kristi's door? He was so mad at himself for how childish he'd been earlier. And how with so much else on his shoulders he'd let slip away the rest of the day without going to tell her. He checked the time. She'd be getting ready for bed. But if he hurried he might get there first. She needed to know. The Angels of the Lord were coming soon.

9:41 PM

Ryan finished the last sip of his third rather large pour and with it his desire to sit on the floor of his bedroom and sulk. It was time to confront Tristan, to hear it directly from him, to squeeze it out of him if he had to. The five-year-old kid in Ryan still holding onto Tristan on that promenade after all these years needed to know what this was he'd held onto for so long, what this support of his closest childhood friend was truly made of, and would, under pressure, its structure, once so solid, crumble to the ground as dust?

He picked up his phone and found Tristan's name.

.   .   .

Tristan was hitting his stride. He'd knocked out maybe another 60th of the paper, it felt like, in just the last 20 minutes, it felt like, fueled as he was with rage courtesy of Candidate Kill 'em All's latest contribution to what a future Gibbon would surely write in the *Decline and Fall of the American Empire*.

But then his phone buzzed on his desk. Crap, he'd forgotten again to turn it completely off. He flipped it over and the first thing he saw was not the text, but the name of its sender, and everything he'd been trying to avoid thinking or worrying about from his stupid fucking stump speech yesterday, and hoping maybe Ryan didn't quite hear or catch all of, now came rushing back like a tidal wave that had at first been quietly receding out to sea gaining its power, barely noticed.

He read the text. "I'm coming over. Be there."

Crap. Fuck, fuck, fuck, fuck, FUCK!

.   .   .

Ryan shouldn't have been driving. He knew that. He actually hated people who drove drunk. But he wasn't drunk. He could handle his booze. And the walk would take too long. He hit his brakes as the light turned red and students from every direction started crossing the intersection of this heavily bar-ed area of town. Several seemed more intoxicated than he already. They seemed so carefree walking by him. Like they were living in two different worlds, he and them. Like maybe a few blocks away there could have been a massacre going on like the ISIS attacks in Paris and Ryan knew all about it, had just come from its carnage, but here, people were smiling, they had no idea, didn't notice the sounds.

.   .   .

Tristan was sitting calmly in his chair thinking about how he'd handle this, what he'd say. You had to choose your battles. Was this really the time to have this battle with Ryan? Why now? Because of some chance fuckup that Ryan would have been standing there on The Commons yesterday? Something like this, something this important, should be planned for the right moment, when it could somehow be addressed calmly and rationally, not fucking *now*. He could point out the many, many problems with the Official 9/11 Lie to anyone, easily, no prep needed, but *Ryan. Fuck, fuck, fuck,* what a fucking impossible conversation to have.

His eyes started wandering around his room. It had been a long time since Ryan had been over here. They'd drifted so apart. Tristan was a bit of an artist, sporadically, a pretty decent one, and had made some posters, mixed messes of photos and graphics, which now hung on his walls and recaught his eyes: a black and white photo of The People listening to Kennedy speak (at Cal, maybe?, Tristan thinks that's where he got the image) covered in the center with a blazing red All Seeing Eye atop the Illuminati Pyramid, taken from the back of the one dollar bill and blown up large, with the words above and below it, "Democracy is Dead. The Oligarchy Rules;" the kill-shot from the Zapruder film blown up in color with the red blast exploding from the front right side of Kennedy's head, a sniper's target around it and the words, "The CIA Killed Kennedy;" and, of course, those burning Towers that dominated Tristan and Ryan's lives, and the words, "Never Forget," an ellipsis, and, "Who Really Did This."

He shot up from his chair, stood on the missing-roommate's-bed-turned-sofa and began taking down the posters, starting with the Towers.

.   .   .

Ryan parked his truck on a curb in the dorms' turnaround, wholly aware that the bullshit Campus Ticket Nazis would be here inside of 3 seconds to leave the bill on his windshield, and headed to Tristan's building.

.   .   .

Tristan rolled up the posters and put them, fully aware of the irony, but no time to give a shit, in his closet. Then he went for the books. Everything by Professors David Ray Griffin or Steven Jones had to go, *The New Pearl Harbor: Disturbing Questions About the Bush Administration and 9/11*; *9/11 and American Empire: Intellectuals Speak Out*; *Debunking 9/11 Debunking: An Answer to Popular Mechanics and Other Defenders of the Official Conspiracy Theory*; *9/11 Contradictions: An Open Letter to Congress & the Press*; *New Pearl Harbor Revisited: 9/11, the Cover-up and the Exposé*; *The Mysterious Collapse of World Trade Center 7: Why the Final Official Report About 9/11 is Unscientific & False*; they all had to go. All the printouts too. Anything from Architects & Engineers for 9/11 Truth, Scholars for 9/11 Truth & Justice, Firefighters for 9/11 Truth, 9/11 Truth.org, Patriots Question 9/11.

To be safe, even, Philip Shenon's *The Commission: What We Didn't Know About 9/11*, what else ... he looked around, knowing how ridiculous this was, but just on the off chance that Ryan wasn't going to go there, not now, he needed to put it all out of sight at least, but then he heard the three loud bangs on his door.

Tristan turned and went to his closet to drop the books on the floor. Just the fact that there was a fucking knock said so much. They used to walk right into each other's houses, bedrooms, without a thought of acting like it wasn't their own, and now a fucking knock? And not only that, but one that sounded like the Goddamned police! Tristan shut the door to his closet quietly and turned to open the one that stood between him and Ryan and accept his fate.

9:47 PM

Kristi unlocked her door to let him in—fearing after all her reflection of late what she was letting in—what she'd long been letting in—to her heart. And as soon as she saw his eyes, she knew her fears were right. They weren't the sweet, hopeful eyes of the handsome boy who first walked up to her at lunch to say he liked what she'd said in class that morning. They were the eyes he'd looked at her with at Todd and Connie's this morning—holding the Bible so firm to her—"read it and follow it."

They walked back to her room to not disturb her roommate. He held her hands and sat down with her on her bed. She, in her cozy pajamas, on top of cozy blankets, feeling the opposite of comfort.

He was saying something about Lot. Why on Earth? She'd been brushing her teeth, and he'd called saying he needed to talk and was coming over. And here he was with these eyes and now Lot.

The worst part about her discomfort was the growing knowledge that maybe her deepest fears had been right. And that tonight, in her pajamas, her teddy bear sitting on the bed behind her, her teeth freshly brushed, she'd have to do it—to say it.

Lot. And how he'd prepared his house for the Coming of the Lord. She never understood that story. There was a lot of the Bible she didn't get. Why God had been so awful, so childish even, before Jesus. Jesus she got. Jesus was everything. Jesus was her Lord. The story of Lot and Sodom was especially difficult to accept as God's Word and ... it was just plain strange. Preachers had said it meant that homosexuality was wrong. Maybe that's why he was bringing it up. Maybe he'd found out about Kyle, whom he always seemed agitated with at Bible Study. Still, she thought the preachers wrong who took that meaning from the story. When she'd heard a pastor from her youth say that and had gone home to read the story for herself—for even early on she'd become someone who was not willing to take what others said was the truth, as the *actual* truth—that was the moment she first remembered thinking that pastors weren't always right either. And even besides the homosexual issue—which definitely did not seem to be the point of the story to her—how in the world anyone could take from that story that Lot was a good guy whom we should emulate ...? Lot? The guy who offered up his virgin daughters for mass rape? And his daughters who slept with their father? Got him drunk so they could rape him? These were the *good* people we were supposed to follow? The ones God chose not to punish while He burned the rest?

Kristi's faith had little to do with the Old Testament, she had to admit. She wasn't a Genesis Christian or a Leviticus Christian, but a Jesus Christian.

And now Luke seemed to be coming to his point. Kyle. Yes, poor, sweet Kyle. What could he have possibly seen to—*oh.*

"I don't need to hear all the—" details, she meant, but fortunately he stopped describing; what she'd heard was self-explanatory even to a good, sheltered, Christian girl like herself. She figured Luke would stumble upon Kyle's sexuality at some point—though she'd thought the revelation would be a bit more subtle—but seriously?, she didn't think he'd be *this* upset, this day and age, wasn't this something older people had a problem with, not the young?, though Luke was a bit of an old soul, wasn't he? *But oh, I see,* it's not just that, he's using that just as an opening to now go back and bring up other grievances he'd been holding for some time, bringing up things he'd remembered her saying nearly word-for-word in her Bible Study or to friends or to him. He was on a bit of a roll now, or more a downward spiral headed toward depths she did not want to go to with him.

"Luke. Stop," she said, but he wasn't stopping.

It was so hard to do it, she thought. It. All the its involved with this mess their lives had knotted into. To hurt another person to whom you were so close. Who'd opened themselves up to you, made themselves so vulnerable to you. But he was hurting her, wasn't he? That concern didn't seem to concern him. How we hurt each other in relationships, she thought. The closer the relationship, the more the pain. She wanted to explore that in her journal some.

But now Luke said this: "I fear, Kristi. I fear for your soul."

And his fear for her, on her behalf, was so real, so palpable, there was love for her, great love and concern, behind that fear, but that just made it all the worse, made it pierce her heart more deeply.

She wasn't going to say it to him, never like this, never so bluntly, but the pain of the strike he just delivered with those words hurt her so thoroughly and so suddenly that her words came out at first as self-defense.

"Luke! I think you betray Jesus …" she shocked herself with her own words, but had to keep going "… with the words you force into His mouth!"

She knew her words had stabbed him as deeply as his had her. But it didn't feel bad to do it. It felt like a much-, much-needed release.

She continued on, for once not letting him speak, for once over-talking him, letting him see how it felt—fueled as she was by so many thoughts long-building, long-looked-at and reestablished in her mind through her journal pages—and fueled too, she'd later have to admit to herself, by rage—the rage of the pain still burning inside her someplace she couldn't quite pinpoint from those blank lines—from the cold, hard emptiness of why he loves her unanswered, or worse, that he doesn't.

How could two people read the same book and come away with such different views? She found herself repeating something she'd almost forgotten she'd ever heard, but it was so pertinent now her mind had retrieved it from somewhere in the files of her psychology studies: "Maybe the Bible is the greatest inkblot ever created. Because it tells us so much more about the soul of the reader than it does of its author." From Luke's face she could see he didn't get that, she'd have to remind him of what inkblots were, but she couldn't now, she was on a roll and needed to get it all out, needed him to listen to her for once.

She went on about the many evils that had been done over the centuries in the name of God, Christ, the Church, and then, feeling herself nearing her end, she quoted scripture to him who knew it so well in words, but maybe not well enough in meaning, "'and the greatest of these is Love.' And that's how I intend to live my Christian Life."

She finished. There was silence in the room for a moment. She had a fleeting worry that her roommate might have heard all this.

But then Luke said it, the word he was still stuck on from the very beginning of her response—and his questioning repetition of it showed how little he'd heard or taken in truly about everything she'd said after it, how his focus was still stuck on that first—though, yes, perhaps greatest—accusation:

"Betray Him," he repeated, looking at her with such depth of pain she felt good and horrible about causing. "Betray Jesus Christ?"

There was another awful silence. And she knew what was about to happen. He was putting his words together to launch a counter-attack, to teach her a lesson, high and mighty, as the greater scholar of the Bible, he thought, but she was not about to hear it, again, for the tenth, hundredth, thousandth time. She stood up from the bed, walked away from him a bit and then turned back, arms crossed across her chest to somehow, feebly, try to protect her heart as she let escape from her mouth the words that would hurt her as much as him, but had been gaining a now unstoppable momentum inside her these past few months: "Maybe we aren't meant to be."

He looked at her, not yet sure what she meant, somehow his face softening from a man enraged to a boy scared, as she clarified for him: "Together."

"That's why the workbook, why the classes ..." she continued "... God wants us to be certain and ..."

He was completely a little boy now, fragile. She realized suddenly she was holding his heart in her hands. She needed to be careful. But she needed also to finally speak the truth: "... I'm not certain, Luke," she whispered, tears wetting her lips. "Not anymore."

9:57 PM

It seemed like a very long time Ryan stood there waiting for Tristan to open the door. He should have just barged in, he thought. But at the same time, he knew why he waited: they were strangers now.

He went back to the thought he'd had on his bedroom floor before getting up and coming here, the thought about why Tristan's words had hit such a nerve, a thought inspired by his years of counseling as a kid: that his sense of how the world, how life, was supposed to work, his "map," his counselor had called it, had come crashing down that morning along with the Towers. And he remained lost, without a way to understand the world, until a new map was given to him, when the full story was revealed: there were these people who hated us and our way of life and they came to kill us for it. Tristan was trying to tear down his map again. To send him back to the kid sitting on the floor of his childhood bedroom with no understanding of what was real or not anymore, with no understanding of why God did what He did or allowed what He allowed or if He even existed. With no sense of what he'd done to deserve this, or his dad, or his mom. Ryan couldn't go back to that. That emptiness. That adriftness, that Godlessness, that rulelessness, that meaninglessness.

Tristan opened the door. And like always between them, no matter how long had passed, it was like they'd just been hanging out together the day before.

"You're really fucking losing your mind, you know that?" Ryan said, and not waiting long enough for a reaction, pushed by Tristan into the room.

Great, Tristan thought, closing the door, *this really is going to be an impossible conversation.*

"There's an *oligarchy*? Is that it? And how the fuck does this oligarchy benefit from killing 3,000 Americans?" And as soon as Ryan heard himself say that, he knew exactly the type of bullshit Tristan would respond with, and so he put a stop to it, "Jesus, don't answer that. I know your fucking answer to that. I don't want to hear it."

Tristan saw through that, what he was doing, despite the macho (perhaps to some it would seem intimidating) energy as he paced around the little room, Tristan could see in the tiniest little details of Ryan's face what he really meant, what he was really feeling. So he said it. To call him out. To remind him he wasn't going to get away, with Tristan, with the easy facades he threw up for everyone else.

"Then what'd you come over here for?"

As soon as Tristan said it, and saw the changes in Ryan's expression, he was sorry he did. Tristan's mind and heart seemed to be fighting their own internal battle here. He'd so long wanted, needed Ryan to know the Truth, but for just as long been frightened to death to tell him for the pain he knew it would cause him, for the severing it would certainly cause between their souls.

Because I do want to hear it, Ryan thought. Because of the fucking rumors he'd heard from time to time, because of Tristan's snide little disbelieving remarks he'd make sometimes about the wars we'd recently fought, about Bush, about the new candidates for President, about the threat of terrorism, remarks he didn't think Ryan would see too far behind. Because now that it had been confirmed that Tristan believed this shit too, as fucked up as Tristan was sometimes, still, it somehow had more weight now. Maybe even, he hated to even mention the word, credibility. And because his third childhood therapist, the one he finally liked, had said you can't run from the things that cause you fear, you have to face them down, see them for what they really are. If they can really harm you, then you act rationally to protect yourself. But most often, you will find that they can't really harm you, that your fears are unfounded. *So lets do it. Lets see this bullshit for what it is.* He sat down on the spare bed/sofa and threw his arms up in the air. "Because I do want to hear it." He gave a look that said, *okay, you're right.* "I want to know what the great Tristan Harris has figured out that everyone in the White House for two presidencies, in the military, the CIA, that all our partners in the world, that no one's figured out, but you, Tristan Harris, you've got the answer. Come on," he said, raising half-up, grabbing Tristan's desk chair, pulling it closer, slapping it a couple times, and, as he sat back down, looking up at Tristan with these eyes that looked to Tristan for the first time in their lives like they could be the eyes of a killer. "Tell me why everything we lived through that morning was a lie."

Tristan had never feared Ryan before. They were the same age, but Ryan had often felt like a big brother to him growing up. When Tristan finally started telling everyone he was gay in high school, it was mostly fine of course, it was New York, but still there were a few kids he thought might tease or bully him, but he knew Ryan would protect him. Ryan, the star athlete, no one would mess with. But the way Ryan looked at him now, he looked like someone who could snap and suddenly be this whole other person, this terrifying animal. Tristan suddenly, with someone he'd known his whole life, felt he had to be very, very careful now not to let out whatever that animal was within, so clearly just behind Ryan's eyes, ready to push through the personality Tristan knew, and loved even, and pounce on him with nothing but an animal's pure rage.

But Ryan was in there somewhere, Tristan knew. And his friend, who had been hurt so bad—he needed him to know who it really was who hurt him. He needed him to stop chasing the scapegoat, the patsy, the fiction. For Ryan's own sake. For his father's. To focus his pain upon the real killers. The psychopaths in power.

Tristan reached out to grab the back of his chair that was turning slowly from Ryan's rough handling of it, and to move toward sitting upon it, as his mind raced. This was it. There was no time to plan it properly, a chance cockup yesterday, and here they were now, old friends, having come so far and seen so much, but still stuck there on that promenade that morning, and now finally, about to look back at those burning buildings and see them for what they really were, for the first time, together.

Tristan sat his butt in the chair. His mind flew past the hundreds of things he'd studied, the dozens and dozens of gaping holes in the Official al-Qaeda Conspiracy Theory: the pilots who couldn't fly; the "hijackers" who would later be found alive; the paper passports the FBI claimed to find laying around on the ground, which somehow jumped out of the pockets of the terrorists to survive fires and explosions and impacts that supposedly disintegrated airplanes and brought skyscrapers crashing to the earth at near the speed of free-fall gravity; the rushed cover-ups of the crime scenes, hurrying away the physical evidence to be melted down and destroyed before anyone could ask to test it; the evidence that Osama and Atta and others were CIA assets set up as patsies in the same old fashion as Oswald himself once was; the cover-up job of the 9/11 Commission and others; the military's blatant violations of its own longstanding and always-followed rules and procedures; the stand-down order to the Airforce ... maybe that was the place to start with Ryan, the military ...? No. *No, start where it all started for you, Tristan.* The most obvious. And Ryan, with his engineering mind, would *have* to face the truth of it.

"Do you remember," Tristan asked with a voice quite quiet for him, "the other tower that fell that day? The third one?"

Ryan didn't know what the hell he was talking about.

"Building 7? World Trace Center 7? It was a 47-story building just north of the Twin Towers. And just like the Twin Towers, it dropped completely to the ground, into its own footprint, at near the speed of gravity's free-fall pull. But it wasn't hit by a plane. And all the photographs show that it was barely on fire at all. Just a few sporadic fires can be seen in some windows. And yet, at five-something that afternoon, it suddenly fell completely to the ground. But steel-framed buildings had never done that: collapsed because of fire. In the whole history of humans building skyscrapers, the only time they've ever collapsed for the reason the government tells us they did on 9/11—*was* on 9/11. Three of them."

Tristan whipped around and grabbed his laptop, started looking for something on it.

"What the fuck was Building 7?" *And,* Ryan thought, *how could I have never heard of it?*

"This." Tristan said, turning his laptop around for Ryan to see a YouTube video of the building standing there on the afternoon of 9/11, its 47 stories perfectly still, just a few small fires burning, and then, suddenly—"The whole thing falls completely to the ground, perfectly level, into its own footprint, at near the speed of free-fall."

Ryan had never seen the video before. He grabbed the laptop from Tristan and started it again.

"Ask your engineering professors," Tristan said, "how a steel-framed building suddenly falls completely to the ground like that from fires, and supposedly, a gash on one side of it from the antenna of the North Tower. The government first told us the fires were raging and fueled by gas stored in the basement and that that melted the steel. But scientists laughed so hard at that explanation the government had to scrap it. Fires from gas—even jet fuel—and all the other building materials aren't capable of getting within a thousand degrees of what's needed to melt steel. So then, the government just shut up about it. The 9/11 Commission Report doesn't mention Building 7 at all. It took the bullshit NIST report like seven years to come out and no one with a brain believes its absurd explanations. But even though structural engineers and physicists keep calling 'bullshit!' on how it could have possibly collapsed under these conditions, on the day of the attacks someone kept spreading word that the building was going to collapse. There's even a video of a BBC news reporter announcing that the building *had* collapsed while it is still visibly standing in the background behind her."

Ryan watched the video of the fall again.

"Look at that. What does it look like? What's the most obvious answer?"

Tristan waited. Ryan's face watching the fall again. Tristan knew it was sinking in. So he decided to go for it.

"Controlled demolition."

"Jesus fucking Christ, Tristan." Ryan tossed his laptop on the bed. "Do you have any idea how long that would take to prep? How few people can do a thing like that? There's no fucking way terrorists could get in there and—" Ryan stopped himself realizing the trap Tristan set for him. "So that's what you've got, huh? Because to your untrained eye it looks like a controlled demolition—"

"Not just to my untrained eyes, to many trained eyes—guys who actually *do* controlled demos—and not just because of the way it looks, but because of the evidence—"

"What fucking *evidence*? That video?"

"Because metal did melt! Steel. Molten steel was found in the pits of all three buildings, photos of the cleanup show beams dripping with it days after the buildings dropped. Firefighters said when they got down there metal, metal, was still flowing like lava! The core of those pits was still a thousand degrees *weeks* after the attacks! In some spots the debris core was more than 2,000 degrees Fahrenheit! Jet fuel can't do that! It can't even come close. And anyway all the jet fuel would have burned up in minutes. We're talking *weeks* later. The only thing that could do that, the only thing, would be powerful demolition explosives like thermite—or, more likely, thermate, the military's version." Tristan stopped himself. Fuck. Seeing Ryan's face at that word.

"The *military's*?"

Keep it going Tristan, it's the only way, the truth, the facts, they're all you've got. "The military developed an even more powerful grade of thermite called thermate that—"

Ryan jumped up and grabbed the arms of Tristan's chair, getting in his face. "The fucking US Military, Tristan? The *military* did 9/11?"

"No. Not the military. Not all of it. A rogue element within our government—it's not just military, it's CIA, it's the White House, it's—"

And Ryan lost it. "Jesus fucking Christ, Tristan!" he said, throwing Tristan's chair over. Tristan scrambled to his feet as the chair hit the floor. Ryan charged after him. Tristan backed up to the wall, his hands out to protect himself. "Ryan, there's a lot more, okay, this is just the start, but you've got to hear it, you've got to know the truth—"

"*Truth*?! Fuck you, Tristan. You are so fucking far from the Goddamned truth, you're in fucking psycholand!"

"No, fuck *you*, Ryan! You're the one who chooses to believe a fucking fairytale about how your own father died!"

And then it was like slow motion. But it was somehow so fast too.

Ryan's hands were on Tristan's throat.

Ryan was squeezing. This wasn't fucking adolescent play. This was real. Tristan couldn't breathe.

Tristan's hands were grabbing Ryan's arms with all Tristan's considerable strength, but Ryan's arms weren't budging. They were an immovable force, literally squeezing the life from Tristan as the milliseconds passed.

Tristan pulled up his right hand and slammed Ryan's face with his fist. Ryan knocked back just enough for Tristan to break away the lock of Ryan's hands with his left arm and grasp for air. He turned, falling, lightheaded, and Ryan knocked him the rest of the way to the ground, slammed his fist into Tristan's face twice. Then Ryan, straddling him, began to strangle him again. Tristan thought he would pass out. He tried to kick Ryan with his knees, but it didn't work.

"That's my fucking dad, Tristan! My fucking dad."

Tristan thought: *Exactly. And don't you want to know who killed him?* But he couldn't talk. Air—you never thought about it until you couldn't get it. Could this really be it? He really couldn't breathe. Really hadn't breathed in far too long …

Tristan's face was so red. His life in Ryan's hands. The boy on the promenade who held him up …

Weird a connection as it was, Tristan, with Ryan's face so close, thought about when they were kids—holding Ryan on the promenade as tight as he could. Was this really going to be it? There was poetry in that.

And then, finally—air.

Ryan let go. He was crying, he noticed. Tristan was too. The five-year-old in Ryan stopped him. Kept him from killing his friend—the five year old still somehow there in memories looking at Tristan's face so close. The children in both saved them now. Had it been just the adults, Ryan knew he wouldn't have stopped.

He got up off of Tristan who turned into a fetal position—gasping and gasping for life.

Ryan watched him for a moment. Then turned away.

Thursday
October, 20th

5:13 AM

"Betrayal," she'd said. "Betrayal of Jesus Christ."

Luke had barely slept. Desperately as he wanted to, he could not quiet his mind. It was nearly the worst thing she could have said to him, short of betraying the Father. The Father, she didn't understand, that's where Luke's true loyalties lay.

It had taken Luke a long time to realize that. Jesus was not the Father, despite the myths manufactured by those with flawed beliefs. Jesus, like the rest of us, was a servant—though as Son, a privileged one. Jesus spoke of love as the greatest commandment, though he knew well His Father's pain. Pain that His Creation had betrayed Him. Time and time again humanity betrayed its Father. What sorrow, what anguish, He had to bear. To watch through the centuries as those He had given life used it to mock Him. To laugh at His Commandments. To ignore His Promises. To choose to live in filth and sin rather than His Righteousness. There couldn't be a greater betrayal in all of existence.

No, Kristi. No. What you call betrayal, I call the utmost loyalty.

8:44 AM

"Fairytale." That fucking piece of shit.

It was such a Tristan thing to say. And Ryan knew he'd been thinking it for years now. It was the only way he could have hit him with the real question he was asking: "How can you not want to know how your father died?" Tristan hadn't actually said those words aloud, didn't need to. Ryan could see them; in the way we could somehow see hidden truths in the face of someone we'd known all our lives. But he saw also that Tristan didn't say it with anger. He said it with love. As if in some ways he was "our" father to Tristan. In some ways, Tristan, the brother to Ryan he'd always been.

The hatred would be easier to hate. And thus to hide from. The love kept seeping back in through the cracks. Ryan couldn't force his mind away from it.

He turned over on the sofa to grab another drink from the bottle of whiskey. No longer his father's, he'd finished that off, but a cheap bottle he swiped from his roommates' stash.

He'd been sleeping sporadically on the sofa all night, Houston laying on top of him sometimes, other times on the floor nearby.

He'd never attacked Tristan before, never even thought of causing him harm. Any smack or punch before had been playfulness. This had been the other extreme. Perhaps, the thing that scared Ryan the most was the certain knowledge that a part of him could have held Tristan's throat shut a little longer.

An evil part of himself he'd been trying to control for so long, after first, for so long, trying to live in denial that it even existed. If that evil part of Ryan had done a thing like that last night … how would his better half seek justice?

Goddamnit, Tristan, the shit you put in my head!

He knew the physical response was a defensive blow. He knew that. And it made him feel weak. That his body would need to protect his mind from thoughts.

And that same offended, kneejerk, "I'll kick your ass," response was trying to occur between one side of his mind and the other—but the mind is not so easily intimidated as the body. The brute was useless there.

And that, Ryan knew, was his Achilles' heel that Tristan had just struck with his arrow, knowing it too.

It was the passport.

The passport had given him hope. And then his hope had been stomped out with the cruelty of adults mocking a child's dream.

They'd found the passport of one of the terrorists that flew into the towers, the press had said. And with that discovery Ryan's younger self had found something new to hope for. Something he could hold onto for a little while. Something small. But still it was hope. Hope after only despair.

A passport was made of paper. It had been inside the plane that slammed into the building and yet had survived that massive fireball. Some guy running from the towers had handed it to a police officer. Charred a bit, around the edges, but still the photo clear and name legible. The news was elated. They'd found their man. One of them.

But Ryan was elated too. If they'd found that, if that had survived, then maybe too, one day, someone from the government would show up with something from his dad's office. Ryan would take anything. A piece of his chair, something. But in the recurring dreams he had about if for years of his childhood—it was his dad's Jets jersey the man brought to the door. It was charred a bit, around the edges, like that passport, but still the name and number clearly legible, still clearly his father's, the one draped over the back of his desk chair, unless he was wearing it over his shirt and tie in preparation for the big game—any of the big games.

When little Ryan finally voiced his hope one day to adults—the adults reminded him of reality—of what was possible and what was not—that nothing, nothing could have survived. Ryan protested, *but the passport!* But that was an unexplained (and unexplainable when he protested more) fluke. A gift from God, perhaps, that justice might be done. His father's jersey, he'd have to accept, and his chair, and his pictures, and the glass of the window Ryan face-planted so often—had all been cremated with the countless rest.

As he grew older, and rumors started to creep into his consciousness, it was the passport that still bugged him. If anything felt like a plant—if the props department for some old movie had ever burnt a document just enough around the edges—if the FBI needed to give The People answers— that was the one for Ryan.

But at worst—worst—that was the government needing to prove in simple 5th grade terms to The American People the complicated and nuanced truth it was already putting together—already sure of. The government giving the people what they needed to see it all clearly. The government would never have been behind the terror itself. This was America. Not Hitler's young government burning down its own parliament building to blame it on The Others and seize the power it wanted thereby, to "protect" The People. Ryan had learned about that recently in Military History of WWII. That was a sick man, a psychopath. We could never ....

Ryan couldn't complete the foolishness of his own thought. Blind faith in American Perfection was not his religion. He read history and had seen the corruption of power too often in its pages.

And motherfucker the way that building fell. Why did it have to fall so evenly? So quickly? So suddenly?

Why did they all?

He'd heard of Building 7, sure, now that he thought about it. But he never thought about it. Why would he? His father's Tower had dropped that morning. After that, nothing else could have begun to matter.

But Ryan was an engineering student now. And buildings didn't fall like that, did they? The first two, hit by planes, the equations and variables too complicated, the possibilities too hard to accept. But this third building? No plane. No father's office. Forty-seven stories falling so easily, so evenly, so suddenly. The soldier in Ryan would have to accept things on order. But not the engineer.

And not the son.

He sat up, waking Houston, pulled his laptop out of his bookbag, opened it and for the first time his own fingers typed in those search words. Those betraying words. "Building 7 collapse."

He found the video.

He watched the fall.

Again.

And again.

Even. Perfectly flat across its breadth. The dip in the middle of the roof structure first. The speed at which all those support columns would have to fail at once. All the way down. So little smoke before, so little fire. And then nothing.

Gone.

9:07 AM

Life's continuing on seemed inevitable.

And maybe that was the problem.

Unquestioning belief that our existence would never cease.

"I think, therefore I am." But it was the physicality that Tristan was stuck on, lying in his bed, staring at the countless little holes and divots and bumps of the cinderblock wall before him. The muscle memory of his throat still reliving the trauma. Its walls pinched together. His lungs unable to suck even a sip of air through. A little longer and not even blackness to contemplate. As insentient as the bricks before him.

People didn't think about that enough. Especially young people. All the faces he passed on campus. All the conversations people had that mattered as much as all these little holes and divots and bumps in these thoughtless, and thus unaware of their thoughtlessness, blocks of cinder.

Ryan's skin on Tristan's throat. Skin he'd sometimes had wet dreams about in his early teenage years. The memories, seared in his synapses, of Ryan's shorts falling too low at the beach or practice; his body in the sun as the two of them jumped into the pool together; or that morning Tristan went in to wake Ryan for an early run and found, to his flushed-face,-pounding-heart curiosity, Ryan's morning wood pushing up against the sheer cloth of his boxers with all its might, and Tristan crotched down to catch a glimpse of its vein-ribbed skin through the stretched-open fly, before disturbing him.

Ryan's skin on his. The smell of his breath, his hair. The eyes that have seen in life so much the same as Tristan's.

The irony after all this time, after all this longing, that they weren't there finally to please him, or to love him, but to end him. To cut "I think, therefore I am" off midsentence. Ryan's cold response to his unrequited love, his cold soul unsatisfied with the pain caused by his unrequital, should now finish the job of strangling his emotional heart, by ceasing the monotonous beating of his physical one.

Finish the job, Ryan. Lest I finish it first.

■　■　■

9:15 AM

She couldn't understand where it came from, the gunk. All her products, all her cleansing, the money saved up and spent on facials, but still it got in there somehow. Like some pollutant we just got from being out and about in the world.

She stood up and adjusted her eyes from staring so long at her larger than life face in the magnifying mirror, and surveyed the instruments in one of her vanity drawers to select the right tool. She had to be careful. Wrong move and this could get ugly. She selected the pointed metal butt of a pair of tweezers and went back to her enlarged face.

Right there at the crease of her nose was the gunk. The poor little pore just choking with it.

She placed the tweezers' butt to one side and pressed against the skin. Nothing. She tried another side. Nothing. She pressed firmer, *crap*. It slipped a little and almost left a red mark on her cheek.

She tossed the tweezers back in the drawer.

She'd have to attack this with fingers. She went back in.

Two fingers north and south of it—she pressed, squeezing it.

Crap, crap, crap!

The gunk just stayed there in the little hole absolutely unmovable, but now the area was turning reddish and getting a little swollen.

Crap, fuck, shit.

What if she pushes too hard, the fucking gunk still won't budge, but something pops inside of it and it becomes one of those red, under-the-skin mountains?

She thought about getting a fork from the kitchen. Maybe the pressure of a prong on either side?

Oh, Jesus, Tracy, you can't use a fucking fork on your face!

She took a calming breath.

Thought.

Grabbed a swab. Dabbed some astringent on it and wiped the area to be sure it was dried of any microscopic oils. She did the same to her finger tips. Then she went back in. Found a different angle. Inside her head she said the word, *Please.* To God, maybe? The kind universe? And pressed.

The gunk popped out like a little worm shooting from its cave!

"Yes!" she said aloud. "Thank you!" Again, not quite sure to whom.

She grabbed the swab again and wiped the vanquished gunk away.

9:17 AM

Kyle was looking at his hands.

His bookbag was laying against his legs and there was work in there he needed to do, but the quiet of Library Lawn led him instead to want to think. Kyle cherished his moments to think. Quietude. Solitude. Dorm life wouldn't hear of either. Even in sleep he often felt denied these.

But he was leaning against one of the columns of the surrounding colonnade and it was quiet, mostly. And his hands, as always, looked so small. He thought his hands looked like a kid's. Like a middle school boy's.

And that was part of the problem. Because he still felt like that in a lot of ways. Like just a kid. And yet so much was in his hands now.

A lot of the other students didn't have the pressure Kyle had. Pressures put upon him by others. And the ones he'd chosen for himself.

Well ... sort of chosen.

The first were mostly his father's. Immigrant to America. The great hope of the great society. "Opportunities you have that I never had, that no one on this side of your family ever had." All that. Four years and that's it, Kyle. No fifth or sixth year, no grad school, no! Four more years and you get a job and you're on your own. You support yourself. You're on your way. The Land of Opportunity.

Which was weird since the joke was most Persians supposedly said to their kids: Doctor or Lawyer? You get to pick. But Dad was no joke.

And now it was less than three years. And he had to know what he'd do for the rest of his life. And he was pretty sure. More sure than a lot of students. But still, not sure enough. Because ... because of the other pressures.

Because of the purple liquid.

He saw it now as clearly as when he was a boy. That first time. The purple liquid entered the long IV tube and he watched as it went down the tube's length, nearly to the floor, and then up—closer and closer to him—and then disappeared, as did the tube, under his t-shirt. He imagined how much longer it would be, how many milliseconds, until it hit the port they'd put under the skin of his right pec and entered his body.

And then everything changed. Again. Then he was a chemo patient. Then it was in his body, swirling around his cells. Then he'd attend his middle school classes via a TV/internet setup from the hospital on "Chemo Days." 'Cuz he could really concentrate on what the teacher was saying with that fluid in him and with every bit of his mental capacity focused on not throwing up. Not again. God, he was so tired of throwing up.

So there was that. Sometimes Kyle wondered if his hands stopped aging then. But the new doctor last year had laughed at the silliness of the idea.

Now, at the colonnade, Kyle yanked down the bottom of his t-shirt, which was already down. Some weird un-thought-about response that didn't want the purple liquid coming up through it again. Though, of course, he was forever grateful it had back then.

He had to choose right. Life was short and he'd been granted a second chance at it.

But how could he answer the question of what he'd "*do*" with his life, when the more fundamental questions had yet to be answered?

And one of the biggest was what the heck we were all doing here, anyway? And not just on this campus, but on this planet. What is the point? What is the meaning of life? Which religion is right? Are any of them? Which philosophy? *Don't I need to know some of these answers before I make that other decision?* That biggest of all the questions that college asks of you? That thing behind all the other things that we're all really here to figure out: *what the heck am I going to do with my life?*

Shouldn't there be more answers here? For all the tuition dollars Dad worried about. For all the people who seemed to want to tell you they'd found them. For all the time spent studying. *Shouldn't I have found more answers? But all I've got is more questions. And I'm trying to hold them all in my little hands but ...*

He wiped his hands on his legs.

He looked at the students walking to and from the library. They seemed so much more confident than he felt. They seemed to know. Or maybe they just didn't care.

9:19 AM

This was going to be a great day, Tracy thought as she began applying her makeup. She was back in business, just like the boys of Sig Chi O would be tonight. For she'd figured out her next big move. A meme. Tonight. And this bitch was going basic viral.

A gif, to be precise.

First Shot: Hot guys and girls dancing at the biggest party of the year.

Second Shot: They turn toward camera.

Third Shot: They start to lift or unbutton their shirts.

Fourth Shot: A little more skin and we start to see body paint.

Fifth Shot: Shirts totally off or open to reveal their seven torsos spelling out "N-o-v.-8th!" in body paint.

It was brilliant. How do you sell politics? Like anything else—with sex. If she got a couple more students she could just add more exclamation points. Or maybe even spell "V-o-t-e."

This was going to dominate the internet.

The biggest concerns were (A) boobs and (B) faces. On the boobs, she'd work the girls beforehand to make sure they were wearing bras they were good with the world seeing. But they'd be dressing to undress anyway, so that would probably already be the case. Faces were harder. The guys wouldn't give a shit, but the girls def wouldn't want Mom and Dad seeing this. She'd have to triple assure them they'd be covered in post—

probably with the school's cartoon Sand Tiger head—just to make sure as this thing spreads credit comes back to where it's due: Tracy Reynolds.

The next thing was to get Ryan aboard and to take this seriously. That way the rest of the guys would take it seriously. Everything had to be done right. Tracy would direct and shoot. Then maybe tomorrow morning she could get that blue-haired girl to help with the special effects.

She finished foundation and started in on lashes.

But her phone whistled. She looked at the sweet and gorgeous face of her baby sister and swiped to answer.

"Hey, Little Me."

"Why is Mom such a fucking controlling cunt?!"

9:20 AM

Kyle was thinking about a similar conversation he'd overheard sometime freshman year. That was one of the things Kyle liked so much about being a quiet person—you got to hear a lot more.   And think about it. Eavesdropping was a great way to learn about your fellow humans. And campus had some of the best there was.

Kyle had brought a towel to campus that day and laid it down under a tree to set up shop studying. A guy and girl were sitting on their own towel not too far away talking about it: The Question: What will we do with our lives? The guy was a History major and someone had asked him what he was going to do with that and he said he'd responded, "Just ... *learn*. What's wrong with that?" The girl laughed along with him, in on the joke. "I mean why does it always have to lead to some job? This isn't a technical college, is it? I just wanna ... *know shit*." The girl laughed more.

"Just … learn." Kyle liked that. He thought about it sometimes. He remembered thinking then that he'd like to get to know that guy, maybe become friends with him. He'd figured he was bound to run into him again, have a class with him or something. But he never has. It was crazy how campus seemed so small and so big all at the same—

"Don't get left behind!"

Kyle was pulled out of his thoughts by a nice older lady who was smiling at him and handing him a flier.

"Thanks," he said and took it. She went on down the colonnade interrupting the other studiers and thinkers of Library Lawn with her flier and her talking despite the silence signs.

Kyle looked at the flier. "DON'T BE LEFT BEHIND," it said, from "Billy Graham."

The lady seemed sweet. And maybe it was a sign from God, given what he'd been wondering? He decided to give it one or two of his minutes. Tristan probably wouldn't finish with his paper until 10:00 on the dot, anyway.

He opened it. "Jesus is coming back!" it said. He'll take his followers with him and leave the rest behind, it said. "The Bible made clear predictions about the times leading up to Christ's coming," it said. "Clearly the evidence of those predictions being fulfilled is all around us." it said. "All the signs seem to indicate that something will happen soon," it said. "It all leads up to the ultimate rebellion against God—Armageddon," it said. "You're in danger of being left behind!" it said. But, "He loves you," it said.

That didn't feel like love, Kyle thought.

He and his mom talked a lot about that. It's one of the reasons she left the Christian church. This idea of a god who created all these souls just to demand allegiance and worship from them. And if they don't give it to him, he'll torture them for all eternity. It seemed so silly. What, he was sitting around all lonely as the only being in existence and thought, "Ooooooo, I know, I'll create a bunch of souls who can worship me and if they don't I'll burn and torture them forever and ever!" *That's your god???*

Kyle didn't have any interest in worshiping a childish, silly little god like that. That was the uncontrolled-adolescent-outburst god of the Great Flood story. That wasn't the god Kyle knew in his heart.

He didn't even know if he should call it "god." He just felt and believed in this benevolent presence. That's what he wanted to find out more about.

When he was sick. When the chemo was in his body and the slightest wrong move or even the taste of the air could be enough to make him throw up again. He would sit there as motionless as he could. He couldn't talk for fear of tasting the air. The smell of the place—which no one else seemed to smell, but which was overpowering to him even 50 feet down the hall from the front door—was bad enough and remembering it now made his eyes automatically search for the nearest trashcan like they did so many years ago for fear of needing to puke again, even now, even here.

But it was then, in that stillness and silence, when all else in life seemed to fade away, that it was made clear to Kyle that there was nothing left to hold onto but this one thing. This benevolent force. And he grabbed it. And he held it with all his might.

And he survived.

He knew that.

But then, when death had released its grasp on him, when normalcy returned, when caring about grades or traffic jams returned, all the things that had faded away now again cluttered and obscured that one thing that he'd been left to hold onto. And his grasp on it wasn't as strong. And his certainty in its existence wasn't so certain anymore.

And a part of the clutter were the people who claimed to speak for that benevolent force—but they didn't. Instead they gave you this pamphlet about a silly, childish god who claimed to love you, but who doesn't know what love is.

Kyle stood up and went to the trashcan not to throw up, but to throw the flier he just noticed he must have crumpled into a ball at some point away.

He didn't remember crumpling it. There was an anger there, he thought. An anger within him about those people and all they believed. Surely that nice old lady would tell him he was going to burn in hell forever and ever if she knew how much he liked it when Tristan's cock slid slowly into his ass.

Urg! It was always the outsiders that got under his skin. Why did they let them on campus anyway? They weren't students here or professors. They didn't belong here. And it was almost always the Christian Conservatives that came. They were here more than Red Bull!

Kyle chuckled at that as he sat back against his column.

God, he was really sounding more and more like Tristan sometimes.

Where the heck is Tristan anyway?

He picked up his phone to send him a text. "Hey U. Almost done?"

9:21 AM

Tracy rolled her larger than life eyes in the little round mirror as she applied her mascara and awaited the onslaught from her little sister, Aubrey.

"What now?"

"I'm eating toast. Toast, at breakfast. TOAST!"

Tracy's eyes widened knowing what was coming.

"And she hits me with, 'Carbs, hun.'"

"Urg. Tell her to mind her own anorexia."

"She's been on my fucking ass lately. Like, I know! I can see it! I've been a little stressed lately. I'll work it off. I don't need your snide little remarks at fucking breakfast!"

"She's a bitch. She's always been a bitch. We just have to ignore her, right?"

Tracy moved on to lipstick.

"I know, I just—"

But there was a silence. Tracy looked at her phone. She knew what the silence meant.

She put down her lipstick, picked up her phone and walked out to sit on her bed.

"You okay, Aub?"

"Yeah," she said, through clogged throat.

Tracy let out a long breath.

"I'm sorry, sweetie."

Tracy thought about what to say.

"It's not much longer now. Senior year's going to start flying by, I promise you. And then you'll be out of there and starting your new life at VT and you can put her behind you."

"Have you? Put her behind you?"

Tracy was silent for a bit. Both phones transmitting the silence to each other.

"She's our mom. She'll always be in there somewhere, but ... we can choose ... to not be her. And I'm ... trying to do that, I guess."

"Yeah."

"Yeah."

The phones waited.

"College lets you ... start with a clean slate if you want. New place, new friends ... new you. I'm not free of her yet, but ... I'm moving there, I think. I don't let her affect me anymore."

"She's been saying things about you."

"What?"

"About what a loser Ryan is. About you picked someone who's going into the *army* and will just get PTSD and be fucked for life and never make any money."

Tracy tried to will the tear back from her new mascara.

"About how she thought she raised you better than that."

"Fucking cunt."

"Yeah."

"Yeah."

The seconds of the call ticked off for a while longer.

Ultimately, Tracy had to wipe.

She looked at the mascara on her finger. Heard her sister sigh. And was glad to know she was there.

10:17 AM

Kristi very much wanted a respite from all the heavy thoughts weighing down her mind, pulling it to the floor almost as physically as Luke had pulled her off the bed to pray the other night and keeping her stuck there, unable to think about anything but the weights which held her. But class this morning wasn't going to give her that and she'd seen the problems of it coming since being given the syllabus on the first day. Today, of all days, her professor wanted to talk about religion.

She really just wanted, needed, to sit here like normal and transmit her professor's words to her page while happily thinking in the background how she'd one day use this knowledge to help her patients. But today, her professor's words would not flow so easily from his mind through hers to her notes to be studied and pondered later. Today, his words stung. Today, they were offensive. Today, they snagged with jagged teeth all the way down as she tried to digest them. Today, was another one of those days when her chosen field of study and her chosen most fundamental beliefs in life couldn't exist very well in the same room together, much less the same mind. Her heart was doing its best to stay out of it. It had its own overwhelming problems.

Her professor was saying if your patients have religion: use it. But it was the way he was treating it that was the problem. A trick to relax the mind. Like belly breathing or thinking about your happy place. If religion brings them comfort, meaning, then let them have it.

It was the way he was describing it. Like Santa Claus for your kids.

If it helps them stay in line, if it gives them a sense of peace that there's a point to everything they're doing, that there will be a reward in the end, that God or Santa Claus cares about them—then what harm done?

True Believers sleep better at night, he said. Death isn't so scary. The loss of loved ones, less painful. The daily pressure to do some important, grand thing with your life tends to be less imposing, demanding upon the psyche, tends less to lead to a feeling of despair when lofty goals are not reached. You've told Jesus you love Him, you've followed the rules of this book or that as best you can reasonably be expected to. You're good. No reason to worry. Everything will be fine. God or Santa will take care of you.

"Use that," he said. "If I could prescribe it in pill form, I would!" And he laughed at his joke along with maybe half the class.

Kristi was just trying to get his words down in her notes, but she knew when she came back to them it wouldn't be to study them, but to fight them.

Obviously, he had no idea the struggles religion was causing between her and Luke lately. Much less, what the Truth really was.

The thought occurred to her that she was fighting more and more things in her life lately. She wondered how she'd gotten herself into such a bad place, when just a little while ago everything from her boyfriend to her career choice had seemed so perfect.

10:21 AM

Kyle got in the elevator and looked at the numbers. He pressed 2. It was a protest, pressing 2. His floor and not Tristan's. He stepped back and let his body fall against the wall cushioned by his bookbag as he waited for the doors to close. He was so mad at Tristan. It was the amalgamation of small things that showed you how someone really felt about you. And what had gathered together was an ugly mosaic of Tristan not giving a shit about Kyle's time.

The doors closed. *The little shit. He knew he told me to meet him at the library. He knew I'd be sitting there waiting like an idiot because I always do what he asks. I'm his little well-trained puppy. And why had I even gone in the first place? Why did I think he'd even care that I walked with him to turn in his stupid paper, that his hardened mind would even begin to notice that as a kind little act of love that one boyfriend could do for another? It showed exactly how much he cared that he couldn't take the 1.3 seconds needed to text me that he changed his plans.*

The doors opened on his floor and Kyle stared at the hallway. Then he lunged forward and pressed 4. Not as a protest. But as a someone's-about-to-get-bitch-slapped.

.   .   .

Tristan really hoped Kyle wasn't on his way over right now. He knew it was shitty that he forgot Kyle was waiting for him at the library. But he really couldn't deal with Kyle's eyes, the way he imagined they'd look seeing what he'd seen in the mirror when he'd gotten up to take a piss this morning. The litany of things it would all mean about him.

That he was weak.

Physically weak, that he couldn't protect himself.

Emotionally weak, for keeping the brute, Ryan, in his life.

Intellectually weak, for not seeing all this coming and acting rationally to avoid it.

That Kyle'd been right all along and Tristan wrong.

And then, even the simplest—that this really did happen. That Ryan really did attack him. That he'd have to face that. Act upon it.

And that. What was that? The follow-through? What would he "have" to do? Kick Ryan out of his life? Why? To save face with Kyle?

But the door handle jerked down. And the door pushed open. And Tristan sat up a little. And there were the eyes he feared.

Kyle forgot what he was going to say.

He just kept staring at his boy's neck, trying to comprehend. At first he thought they were hickies, but clearly they weren't, the bruising was too big, too awful.

"What ..." was all he could manage.

Tristan thought about a joke. He was into choking now. But there was pain in Kyle's face. A face he loved and didn't want to hurt anymore.

"Ryan and I had a little tiff."

It felt good, so good, to let it out. In that instant Tristan realized how much he needed Kyle right now. He wished he'd come over and hug him, touch him, something. But he just stood there staring.

"I ..." There were so many different things to say in Tristan's mind. But none of them made any difference.

He had the feeling that he should cry. That he wanted to cry. But somehow it seemed not physically possible at the moment.

Kyle started to allow his field of vision to retreat from Tristan's neck and realized he should shut the door behind him as he heard people coming down the hall. He let it close and stepped over to sit on the edge of Tristan's bed.

"He *choked* you?"

"It was kinda hot, actually."

Some part of Tristan's mind insisted on trying the joke. It was in self-defense. It didn't work.

Kyle touched Tristan's collarbone. For fear of touching the actual bruises.

"Tristan. This is really, really serious. He had to be really, actually *strangling* you to cause bruises like this."

Tristan had to look away. He focused again on the little holes in the cinderblocks. There was something comforting there. In their unawareness.

"We have to tell." Kyle hated that it came out that way, he knew it sounded so ... "We have to report this. We have to go now so they can see this before they start to heal. Come on, get up, we're going—"

Tristan shook his head, but stopped because it brought Kyle's eyes back into his field of vision. He refocused on the little divots.

"Tristan!"

"No. Okay, just ... no."

The most uncomfortable, energy-building silence ticked by until Kyle said way too loud, "No, it's not *fucking* okay!"

Tristan went back to the blocks.

"Tristan, he physically attacked you! How long was he—" it was hard to get the word out this time "—*strangling* you to cause this much ..." The thought of how many long seconds it must have been plus the snot that had formed from nowhere seemed to suffocate Kyle and he sucked in some air and tried to stop the path his thoughts were taking.

Tristan was looking back at Kyle now. His tears felt good. They were the tears Tristan needed. He pulled his hand out from under the sheet and took one of Kyle's.

"I deserved it. I said something I—"

Kyle's look cut him off. "You *said* something." His point was blatant. How absurd it was that saying something should lead to this.

10:56 AM

Ryan had found the "debunkers," they called themselves. Engineers, they called themselves. And his heart rate had calmed once he did. He'd watched more videos, read a manic mess of shit, and had gone in search of reason, answers from those with credibility. But the problem now was, and the reason he could feel each pound of his heart in his chest again, was the answers from those with credibility were incredulous. There wasn't a single article he'd read yet, that had it been hurriedly scribbled as an answer to an exam question, any of his professors wouldn't have drawn a big red "X" through it, and called the student in to ask if he'd/she'd paid attention in any of their engineering classes, ever. It amazed Ryan the crap a bureaucrat or a media figure could get away with that a student facing his professor's red pen never could.

There seemed to be three key arguments the debunkers had come up with over time and at best they seemed designed only to convince the mind of someone for whom science and math were foreign languages.

The first was fire, and it was patently absurd. The second was building design. The third was the first two, plus a falling antenna.

Then there was another argument, actually, and it was the most prevalent: pretending it didn't happen. The 9/11 Commission not even mentioning Building 7 at all—no mention that a 47-story skyscraper had fallen to the ground that day. The media: every anniversary they show the Twin Towers fall again, but never Building 7.

And the worst part to all this was that Tristan's little quips last night had been right about them all.

Fire melting the steel and dropping the building to the ground. It was a fucking cartoon explanation. What, engineers had never thought of the fact that there could be a fire in a building before? The entire building could have burned for months until there was nothing left but the steel. The steel would still be standing!

To be sure, he looked up the melting point of structural steel: 2700°F. The hottest possible burning level of the office materials, which the government told us brought the building down: 1500°F. It was simple math. This was nonsense. "X!"

Weakening the steel, some morons said. Weakening. Are you fucking kidding?! The building dropped straight to the ground all at once! It didn't slouch where the fires were and stand firm in the rest. Weakening?! No fucking way. "X," These people couldn't pass the undergrad classes he was taking and they were supposedly government *experts*?!

The building's design? *Oh, it was some flaw in the design, was it?* This is a unique building with this problem? Then how come the other two skyscrapers fell in exactly the same way that morning: straight to the ground, nearly the speed of gravity?! Did they also have this unique design? Nope, couldn't be more different. How was the firm that designed the building not screaming defamation, much less bloody murder! *And the fucking antenna?* Hitting one corner of the building? But the whole thing dropping completely flat across the board?!

Jesus Fucking Christ, these arguments! Ryan hadn't taken a swig since finding the debunkers, but now he needed another one. He knocked them back, two big ones. He needed to talk to some of his professors about it, like Tristan said.   He'd make an appointment with Professor Woodard. She'd be willing to talk about this. At least she'd be willing to with Ryan. She'd help him find the answers, the explanations in physics, in science, in math, in reality. The truth.

Houston suddenly jumped off the couch and ran to the door to sit and wait without a sound and then as Tracy opened it he leaped his paws to her breasts and basically motorboated her with kisses. Definitely Ryan's dog. One of the Ryans, anyway.

Tracy pet Houston and kissed him back, then looked over at Ryan clearly having slept on the couch, the bottle of whiskey on the coffee table and the smell of it in the room, the bags she'd never seen before under his eyes that made him look 10 years older, and his laptop inches from his face playing some fucking internet videos.

"Well, clearly we're making some moves today."

And her mom's words about Ryan squealed in her head as she went back to Houston.

Ryan didn't say anything. Great. That's when he was the most pissed off of all. When he was silent.

She walked over and sat down on the sofa chair next to him. He shut his laptop. She looked him over again.

"Have you just decided to accept your fate as a loser and start drinking yourself to death or what's the plan here?"

"God, why are you always such a fucking *bitch*!?"

The word stung. It took her a second to realize why as it certainly wasn't the first time she'd heard it ... it was the first time she'd heard it from him. Saying it to her.

He had never. Not bitch or anything like it. He had wanted to, for sure, but had never.

She sat back in the chair. Houston laid his head on her leg. She looked at Ryan again. Looked at the ceiling. Looked at Ryan again. Then down at Houston.

At his innocence.

And her guilt.

"I was raised by the best, I guess."

Ryan kept staring at her but something inside of him changed as he did.

"Do you know what my mom says about you?"

But looking at his face, she couldn't do it. Didn't want to do it. And why would she let that bitch into this conversation, anyway? *Stop it, Tracy. Stop being her.*

She changed course.

"Once. When she was really in her zone—she told me I ruined her life. Getting pregnant with me. And she meant it. There was nothing hysterical about it. It was just the cold hard truth."

They looked at each other in silence a moment.

Then Ryan realized something. And he decided to say it.

"That. Right there. Was the most real you've ever been with me."

Their eyes remained locked. They both thought that that was sad, that truth. But also that it was good. It was a start.

11:32 AM

His professor was saying something. But something in what he'd said was reminiscent of something another professor had said years ago. Freshman year. World History. This earlier professor had gone off on one of his tangents, straying from the facts he was supposed to teach to pontificate as was not his right.

"Beware of the person who knows for certain the truth."

That's what he'd said. He said, in his humble experience, humble though he wasn't, it was the learned man who had learned how often he and others were wrong. It was the learned man who saw how often there were exceptions and nuances. Who has learned how very much he doesn't know. It was the ignorant man who knew the answer at all times.

And therein, thought Luke, laid college's greatest sin.

And that's what had happened to Kristi.

In a place supposedly meant to teach truth, it instead meant to kill it.

He looked around the amphitheater classroom at all the others taking their notes. Gulping down what today's professor was saying. Others with social media on their screens, some with games, one next to him working on her resume.

They hadn't come for truth anyway. They came for fun and games. And then their career. *Their* career. *Their* path in life. The meaning they chose to seek. They, they, they. Me, me, me.

And the university fueled their wildest golden calf dreams, supported and coddled the supreme importance of "me." And of what "*I* think." Let

184 | WILL KANE THOMPSON

them drink the bottomless cup of life's pleasures, tipped it forward for them to indulge a little more, to keep them happy and signing their promissory notes for tuition and room and board and keg party dollars.

The silliness that they thought all their planning could make much of a difference anyway. That the Lord had not already preordained humanity's fate, and not only that, had spelled it out for us. The pitifulness of that, rather.

Poor Kristi wasn't ready for all this. Not strong enough yet.

And I've failed her too.

Perhaps, I've been weakened by all this. Perhaps, I should have listened more to Meeks.

Not ready yet?

Is that me?

Dear God, please show me the Truth. Point me the way to Your Glory.

11:44 AM

Bret drove precisely like somebody who grew up in one of those southern towns where the cops only ever pulled cars over that had foreign license plates and most certainly never a pickup truck like his with both a Rebel and American flag flying on poles off the back, each too large for even Bret's too-large truck. Ryan's "Empire Gold" New York plate got stopped nearly every time he drove through The South to Florida and back. But Bret was clearly good-ol'-boy'ed into the system. A stop sign meant he'd slow the truck to 15 miles an hour if he was turning and if you were lucky. If Ryan was lucky, sitting in the back of the four-door cab holding one of the frame handles and feeling a little nauseated already after his morning of cheap whiskey.

Tracy had told him to get out and blow off some steam, and Bret's offer had been hanging there from yesterday. Ryan's sprits lifted a bit more when the truck pulled over in front of his Fraternity House and Miles jumped in the back with him. Miles was the only friend of Bret's Ryan actually liked. The guy found shenanigans to be had in everything he did. *Shenanigans. Mom's word.* That brought him a little smile.

The other great thing was the guy was the most notorious streaker Ryan knew. It was like the second the kid got drunk he couldn't stand having clothes on. Drunken memories swam through Ryan's mind of Miles running out to the House's backyard one afternoon, butt naked, cradling a bunch of water balloons in his arms and pelting random brothers until they found ways to retaliate; countless times running bare-ass through parties trying to get girls to join in, so far, always unsuccessfully; and a couple times just standing there with a beer in his hands talking with his fellow partiers totally nonchalant about his cock and balls hanging there for all to see. So Ryan knew he'd definitely get Miles locked down for Trace tonight.

Woah. Trace. He hadn't called her that in … it'd been a while. He really was grateful for the talk they ended up having this morning. Grateful she got him out of his funk, even made him laugh. Made him get up and get out. *Trace.*

"There's that cunt right now."

Ryan hadn't caught the guy's name sitting shotgun and hadn't cared to. Now he was even more certain about his initial instincts about him. He seemed to be referring to a knockout girl pulling a massive box out of the back of her Mercedes just a couple blocks up the road from the House.

Bret slowed the truck more than he would for a stop sign to look at her, almost seemingly hoping she'd notice, but she'd turned and was walking toward her apartment building. All Bret said was, "Yep." But the word seemed as full of hate as his mouth currently was with dip spit.

"She turn down your killer moves or something, Bret?" Ryan said knowing Bret would never begin to have a chance with that girl.

"Shit, like I'd touch that."

"Oh, you ain't know who that is?"

"No Miles, I *ain't know*." What the hell? Miles didn't talk like that. Bret just brought out the redneck in everyone.

"That's Senator Carlyle's daughter, bro. You don't know this? She lives across the street!"

Miles seemed astonished that Ryan could have missed out on this fact.

"Nope. Didn't know," Ryan said glancing back for one more look at her ass, that the clothe of her little shorts clung so intimately around as if with static.

"His half-breed," said Shotgun Guy.

"Yeah. Her mom's Cuban. Thus that ass." Miles was staring too.

"Should have run that ass over right now."

Jesus, this guy. What the fuck? And how old was he anyway? Like twenty-eight *or some shit?*

"Nah," Bret chimed in. "She deserves better than that don't you think?"

"I'll give her better than that," Miles was saying and making some awkward sexual maneuver in the back seat that one of the Ryans, at one point, would have found funny, but his thoughts now were still stuck on something in Bret's reflection in the rearview mirror that he couldn't quite articulate to himself.

He was glad Miles was here. If it were just the other two, he would definitely have told Bret to pull over, and gotten out.

11:53 AM

Kyle had kissed his bruises. "I'll kiss them to make them better," he'd said. His skin could still feel Kyle's gentle lips now. As if choosing to remember their sensation after such assault.

"We'll just stay in tonight," Kyle had said.

The world outside. People seeing his bruised neck. Questioning.

But Tristan didn't want to hide them, the bruises.

"I'm out now," he said to himself. Alone now. In bed still. Out. Of another closet he'd somehow put himself in. Slowly. Hidden from self-analysis. He'd stepped into the comfort of its darkness and shut the door.

To hide it all from Ryan. That was only the beginning. Only the outermost and easiest layer of what was peeling back now somewhere in Tristan's vision between his eyes and his cinderblock wall.

Ryan. And all the pain there. All the fear. All of that only led to something deeper. To something else he'd kept hidden. To his dad. Tristan's.

The War Profiteers. Unintentionally, perhaps. Unknowing of the real depths of it. Of how it all actually came about. Of how strings were held and where they led to. But still his father happily accepting their money. Crumbs from them; feasts for him. Proud of them too. Helping to protect the country. To bring the world peace.

As if working for them was the same kind of "service to the country" as being in the Army. Though, of course, rather than sacrifice you shared in the plunder.

The thoughts he hid from his father. *Time to be out, Tristan. With all of it.*

But Dad. All the pain there. All the fear. That too only led to something deeper. To something else he tried to keep hidden. "The man in the mirror."

The boy. The scared little boy. The boy who could read. Who could think. Who, even, had found the courage to talk sometimes. But not to act. For to act would change everything. For to act, to truly act, to do it right, to take a stand—you could not come back from that.

You scared little boy. Fuck you. Fuck you, Tristan. Strangle him out as Ryan tried to do to the whole of me. But have the guts to keep going. Squeeze until he kicks no more, tears form no more, inner protests and begging pleas scream no more. Say goodbye to him. Burn him to ashes and toss them in the nearest dumpster.

The scared little boy must die. For if I let him live—he will keep the rest of me from my destiny. He'll keep me here. In my little room. Under my blankets. Believing that mother's kisses could heal my wounds.

Tristan grabbed his covers and threw them off.

12:01 PM

Jasmine walked around the large island of her modern and immaculate and barely used kitchen with a 10-inch knife in her hand made of some new material so sharp you had to be super careful lest you slice away a finger.

She approached the boxes in the middle of her tremendous living room, stabbed one side of a box, and began to slice away the tape.

She only had one roommate now, having gotten rid of the rest, but she might need to ask this bitch to leave too because she was not being helpful at all or happy even about the party. But it was her place and she would do as she pleased with it. It was one of the few nice things Daddy had done of late: buying these two old apartments, gutting them, connecting them and upgrading them. Everything to Daddy was a potential investment, and on this one, she was quite sure, he was hoping to lose big. A cover for other things. But that did have the side benefit of making the place all the nicer for her college experience.

Her tank tops began to appear. She ripped the plastic and held one up. It was the Homo one. It looked great. Even the line above the butt. The company had done a fantastic rush job.

She went on opening others, searching for hers.

She found one of the ones she'd come up with at the last, last minute. She wasn't crazy about the rhyme—rhyming was not her thing—but she liked it well enough:

> Molly, Molly, Molly,
>
> I'm so cool!
>
> No way, bro!
>
> That's so 2002!
>
> Shit then man,
>
> what's the new thing?!
>
> Don't worry, bro!
>
> They'll tell us ...
>
> ... we'll follow.

She was so over drugs and what people thought they did for their status. But where was her shirt? *Don't tell me they forgot the most important—oh.* Here. There was one shirt wrapped alone. She ripped the plastic bag, opened and held it up.

Back in Business!

Thanks for the call,

Senator C!

And for caving,

President V!

#BoysOfPrivilegeWinAgain!

This one she'd wear and post all the pictures of. This time not throwing aside her drink the second a phone looked poised to steal incriminating evidence. This time holding the drink clearly in shot—possibly even artfully spilling a colorful one across her breasts and their politically incriminating words. And the leak to the local press would come from her.

For what no one yet knew, but of what she was quite aware, was Daddy had made a call to FSCU's President Voorhees to pressure her to get his old frat Back in Business.

Daddy, who had written her last week the cryptic handwritten note on unofficial paper—

Stay. In. Line. Sweetie.

—worried about her behavior and his good father image.

Daddy, who had threatened Mommy this week to leave her high and dry, to excommunicate her mother from privilege in a brilliant campaign already scripted for the media by a far-outside-the-beltway consulting firm complete with incriminating evidence on how it was all her mom's horrible fault.

The boys of Sig Chi O were just cover.

Daddy was the intended target of this shot across the bow, this tiny round from the armory of ammunition she'd discovered.

Daddy was fucking with the wrong daughter.

12:37 PM

A thought was forming. It wasn't quite clear to him yet, but the pieces were coming together, he could feel a gravitational pull in his mind finding each element buried in the layers of different memories—experiences, things he'd seen, things he'd read. He was looking for a book, maybe several books, in which his mind seemed to know it wanted to pull together its thought from words it had once read there but could not quite remember all of.

Tristan's books were stacked in every place they could be around his room, little not-terribly-sturdy towers of thought which never went together, or rather, seemed to to others. His own private library was his most prized physical possession. The only physical possession he actually cared about. The notes and underlines in these books. The history of his own intellectual and emotional development in their pages. Memories of where he was when he first read the great ones. Of who he was then. Some old scratchings of notes seemed so elementary to him now; some surprisingly wise, precocious, happily so.

His mind was skimming through memories as well as occasional new thoughts inspired by book covers and spines half-read in his search.

All the protests of his generation that had meant nothing in the end. Even the ones that "worked," had worked so little. They got the name of a campus building changed from that of the man who donated money for it, money he half-made because he owned other people for their labor. Good, yes, but so little. A baby step. They got some liberal-leaning people to agree with a more liberal thing. Got the choir to sing a little louder.

That was all it ever was. For any of them.

Even his generation's greatest successes—the Black Lives Matter Movement, the energy they'd unleashed for Candidate-To-Good-To-Be-True's primary run—made waves, big waves, but waves that only crashed upon immovable rocks.

And mostly it wasn't even waves, but drops in the countless buckets. Frat boys will drop and do pushups on the campus lawn if you donate some money to some cause of the semester. Whip cream pie a professor in the face to raise money for a woman's domestic violence rescue charity. Take a cookie and sign this petition to—

Here. Were these the books he'd read it in—the thing he was looking for? *At Berkeley in the '60s* and *Berkeley at War*. He pulled them out, proud of himself for stacking them together, holding the books above them in place as he did, and then sat cross-legged in the middle of his floor to flip through them.

Cracking open the pages of a book he'd read and liked. What a pleasure—a comfort—that was. Memories of what he'd read and the thoughts about those thoughts reconstituting themselves as the author's underscored words and his own in the margins were rediscovered on the pages.

He thought maybe the thing he was looking for had been done before. But not done quite well enough. Those who had done it had stopped short of some key component Tristan would add. It wasn't enough just to do an act, it was how you marketed it.

"FUCK! FUCK! FUCK! FUCK!" he'd written late one night across the top of one page. The right to say "FUCK!" Hard to imagine that was a thing in America, land of the free. The Free Speech Movement. That was one of the early Berkeley protests. A young guy fresh arrived in Berkeley from NYC got a piece of paper, wrote "FUCK!" on it, sat down in front of the Student

Union and held the paper to his chest. He was arrested. Students rallied on his behalf. The "Fuck Defense Fund" was established. Tristan would have liked these guys.

They started their own newspapers, ran the prints themselves, to say what the corporate press wouldn't about racial equality, the people in power, the growing "conflict" in Vietnam, and everything else. SPIDER magazine was one. "Sex, Politics, International Communism, Drugs, Extremism, and Rock and Roll." Tristan had a note on the side of the page to try to find old copies of it, maybe frame some, but he'd never gotten around to it. He wanted to again now. He wished his generation would start something like this. Not just the anything-goes-ness of most of the internet. Mc was right about that. Some degree of control was needed: smart people, empirically led minds, editing it, guiding it. Otherwise it leads you away from truth, not toward it.

Fighting the neighboring campus businesses to treat blacks equally. Protesting their stores. Fighting to get the speakers they wanted to be allowed on campus. Communist leaders, if they wanted. Malcolm X, for sure. Fighting to liberate campus as a whole for political activity. Imagine that, Tristan had thought. The university telling them they couldn't be political on their own campus. Treating them like children. Like "where's your hall pass for the bathroom?"

And the irony that now students were fighting for the opposite—to keep speakers away, to shut them up—begging to be saved from hearing the free speech they disagreed with. Tristan didn't want to hear that conservative bullshit either, enough lies had been spread with bullhorns of far more power than he would ever wield. But still, the irony.

Debt was owed to these old students for fighting these early fights. But an emptiness returned to Tristan's gut when he thought of the generations since, including his own, that had failed to take up the torches when necessary to continue the fight to one day create a True America, a true land of the free. Or even if they took up the torches, the failure to carry them to the castles and burn them down.

These students in the '60s fought all their fights in the face of the suspensions, the arrests, the police beatings and other brutalities, the "careers ended," the political trials, Fucking-McCarthyism, the Fucking House UnAmerican Activities Committee witch-hunting every American for hints of communism and turning its brainwashed eyes toward Berkeley. The students protesting HUAC when it came to town and the police using fire hoses to literally wash them down the front steps of their City Hall, a peoples' building. Law enforcement and politicians hurling the word "communist" as much, and much the same, as "terrorist" today.

Mario Savio and his boys. Tristan would have liked him. Where were the Mario Savios today?

The FBI files on the students. American students. Citizens. Voicing their opinions. The police state campus became. Capturing the car. *Ha!* Tristan loved that one. Even now he had to smile.

The students, defying the administration, choosing to be political and exercise their free speech wherever they damn well pleased on their campus, had set up tables in Sproul Plaza. University Police came to arrest one of the activists and the students weren't about to roll over and take it. Hundreds of students surrounded the police car, not letting it move. They climbed atop it, one stuck a potato in its exhaust pipe, others slashed its tires. They controlled the car all night, taking turns mounting it as a podium, a pulpit to preach to the assembled, enlivened crowd.

How Tristan would love to have been there. To climb atop the roof and say a few words, get a few cheers, look out on the faces of an empowered youth, a believing youth, a youth ready to take their freedom back.

He'd thought of trying to get into Berkeley, but the grades from the classes he didn't give a shit about were in the fucking way. And he also had some gut instinct that it wouldn't any longer be the Berkeley he wanted. It would be a sad reminder of a place where students once fought the assimilation, but now strove for it. Begging to do everything they were supposed to to get those high-paying jobs.

Then, the good ones anyway, had fought the "Robot Factory" of the university, the assimilation into some automaton purpose they were being bred, mass-produced, into for some ultimate purpose in the machine of society. They fought for an education revolution.

Then, they fought for an American revolution. Then, even, a Human one. Berkeley, Columbia, the first of many campus revolts in a student revolt movement that would become global. A radical Berkeley the first step toward a radical America, a radical humanity. No longer liberals sitting around and talking, no more coffee shops and late night joint-sharing circles, but radicals demanding change with action.

Racial equality, school desegregation, Black Power. Eldridge Cleaver. Huey Newton. Where were the new ones?

And then the war.

Burning their draft cards. Hanging Lyndon Johnson in effigy. "Hell no! We won't go!" "Hey, hey, LBJ! How many kids did you kill today?!" Tristan's marginalia on one of these pages, "How often we Americans throw away our principles like worthless trash in the face of fear." Fighting the "Blood and Napalm vote." Confrontation politics. The battles against fucking Ronald Reagan as California's governor. Reagan's hatred of the students and accusations about them. Accusations by even some of their own professors of "treason." *Treason.*

To look at what the students fought for ... and what those in power fought for ... and then to call the former treason ... it was straight out of Orwell's pen.

Hell's Angels attacking the student marchers, a Republican org bailing out the *one* of the biker gang thugs to get arrested for it.

Students crossing the tracks and stopping the train carrying more young men to the war effort with a banner that read "Stop the War Machine." How different from the students of another of Tristan's favorite books, *A Separate Peace*, helping to dig out a similar train through the snow, he thought. How long we've been fighting this war, or should have been fighting it. His scribbled words in the margins, "Is it Eurasia or Eastasia we're fighting?" thinking, as so often, of his Orwell. And whom will we be fighting again so soon?

He thought of standing with his mom and a hundred thousand others in New York City at 7 years old. She'd taken him against Dad's will to the 2003 protests to try to prevent the imminent Iraq war. He remembered after all these years the signs held by the group near them: The 9/11 Families for Peaceful Tomorrows. The corporate media had whitewashed it all, Mom had said. When he grew older and looked back at the coverage, he knew she'd been right.

Was this where it was? The thing he was looking for? Confrontation politics. Johnson's war profiteer friends. Dow Chemical's death profits from manufacturing the napalm. "The Resistance." Here. This was it, wasn't it? The Resistance Movement? He saw those words again. To "harass and disrupt" the Selective Service System. Thousands of "militants," they were called, blocking the induction centers. Police thugs in riot gear beating them back. The police firing tear gas. The students hurling back rocks. Barricades built in the streets. Fires set. Riots. Store windows broken in town near campus. Curfews put in place. Militancy worked.

Wait, what? Did it? Was the war stopped from this?

He kept turning the pages. Where was the thing? He thought it was here. The street protests were becoming street parties. We were off to hippie land because we couldn't get anything done, and we might as well accept our powerlessness over it all, and focus instead on escape into drugs and sex and their illusions of happiness. We might as well pretend.

As always, it was fight or flight and after some had fought and been smacked down hard for it, the rest were choosing flight. LSD and escapism. *Those weak pieces of shit!* Allow the powers that be to continue ruining this world and hoarding humanity's fortunes for themselves while you drop acid and ruminate on your meaningless dreams—*FUCK YOU!*

... *Fuck you too, Tristan,* he thought. For how often he'd done the same. *Fuck you too.*

That picture as he turned back the pages again, back from the hippies to the radicals. That officer standing triumphantly over the fetal-positioned crying body of the student protestor he'd just beaten down with his billy club. Hard to tell in his grainy, black and white face—hard to know if Tristan was just projecting—but he thought he saw something in the officer's face of a dazed, stupefaction of a "What have I just done?"—of a "Who am I fighting my own for?"

Rage. Rage was in that picture. Rage was Tristan's reaction to it. Rage.

Days of Rage. That was it! The thing he was looking for was in there, wasn't it?

Tristan crawled around the floor on his hands and knees looking for the book amongst the stacks.

There. He pulled it out roughly, letting the books atop it tumble over like blocks of a Jenga game, its red cover, the smoke of the bomb, *Days of Rage*, "America's Radical Underground ... Revolutionary Violence," this had to be it. It was in here. Somewhere amongst "The Army of Angry N-----s," the revolution, the Weather Underground. He sat again and opened the *Days of Rage* on his lap. Searching. Searching for what it was.

12:40 PM

"Bitch." He'd called her a bitch, the little shit.

Why had she let him off the hook so easily with that?

Just because he was right.

She passed another store window and caught another glimpse of herself.

It hadn't been as freeing as she'd wanted it to be, her little trip up to Naples to do a little shopping. She should have brought friends, but she'd wanted the alone time, the escape.

She wanted new lingerie for tonight, and you couldn't get that anywhere near campus unless, you know, you wanted a cartoon Sand Tiger on your ass.

She smiled a bit as she walked thinking that she did used to have a pair of adorable cotton shorts with a smiling Sand Tiger on the butt. She'd worn them to the beach that day Ryan first took her to Floatopia and left them in the sand when they launched out on the little girl raft Ryan brought that she thought was so cute of him, that he'd show up with that. She never saw those shorts again.

She caught another reflection of herself. Carrying her lingerie bag on her arm like a purse. This street and the other people shopping on it. Its palm trees and fancy stores, trying to be the Rodeo Drive of Naples.

"Façade." Tristan's word. He was right too.

That pic he'd posted of her doing—or trying to do—the hula-hoop on his raft. It was such a happy moment. Maybe one of her happiest in college. Maybe one she'd look back to in old age and smile. Maybe one she'd cherish more than so much of the rest of it.

They'd slid off Ryan's little raft and onto Tristan and his friends' gigantic float with the blowup palm trees. One of the gay boys even had a hand-cranked blender out there and they were making drinks. Someone had brought a hula-hoop.

Tracy had had a solid moment in her youth with the hula-hoop. It was her favorite thing for maybe a month. Tristan tried it first and looked like such an idiot doing it. The float was big but it was still a float. You had to really spread your legs wide to get anything close to balance. He'd fallen back in laughter and to the cheers of his new friends after just a few spins of his hips.

Tracy surprised herself getting up to go next. Especially since—as she'd remembered later, to even more of her surprise—she'd actually had nothing to drink yet.

Ryan had brought whiskey. In the sun. Who does that? And one of the boys was still working the hand-crank to make her beverage. She was stone-cold sober. But, no, she wasn't. Just sober from alcohol. Not the adrenaline of the day.

She got up and did it. She made it three times as long as Tristan, though Ryan's help was cheating. She loved that he did that. He laid on his belly and tried to help hold her up by the thighs. She whacked him in the face with the hoop a couple times on accident. He laughed and didn't stop holding her.

She thought about that on their walk back to campus from Floatopia that day. They could have gotten a ride, but chose to walk. And in that walk had a great deal of comfortable silence.

200 | WILL KANE THOMPSON

She thought about what an idiot Tristan had looked like and what a fool she looked too, and she thought about how wonderful it was that in that actual moment—not the photo of it—she could hardly remember ever loving being a fool so much.

Ryan did that. In his best moments. He made her forget her worries about what everyone around them thought. Her cute little shorts with the Sand Tiger on the butt and the towel she'd brought had been stolen, so she had to walk back to campus in just her bikini and at first was worried what people would think driving by but then, arm around Ryan's, forgot all about it.

And on that float before. Swinging her hips around—smacking Ryan in the face—all the other eyes on that sea of people became a blur—and all her thoughts about their thoughts about her blurred just as much—and her little world narrowed down to that small circle around that hoop from childhood. Ryan holding her up and Tristan scrambling to get his phone out of the plastic baggie to take some pics in time.

And she'd thought about that a lot in the years since.

She knew a lot of people didn't "get" her and Ryan. Thought they were just yet another of those couples in college or high school that were just together for no apparent reason. Just two hot people, so why not?

But she knew, in her better moments, they were so much more.

She knew she helped Ryan stop his constant focus on the future and the past and live instead in this wondrous present. He'd told her about his multiple Ryans. She knew she helped him be College Ryan, and she knew that College Ryan was something his poor hurt soul needed to be more often.

And she knew that just as she helped Ryan focus himself in time, he helped her focus herself in place—to stop always thinking about everyone else around them—to let all their eyes become a blur while she let loose in that happy little circle of being free.

12:43 PM

It was a long trip. Longer than Ryan thought it would be. But in this moment, he wasn't regretting it. Not yet. Because the road was so nice.

Miles had long ago fallen asleep, head back against the doorframe, mouth agape, occasional weird noises. Bret and Asshole Man had been silent under Bret's twangy music Ryan had finally begun to tune out—the wind from the open windows helped. They'd left the protected lands a long while back. This was the "real" Florida, as Bret might say. Old roads that cut deep into the peninsula's center and looked like they'd never once been repaved. A vast stretch of forest that must have caught fire once—all black tree trunks up to the tops where new growth had found a way to start again. Cows and farmland and an occasional wetland still, left to itself, to what this entire peninsula must have once been. Some mining companies digging up the great sandbar of Florida into massive white mounds. A lot of ranches with free range cattle—the kind you hoped to see. But a couple massive cattle houses with the cows packed in skin to skin and troughs dug all the way around like a moat that must have been filled with something awful. And lots and lots of churches. There must have been one church for every six people who lived out here. Baptists churches. "Jesus is Real," "Real Life" churches. A couple of modern mega-churches, but mostly small rundown churches and one or two made from buildings clearly meant for other purposes.

They drove through one of those small towns where the speed limit drops to 35 and Bret, to Ryan's surprise, did slow down. He drove slower than Ryan had ever seen him. At one point, looking around at the buildings, some of the people walking by, Bret glanced back to Ryan and let out, "Quite a thing to protect, huh?" Quite a surprise that was too—a poignant phrase from Bret.

As they were pulling out of the town Ryan noticed a yard sign for the guy Tristan called "Candidate Kill 'em All" so consistently that Ryan now thought of him as that too. The sign was in front of a rundown shack of a house. That was an image Ryan had seen before and couldn't get. Why people who lived in such poverty would vote for a man born into such immense wealth who had clearly never, before running for office, given two shits about people like them. Hope. That was it. The power of hope. That that man, and the class he came from, might let some of their fortune trickle to them. A fool's gold.

Fuck, he was sounding like Tristan. And Tristan was precisely what he wanted out of his mind. Back to the open spaces, to Florida, to the peace of that. But even his appreciation for this old road reminded him of something from Tristan. That book Tristan had made him read in high school. *Zen and The Art of Motorcycle Maintenance.* Ryan hadn't wanted to read it, but Tristan wouldn't let up until he did. And he'd ended up really liking it—the beginning part anyway, that was all Ryan had read. Somewhere in between lacrosse and college apps and everything else, the desire to keep reading got lost. But he remembered finding some of his own feelings put to words in it. His respect for "the machine" and how it worked. It had helped cement for him that civil engineering was the path he'd take. Again that ever-present problem with Tristan—that there was so much good there too.

Another huge mound, the biggest yet. What were they mining here? Birds everywhere. Oh. Oh, wow. *That's* all garbage. Landfill. It must have been a mile long. *We just bury it.* This was definitely not the Florida the tourists see.

A flash of another field. Another hole in the earth. Debris in the soil. But not here. The thought Tristan triggered with the line of thought he'd led Ryan to this morning. Those thoughts still warm, now touched by views of the vast fields he looked out upon, brought back that hole in the Pennsylvania field into which one of the planes disappeared on the morning of 9/11.

When he thought about that hole there was this feeling, this mystical knowledge that the vast part of his mind that was subconscious didn't believe for a second that a plane would disappear into that soil—but a knowledge too that the conscious part of his mind had fought to keep that damning thought hidden. There was an off-balance-ness he felt again, the world, the landscape before him, starting to tilt a bit. A sickness in his stomach. What he'd felt this morning, but he had his whiskey then to reach for and calm it. The danger of the knowledge: what if Tristan was right this time too? With even the possibility of this, his world felt like it was crashing down around him. Like he himself and everything that constituted him was falling or could fall apart.

He wasn't so dissimilar, was he, from that guy with the Candidate Kill 'em All sign in his front yard. Ryan was voting for him too, but for different reasons. But were they different? Was he just as much a fool for believing?

Bret was talking. And Ryan was glad about it for once. Actually, relieved to hear Bret's voice. Something about when they got there. Ryan nodded like he'd been listening.

"I'm just sayin'," Bret kept saying, "some of these guys—they're real serious dudes. You know? Real serious. So … try not to be too … New York." Bret and the other guy laughed a bit at that, but a laugh that tried to maintain their own "seriousness."

Ryan gave him another nod and looked away again. Fucking Bret. What the hell would he know of anything serious?

They slowed and turned in to what must be his uncle's ranch. Ryan was a bit let down by it. Just a dirt road with a metal cattle gate across it. Not one of those wooden structures of a beam and two posts that you drove under. Ryan had thought those obligatory for a proper ranch. Just that metal gate. No sign except "No Trespassing." No lock on the gate either except the nerve to get out of your car and go open it. Which Bret was doing right now. The thought crossed Ryan's mind that maybe this wasn't Bret's uncle's ranch. Maybe Bret just had that nerve.

12:52 PM

Their words hurt, "bitch" and "façade." But maybe they caused the kind of pain she needed. What her new hero had talked about in Make Moves— some of the pain was good for you—you had to figure out which helped you grow and which held you back. And the stuff that held you back you had to …

"Clean House." That was her chapter on getting rid of the bad in your life. Tracy loved that the author took historical things women were told they needed to do and flipped them around into things that would actually help them.

She'd said, "You *do* need to 'clean house', but I'm not talking about the kitchen or the bathrooms. I'm talking about all the negative influences in your life. Every*thing* and every*one* that holds you back—they gotta go!"

Tracy was walking faster now. She was headed back to her car. Damn right it was time to clean house. And there was one big negative influence above all the others. And it was time to start with her. The Queen Bitch herself.

She wasn't gonna let her do this anymore. Not to her or her sister. For Dad, it was too late. Mom had already destroyed the poor man.

She needed to get to her car and get on the highway where she could put her mom in her place with no one around to hear.

Her flip-flops were slapping against the sidewalk as she moved. She wished she'd had on heels. Make Moves said, "Yes, you need to wear heels! But metaphorical ones. The things that make you stand taller. The fabulous Manolo Blahniks of your own self-image that let you know you've walked into this boardroom to own it! ... Or maybe just to kick some ass!" Still, she wanted the physical ones too now. The sound they'd be making, the posture they'd give her, would be more fitting for what she was about to finally do.

1:07 PM

"WARNING!" it said. Hand painted in red across the top of the massive sign. He held it by a 4x4 wood post, maybe twelve feet tall. It had to be heavy. The corners of the wood had to scrape at his hands all day. A cross to bear, Luke supposed. That was probably why he made it that way.

Luke had found himself in the middle of The Commons again. Something inside him drawn there—not willing to take the long way around. And there was this man he'd seen once before. Maybe a year ago. He seemed to be a traveler. Going from college to college with his massive sign.

"WARNING!" it said. "GOD IS COMING! And He is ANGRY with YOU!" He turned the sign around to the other side where in smaller text he'd listed The Lord's grievances.

There was a lot of yelling. Some by students who thought themselves Christians, yelling that he had God wrong. Kristi wasn't among them, but she could have been. Luke almost had a vision of her there. Saying one of the many somethings she'd said so many times now of late, now she was changing or being changed by this place. One frat-looking guy was skating by in front of Luke, and had slowed his board to take in the man and his sign, and, almost in slow motion, it seemed to Luke, had extended his arm to a very firm, solid, middle finger pointed at the man, as he continued on.

Or was it at Luke? And would Luke be this man? Was that his future? No. Never. God had more in store for him than this.

"That skirt will lead you straight to Hell!" the man now yelled at a girl walking by. Her skirt was short. Her legs long and tan. She screamed back something about, "Get out of here! You don't belong here! No one wants you here!" *Was she screaming that at me?*

A water balloon went flying by. One of the tables had them. Something about a fundraiser. It pelted the man's sign. He turned his chest in the direction the projectile came from. Hoping to catch the guilty on the GoPro camera strapped around his torso. But it was probably too late. More things were being thrown. *Sticks and stones,* Luke thought. *And words. Lots of words.*

It needs to begin. The arguments never win. Never will. An endless battle. Truth, the greatest casualty. He'd read that somewhere or heard it. Truth, war's greatest casualty. But the Lord of Lords had planned a war to end all wars. And it needed to begin.

The Lord's draft had begun. It began long ago. And these students around him had held up their draft cards to Heaven and lit them aflame. As the Lord must now one day light them. Their eternal souls.

Soldiers. Who would be God's soldiers? The *Soldiers of Christ*. That was the question. The only question. And the weapons God would give them—the weapons of all the world's armies would be but water balloons against them. But words, hurled in anger.

But …

"'To the one who conquers, I will give the morning star.'"

1:09 PM

She was trying to get around yet another slow-ass driver on 41 South. She could see the road was clear ahead of the old fogy and just needed the car to her right to slow a bit so she could zip over and around the one in front. She wanted the clear road ahead for this. The phone was ringing loud on her speakers.

"It's my beautiful College Girl! How are you, dear?"

Urg. She must be in public.

"Heard you all had a nice family breakfast this morning."

Finally a break. She gunned it and made her way around the car. Freedom ahead as far as she could see. Tensions lessened. Time for this.

"Excuse me. She seems to need me a moment. Exams and things." She heard her mom say to who cares who. Then, clearly walking away from earshot, her heels clicking on a sidewalk, "Oh, so you've called to pick another fight. How thoughtful of you."

"Nope. No. You know what Mom? I think I've called to end one."

"Oh lovely. Which would you like to end, darling? The one about your credit card statement?"

She started driving faster. Screw a speeding ticket, this was worth it.

"No Mom, I think I'm just going to end *all* of the fights, actually! And I'm going to do that by cutting the person out of my life who really, deep down, the more I've thought about it, is the actual cause of every fight I've ever had!

I believe you know her well. You see her ugly face in the mirror every morning before you cake it over with an inch of makeup."

"Uh … Tracy, that was a bit much, don't you think, even for you?"

"Oh don't play innocent with me, I know the things you've been saying. I know what you're doing to Aubrey with the goddamn toast. I just can't wait till I get to help her through her anorexia in—how long you think she's got Mom, another six months? And I know what you've been saying about Ryan."

There was a pause.

"Good. I'm glad you know how I feel about Ryan. Do you really think that's a healthy relationship for you?"

"Oh! This is full of it. *You* telling *me* about healthy relationships. What, like your relationship with Dad, where you tell all your friends that Dad's a *lawyer* even though, you know, he like, never went to law school and his title is Senior *Paralegal*. Or, how about the fact that I'm currently taking out huge college loans because you convinced Dad that we needed a *pool*—in *Ohio*—where we use it what?, three times a year?"

"Oh, you ungrateful little bitch. I always—"

"Nope. Gotta cut you off right there, Mom. Been called a bitch too many times today and I'm not going to hear it from the Queen Bitch herself who made me all of who I am. I called to say I'm done. Not taking your phone calls anymore. You got something you need, have Dad call. And you're not coming here anymore either so you can try to Mrs. Robinson one of my fellow hardworking studiers. That's it, Mom! I'm done! No phone calls! And you're *not allowed to come here anymore*!"

There was silence.

"And I can't wait for Aubrey to get to Tech so she can tell you the *exact same thing*!"

There was more silence.

She just noticed her cheeks were wet. She was driving down a newer cement patch of road. The creases in the cement made a repetitive thump. Ticking away the time.

She breathed in deeply. She heard her mom doing the same. Pictured her mom, back to friends, index finger to eye to save the mascara and the face that hid behind it.

There was the deciding to say a thing like this ... and then there was the saying of it.

And then there was this awful silence.

1:12 PM

"You're the n-----, baby, it isn't me," Baldwin said again through the years as Scotty watched him again on his laptop. Baldwin, so many things America said he couldn't be, America said he *wasn't*, and yet there he was touching the scarf on his throat, his immense mind pulling all life's lessons down into their most elemental expressions for us to hear them clearly. There he was. And still is. Just as his uncle had described him. Scotty's mom's brother. The reader. The librarian. The one always, relentlessly, annoyingly, pointing to history for all answers, always, to every question. The one who'd given him this book with the strange and somewhat fearful, "Don't tell your dad I gave you this," librarian's whisper.

It was open on his lap now. The first time he'd really opened it—opened it to actually read it. He went back to it now. To the quote of Baldwin's the author chose to put before the final section. It was that quote Scotty had first read the first time he opened the book to skim it over a bit after his uncle had given it to him that day. Baldwin: "And have brought humanity to the edge of oblivion: because they think they are white."

The line had confused and intrigued Scotty when he first saw it and so he'd put down the book and gone to the internet to find out more about this Baldwin his uncle so praised. And that's when he'd found the video he'd watched again now with much greater understanding having spent the day actually reading through this book until the page of this quote, rather than just thumbing his way there—this amazing book he couldn't put down today, for which he'd texted friends and professors alike to say he was sick, for which "brothers," white brothers, had to come to get the waterslide to put it up today and he pretended he couldn't talk, something with his throat, because he couldn't stop reading it, because for reasons he didn't understand when it happened, the first word, the very first word hanging there by itself when he cracked it open this morning made him cry:

"Son,"

Because he saw why his uncle had said don't tell your father. Because the book was a father's advice to his son. Not his uncle's place to give. But advice he needed. Advice he wished he'd had years ago in his own father's voice.

And he'd been holding the book's hard cover in his hands all day so tightly the joints and bones of his hands hurt and his fingers often lost their blood. He'd needed this book for so long and so, so needed it right now.

Ta-Nehisi Coates's *Between the World and Me*.

He turned the page and kept reading. His hands hurting. His eyes worn from their swollenness. But his soul, or what he called his soul, feeling fed like never before.

1:18 PM

Kristi was seated at one of the study carrels along the walls of the Great Hall of Reading. She liked the quiet energy of this space. Every so often a whisper, a chair squeaking back across the floor, an earbud playing too loudly. But mostly quiet and yet surrounded by so many from so many different places, but just like you in their intent on study, or bettering themselves, or achieving our goals no matter how grand. (Though, yes, quite a few were likely just wasting time online.)

Todd had set up a "Christian Study Spot" on the fourth floor of his new building. There was even a coffee bar—"Coffee for Christ." The name didn't quite make sense for her. She liked studying there with her friends sometimes, but she also liked coming here, to this sort of intellectual heart of campus. *We're getting so secluded in our different groups,* she thought. She wanted to be among the full campus more often. Though the mural above her head here felt oppressive. The search for the fountain of youth. What a silly, secular thing to seek. Everlasting life was not to be found in our young bodies, but in our souls, given to Jesus.

And who would want everlasting life on Earth, anyway? This world was so fallen, so cruel.

She didn't like that thought. It didn't quite sound like her. But it was what she was reading that brought her low.

The text was on violence in families. The chapter was on the Cycles of Violence. It said there were two types of cycles. Episodic and generational. The first was within relationships. A violent act, the begging of forgiveness, a period of normalcy, and then a building toward violence again. Round and round the cycle went, and most victims of domestic violence found ways to numb themselves to it. The text had said victims often don't see the cycle.

But Kristi didn't believe that. She knew people too well. They saw it. And chose to bury it.

Then there was generational violence. The child exposed to violence by his or her parent grows up to express his or her anger in violence, perhaps even to his or her own child.

The text said, so much depended upon one fundamental question we answered for ourselves, or had answered for us, as children: Do we fundamentally view the world as a safe and good place, or as a scary and bad one? So much that would happen in the rest of our lives, so many decisions we'd make, grand and seemingly insignificant, would be based on that worldview. Our whole lives might depend upon it.

And the cycles continue on and on. What can break them?

And it comes in so many forms, violence. Violence could even be a mother who shows her child no love, a side box in the chapter had noted.

Luke's face, holding the Bible at her yesterday morning. Was there violence in him? What happened to his poor soul years ago with his sister's passing? Against whom did he hold such blame, anger … violence?

The violence upon that girl in her Church Family in Winter Park who did the "unspeakable" thing.

The violence growing on campus. Her walk here today. Through The Commons. A man holding a giant "WARNING" sign. Yelling about a Jesus Kristi couldn't recognize. A violent one. The anger in the crowd toward him. Anger for many different reasons.

She drew in her notebook a couple of concentric circles and titled them "Cycles of Violence." In the inner circle she wrote in her tiniest handwriting, "w/n a Relationship/Episodic." In the bigger circle around it, "w/n a Family/Generational."

But then she had a thought that wasn't in the textbook, and she drew another, larger circle around the two and wrote in it, "In Society/World." And then another tiny circle in the middle of them all and drew a line to it by which she wrote, "w/n Ourselves."

She looked at her four concentric circles and saw that these cycles of violence were much bigger than just what her textbook was talking about. She thought about how contagious a thing violence was. How easily it jumped from one circle to the next. They were so massive and so intimate, these cycles, they existed on so many levels—how could we ever stop them?

And where would you even start? The biggest or the smallest?

She thought of her other circles she'd drawn yesterday in her journal. She thought of her career to come. How would she help people who would come into her office and might be the victims of violence—domestic or otherwise? Would a perpetrator of violence come in? How would she help him or her?

She stared at the blank, dark wood of the carrel for a moment. The concentric lines of the life of the tree it once was. And all her circles began to coalesce for her. And for the first time she thought she was beginning to see an answer for the type of "strong woman" she wanted to be. That she could stand in the path of these cycles of violence for her patients and break them. Not with some fantastic superhero power. But with what she would learn in many more books like this one, in many more hours of study, and in continuing to grow her empathy muscle, which she'd been working on her whole life.

Yes, Kristi. Yes, she thought. *That does seem like a pretty darn good goal, doesn't it?*

She smiled.

Then got back to work.

1:23 PM

"Revolution," that's what they thought they were igniting with their Molotov cocktails thrown at ROTC buildings, a bombing of Columbia's Law Library, Berkeley's Hall of Justice, and other campus buildings and centers of financial or military or other power around the country—to bring America down—"America," what it had become—so that a place built on American Principles could be built again, better this time … perhaps.

A revolution like Ché's, tactics like the Viet Cong's.

And like the Panthers'. And wanting to be them. The Panthers who learned from Malcolm. Malcolm who compared King's followers to "house negroes" and his own to "field negroes;" one who wanted to ask, the other who was ready to take.

To bring the terror back home to those who feigned ignorance of the terror they imposed upon others in foreign lands like Southeast Asia or those in the wrong quadrant of the nation's capital. That was the strategic theory: if they felt the terror themselves, then maybe they would stop imposing it on "The Others."

But it was a strategy that misjudged the privileged. For their response was not to back down, but to double down.

Tristan flipped through more pages about these days of rage.

"Ivy League Revolutionaries," the students were called.

JJ at Columbia.

Bernadine Dorn, blouse open illegally low, dripping with sex and intellect, and her fellow Weathermen wanting to be the same, wanting intellect and raw power and the occasional orgy too because "people who fuck together fight together" like the old Spartans.

Panthers leader Fred Hampton murdered in his bed by Chicago's police.

Villages of innocents in Vietnam had to be destroyed in order to be saved.

The bombs the Weathermen made used watches as ignition devices. A tiny screw in the face of the watch closed the circuit when the minute hand hit it: the point at which time would stop, for some at least.

But they retreated from stopping time. They didn't want to kill anyone. They called in warnings to clear buildings of the innocent before their "terror" took place.

Though they couldn't warn themselves of fate. One accident in the bomb making with all their supplies around and their first bombmaster blew himself up in their privileged brownstone in Manhattan's village—kids at play while their parents were away.

And no one came to their Days of Rage, did they? Their dreamed of massive protest to fight back against the police. Only the Weathermen showed. No one stood with them. And the police—our protectors—beat them down.

Tristan hated to see it as he sat up and more distant from the book, now flipping aimlessly through its hundreds of pages of history. But it kept appearing in his own hand. He'd written it so many times in the margins.

"Fools."

"Fools" and "Fools!" and "FOOLS!"

From the first pages of the book he'd tried to guard against the author's admitted political differences with the book's subjects. But whatever ugly gloss the author might have put upon them, their actions were still their own, and all Tristan saw as he read the pages was his once heroes turned to morons before his eyes. Morons when it came to understanding power.

Bombing empty buildings and thinking that would stop the war. Shooting police officers and thinking that would make them stop shooting back. Kidnapping an imbecile heiress for the press of it. Declaring war on the United States. The belief that they *could* start a revolution and much more that they *were*.

There was no revolution, of course.

In their old age, they looked back at their younger selves and admitted those now-distant kids deluded.

Today, Ché was a t-shirt. A poster. Bob Marley. An evanescent sense of protest to market yourself as distant from the beating drums to which you marched.

Tristan closed the book.

It wasn't here, the answer.

Where was it?

■ ■ ■

1:28 PM

More like his mom. That's what he wanted to be. She was small. Her voice was quiet. The stereotypes of strength were nowhere in her makeup. But her strength surpassed all those who pounded their own stereotypes with gusto, with machismo, by a factor too important to number.

When Kyle was sick, his mom told the doctors how it was going to be. She told him how it was going to be. Indeed, she seemed to tell Existence, the Benevolent Force, God itself, how it was going to be. Her baby was getting cured. Period.

That's when her strength came out. When any force, no matter how strong, suggested it might try to hurt someone she loved.

And Kyle loved Tristan. He did. The threat of harm to him made this clear.

And that's why Kyle had made it to this bench outside the Student Health Center. To protect someone he loved.

But he'd not yet made it further. Because there were voices from his elementary school still talking at him. Calling him "tattletale." The ever-present pressure of what others thought of him. The desire to fit in. To assimilate. He was still so much the only "Arab" or "Muslim" or "Middle Eastern" in his elementary school and his middle school until 7th grade when that other kid came and benefited from all the ground he'd paved as "his people's" only representative.

To be liked.

Mom didn't care who liked her when she was protecting her baby.

So Kyle couldn't let himself give a crap now.

He stood up and went into the building.

1:30 PM

Nothing focused Ryan's attention like holding a weapon in his hands. His finger taut against the side of the barrel until his mind was made up. The knowledge of what was to happen inside the "machine" inches from his face once the simple sequence was initiated. The care and process of having checked it thoroughly before. The line of sight down the barrel to target. The breeze on your face. Moving the index finger to trigger. Ready. Squeezing.

The controlled force exploding so near your center of thought. The hole in the distant target. Finger back to weapon's side. Adrenaline suddenly present throughout your bloodstream. Because there you stood on the ledge between life and death. The power of it in but that little squeeze of your finger. The decision yours. Accident possible all around this ledge. Power not as something understood, but as something felt.

And even Ryan had to admit it was fucking fun.

He approached the firing range with Bret. Time to let his tensions loose on those distant targets.

1:32 PM

"That's not how it works," the woman at reception said. "If you want to see a counselor you need an appointment. The first intake I have is January, 12th at 3:15."

"That's …" Kyle tried to explain again. "I'm not here for counseling. I just wanted to report something. The website said we should tell a counselor if we wanted to report something, but then it didn't really tell us how to do that. So I'm here just to …" Kyle didn't want to say it. There were two other students waiting in the sofa chairs behind him for their appointments.

"Just … isn't there a form I could fill out or something?"

"A form for what?"

"For …" Kyle had said this already when no one was looking, but now there was a scene, he couldn't see them, but he could feel the two kids behind him staring, listening intently, and this stupid woman wanted him to repeat it because she clearly wasn't listening at first because she probably never listened to a freaking thing in her life, *don't they train the freaking people who work at a counseling center about being, you know, discreet?!*

Kyle. Calm down. Do this.

"There's a student I'm worried about."

"We can't force someone to go to counseling. They have to come in on their own."

Kyle had had enough. He no longer gave a crap who heard. He declared loud and firm: "The school website said if we're worried a student might harm someone else we should call the police if it's an emergency or come here if it is not. Should I pull the website up for you?"

Finally something seemed to click in her stupid, unhelpful, uncaring mind.

1:41 PM

In most things ROTC sanctioned they had no weapons. Just Ducks. Rubber formed to look like a weapon, have its weight and clumsiness as you ran up a hill. Their "rubber duckies." Little changed from the toys of childhood.

Ryan had brought his weapon today. A SIG-Sauer M11-A1. Unlocked its case. Checked, prepped, aimed, breathed, moved finger to trigger and fired, and heard Bret's laughing. While Ryan was focused on where his hit lay in the target, Bret was focused on the size of Ryan's weapon. But Ryan wasn't complaining about the AR-15 Bret then handed him and which he was now firing. It was unquestionably badass.

Some of the others were assembling. A group of a half-dozen came together after work. Construction, it seemed to Ryan. Ryan paid them little attention. His attention now focused on what Bret brought out from the back of his truck to impress him with next. And, Ryan had to admit—it was impressive.

A Vietnam-era Pre-Ban AK-47. Bret worked an entire summer just to buy it. It was legal, he assured Ryan. You could legally get one the way Bret had done it. Purchase a pre-1986 one, legally acquired by its present owner.

Ryan figured Bret the type to purposefully buck gun laws with pride. But he also knew Bret wouldn't ever pull anything illegal out of the back of his truck to show Ryan. That would be too much weapon to put in Ryan's hands against Bret's ROTC career should their "friendship" ever sour.

Ryan had never held a weapon like this, much less fired one. As he put its heft to his shoulder he thought about the weapon's history. He wondered if it had been to war and whom it may have killed. He wondered about the soldiers who might have held it. Had they lived? Had they died holding it in their hands, laying fire into the bush in one last effort in their final seconds against the enemy? And since it was an AK, was the enemy us?

He slid his trigger finger into position. He squeezed. And the recoil in his mind was the most powerful he'd ever felt.

1:43 PM

The guy said he had five minutes. One of the two students in the sofa chairs was waiting for him for their appointment.

Kyle sat. The guy sat. He looked at Kyle. "You're concerned another student might harm you?"

"Not me, someone else."

"Okay. Tell me why."

Kyle would really have preferred a form. A box on the website. But obviously the counseling department hadn't thought about what it must feel like to come in and tell them something like this. You know, the *psychology* of it.

"He choked somebody. For real."

"That's an assault. You should go to the police. Or, well, the person who was assaulted should."

"Okay, but that's ... not going to happen."

"Okay."

"And it's not just that. He has a history. He's getting worse. And I think someone needs to talk to him."

"Well, we can't bring someone in against their will here. We don't have that authority. Unless they've violated certain rules and regulations and the Administration requires them to come in."

"Like what regulations?"

"Like the police find they committed that assault. Or they're arrested for underage drinking. Things like that."

Kyle hated this office. He hated everything about being here.

He just thought someone would give a shit that there was a student that had a tendency to freaking choke or hit or whatever—*harm*—another student.

"I just thought you'd like to know there's a student here who might harm another one. Thought you might give a shit."

"Okay. Let's not use profanity. I can make a report of it in case there's another incident. But I'm just letting you know, there's not much we can do. I think it'd be better if your friend went to the police. ... Or was this really you who was assaulted?"

"No. It's ... *not me*."

"Okay."

The guy found a form. Kyle read the top of it upside-down:

"CONCERNED STUDENT REPORT"

Yep. Would have been nice had one of those just been hanging out on a table in the lobby or, you know, *online*.

He'd thought before coming the hardest part was going to be giving the name. Ryan Sheridan. But nope, he gave it with ease. Because everything he thought would suck about this—all the internal stuff—didn't suck a hundredth as much as everything in this stupid office.

He finished and got out of there as fast as he could.

2:08 PM

The exercise had commenced. And it was classic Bret. Sloppy.

It was live fire. And more precautions should have been entered into the planning. Targets were set up around the ranch and the now fully assembled group of about 20 guys formed into two squads and moved out to take them down. Ryan and Miles were in Bret's squad and subjected to the privilege of Bret yelling his various commands, initiating different mock scenarios along the way. The guys seemed like a pretty decent group. Ready with advice on a defensive maneuver or approval for a solid hit. Maybe half of them were veterans. Most were in their late 20s, early 30s. All white. Ryan had expected that.

But Ryan wasn't firing his weapon during the exercise. He knew he was being mocked for it. He could clearly see Bret's disapproval and embarrassment for having brought him.

The firing range had been properly set up, as best Ryan could tell. An earthen barrier behind the targets. Clear as far as the eye could see beyond that.

But Bret had set up his targets for the exercise at random around the compound. And everyone else seemed perfectly content to accept Bret's word that no one else was around for miles. Don't worry, fire away. There was a trust there Ryan couldn't comprehend and would never want to accept. Bret showed few signs of competence worthy of that trust. And this was not a war zone. This was a ranch in Florida. Accidents here were not collateral damage. They were manslaughter, reckless endangerment of human life, or just murder.

They'd finished an exchange of fire with the first set of targets and the squad was moving on to the next encounter. As they walked, one of the young vets neared Ryan.

"You know, we call 'em the Greatest Generation and all. But a lot of those guys in World War II, when they got to the front lines and saw the enemy—they didn't fire. They froze."

Ryan knew all about it. He'd read Lt. Col. Dave Grossman's *On Killing*. It was one of the most fascinating reads of his life. It talked about how the army had to devise ways to turn young men into killers. Almost like engineering psychopathy. The firing rates in World War II had been very low. But by Vietnam, they'd skyrocketed. The army had overachieved in figuring out how to make killers of boys.

Ryan was forming his response. He wanted to respect the man's service, but make his point as well.

But some more of the guys apparently smelled blood and approached for the fun.

"Yeah, where'd you leave your balls, bro? You forget them back at campus with all the other pansies?"

Okay, maybe they weren't all so decent. This guy didn't seem like a vet. He seemed more like a basement gamer brought out in the light and given a loaded weapon in place of his remote. His overhanging belly wiggled awkwardly as he laughed at his own joke.

Then Miles was behind him. Hands on his shoulders. A mock massage. "Aw, buddy, is your pussy hurtin'? You want daddy to give it some lovin'?"

The guys really laughed now. The vet too. And big belly guy laughed so hard he started coughing up the resin of old cigarettes.

Guys like these and "balls" and "pussies." It was all they ever talked about. Ryan responded with silence.

Bret yelled back to quiet the men and keep them focused. The enemy could be anywhere.

■ ■ ■

2:33 PM

The white redneck n----- who pulled him over yesterday yanked off the covers of his long, deep, rapid-eye-movement dreaming, and left him naked with all of the nightmares, all of the knife jabs of prejudice, of you-are-not-equal-to-me-ness, stabbing back at him, stabbing at, but through, his skin to whatever it was that was in his depths, beyond the stupid boundaries of its color.

There were so many such stabbings. His skin was smooth and flawless to the physical eye, but to the emotional one there were scars everywhere, trying to heal since even the days of elementary school, but the ugliest wound, the sickest, the one that would not heal because to let it would be too unbearable a betrayal, was the gash from the shrapnel of the bullet that sailed so easily through the young skin and body and once-beating heart of Trayvon Martin, broke into millions of metal shards and burrowed into millions of bodies like Scotty's. And like Coates's son's.

When Scotty read about Coates's son excusing himself to cry in his room after the acquittal of Michael Brown's killer, he was reading about himself. A different life, yes, slightly—but not too. Different paths—but still him. Still a "privileged" young black man who lived in a nation sickened with a pandemic of killing or imprisoning young black men and exonerating those who steal their bodies from them, as as necessary as the laws of nature.

And all covered by a dream. A myth. One his uncle had to help express by giving him Coates's book behind his father's eyes because his father was the most overbearing believer of the dream, the myth, in Scotty's life.

"Dad,"

He wanted to write him back. Like Coates had written his son ... and Scotty.

Dad. Who'd found what he thought was "happiness" by sitting in the comfort of his home and pretending his comfort was given to him by the myth in which he devoutly believed and thereby pretending the discomfort of others was the fault of their own making because of their lack of faith. If they'd only believe in the American Dream and work hard for it, they too could sit in comfort.

But Scotty didn't want to find "happiness" by pretending all the pain didn't exist. The myth was a mask. And he'd worn it too. That was the thing that struck him most in Coates's pages—he saw himself looking in the mirror in his childhood bedroom and realizing he'd donned that mask too. Today, in his college bedroom, he'd found himself being forced by Coates to admit that.

Somewhere in Baldwin's words—"because they think they are white"— somewhere in Coates's—somewhere in the conversation with them, what Scotty was thinking about were the layers. White people's layers. White people created them and wrapped us all up in them.

It was the opposite of, "I don't see color." For Scotty, there were layers upon layers of color on our skin. Layers of meaning, that white people had put upon his skin and upon their own.

The mask Dad wore was one of those layers. A layer that made him acceptable to whites. A layer called, "One of the good ones."

Scotty'd worn that layer too. Accepted it placed upon him.

Layers of myth. White people's myth.

Coates wiped the white people's layers away.

Coates vanquished the dream.

Coates brought not just Scotty's scars back to him, but the old scars of his people, the ancient ones too. For it was all built upon the plunder. The plunder of their bodies. The un-admitted billions of dollars their labor had been worth. Their bodies. America's "greatness," its "exceptionalism" had not come from God, but from the very human evil of stealing the life from millions to add to the bounty of your comfort.

The waves of black bodies from Africa, the first black gold the whites would rape from the Earth.

And to give us some outlet, some release valve for this long-sustained terror, they wanted us to follow King and nonviolence, and not Malcolm. Scotty hadn't ever thought about it in that way. But Coates showed him the way to truths behind the myths.

His tired hands flipped through the pages of the book again as he let it all sink in after finishing it. Fingering now through pages made intimate to him. So many hard underlines and circlings and thoughts written around the edges. There toward the end Scotty had written, paraphrased, back to Coates, in conversation with him—The Great Conversation, a teacher had once called it—books—"They give 'nonviolence' to the weak, while the powerful act with the greatest violence of all."

And on another page, "Evil always clothes itself in religion, morality, righteousness."

And another, "We must awaken the dreamers from the dream ... You, Scotty. You must awaken."

He closed the book. He looked at his hands as they held it. The layers upon them he wanted to pull off. White people's lies wrapped around his soul. To pull them off and see only the truth of his own skin, in its purity. His skin was not what white people had said black was. It was his to see in it what he chose.

And right now it seemed somehow both smooth and young, and scarred and old. Somehow both tired, and full of a new and ancient energy.

2:48 PM

Different. That's how he'd been made to feel so often. Before his metamorphosis.

Ha. He liked calling it that. It wasn't as big a metamorphosis as others'. Nothing like Fin's. *God, the struggle Fin had to go through.* He couldn't imagine how hard that had to be. The realization you were born with the wrong genitalia.

His was far subtler. And it was just given to him. There was no need to raise money, to find doctors, to cry and beg and have your soul torn in two with family and friends and yourself.

His just happened. It started about junior year of high school and seemed to finish up over this last summer. Somewhere, somehow, he'd gone from the ugly redhead with freckles and damn near see-through skin to the super cute ginger with freckles ... and, yes, still super pale skin.

It felt like two metamorphoses. Both external. One of his skin, his body, the smallest changes in the lines of his face, something in or around his eyes maybe. And the other of the society around him that just, for whatever reason—maybe it was TV or something?—seemed to do a 180 on redheads. All his life he'd been an outcast, physically, and now suddenly he was desired. A lot of times it was the latinos and latinas. A lot of times black boys and black girls. And then, yesterday, in the library, for the first time really—and blatantly—*so* blatantly—a blond white dude with tats and quite a nice cock too.

Before he'd thought being "no labels" sexually was like an added curse because no one wanted him anyway, so it just meant twice as much rejection and unrequitedness. But now it was like the floodgates were opening, and he was definitely game for making up for lost time. The hot tat boy would have been one of the ones making fun of him in middle school, he knew it. And now he was opening up his shorts leg to show him his half-hard hot penis! *What?! How did that happen?!*

Life was strange like that. The things that could change.

And how quickly you could be pulled back too. Put back in your place.

He couldn't be sure they were making fun of him. But their barely hushed little laughs carried to him by the breeze over the beach sure sounded familiar. And it was in their eyes as they turned away from him when he caught them watching him as he sprayed on his sunblock for the third time today.

One of them gracefully tossed the volleyball into the air, up against the blue sky, and then leaped up with his long, perfect body, darkened by the sun, to spike the ball across the loosely defined court, and their game resumed. But they'd paused in their fun to make fun of him.

And in their distant laughs so many memories rushed back and turned him into everything he was before the metamorphosis, and he sat down under the shade of his umbrella because it would hide him a bit.

And he wanted to put his shirt back on and leave.

But no, he *fucking didn't!*

He wanted to stand proudly, fearlessly, nearly naked as they were out in the sun with no umbrella and no sunblock, just come here and pull off his shirt without even thinking about it—just enjoy the heat of the sun on his skin and being mostly naked with the rest. Because he loved the sun and the beach and probably way more than they did, especially as the freedom to enjoy it like they did was something he would never know. It was unfair that he just wasn't born with the right skin for it, and that wasn't his fucking fault!

Had he been born with their skin he would have been a surfer. He wouldn't be able to get enough of the sun and sand lifestyle. He would have had a dozen boys and a dozen girls as hot and as tatted and as shaggy blond haired and as growing more and more hard for him as the one in the library yesterday.

But he wondered too how he would have looked now down the beach at the pale-skinned redhead lathering on his sunblock for the third time today just to get back under his umbrella.

He wondered if he'd have mocked him too. He wondered how much he'd appreciate the skin of his own body. How much he'd take it for granted. How much he'd assume he deserved it. How much he'd assume it *was* him.

"Well aren't you just the cutest little thing."

A girl was handing him a flier. She was stunning. Latina. And probably all the guys and half the girls on Sand Tiger Key were staring at her right now, but she was staring at him.

He said, "Thanks," and took the flier. Raised his sunglasses to look at it. It seemed to be for a party.

"Uhhhh. Are those freckles on your little cheeks?"

He felt his embarrassment coming back. Felt like a small kid with this girl even though they were close in age. "Yeah. They come out in the sun sometimes."

"Well I hope the sun brings a few more out to play by tonight. They couldn't be more adorable."

She smiled, turned, and headed off. She had all the confidence in the world, this girl. And God her skin was … perfect.

He looked over and yes, thankfully, the guys who'd laughed at him had paused their game again and were looking back. Was it jealousy? Was it a new respect for the ginger?

Ha. Life was funny sometimes.

You just never knew what might happen.

2:49 PM

Jasmine continued her saunter down the beach. The volleyball guys had stopped their game and were awaiting her approach, staring like a herd of dumb animals, as boys will.

"Excuse me, ma'am." One of them shouted to her in his best impression of a gentleman. "Could I please have one of your fliers? I'd like to sign up or … donate … or, you know, whatever you tell me to do." His friends laughed.

"Sorry boys. I'm throwing an *Anti*-Frat party and, alas, you just don't seem the right type."

"Oooooo! Burn!" etc., the herd went. Jasmine smiled.

"I'm not in a frat. I hate frats. Stupid. I spit on them." He spat.

"Oh? What are those giant letters on your ass then? They seem, oh what's that language … Greek?"

He grabbed the ass of his shorts. "Uh, these are my friend's shorts. *His*." He pointed to one of the other guys. "Don't invite *him*!"

"Well then there's the other problem with those shorts. You know. Around the front. Little mesh shorts and yet … no outline of anything."

The guys lost it. One fell down.

"I'm a grower, not a shower!"

"Mmmm. Better to be both, don't you think?"

She smiled and kept walking. She just loved putting these "King of the World" boys in their place.

3:02 PM

"You were born into violence, Habibi. What the worst in men makes them do to each other. We protected you from it. But it surrounded us."

Grandpa had only said things like this a handful of times, but when he did, he said them with such a force behind them that Kyle remembered these moments. Though he couldn't remember the history. He was too young then.

"Your sweet face was so innocent. It was innocence itself—the innocence in all of us—we were trying to protect when we protected you. Sometimes I think that now."

Grandpa often wanted to talk about it. Dad almost never did.

Grandpa wanted Kyle to know where he came from, who he came from, what they had protected his innocent eyes from then.

So Kyle was walking now, finally, toward not just learning, but maybe feeling a bit more of that history and that present.

It was a big day. First, to try to walk a bit more in the steps of his mom (though that didn't go so well) and now in the path of his grandpa. He hoped this would go better. But he feared it wouldn't. It was in his stomach, the fear.

Kyle only knew bits and pieces. That was the problem.

He knew Grandpa had left Iran in the 60s, moving the family to "The Paris of the Middle East," they called it, Beirut. That was one of "The Great

Shining Moments," Grandpa had said. The western countries had pulled out and Lebanon was free, democratic, the economy was booming.

Grandpa had had that hope for Iran, he'd said. But it had all been pulled out from under them, he'd said. Their President had been assassinated by the American CIA, he'd said. And the Shah installed. When Grandpa said this, and things like it, it never sounded like Tristan. It was said too plainly and too much from a history a man had lived through himself. It just sounded like truth.

He'd suffered prejudice in Iran, he'd said. Being Sunni. But Lebanon was a melting pot. Sunni and Shi'a in equal numbers, and Christians and … Kyle couldn't remember the others, but there were lots there from every walk of life.

But then it all fell apart somehow. Civil war. What was and should have been so beautiful in that melting pot turned so ugly.

But then it got better. It was another "Bright Shining Moment." That's when Mom came. *And later she and Dad had me.*

But then the violence started again.

And then, of course, 9/11.

And so we came here.

Grandpa said the family was always moving West to try to escape the violence, the corruption, that thing in men which makes them do so much evil.

"So now we're here. In the land free from all of that," he'd once said, looking at Dad in a way that made Dad so angry he left the room and they didn't see him for hours, though there didn't seem to be any anger in Grandpa's voice, not to Kyle.

There were things Kyle didn't understand. And he had to admit he didn't want to understand them.

As soon as he was really old enough to learn more about the harshness of their past, he'd been hit with his own war to fight: cancer. And once he'd been cured of that, the last thing he wanted to think about was that violence he'd been born into. He wanted the good, the beautiful, the innocence.

So there were things he didn't understand. He didn't understand how, if Grandpa had suffered so much prejudice as a Sunni in a Shiite country, and now as a Muslim in America, then how could he *possibly* have prejudice himself? How could someone who knew what that violence felt like turn around and lay its pain upon the soul of another?

Kyle couldn't tell his own Baba Joon he was gay because he knew the deep *hatred* Grandpa held for that. *Hatred.* For his own Habibi?

Kyle knew he wouldn't be "Habibi" anymore if he told his Baba Joon that truth.

How could Grandpa not see the violence his words, his beliefs cause me?

There was so much love there. And so much pain. And all wrapped up together in a way you couldn't pull one out from the other. Like the love and fear in and of Lebanon. Like the cancerous cells growing around and through the good in his young body.

Kyle's tumor had pressed up against the walls of his heart when they found it. It had wanted to pierce through. He could never forget that. What evil had aimed for.

3:07 PM

Scotty was walking. That's all. Just taking a walk. On a beautiful day through a beautiful campus. Not a Mecca like Coates had said of Howard, not at all. But still his own Mecca, he guessed. The one life had brought him to. Not a coming together of all those different peoples thought to be black, but one of many different peoples thought to be many different colors, though, yes, mostly shades of a skin thought white.

But he wasn't just walking. He was on a new path. A path that shouldn't have had to be his. His path was supposed to take him today to a fraternity house to set up a waterslide. To a class to learn a little more. Maybe to the gym to tighten up his skin should it be exposed after the party tonight to a pretty girl.

But his path had been altered a long time ago. The course correction for Scotty began the night Trayvon Martin took a walk in the rain with a bag of Skittles for his friend and a watermelon juice for himself.

Trayvon was walking. That's all. Just taking a walk. On a rainy evening. But he was also being hunted. Hunted by a man who saw his skin, and for some reason his hoodie, as a source of the man's own fears. The man said it had nothing to do with Trayvon's skin. The court agreed. But it didn't pass the "but for" test. Scotty had learned that somewhere along the way. *But for* the color of Trayvon's skin, who believes that he would have been hunted that night? A white boy, hoodie or not, raining or not, Skittles and juice in hand, would have never met Trayvon's killer. *But for* the color of Trayvon's skin ….

Scotty and his friends had been walking. Around his own neighborhood. Back in 8th grade. Walking up to each home's door. If the people weren't home, hanging a flier on the knob. If they were, asking them it they'd like to know more about their candidate for US Senate. Scotty'd had a brief moment of interest in politics. They were "canvassing," this was called. A woman in the neighborhood called the cops. A group of young black teens were "casing" the neighborhood. Walking up to each door to see who was home. The cops came. Checked out their fliers. Called the Senator-to-Be's election office with a *description* of the boys to make sure this was all legit. It was. Legit. Legit in society's eyes that the cops should come because a group of black boys were walking in a "white neighborhood."

The day Trayvon went on that walk started Scotty on a long and painful path with him. It started simple and clear. But simplicity and clarity soon left his grasp.

It started with the pictures. The boy—young and cute in his hoodie. And the man who hunted him down and killed him. And society didn't even want to prosecute the man. All he'd done was "Stand His Ground" against a young black boy taking a walk in the wrong neighborhood. But the blacks yelled and screamed until they did prosecute him. But then the all-white-but-one jury let him off. No harm, no foul. Another "black thug" off the streets. The "good people" safer in their homes. A story told—and not told—too, too, too many times in America.

But then, unable to let go of it and move on, a teacher—a good one—suggested Scotty write about it for class.

So he did. And a thing started to happen that Coates had talked about. Putting words onto paper helped one find clarity. He researched. And not just what the 24-hour "news" bullshit artists said about the case. But he found court filings, testimony, analysis by a seemingly fair law school professor. He got closer to the truth. And the truth, he didn't like seeing.

The pictures weren't so simple anymore. The actual, *real* Truth, of course, would never be known. But the best guess at truth he could make, based on what evidence there was available, seemed to suggest that maybe, after being followed, Trayvon did turn on the man and beat him down. And that maybe it was in this reversed assault, that hunter pulled out his gun and fired that bullet that pierced through Trayvon's hoodie, his heart, and ricocheted into Scotty's and countless others'.

And, at first, and for a while, Scotty didn't like seeing that version of the truth. His young innocent martyr was gone. The forces that killed him and accepted his death were less clearly, pure and simple evil.

But the terrorism of that ricocheted shrapnel ripping through his heart was still real. And he felt lost with nowhere to throw his pain.

But in time, history, like his uncle always promised, brought him a better answer.

It came in another book. A very different book. One his dad actually gave him and in which he would have never expected to find it. And it was from a very different Malcolm. Malcolm Gladwell's *David and Goliath*.

This Malcolm had written about another picture. A more famous one that came at an earlier time in the long history of black people fighting for their humanity.

This was a photo of a young black boy being attacked by a snarling police dog and leaning in as if to say, as this Malcolm said, "Take me, here I am."

It was a photo that helped to change the course of history. It changed people's minds about what was happening in Birmingham and how blacks were really being treated in the South. It became a national embarrassment before the eyes of other—more advanced—nations.

But it wasn't quite the truth. Not all of it. Not of that one incident in time.

For as it turned out, when the press's shutter snapped shut and time was imprisoned in an image forever, the boy—15-year-old Walter Gadsden—was not leaning in as if to say, "Take me now," but was rather steadying himself to fight back. He hadn't come as a marcher that day, but as a spectator. He'd just taken a walk too—to come see what was happening. But when the dogs were brought out against the people and people were bitten before him—he couldn't stand the sidelines anymore. He chose to fight back. And in the seconds of time after that shutter-flap shut, Walter kicked that dog in the face so hard he broke its fucking jaw.

And that helped Scotty see what Trayvon had done. And what he knew and feared and hoped in his heart he would have the strength to do.

Trayvon and Walter had had enough. They'd been pushed past their breaking points. They chose to turn the tables. To no longer be treated as prey, but to pummel the fucking mutts who hunted them right in their stupid, snarling, hate-filled faces. Hate-filled they knew not why. Other than that their masters pointed and gave the command.

Walter was Standing His Ground.

Trayvon was Standing His.

And now—finally—so was Scotty.

He arrived where his path was taking him. To one of the groups on the Campus Commons. To the hand of a friend's who grabbed him and pulled him in. Black hands and black arms hugging black bodies together. To hold up signs. To march their own marches and continue others from history. From Birmingham, through Baltimore, through every last mile. To turn on their hunters and Stand Their Ground. Because this world must finally fucking face the simplest Truth: that Black Lives Matter too.

No. Not "too." Fuck saying "too."

Black Lives Matter, period.

3:22 PM

The fear in his stomach was growing as he neared the place—the Religious Studies Building. His feet slowed, pulling back against that part of his will that had determined to go forward. It was a fear of the lostness he was walking into.

He knew who he was in Tristan's arms. He knew who he was at home with his family. He knew who he was back in middle school as the sole Arab representative. They were all different Kyles, in a way, but at least he knew them.

But these would not be the "Arabs" he'd tried to portray, perhaps wrongly, to his elementary and middle school peers. Back then, his focus was entirely on convincing his peers that he was not at all different—that he *was* them. "See, I play soccer too, just like you. See, I'm laughing at that joke too, just like you. See, I'm just like you … just like you … just like you."

But this event, about understanding Arab-Americans, meant that, "we aren't just like you." Because if they were, then why did you need to go to an event to understand that?

Walking into this room would be like separating himself from everything he had tried to build since that first day of school in suburban Maryland when his parents dropped him off with his lunchbox and he was suddenly alone, amongst them, and all he wanted in the world was to not be any different from them.

And what would be in the questions? What only slightly hidden poisons would they contain?

And what, too, in the answers? How would that guy Tahir respond if he was leading this? His Arab dress definitely did not say, "I'm just like you"—it said, "I come from a completely different world and I want you to know it!"

And what poisons would be in the answers not just to sicken the audience, but to grow the sickening pains in Kyle's stomach too?

The prejudice of his grandfather against gays? Would that be there behind the doors to the room Kyle now suddenly found he'd too soon (though he knew he was actually quite late) come to?

The Arab dress of Tahir was what they wore, was it not?—those in the pictures who looked on with approval at the hanging bodies of the gays.

The image made it harder to turn the door handle, but he did it if only because it was the natural momentum of things.

But what he saw inside was not what he expected at all.

Cakes. Little cakes. On little doilies. Down all the long rows of the curved tables around the amphitheater-style room in front of all the empty seats.

And down in front of the room, Sara, friends around her, touching her shoulders, and she was crying.

Kyle walked down the center aisle in a bit of a daze. It could easily be something from a dream, this room. All the little cakes on all the little doilies in front of all the empty seats.

Sara had made them, he'd find out in between her sobbing. They were basbousa. She'd written it in her pretty handwriting on every single one of the little doilies so people would know. And she'd capitalized the last three letters in alternated markers of red and blue.

But that was nothing compared to the work of actually making the cakes. She'd been quite diligent to make them precisely as her mother and her grandmother and her grandmother before had all made them. With the rose water. She'd gotten the flowers herself. She'd wanted to tell them about the rose water during her time to talk. What her grandmother said it meant. Why she'd put in the effort to make it just right for them.

But no one came.

Not a single student outside the Arab-American Student Association.

They'd been tabling and posting for weeks. They had so much they wanted to say.

Tahir had left already in an outbreak of "I-told-you-so" anger, they'd said. Sara, had told-them-so too. See, she'd said with just a look of her eyes and a sad contortion of her face. He's a very, very angry young man.

3:26 PM

He came here because he needed others. He didn't like to admit that. And probably never would have, had he not been spending so much time lately taking a good hard look at all things, including himself.

He knew too that it was dangerous coming here. But he was confident he could protect himself.

The site was on the dark web. The vast space behind the internet most used. Here people's thoughts could be unsurveilled, it was thought. And so they let it all out. All the things they must hide from the "others" they fear and yet so long to share with the "others" like them.

You're free to explore here. And your exploring, where your search takes you if you let it, shows you things about yourself you might not have known.

He first came here freshman year when he found mention of it on another chat room, having clicked deeper and deeper into the surveilled internet away from a site linked by Pat Robertson. He watched a video on his phone on how to get to the dark internet. It was far easier than he'd worried it might be. Things almost always were once he put his mind to doing them.

There were thoughts here he didn't like. He still had to weed through the bad. A lot of the community, Christian Identity and such, were racist. Luke didn't like that. He didn't see that in the Bible. Meeks had always embraced different races. Proudly welcomed them into the church. All except Arab. But that was about the Word of God, not skin.

He came upon a particularly egregious one now. It argued, by not very intelligent means, that America's slow downfall began with the end of slavery, the integration of the races, and disobedience to God's Rightful Order. It called for great violence. New lynchings. Luke clicked on the comments box and started to respond ... but he stopped and erased what he'd written.

Instead, he printed the post, opened a drawer in his desk and added it to a pile of others.

He went back to this other world and kept on. For the most part, the site, *Soldiers of Christ*, was the community of peers Luke had so long longed for without even knowing what it was he sought.

Meeks was a great light in the darkness, but he was a mentor, a sage, a man coming to the end of his Earthly existence. Here, Luke found energy, hope, rejuvenation, assurance amongst others who seemed like him and were not just looking back upon a life lived, but forward to doing something momentous with this life, something worthy in their Earthly existence of their Heavenly one to come.

It struck Luke that this was the college campus he needed, this The Commons, the Community Square of ideas where he could explore and learn and share and grow. This, an oasis from the outer world he found so barren, so chained upon a path to its own demise.

The anonymity of the posts at first made them seem impersonal, but as you read them you realized the namelessness frees them to be so much more deeply personal than the named. Sometimes when you'd spent long enough in this world, when your mind got into that pace of search for more and more, you felt such an intimacy with these others, it was as if you could be them. Their thoughts your own.

Manifest Destiny. So alive at our nation's founding and in its early years, so forgotten now. The heritage of why the Lord gave us this country, the beacon of light we were supposed to be in this world, the reason for our exceptionalism. We were losing our way. The America we needed to get back to. The True America.

The battlefield for the coming Revolution was being laid out. Satan's terrorists—from false religions or the secular, the atheists—could not be negotiated with. They must simply be destroyed. The point of crisis was coming.

A return to old ways. When men and women of the early church chose martyrdom over denial of the Lord. Revenge. Empowerment. Men being men again. The destruction of this effeminated, emasculated society.

Voices that repeated the same message from so many disparate parts of this great nation. A hidden army spread throughout, ready to rise.

And it wasn't all so anonymous. You did get to know some of the handles whose posts you regularly liked, and, it seemed, the personalities, the people, behind them. People seemed to be crying out to still be noticed, recognized for their individuality, despite the trouble gone to for anonymity or the constant repetition of others' thoughts.

Luke went back to one he'd found a few months ago and felt close to—it was titled, "The Liberal's Poisoned Apple." It was about the election. A lot of posts were now.

The stakes of the election were laid out so clearly here. The article read differently from many other posts: reasoned, researched, perhaps even the work of several minds. The Secular Jihadists were winning this great war. Hijacking America. The public schools promoting godlessness; the media, heathenism; the government, a moral permissiveness that led only to immorality, for evil was at the heart of men. We were under siege! It was Nazi Germany again except this time the Jews, Christians; the Nazis, Liberals. History repeating itself. The "tolerance" they preached was but masked intolerance—intolerance for us. Intolerance for Christianity. Intolerance for the One True Lord. Intolerance for our Manifest Destiny.

He felt himself calming, being here. Not on the real Commons with the angry students pelting him with petty weapons and insults. Not laughed at, teased. But on this hidden Commons. Where things he believed were cheered. And where the path to the Lord's Destiny for us was not distorted by the Devil's uncertainties, but was laid out clearly by fellow followers of Christ, and no, not just followers, but *soldiers* ready to take up arms for the Lord in the battle that had long been foretold, but not yet been allowed to us. These were men ready for action.

Some even posted pictures and videos of their preparations. Some were a Christian rock group popular at the concerts of the Christian youth movement BattleCry who often posted photos with their SIG-Sauer semiautomatics and other weapons they called "the swords of today."

Peace. That's what Luke felt among his own. Calm. Long, deep breaths.

3:37 PM

He'd thought there'd be some release coming here. That the pressures building inside him would escape his system a bit. He didn't like all this anger within him, but it was there and filling so many other thoughts, normal thoughts, thoughts that were never angry before, with its rage.

This wasn't how Scotty wanted to live his life. He was, by nature, a fun-loving guy and just wanted to stay that way. He wanted to be taking the honorary first slide down the waterslide right now after taking his first shot of the afternoon.

But his rage wasn't escaping. It was finding deeper spots in which to burrow, to pack itself in tightly, to make room for more to come.

Because after the initial togetherness he felt with this new group, he was quickly made to feel their—and his—separateness from the students on The Commons to whom they were but an annoyance.

Occasionally, a black fist would go up from a passerby, once even a white one, in solidarity. (Though the white face had to be checked first, lest the fist have been in jest. But the face said solidarity. And that felt good and not good too.)

The firing synapses of his brain lit up another memory: Zimmerman auctioning off the gun he used to kill Trayvon to his "fellow patriots," calling the gun something like, "An American Firearm Icon."

Scotty didn't want to hold the sign he was holding. He wanted to crack its wooden post hard enough across the snarling mutt's face to break its jaw.

He wanted to yell at that stupid lady in his old neighborhood that it was his neighborhood too, "you racist bitch!" and that all they were doing was what packs of white kids were doing all over the state that day, yet no one would have even thought about calling the cops on them, but rather praised their sense of civic duty!

He wanted that stupid redneck prick who pulled him over yesterday to be jealous of his car and his life. He wanted him to know that he *was* better than him, and not because of his car or his cushy life, but because his hatred was a better hatred.

That asshole and others like him hate because of the color of skin. They hate because of things they assume about you, when they know nothing of who you are. *But I know who you are. I know what you believe.*

And it's your belief *that I hate.*

He wanted to yell at that prick loud enough for King to hear through the ages:

I have judged not the color of your skin, but the content of your character!

And I find you guilty.

3:59 PM

The sound of so many weapons being discharged around you at once was all-penetrating. You *felt* the sound waves hitting your very bones as the bullets clanked into the old metal of a long-dead and scrapped truck frame and a tractor that certainly hadn't worked in his lifetime, and probably not even in his father's. The noise sent Ryan into a deeper cocoon of his thoughts.

The thoughts started simple, strategic. They were in a barn that seemed one more hurricane away from total collapse, firing out between the slats of wood at the rusted machines. Bret was more energized than Ryan had ever seen him, yelling out the worsening scenario over the gunfire: they were surrounded by the enemy, and now the enemy sent in these two armored vehicles to light the barn aflame and burn them all to ashes.

But why were they in the barn? If the enemy were closing in, Bret's leading his men inside the barn was tactical stupidity worthy of court-martial. Ryan would have sent at least two snipers climbing up to the barn's roof to take the high ground. Always. Always, the high ground. He would have spread the team out to triangulate fire and disperse the target for the enemy. Run into the barn? It was running upstairs in a silly horror movie. It was child's play.

And that's what all this was. Grown men suiting up to play war. As the group started coming together earlier in the day, Ryan had thought maybe Bret was involved with one of the Watchmen groups he'd seen a documentary on. They were training to protect themselves during doomsday scenarios like another Katrina where the government left people to die or pillage each other's belongings. Or a nuclear facility meltdown, or a dirty bomb terror attack. The government wouldn't be there to help you; you'd have to protect yourself.

But as the afternoon wore on he knew these guys weren't that. These guys were he and his friends in the woods behind their suburban houses in the 3rd or 4th grade playing Army like in the movies, except now they were far, far more dangerous. The bullets ricocheting off those old vehicles could easily pierce the old slats of the barn and take one of these 3rd graders in adult bodies to the hospital.

Miles had lowered his AR to his groin and was firing in a way that made it clear what a weapon was to him.

Ryan had turned and walked back out the way they came in and was standing outside on the safe side of the barn when he heard it amidst the onslaught. Bret's voice. He'd let out a holler of joy in the moment, of pride, of ecstasy, even, in the kill, and then the words:

"Y'all killed those FBI motherfuckers dead!"

Maybe he'd thought Ryan had walked back to basecamp. Or wouldn't hear over the gunfire. Or maybe he'd forgotten Ryan existed. But there was no mistaking what he said.

The whole time, for Ryan, this ranch had been a village in some foreign land, maybe Iran, maybe Northeastern Africa, maybe Iraq again. But in that one line, Ryan realized what a fool he'd been to not admit it to himself before. For Bret and his boys, this battle was taking place precisely where it played out: on a ranch in Florida. And the enemy was not a foreign invader or "bad people" run amok come to steal your family's dwindling food supply. The enemy they fired upon with such vigor was our own government.

The fire ceased in victory. Yells of triumph erupted. Ryan walked back in as the others opened a door on the other side to survey their kills.

Asshole Man from the ride here announced, "We got one still breathing, fellas!" walked up to one of the target cut-outs, pulled a KA-BAR from the sheath strapped around his thigh, and stabbed the survivor in his heart.

His brothers-in-arms cheered.

4:21 PM

He had books all around him now. He'd made a mess of them. His body was aching in different places from the way he'd been sitting there with them on the floor all day. His wounded neck still hurt. But the real pain that was swelling inside, deeper than skin and muscles and bones, was one of despair. For as he looked at all of his reading, all of our history, a very difficult truth screamed back at him.

He thought of the poster he'd made on his wall behind him, "Democracy is Dead / The Oligarchy Rules" around a blown-up image of what people call the "illuminati pyramid" from the one-dollar bill. There were several meanings to see in this symbol from our history, from those who have ruled us for so long, but the one Tristan preferred was the simplest. The mass of mankind was represented by the bottom pyramid, and those with the knowledge and the power to rule over us by the top. The oligarchy.

And the hard truth that screamed back at him now, from all of his books and all the history of this American experiment in democracy, is that we had never dislodged our masters.

One of our greatest American myths was that we had done this at our founding. That we, the strong, united Americans who believed that "all men are created equal" and had a God-given right to "life, liberty and the pursuit of happiness," had bonded together to throw off our masters in the Revolution and thereby secured our Destiny as the Land of the Free.

What a brilliantly scripted piece of bullshit that was.

Read your Zinn. That great book there on the floor before him: *A People's History of the United States*. "Tyranny is Tyranny" and we the "Persons of Mean and Vile Condition" were as controlled as we ever were before.

The brilliance of a "Democratic System" to bring legitimacy to their rule. *To fool us into thinking it was we who ruled. Ha!*

Our Founding Fathers, who believed only that *they* were created equal, that *they* had the rights they spoke of, drummed us up into war as easily as they always had and always will to throw off the competition of another oligarchy so they could rule us as their own. We thought we were fighting for Equality, Freedom and to keep our Sacred Fortunes. But we'd been played. We were only fighting for the myth of those things for ourselves. In reality, we fought for, and won them for, our masters.

All the uprisings. All the rebellions. All the protests and skirmishes with law enforcement and actions and Get Out The Votes and we were still as ruled as ever. For Democracy itself was the greatest myth of the land.

If our protests from the bottom pyramid to the upper ever succeeded, they did so only in getting a few more crumbs dropped down here and there.

"Fine. We'll free the slaves," they said. "We'd come to realize they were too costly to keep anyway, and as their numbers continued to grow, their threat of rebellion too dangerous to our interests. We learned eventually it was cheaper to pay a man less than a 'living wage' for his labor than to buy his life and then house and feed him and pay others to beat him continuously into work and submission and guard constantly against his savage nature against us. We can spend less on the 'free man' and inspire a greater work ethic by giving him pride in his pennies and hope (pitifully fake as it is) that with harder and harder work for us, maybe, one day, he can be us.

"Fine. We'll cut back a bit on racism. We only fueled that in the first place when we feared that the Negroes, the Poor Whites, and the Indians would band together in common interest to overthrow us. Divide and conquer. But now we have other means—all those pennies and all that hope given to a tamed beast called the Middle Class to buffer us from the poor. So we can cut back on the racism to keep you quiet.

"Fine.   Women and the un-landed can vote.   What difference does it make when we turn the whole thing into a stage production anyway?

"Fine.   Gay rights too.   Marry whomever the hell you want.   And fine, smoke pot.   We'd rather Monsanto it anyway.

"But don't you dare try to get in the way of the economic machines that suck *The Wealth of Nations* from the bottom pyramid up to us.

"Peace, not war?   Save the environment?   No chance in hell.   Nothing in the history of mankind has made us more money than war.   Though a good distant second is oil."

Crumbs.   That's all we ever knocked down from the top.   We never dislodged the upper pyramid.   Not even a single member of it.   They only took out their own who strayed too far from the cause or who tried to harm them.   The assassinations were made to look like they were done by some nut job from the lower pyramid, but all the evidence always proved they were orchestrated from the top.

Prison?   When?   Never the people at the top, only the peons from the lower pyramid who worked for them, and out of love, loyalty, belief in the myths or, more often, future financial payoff, took the fall on their behalf to give The People their myth of Justice.

Watergate was supposed to have been that one time.   Remember that one time when the American People had enough with corruption and overthrew a president?   That was the fairytale.   First of all, lets not give the American People too much credit here; it was a handful of them smart enough to notice, concerned enough to dig deeper.   Woodward and Bernstein and Deep Throat.   Some people at the New York Times, a few others here and there, but most would rather not bother with such dull and unpatriotic things.   Most simply wanted to trust their president.

And when all was said and done, what was really said and done?   Some peons went to prison (and even then, just for a little bit—a month in jail here, a few more there, a $100 fine). Nixon on tape talking about getting them a million dollars to keep them quiet about other, more important, things, how easy that would be. Impeachments brought against him, Nixon deciding to step down rather than go through the trouble, Ford, first thing, granting him a full pardon, the money flowing again; "The System worked," we were told and that was finally a bit of truth; The System had worked, and kept on working, just like it did before. A figurehead was switched out, but the real players stayed in power and in the end, it was only the surface of a great and hidden pyramid that had been a tiny bit exposed. Watergate was about a simple break-in at the DNC, we were told. Dirty tricks (illegal as they were) in the shit-slinging stage productions between Republicans and Democrats fighting to lead us. But there was so much more to be revealed than that. Clandestine elements within the clandestine services, whom they really worked for and what they really did. "That whole Bay of Pigs affair" we didn't want opened back up. All the easily gotten millions behind the scenes, and where did it all come from? How easily and often the American People were lied to. Questions we didn't even know, even to this day, that we should have asked. All that gets properly buried again with Nixon stepping down, no more public inquisition, and The System can continue to work. The Oligarchy can continue its rule.

Truth Bombs, Tristan called these. Every so often some scrappy, hungry reporters, a hacker, a whistleblower like Chelsea Manning in the military would come along and drop one. A little truth would squeeze out. Some pawns would fall for their king. The dust would clear and all would be the same again.

Tristan'd even thought to himself sometimes about trying to drop a truth bomb of his own, before coming to his conclusions about them. He didn't have the hacker skills, but maybe he could pull a Manning. Get inside, find the goods, and dump them on The People.

For a while he thought seriously about cutting his hair, covering his tats with some nice button-downs and slacks, telling his father he was coming around, learning the errors of his ways and asking if he could put in a call to any of the swarming hive of war companies around Tampa, and Tristan could get a summer internship at one. *Let me get that coffee for you and organize your receipts and please stop looking at me like that, creepy old man with all the porn on your desktop, and let me make a copy of that file for you and keep one for myself.* Maybe someone would slip up in front of him and he could nonchalantly open his cell's audio memo app while the cunning little old lady in her hot pink lady-politician-fuzzy-blazer talked about getting some more big government names to float the draft idea in the press, lay the groundwork for majority approval of massive military contracts for their new line of weaponized robotics; drones were just the start; we could build you an entire ground force, screw boots on the ground, rubber treads instead, and make us very, very wealthy in the process.

Or maybe he'd just drive up to the Military Industrial Complex's complexes around Tampa, hit up Grindr, get some closeted, Republican, married, mid-level War Profiteer out to his Jeep to give this hot young boy a blow job, and ram his ass with some blackmail video once the deed was done.

But he had to go back to the truth laid out before him on his dorm room floor: Truth Bombs never stopped the truth they exposed; at best they just made those in power find another way to keep doing the same.

The Pentagon Papers, Abu Ghraib, Edward Snowden, Iran Contra, Mai Lai, Seymour Fucking Hersh again and again dropping his Truth Bombs, Zinn and Chomsky tying it all together for us, WikiLeaks, before Assange went stir crazy, Anonymous, the good ones anyway—there, half-hidden by *A People's History*, laying under it, *The Burglary* by Betty Medsger, the story of the badass William Davidon and his friends who burglarized an FBI office to show the world the files the FBI was keeping on patriotic Americans—college students demanding justice, blacks demanding humanity, professors demanding truth—it was a small mountain of books exposing a history of racketeering, but the criminals remained our masters.

Truth Bombs.

You could drop a Truth Bomb of Mass Destruction in front of them, and The People after a brief and irritable awakening, would fall right back asleep.

You could drop ...

Skyscrapers in front of them. The worlds tallest buildings to the ground at near the speed of gravity, and they'd remain blind to the truth imploding to the ground before them.

That was it! That's where the thought was. 9/11.

He jerked around and looked at his closet. He'd hid it in there.

4:31 PM

Treason. There was one the few words that was still supposed to mean something. But if he'd said it out loud, its meaning would be pounded into the dirt along with both their bodies in a rather evenly matched fight. Dumb as Bret was, his body was just as in shape as Ryan's.

To turn your weapon around and fire it upon your own government, your own country, your own people. That's what Bret and his friends were training for? That's what Ryan had associated himself with on this fucking ranch? Ryan was fuming. His own patriotism could be called into question just for being here. By being associated with these shits even for an afternoon.

But again, Ryan's anger helped. Rather than exploding in rage, he used it to focus himself on target. The trigger finger of his anger, taut against weapon's side, waiting for the target to properly reveal itself.

He wanted to maintain control of his voice, his facial and body expressions, his words, to ask questions—to "know thy enemy" first.

He approached Bret on the walk back to "base." Once he noticed the approach, Bret slowed his walk, it seemed to Ryan, to keep the others from hearing what Ryan would have to say, fearing any further association with the loser who wouldn't fire his weapon.

"So this was what? Waco?"

Bret cut his eyes at Ryan hard, then looked away, shaking his head. "Man, you don't have a fucking clue, do you?"

"So read me in."

Bret slowed even more, more distance from the boys, and now a seething whisper, "Wake the fuck up, Ryan. This country's about to choose between the nation of our Founding Fathers or *enslavement* to those who would be our masters. And there's a damn good chance they gonna choose wrong."

Ryan maintained the cover of his steady voice, the mask of his unchanging face. He processed the different voices with which Bret seemed to speak—his own and someone else's.

"In which case you would do what?"

Bret turned on him, forcing Ryan to take steps backwards, as Bret moved forward, lest they end up in that brawl in the dirt.

"Maintain my Oath!" Bret's whisper hissed. "Foreign and Domestic, motherfucker. *All* enemies. Foreign and *Domestic*."

"And for that," Bret continued, grabbing the barrel of Ryan's AR, "you gotta have the balls to fire your Goddamn weapon."

Bret turned back to catch up with his boys.

And Ryan had his answer.

4:39 PM

Tristan opened his closet door, and upon seeing the books dropped there hastily, was disgusted with himself again for the scared, weak little shit he'd been last night, for fear of Ryan on his way. For in that fear he'd just dumped the books in his dirty clothes basket. The posters, he'd forgotten, were no longer on his wall but here, having unrolled as much as they could and settled into new warped shapes since last night.

He pulled out the books and dropped them on his bed, unrolled the posters and laid them on his makeshift sofa trying to get them flat again, looking as he did, up close at that pyramid, that eye of all knowledge and power.

He went to the books. Laying on top was *9/11 and the American Empire: Intellectuals Speak Out* by Griffen and Scott. The most important image of his life on its cover—the burning towers, the black smoke. Underneath that was the one he wanted. He pulled it out and sat again on the floor with it, back against his bed, and held it for a moment. Its black cover: *The Commission: What We Didn't Know About 9/11*. He knew it as he held it. This was the book. Reading this was when the thought had formed.

He opened it. Flipped through.

How hard and long Bush & Cheney fought the creation of a commission and stonewalled it every step of the way once it finally formed. The loyalty litmus tests for everyone involved. That most-loyal piece of shit they got to run the commission day-to-day. The push-overs to lead it. The part-time, limited-involvement commissioners for this the greatest crime in our history.

Ignoring the 9/11 Families. Blinding themselves to the most damning evidence. Refusing to follow the paths of leads that led away from the already agreed upon myth and to much darker truths. Every step of the way set up to fail.

The Saudi connections; the War Games NORAD was playing that very morning; the "hijackers" who lived openly in San Diego and were so obviously being handled by intelligence, foreign and domestic (just like their counterparts in Florida); the immediate push to use 9/11 as an excuse to go to war with Iraq; the litany of "failures" of the FBI, CIA, NSA, Military, FAA, etc.; "accidents" and "coincidences" and "mistakes;" why the Bush Administration had repeatedly, blatantly ignored the constant flow of warnings in the spring and summer of 2001 about an imminent al-Qaeda attack; and on and on.

Much of his marginalia was arguing with the book's author, Philip Shenon, for accepting time and again that most well-beaten and blatantly abused of cover-up excuses: incompetence.

Tristan had written in the white space at the end of one chapter in which the author had repeated this most blatant of lies "debunking" conspiracy theories: "People who choose to blind themselves to the possibility that powerful people might use their powers toward corrupt ends, belittle their own intelligence into accepting an absurdly long list of systemic incompetence on one side, instance after instance of unbelievable luck on the other, and a laundry list of coincidence in between tying it all together. What they force themselves to miss every step of the way is that the far simpler, and thus far more likely, explanation is design."

On a later page, the thick ink, deep indentations into the paper, underscores and caps of Tristan's handwriting were screaming at the author: "Why the FUCK do you keep excusing this as incompetence?! They're not the FOOL, it's YOU!!! They were MASTERFUL in their DECEPTION!!!!!!!"

In some more once-blank space at the end of another chapter and wrapped around the title of the next: "These commissions are GENIUS. First Warren and now this one. Scuttle the most damning facts. Don't seek to connect the dots, draw lines of confusion between them, add more dots, lots more, the irrelevant, the unsubstantiated, the made up. Don't approach the thing to solve it, but to make it messier. Denser. Too long to read. Only then connect a few dots, some that you've added out of your ass, to show the preexisting story you were commissioned to tell. Don't worry—<u>The People</u> <u>will</u> <u>trust</u> <u>you</u>."

"<u>GENIUS</u>" on one page, "Nice move" on another, "Brilliant," another.

The more Tristan watched them in between the lines, the more he saw of their conniving ways, the less he found himself hating them, the more he realized he was in awe of them—the ones who pulled these strings.

And then at the end. On the no longer blank pages in the very back of the book. He'd remembered writing them now. These words. He'd been drinking with Ryan. Whiskey. The good stuff. The sniff and small sip and play with the flavors with your tongue a bit before letting it in the rest of the way, the welcome burn down, the tension relieved, the freedom your thoughts were let loose into as the warmth of its goodness came back up your bloodstream to your brain.

But even then, not enough freedom to tell Ryan what he wanted to tell him. What he'd finally started to tell him last night.

He'd been reading this book that week and came home that night after drinking with Ryan and keeping it all inside because of the impossibility of penetrating the wall Ryan had built before it. And looking back over these pages, whiskey bringing him clarity, he wrote a little missive to himself after the "About the Author."

"The only way to beat them, Tristan, is to join them. Turn around and see things properly. Look back down upon that massive lower pyramid, block after block of mankind's near-immovability and see them for what they are.

"Zinn is wrong. There will be no 'Coming Revolt of the Guards.' Not on their own. They need someone, someone through the looking glass, someone who's made it to the upper pyramid to pull their strings."

Tristan thought about that. To do things the way thine enemy does them. To cause events that never were what at first they seemed.

He looked up from the book and let a little exhale of a laugh escape. He'd thought about a shirt of his he'd glimpsed crumpled in his dirty clothes basket. It had the pyramid on it and under it said, "I'm with the Illuminati."

It had gotten some good laughs. But maybe, tactically, it was the way to go. To play the game the way they played it.

4:41 PM

He got down on his knees one at a time to lay the beat-up old box gently on the dirt. He opened its flaps. Inside were four large glass bottles from cheap wine with the corks jammed back in.

He pulled one of the bottles out, and you could see that each had an old cloth wrapped around it, tied on with string. Three of the cloths seemed to be old undershirts, yellowed and rotting. One was a fraying hand towel. He unzipped his Army backpack and pulled out another, smaller bottle that seemed to be filled with a granular substance soaking in liquid.

Then he pulled out a rolled and worn book. Oh, right. Now Ryan got it. He'd seen the book before: *US Army Improvised Munitions Handbook*. Bret opened to a dog-eared page and checked something. All the while the others were looking on with hollers and, "Sweet Jesus!" and, "The hell you got there?" and the like.

Ryan recalled their name from the book: Chemical Fire Bottles. He just never saw anyone stupid enough to make one. Enter Bret.

When Ryan first saw the book, he couldn't believe it said "Department of the Army" on it. All the concerns out there of people learning how to make bombs from the internet or extremist propaganda, and here was the US Army publishing their own How-to-Make-Bombs-In-Your-Garage book. It was a field manual for when our forces might need to engage in unconventional warfare. Every page stamped with "For Official Use Only." That should do it.

Bret's copy seemed very well read and re-read. Well, it did have pictures.

Bret shook the small bottle rapidly to mix the chemical inside together with the sugar. Ryan remembered that. Sugar was an ingredient. Crazy.

Then he unscrewed the cap to pour its contents on the cloths wrapped around the larger bottles.

Ryan stepped a few more paces back, grabbing Miles' shoulder to pull him back too. Miles was hooting and hollering with the others. He'd apparently had a great time today and was now 2-3 beers in.

Bret and three of his boys each grabbed a rag-wrapped wine jug and one by one lobbed them at the large mound they'd made of some of the worst shot-up wooden targets of the day. As soon as the glass broke, the gasoline and other chemicals inside mixed with those soaked into the rags, and the incendiaries self-ignited on target just as the Army said they would, and with this massive display of flames, Bret cracked open a beer to get this party started.

Ryan picked the book up off the dirt and flipped through it again. Pipe bombs, nail bombs, chemical explosives. Unbelievable.

Miles knocked the book aside with a beer for him. "Cheer up, Bro. Victory is ours!" Miles yelled, half-mocking. Miles didn't seem to have heard, or been affected by, what Ryan had about whom that victory was really against. All that mattered to Miles was that "our side" had won.

But Ryan took the beer and accepted his friend's fist-bump-toast. Miles brought him over to a couple of the guys who'd mocked him earlier.

"Miles tells us you're from New York. You should have said. Now we understand, you know." They were still mocking, but seemed to be doing it in good fun.

"Yeah, they just don't raise boys right in New York anymore," said the big-belly gamer, but his smile said he meant no harm. They toasted Ryan a swig and he accepted. Not the time or place for that fight either.

A couple more beers and Ryan was making some rounds around the campfire, talking to the guys, getting them to like him again, and doing a little reconnaissance. He wanted to find out more about who this group was, what they believed, and what they believed they were fighting for. No one seemed to be willing to come right out and say it. Ryan and Miles were both clearly looked at as guests, not insiders.

He noted what symbols he could find amongst the men. Most prevalent was the coiled cobra, fangs displayed, of the "Don't Tread on Me" flag. A few southern Rebel flags on t-shirts, hats, a tattoo or two. One, but only one, "III" tattoo. And one guy who'd been drinking heavily showed Ryan a tattoo of what he called a "Hydra," explaining if you cut off one of the mythical beast's many heads, another one just grew right back. Ryan wasn't sure whether the "beast" in this analogy was meant to be the good guys or the bad.

There was talk of the need to protect one's family, of zero faith in the government, of the terrible things that could happen any day now. But nothing too specific. And Ryan didn't want to push too hard, having been seen as unwilling to fire his weapon when called upon to do so, he knew the guys didn't trust him.

Asshole Man had taken off his shirt by now. He had a lot of tattoos Ryan couldn't make out, without getting closer, but the one he could see from here was a giant one of a snake cut into pieces that ran all the way across his upper back, shoulders. Underneath was written, "JOIN, OR DIE!"

Ryan had seen that before, but couldn't recall its exact meaning. Something with the original colonies, maybe? But he couldn't imagine what that would mean to this fuckwad. He made a mental note to look it up tomorrow.

A couple more beers in and he was sitting on some old crates with Bill. Bill seemed like a good guy. Early 40s, maybe. Overweight and hurting from the day, for sure. Ryan was surprised he'd made the long walk in today's heat. He carried a sweat cloth with him.

Bill was one of those guys who, when you got to talking with them, you realized they really *needed* to talk. Like people didn't listen to him much and finally he found an ear that seemed receptive.

Ryan was reminded again of the simplicity of this tactic: how much some people would tell you if you only acted like you were interested and on their side.

Bill was talking about the "fucked-up economy." But as Ryan listened, he realized what Bill was really talking about was fear. A fear Ryan somehow seemed to taste in his tightly closed mouth as he'd forgotten about the act and was now really trying to hear Bill and understand him.

"I don't know what to do." He kept saying that. He must have said it twenty times during their chat, probably more. Sometimes with some profanity. Sometimes trailing off. But again, and again.

Bill hadn't had a good paying job in years. Unemployment was long gone. He tried for Disability, but couldn't get it. "Hell, half the guys here over 30 have it, the fuckers. Why can't I get it?" Then, he added, "Maybe I need to get more creative with it."

He talked about his dad. "Raised five kids, Mom stayed home, never wanted"—all things Ryan had heard before in the Upstate—"all that on one blue-collar income. What the hell happened?" Bill's eyes were so lost as he said it, really searching for an answer that wouldn't come.

"I've been ubering lately," he said with a laugh of pity for himself. "Can't make it work out here. People just drive drunk, no care. Sometimes I head down your way, drive some drunk college kids around. Good life you all have down there, man. But ... subtract gas and wear and tear on the truck and I ..." He trailed off again.

"I feel like the only reason I *exist* is to pay debts. That's how it feels. The money just passes right through me. Like a ... I remember in grade school they told us about Indentured Servants. Thing of the past, my ass! That's what I'm alive for. Earn a few pennies to pay to my masters."

He paused. Drank his beer. A lot of it.

Bill said a thousand words with his face. And they were all about being afraid.

Scattered memories reemerged to Ryan of his family in the Upstate. Similar moments with his grandfather, his aunts and uncles. His stupid cousins who would have fit in perfectly with Bret and his crew here today. Even as a young boy Ryan felt it. That so much of their bravado was fear. So many of their hatreds actually seemed rooted in something more like jealousy. Maybe it was in part because he was so young then that he saw through these masks. Little difference between the masks adults wore and those worn by a kid on a playground talking big.

Ryan had been an outsider when he moved to Brockport. The kid from the big city, from where all the evils came. They were trying to reclaim him as their own. Trying to help him see the world aright again.

But the world would never be aright again.

Bill found some more words.

"What the hell happened to this country ... I don't know. They tell you any of that in your college?"

Ryan just shook his head. "Not really, no." At first he thought his words were wrong. Memories came back of discussions on the Wall Street crashes, the subprime mortgage crisis, the bailouts. A few flashes of Tristan's conspiracies popped up. But after that flyby, he concluded his answer was for the best, and left it where it lay.

Bill finished his beer and looked at the empty bottle for a while.

"I'll tell you what," he said after some time. "I hate to say it. I *hate* to. But ... I'm ready for the proverbial Goddamn pitchforks. I really am."

And Ryan knew why Bill suddenly got up and walked away. It wasn't the empty beer. Tears had come. And tears weren't manly.

4:43 PM

His bare feet sunk into the cool mushy soil. At first past his ankles, then each time a little less, until stepping firmly upon the dry sandy, pine needle, leaf and twig covered soil in the deep woods. At first the bare feet had just been a necessity of the circumstances. He didn't like to wear shoes kayaking, and even if he did wear flip-flops or the like, they'd just get stuck in the mud first step off the boat. There were countless pricklers and thorns here and there, and the naked crooks of tree roots and creepers to give tiny jabs to the soles of your feet; snakes, insects to watch out for along with signs of gators; but once you got past those tiny fears that keep certain types of modern young men away from nature, the surface of the earth here felt soft, actually. Someone who understood, as he did, felt more at one with nature, feeling it prickle through your toes. And this was a little spot of the Earth he'd come to know well. Trees whose shapes he remembered upon seeing them again. The more time he spent among them the more he knew their individuality. To many, most likely, it was just a swampy little spot indistinguishable from any other back through the hundreds of little islands you could paddle around and streams you could meander up in this preserve of God's Creation, one of the few good things government did.

Kristi had called it an Eden when he brought her here. Maybe she was trying a little hard to show she shared his connection with this place.

But for Luke it wasn't an Eden, but a Gethsemane.

A place of respite, a bit of sanctuary, from a world aligning against him.

He'd come here more and more often of late. It was a place of great decision for him. A place where he could leave all others behind. All betrayers and betrayals. A place where he could be at one with himself and with his Lord. A place where clarity came. Resolution.

He came to the tree. A tree whose scars spoke volumes to his soul. A tree badly burnt, but still standing.

He got down on his knees on the dirty sand, bugs and all, the continuous chorus of countless insects around him. Campus over a mile from sight, more from mind, and he hidden here from their judging eyes. And he prayed to God the Father for release.

The sickness of this Sodom surrounding him. The irreparable harm to come should this country that had been given so much by the Lord betray Him yet again with a vote toward Satan. And all this to bear with the memory of ... his words broke out into a whisper, "... the wrath ... the *pain* ... You once imposed upon me."

The loss of Caitlyn. The death of innocence. All of it hollowing out his soul all over again.

He was that devastated boy again, the day of her death, the carpet of his childhood bedroom rubbing his knees raw as he writhed in pain, as his knees almost began again to now in the twigs and leaves, veins of anger bulging from that young boy's neck as he begged his God to tell him "WHY?!"

And so God showed him.

In a state that felt not quite like reality, Luke had felt God's gentle hand raise him to his feet. He walked to his bureau, picked up his childhood Bible, the one with the painting of Jesus surrounded by the children on its cover, sat on the edge of his bed, closed his eyes and allowed God to lead his hands as he opened the book, opened his eyes, knowing more certainly than he'd ever known anything before or since, that in this gentle suggested action of his body, God was answering his prayer.

And there on the page where his eyes were brought to land were the words that would dominate his vision and henceforth his life.

Caitlyn, despite her own innocence, had to die. Because the Lord had to stay true to His Word.

Because Kristi and all her modern liberal Christians were wrong. The New Testament did not abolish the Old. The Son did not dethrone the Father.

There were His Words. And there could be no painting on of nuance. No distortion of their simple Truth.

And his tears dried on his face as he read them over and over and sat there with their hard truth sinking in and bringing him peace. Hard truths did that. After the pain they cause wanes a bit, you start to feel grateful that at least now you have your answer. And it all makes perfect sense.

"And the Lord passed by before him, and proclaimed, The Lord, The Lord God, merciful and gracious, longsuffering, and abundant in goodness and truth,

"Keeping mercy for thousands, forgiving iniquity and transgression and sin, and that will by no means clear *the guilty*; visiting the iniquity of the fathers upon the children, unto the third and to the fourth *generation*."

The guilty.

Those words:

"… and that will by no means clear *the guilty*; visiting the iniquity of the fathers upon the children, unto the third and to the fourth *generation*."

The iniquity of the father.

Iniquity. He'd had to grab another book, his dictionary. It meant wickedness.

Wickedness.

The Lord had no choice. He must keep His Word. Without His Word there would be nothing.

He was a good Lord. He did love us. But He had to show his wrath too. Sometimes he had to kill in order to save.

He looked up again at the burnt tree. He knew the cross he had to bear.

But he knew too, the resurrection to come from bearing it.

5:18 PM

He drove down the sandy and crunched-leaf dirt drive through the woods. Past the perfect little house with the wraparound porch and all the potted flowers. Past a garden in an opening in the trees. And arrived at a shed at the start of the uncleared woods behind it all.

He got out, grabbed the padlock on the door and turned the dial to the right numbers. Inside, dominating the mess of items, were fourteen five-gallon plastic jugs filled with liquids varying degrees of golden, those more polluted with other substances closest to the door.

It's The People I hate, Tristan thought.

He turned around a moment and looked back at that perfect little house behind the lovely garden. That was The People's dream. And to dream it, they slept.

He went into the shed, bent down to one of the jugs at the end, checked the date he'd written in marker on its lid, grabbed the heavy bitch with two hands and hefted it up.

How could he truly despise The Oligarchy, when in many ways he respected them so? How could he respect The People, when in many ways he despised them so?

He set the jug down and opened its cap. He grabbed an empty jug off a shelf and set it on the ground, grabbed a tall metal stand he'd made, and set it down, straddling the empty jug.

Why then keep this anger toward his father for taking their money? Wasn't it better to profit as they profited rather than play one of the many, many, many fools?

He'd grabbed a series of cloth sacks that had been laying out and were numbered, "1, 2, 3" and inserted one into the other. Now he hung them on the metal frame above the empty jug, which next he inserted a large funnel into.

He grabbed up the full jug again, muscles contracting to heave it up to shoulder height and poured the golden liquid into the cloth sacks until they were full. He set the jug down again and waited as the golden liquid emerged through the bottom of the sacks and streamed down through the funnel into the empty jug.

It's The People's own fault. The Sleeping Giant, they'd for so long been called, for they'd for so long slept.

When Zinn dreamed of "The Coming Revolt of The Guards," he meant the middle class. That's who the guards of The System were, the buffer between what would otherwise be the revolting masses and the 1% who stole the world's wealth. The middle class were kept just happy enough to know The System was Good. And thus to help protect The Oligarchy from revolution.

But The Guard, as Tristan saw it in *A People's History of the United States*, also meant a much more specific group within that sustainably employed class. For when rebellions and uprisings did happen in our history, it was the Army and the Police who must put them down—fools from the suppressed classes fighting, even killing, often imprisoning, their own to protect their masters.

They were the tip of the spear. The ones most dangerous in the direction they chose to attack—whether enemies foreign, amongst the lower pyramid, or within the upper.

When the poor rose up to burn the mansions of the privileged in pitiful attempts in America's early years to level the financial playing field, who put them down? Who brought the peace, but the peacemakers? Who brought peace by force of arms.

These were the foremost protectors of The System, the armed forces. And Ryan and his ROTC boys and their war games were begging to become the next generation of them. Our protectors.

The liquid stopped flowing. He hefted up the jug and poured some more into the filters.

Ryan and his boys.

And Ryan, the worst of all. Because he had every reason to see, all the means to, all the evidence bearing down upon him. And yet ... he chose his blindness. He *chose* it.

Couldn't they see what they were doing? Couldn't they see the tyranny they protected? Couldn't they feel the pain?

The deeply buried pain of a people that had been robbed so long ago, and so consistently since, that they'd forgotten what it was that was rightfully theirs.

5:24 PM

Ryan decided to wander off for a bit. Deep down inside he really was a loner. He knew that. Despite all the groups he was a part of. All the relationships.

Deep down inside he was still standing on that Promenade alone. Looking back at the ghosts of those buildings. The fall of his father's body from the manmade heavens to the manmade pile of rubble.

No one could hold him up. Or stand by his side. Just as no one was there to do for his father. Life wasn't that kind.

He found himself back at the firing range. The light much lower now, long shadows from the trees. He found himself looking in Bret's truck parked there. Found himself checking the AK case. Found it unlocked, as he'd half-expected. Found his hands holding the weapon.

Bret said *he* needed to wake up. His mind went back to the other day on the bleachers. His thoughts that his platoon needed to wake up and that somehow he'd be the one to wake them.

He found himself lying on the dirt mound before the range taking aim. But not going to fire, of course. Not after six beers. Or seven?

He'd heard what Scotty said. When they were leaving the bleachers. Behind his back to the Freshman. That he'd wanted to be the one to cap Osama since he was five.

He'd read everything he could find about it. How it went down. Trying to find some solace in that. Envisioning it.

But maybe he'd read too much.

The old-time investigative reporter Seymour Hersh put out a book, *The Killing of Osama bin Laden*, in which, as seemed to keep happening to Ryan ever since reaching "adulthood," myths, "fairytales" as Tristan would say, were exposed for the lies that they are. The book raised questions about everything in the neat little tale the government told. Maybe it wasn't so neat after all.

Ryan looked down the line of sight of the weapon to the target. What would he have seen had he been on that raid? Down the barrel of his weapon, would there have stood as resolutely as the wooden target before him now the mastermind who killed his father? The man still orchestrating the world's terror from his protected compound? Or would there have cowered a feeble, sickly soul? A prisoner set up for the killing by those who'd captured him long before. A commander of nothing. And maybe, just maybe, one who never really was all we've been told.

Like the story Hersh says we were suppose to be told about how he was killed. That a drone had gotten him in another country. A story we would have been told and retold a thousand times by the press and the movies and our teachers and our elders until there was no question of its Truth. But that story had to be scrapped along with the helicopter that accidently went down in the compound that night and took the night's pre-written myth with it.

And had it been that cowering prisoner at the end of his line of sight — would he have fired nonetheless? As ordered. (According to Hersh, there was to be no, "… or alive," only "dead.") To put a final bullet in the head of this myth like a period in a sentence in the history books. Here lies the truth.

His finger had slipped to trigger. He brought it back to safety.

How did that fucking building fall, Tristan? How did all three of them fall? Who was Osama? What is this government I've pledged allegiance to? This myth upon which I've rested all my hope like that child I used to be resting my hope upon a piece of paper falling from a burning building.

Am I the one who needs to wake the hell up*!?*

Maybe we all fucking do.

Finger moved back to trigger and line of sight to target. Whom the target represented he no longer fucking knew. All he knew—all he needed to know right now—was that the target was the fucking enemy.

He fired. Round after round of automatic explosions inches from his center of thought. Small explosions sending death down that barrel to his target. Eyes now adjusted to the shadows. He could see his target. Still standing. So many holes. But the fucker still wouldn't fall.

■ ■ ■

5:27 PM

"No! I think a raucous, lewd, absurd, ridiculous, half-naked, drugs-in-the-bathroom, who-the-hell-remembers-who-they-slept-with, blow-out party is exactly what this campus needs right now!" Jasmine said, as she stopped mid-step, spun around and confronted her last remaining roommate to her red face. Her roommate had unwisely escalated this to a screaming match. Jasmine was about to end it. She continued,

"This campus has been going nowhere but on a downward spiral lately. Everyone and everything is politicized. Everyone is in their own little angry groups and all our problems are the other peoples' faults and the world's coming to an end and I'm sick of it. I've lived my whole life in politics and I'd like just a little respite from it, thank you very much, for these few years, in

PATRIOTS: BOOK ONE | 271

this little oasis called college. So I'm throwing a party! *Mrs. Dalloway*, if you please."

Her roommate had been ready to retaliate, but was thrown into a moment of confusion with that last remark. So, Jasmine continued,

"And don't think I didn't see you out there on The Commons with your little Republican Girls Club and 'The Government's Not Your Daddy' and the immigrants are the problem and drill baby drill, I saw you out there!"

"Your ... father is one of the most conservative Senators in the ... Senate! I thought I moved in with the daughter of a conservative icon! Instead I got *you*!"

Jasmine calmed her voice. "You see. Look at yourself. Levity ... is what we need. A moment of levity. We're having a party. And by God, some conservatives and liberals are gonna insert tongues and other things into each other and be happy about it."

Her roommate covered her face. Then reappeared. "It's fine if you want to have some friends over. Open the wine. Open *all* the wine. But you've got speakers the size of ... they're gonna blow out the freaking windows, Jasmine!" She was pointing to the massive speakers the DJ and his assistant were in the process of bringing in their apartment and setting down on the living room floor. "Not to mention the cops will be here inside of 10 minutes!

"*And* you're inviting total randos from off the street! Who does that?!"

"I think it's time I made some new friends." Jasmine eyed the DJ's assistant as he put down a heavy crate of cords.

"And what about all your nice stuff?"

Jasmine moved her eyes from the DJ assistant's ass and looked at some of her very, very nice things. And then she shrugged. "If it breaks, it breaks."

Her roommate just stared at her—coming to terms, as she'd had to before, with Jasmine's immovable force.

Jasmine's eyes changed. She took on a face she allowed very rarely in public. Then said,

"Oh. And Noelle. Don't tell me what it is you think my father stands for. It makes me think so little of your intelligence."

With that she smiled again and that look was gone. She brought her eyes back to the assistant, bent down to the back of a speaker, checking something. "Yeahhh!" she said strutting to him. "That's what I'm talkin' about!" And she really did wind up her arm a few rotations before slapping his voluptuous, firm, underwear-popping-out-above-the-poked-out-belt-line ass. "It's time to party!"

5:38 PM

The thoughts of Gethsemane had him thinking about not just the betrayal, but the loneliness at the end of Jesus's mortal life. That all those who called themselves disciples had left. That His Father might have even forsaken Him. But not the women. They stayed by him until and through the end. Only the women still believed in Him.

He was paddling back through the wetlands. Back to the chaos and the fallenness of the "real world." And he was finally seeing clearly what a fool he'd been there.

God had taken Caitlyn from him. But now He had brought Kristi to him. And yet he, Luke, was pushing her away.

She was the only light in his life and he was trying to rid himself of her. Why? Because he preferred his misery?

Was that it?

Was she a way out and yet he chose to stay with his demons?

He did love her. And, God, he needed her. He needed her so much. He needed her to ....

He sat up and forward in the kayak and increased the speed and force of his paddle strokes. Chopping the blade into the water. He knew what he needed to do.

5:47 PM

He was sitting on an upside-down bucket watching the last of the golden liquid ooze through the sock filters and drip down into the nearly full jug.

Purification. You had to weed out the pollutants. "The wheat from the chaff." That Bible phrase that had spilled so much blood.

He'd thought often about the power contained in that simple liquid. What it could do when lit match was touched to it. Something so beautiful there, falling in the late afternoon light. But treat it meanly and ....

His phone beeped. It pulled him out of his daze, but it still took a moment for him to decide to reach in his pocket for it. He'd thought often of trying to get rid of a phone, or at least turning it off for several more hours a day, leaving it at home. He wanted to be lost in his thoughts. And what right did someone have to interrupt them?

But, alas, he was a product of this age. His phone beeped and so thought must stop. He must see who wanted his attention. Trained as a dog of Pavlov's.

He looked at the screen.

It was a text from Mc:

"Paper?"

He must have stared at it for two or three long seconds before a little smile with a little laugh broke through.

He looked up from the phone at the last few drops falling to the jug. And he laughed a little bit more, a tiny bit louder.

Life was a funny little thing.

He got up and grabbed the now full jug, went to his Jeep, opened the back gate. There was a large metal tank sitting in the trunk. He unscrewed the opening and poured the filtered, golden liquid in.

5:54 PM

The doors of Bret's truck slammed one by one. This time Ryan sat up front with Bret. Miles took his same seat in the back next to the guy whose name Ryan still didn't care to remember.

There was that energy between Bret and Ryan that occurs on those rare occasions when two people know there is more that needs to be said to each other, and now. And heavier things yet.

Bret started the truck's massive engine and turned to head back to campus.

5:56 PM

Jasmine ripped open the button-fly of the DJ assistant's jeans and pulled out his manhood. She could smell his musk. A dumb, meaty boy. She knew, despite what she'd said, tonight would be about work for her. She'd be donning one of her masks for the evening. So she should get some fun out of the way now, to help her focus later.

She scooted back on her bed and he climbed after and over her. She laid back and they kissed. She felt his wood poking around between her legs. She liked the feel of his arms, the smell of her worker boy. Manual labor. She pulled his face away from hers.

"Here's how this is going to go. You're going to make me cum. Not the other way around." She began pushing his head and shoulders down her body. "Now get down there and lick until you can taste that you've finished your work."

5:57 PM

She stepped off the sidewalk and into the grass, putting more weight on the balls of her feet so her heels wouldn't sink in the soil. How she would have loved to kick them off instead. Stand in the grass barefoot, feeling the blades between her toes. But that wasn't the image a woman of her stature was supposed to present. She was the president of a university. And her students around her now on The Commons, shaking her hand, glad to see her, needed not someone who wanted to join them, but rather someone who could speak some wisdom from a long life of experience.

Madeline Voorhees shook their hands eagerly. She'd grown tired of shaking the hands of politicians and provosts and donors. These were the hands of her students. The reason she was here in this job. The reason she put up with all the rest of it.

She let students put stickers on her lapels, listened to what they were protesting or tabling for, smiled more real than she did with the politicians as her First Assistant took picture after picture with students' cell phones for them as they stood so near they could be long-lost friends.

In her mind, she was still finalizing just what she wanted to say when she got to the spot they were setting up for her to speak. It was impromptu, walking over here, but the timing felt right.

What a path her life had taken to this point. And what hope and fears came to her now from the past.

Madeline, Maddy, so many years ago now, had grown up in the bohemia of Berkeley, California. Her mom was First Secretary to Cal's President Kerr during the tumult of the '60s as Maddy watched from the sidelines in middle and high school.

All that those older kids went through then. Young Maddy taking her mom's side, who'd taken President Kerr's.

The poetry of her life coming back around full circle, but better. Her mom had been secretary to the President. Typist. Scheduler. A good-looking face bringing in the coffee. But now that secretary's daughter was President.

A bright young lady came up to her with a marker and was sheepishly asking something. It seemed the students were writing "Nov. 8th" on each other as a way to remember to vote. *How cute. Sure, what the heck.*

She pulled off her blazer and handed it to her Second Assistant. And the young lady wrote on her arm to clapping and smiles all around. She laughed with the students, and it was real too. Her louder, less "lady-like" laugh. Not the one for a provost's joke. She was well-loved here. And well she loved in return.

The marker tip snagged on the new little rough spot she needed to get checked. So many skin cancers she'd had removed lately. So many sunny days of her California youth with no protection.

She kept smiling, though she thought about how old her skin looked in the day's late sun, next to the bright young girl's. Her skin looked so tired.

Her back bit. A harsh sting up her spine. She had to readjust her feet in her heels.

Her old body was falling apart. *These bodies we inhabit—and how they betray us.*

The girl finished. She lifted her arm for the cameras. The Sand Tiger Press, right there for a close-up.

She walked to the place her staff had hastily set for her to speak, in front of a non-offensive "Diversity is Strength" banner.

She finalized her thoughts.   Pushing once more from her mind the memory that haunted her more and more lately as campus protests grew across the nation. May 4th, 1970. And where she was when she heard the news.   When national guardsmen opened fire upon the students on the grassy commons of Kent State University, killing four and paralyzing one for life.

She was in her dorm at NYU when she found out. And then she didn't want to leave it. To go outside. She wasn't yet the fighter she would become. This was to be her transition. Listening to the radio reports. Watching the news. Those clips of kids running down the hill away from gunfire. Those images from the Newsweek and LIFE magazine cover stories. Students lying dead on their own campus. Shot by invaders calling themselves patriots. Ten days later, it happening again at Jackson State. Across the country, the largest student strike in US history. More than 500 colleges and universities shut down. That banner she saw hung at NYU when she first ventured out: "They Can't Kill Us All." That woman. That awful woman with her awfully proper hairdo, being interviewed on the street in Kent, Ohio, saying, "I'm sorry they didn't kill more," more of the students, with her properness, her good-American-Patriot-ness.

It seemed like all of Madeline's youth had been dominated by the protests at Berkeley.   And then, her freshman year of college, the government of the United States of America opened fire upon its own youth for protesting against its war. She'd never felt so scared. But soon—her fear did this beautiful thing. It metamorphosed into determination.

She smiled. And began to speak.

"Well! Thank you all! Thank you for—Oh. Oh, okay, why not?" A young man had walked up and handed her a bullhorn. It had been a long time since she'd held one of these, but it was just perfect since—

"A bullhorn for the ol' Bulldog, huh?" she said only half as amplified as the crowd now became.

"That's what they used to call me in my litigator days. Bulldog Voorhees. Ha! I was something, let me tell you. You wouldn't want to be in the courtroom up against this ol' gal!"

The students clapped and hollered some more.

"But you know that's what I wanted to come out and say to you all today. That all those courtroom battles, the ones that made the press and got me the nickname … they weren't really my most lasting wins.

"Sometimes those cases I won, a few years later, they might be reversed on appeal. Other times, we'd win in court, but nothing would change for people in the real world.

"A lot of times, the things that really made a difference in peoples' lives were when rather than duking it out between the two sides, we sat down with each other, listened to each other, and found some common ground."

She felt like she was being a little dishonest here. Some of her bloodiest courtroom battles had made a hell of difference. And she was damn proud of them. But that wasn't the point she needed to make right here and now.

"We're just so *divided* in our country now. It reminds me of other times. Scarier times. And I just know that if we spent more time listening to each other, we'd all be better off for it.

"Will you promise me you'll try that? Let's put down these bullhorns and stop yelling *at* each other and talk *with* each other more. Huh? What do you say?"

There was some applause. But it was tepid.

The corner of her right eye caught again the table of students opposed to abortion. Pictures on their signs of dead fetuses. Did she really want to listen to those students?

"Okay. I care about you all so very much. I hope you know that."

She handed the bullhorn back to the young man and walked among her students again.

She was disappointed in herself. She believed in trying to find common ground, certainly she did. But ... what she said just then felt fake. She should have prepared for this more rather than wasting so much of the day prepping for the governor's meeting. This was more important.

At least she'd added that last bit. At least that was 100% the truth.

She walked to the pro-life girls and smiled for a picture with them. They were her students too. But it was her politician's smile. The one for the provosts.

Oh, Maddy, you phony, she thought. *Do you really accept the politician you've somehow become in old age? And when did either of those happen?*

6:03 PM

Tristan had been sitting there in his Jeep a few minutes, looking out to the sea and the pink horizon beyond.

The AC's parking lot was empty now. He'd waited for the last car to leave. Actually, the last moped. One of the kids who ran the front desk and had locked the gates to the pool at 6:00.

It was weird he'd seen that fucked-up Luke guy again here, leaving when he pulled in, practically running, actually, to his car with all his shit. That was one strange guy. But damn, his face was hilarious when Tristan caught him watching Kyle blow him. *Ha!*

Anyway. Now the place was empty, he got out.

He walked through the little path in the tall grasses out toward the beach. He liked to run his hand through the tips of the grasses when he took this well-beaten path in the soft earth kept open by the feet of men. They tickled a bit on the skin of your palm. He wasn't sure what the grasses were—rye, maybe?

His feet touched the softer sand of the beach. His toes grabbing some of it in a little curl, glad to be back in it again.

He pulled off his shirt and tossed it on the sand as he kept walking to his water.

His feet hit the water and a chill went up his body. His balls gathered together and snuggled themselves into his crotch. With the next coming little wave, he dove in.

He swam a bit further out, turned over and surfaced, spread out his arms and laid back.

This was his thing.

Floating in the sea, head laying completely back so the water and the sound of the manmade world were above his ears.

It required trust. Trust in nature. The waves. In the physics that held you up. That the silly movie-inspired fears of sharks deep in your mind were not worth the harm they caused you. That your idiot schoolmates wouldn't run you over with a jet ski. That you wouldn't float out to sea and awake lost.

Kyle couldn't do it. Float like this. He'd tried to teach him, wanted him to experience the serenity with him. But he couldn't keep the buoyancy for longer than a handful of seconds. It wasn't his body—that was perfect for this. It was his mind. All those little fears that make you lift your head and lose your oneness with the water.

Tristan took a deep breath into his abdomen. He loved hearing the air entering his body in his water-filled ears. It was meditation, this.

Alone on the sea. The setting sun behind him. The benefit that came to your soul when you had the faith to let go of your fears, lay back and let the Earth hold you.

Tensions disappeared.

He came here because he needed this. He needed a moment to breathe. To come back to himself. To be certain in his new clarity.

He breathed in again and thought about what he often thought about in these little stolen moments of escape from the society we'd built.

A more permanent escape.

6:09 PM

His key wasn't working. *What the—?* Had his landlord changed his lock? He paid his rent, right? God, there was so much on his shoulders right now, he couldn't be sure he'd—

"Lock yourself out?"

His neighbor had stepped out to take his beagle for a walk.

"No, just ..." Luke looked at his hand. He was holding the wrong key. He thought about how frazzled he must look to his neighbor right now. It concerned him.

He switched to the right key. "I'm good, thanks. Have a good walk." He unlocked his door and got in to safety.

He got back to his bedroom and there it was on the floor by his desk. His bookbag.

How could he have been so stupid? So careless? Such a damn—darned fool?

He squatted and unzipped the bag. Inside, amongst other books, his workbook: The Marriage Jesus Wants You to Have.

He sat on his bed with it, like Kristi often did across the foot of it, leaning back against the wall, and opened its pages.

There. Those blank lines on why he loved her.

He stopped and stared into the empty space in front of him. He needed to get this right. It needed to be the truth. He needed to win her back.

6:19 PM

Escape America.

He'd thought about that a lot.

There was a family friend who had spent his 20s and early 30s in Costa Rica. He said it was cheap then. He got by—for the things he still had to be a part of capitalism for—making t-shirts with ink he made from berries. Between his gardening and doing a few favors here and there, he didn't need much money.

He ate and read and surfed. It was a life most people worked their whole lives away in the hope of finding in retirement when there would be no surfing and no sex and far less meaning to all the freedom.

But he said that's all fucked now—too expensive, ruined by tourists.

Tristan had researched Thailand and Vietnam, places where the dollar still went far.

He'd managed a month and a half last summer in the Dominican Republic, far away from the parts of the island ruined by American chain restaurants and the people who would eat at them in a place like this. A small "town" near Cabarete. He could hop on motos to the beach. He'd rented a room from a nice older couple.

He turned his head slightly to the south. The sun was setting behind him, laying a warm glow on the water. He thought past all those miles of warmer and warmer water through the Caribbean to his little inlet beach in the DR where he'd laid back in the water and let the world hold him the same as now.

It was Away. But he couldn't make it last. Not without his dollars from America. So he'd taken a TEFL course online when he got back. And maybe that's what he'll do after FSCU's over. Go off to some less polluted society and teach the kids how to speak the language of ...

... the masters.

That was the other thing he'd learned in his summer experiment in the DR, that he, Tristan, couldn't really get away. How could he just forget all he knew?

These escapes were nice. They helped him remember who he was apart from this society. But they were just vacations. Just as futile in some ways as the American family who travels halfway around the world and eats at a motherfucking McDonalds.

It was too much a part of his being now; it had mutated his DNA, this sickness. And the only way for someone who knew what Tristan knew to save his humanity was not to run from this sickness, but to stand your ground and fight against it with all the strength you had left.

Goddamnit, you have to try!

Tristan opened his eyes, popped his body upward, and stood up in the shallow water.

He was surprised how dark it was. The sun had dipped below the horizon while his eyes were closed and his thoughts far away. And his body had drifted north from Sand Tiger Key to the deserted Turtle Key.

Suddenly, he felt foolish being out there.

This isn't fucking "Away," Tristan.

There is no Goddamned "Away."

And clarity. Maybe clarity wasn't something you found, but imposed.

He started walking back, the water up past his knees, making it hard. Those childish fears of something dangerous in the water starting to resurface just because it was dark.

7:41 PM

Boy, was his timing bad lately, Kristi thought as she opened the door to Luke. Everyone was supposed to be here in 19 minutes for her Thursday night Bible Study, some would surely, as always, be early, she'd just barely gotten the brownies mixed and in the pan, and here was Luke wanting another "talk."

"Really, everyone's on their way."

"Five minutes. I promise—no arguments this time."

She let him in and they went back to her room. She shut the door, just in case, as he pulled something from his bookbag. She turned around to see him holding out his workbook for her.

She knew what it meant. Took a solid breath. Took the book. Sat on her bed. And opened to the pages with the blanks that had left her so empty.

The pages were most certainly not blank anymore.

She had to let out a little embarrassed laugh. He'd filled in the blanks and the margins around them and the margins around the book's text, and onto the next page, having turned the book sideways to write from top to bottom. His writing, usually so clean and blocked, was rushed and messy.

She looked up to him a bit hopelessly. "I can't really read this."

He looked back at her full of hope. "Could I read some to you?"

She wanted to say "Yes," but her throat was feeling a little clogged. So she smiled and nodded instead.

He sat down next to her.

"The first reason, is the first thing I ever heard you say."

Time paused there for a moment, it seemed to Kristi.

"We were in that class, remember?" Of course she remembered.

Luke continued, "The student made that remark."

It was a history survey course. A huge room. Kristi couldn't count the number of students. Probably a couple hundred? Maybe more. The professor was talking about the Puritans and asked a question to see if anyone had done the reading. The student who raised his hand answered the question correctly, but then added a wisecrack about how some of the presidential hopefuls wanted to go back to Puritanism. "Christians miss that stuff. That was their glory days. Gettin' to tell everybody what to do and burn 'em at the stake if they didn't do it."

About half the room laughed. The professor even snickered a bit. Then moved on.

Kristi shot up her hand. But it was ignored. So she shot up from her seat and spoke anyway, cutting the professor off.

"You didn't care about the size of the room and all those eyes watching you," Luke continued. "You said, 'I don't think it's right that someone gets to make jokes about Christianity when you wouldn't let them make jokes about any other religion in this room.' You turned around looked at the class and I saw your face for the first time.   Your cheeks were red with nerves, maybe, or anger? You said, so politely, but so resolutely, 'I'd just like to ask that we respect each other's beliefs, please.' You quieted that whole room and got an apology out of the professor.

"I didn't hear anything else after that. I couldn't look anywhere else but at you."

Kristi could feel it in her stomach, that. That he'd remembered her words more clearly than even she had.

"The rest of the reasons are basically everything I've ever heard you say or seen you do since.

"You told me to speak to her. Caitlyn."

The little muscles around his eyes seemed to tighten, to brace themselves. "You were so right. You always say the thing I most need to hear."

He stopped a moment. She was no longer quite sure if he was reading from the blanks or not.

"Even when you said … that I betray Him. You …"

"That was maybe too—"

"It was what I needed to hear. Exactly what I needed."

His eyes went back to the page and she could see there the word written in caps and underscored.

"You have this 'WISDOM.' You know that?"

Kristi laughed a bit and turned, feeling that was a bit—

"No," he said, touching her face and pulling it back. "Wisdom."

His voice was sincere. And his eyes had returned. Those sweet eyes of the boy who loved her.

The doorbell rang out in the living room.

"And you said I was just a child. When she died. And it couldn't have been my fault."

The intensity in his face—there was no way she could go get the door. And she didn't want to.

"And I was wrong. To block you from that. To keep you out. I want to let you in."

Tears fell.

"I want to let you in ... if you still want to come."

She took his hands. She just had to. He let the book slide to the floor to hold her hands in return.

"I'm just struggling too, you know? And all I know is I need you. I'm ... just ... lost without you. I'm ungrounded. I'm ..."

She thought she might have heard the doorbell again, but couldn't let it matter. She wrapped her arms around him. He wrapped his back around her.

"Okay," she finally said as she kissed the top of his head. "We'll struggle together, then."

8:18 PM

"Back ..." she gave a little pause for the drama "... in business."

"Woooooohooo!" the girls cheered as they carefully touched martini glasses too full with Tracy's purple cosmos together.

But they weren't quite back in business yet. They were in t-shirts and light sweatpants and cotton shorts, their hair was only just getting started, and their faces were barren canvases.

Tracy had the best bathroom for Getting Ready Parties. Plenty of room, plenty of light, the double doors opening into it from her bedroom gave even more space, and she did make one deceivingly potent cosmo.

288 | WILL KANE THOMPSON

"Back on some dick!" her friend Kira half-jokingly, half-not added and they laughed and took their second sip of the evening.

Oh Kira, always the studious ones, Tracy thought.

"Mmmm, let's hope it's one of those nights where all the boys end up shirtless," Jordan added.

"Yes, please. God those little muscles that go like this, what are they called?" She traced the v-shape on her own stomach.

"Jesus, I'll drop on my knees and lick those things."

"Speaking of being shirtless—" Tracy did have business to get to "— what do we think, paint tummies now or later?"

"Later, are you kidding? It'll get all messy."

"Okay. We'll have to commandeer an upstairs bathroom at the House."

"Soooooo …"

"What?"

"Can you find someone else to play 'v'. I mean look." Kira lifted her shirt, turned around and pinched an area on her lower back where she was able to pull out a little flab. "I feel like a cow."

"Okay, first of all, you've already agreed, I'm holding you to it, it's your patriotic duty, and second, no one's seeing your back."

"Or our face."

"Or your face."

Tracy couldn't believe she was still dealing with a possible mutiny after all she'd put into this today. But, thankfully, she'd spent a couple hours at the gym herself and had her new classy lingerie, in case one of them bailed. She always ended up having to do things herself.

As the girls moved on with their hair, Tracy stepped out and sat on her bed to call Ryan after two unanswered texts today. She set her cosmo down atop her Make Moves book on the nightstand.

She needed to make sure the guys were good and that he'd gotten the ones with the best bodies.

... And she needed to make sure he was good ... after this morning.

... And she needed to make sure they were good.

But the phone just kept ringing.

And then his, "Sorry. Busy. Call you back."

She hung up.

She'd heard that message too much lately.

She felt ... a little scared.

8:27 PM

Nature has taught us to notice certain things more than others. Movement amongst the relatively still always draws our attention. Movement in the forest, for example, could be predator or prey. Inconsistency in a pattern is another. Good soldiering teaches us to enhance these skills. To notice when our subconscious wants our conscious to notice and to question why.

Bret was choosing his words carefully. Bret. That was an inconsistency in his pattern. Ryan had taken notice.

He was listening so carefully to the words Bret was choosing, thinking about why these particular words were chosen in the small silences in between them, that it took him longer than normal to notice another inconsistency, a difference in sound amongst the music and wind through the windows. Movement. A police siren fast approaching from behind.

8:31 PM

She was trying to focus on the lesson she was leading. It was on some of the Psalms. Fortunately, the Bible Study app open on her iPad was pretty straightforward. Because in the back of her mind she kept worrying about what Abby and Jack had noticed.

They were the first ones here whom she'd made ring the doorbell twice and knock once. Surely they'd noticed they'd both been crying. And there were even more awkward half-hidden looks of recognition after she'd whispered to Luke to clean off his legs. For some reason his legs were all sand-caked again. So out of character. She'd expected him to use a washcloth in the bathroom, but to her horror they could all hear him turn on the shower. Sheri and El had arrived too while he was still in there. What would they all be thinking about how comfortable he apparently felt using her shower? Were they thinking he must use it all the time? That he sleeps here? That they weren't following the Word of God?

And that smile on his face now and pleasantness about him. It wasn't one of his fake smiles she'd seen through before. It was real, for sure. But that was the problem. Why, would they think, was he in such a good mood? It certainly wasn't normal for him lately. Even to be here at all wasn't normal anymore. He'd stopped coming to her Bible Studies months ago.

And now he's sitting there in such a good mood, fresh out of her shower, surely Abby and Jack would tell the others it took them forever to answer the door …

Oh, Jesus. Hopefully, they'll be respectful. Consider it "relationship stuff" and not their business.

But even thinking that in the back of her mind while listening to people's answers to the app questions, she knew what a hopeless thought it was.

8:38 PM

"Of course, it's a Goddamned n-----. We about to get Black Lives Matter'ed, fellas."

"Cool it, man. You want him running your record?" Bret seemed to shut Asshole Man up with that, but Ryan wanted to remind the idiot of the bigger problem for them all as the officer walked back to his car with Bret's license and registration.

"... Or looking into the back?" Ryan still wasn't sure if Bret had anything illegal back there. Or what was left of the chemical fire bottles. "So how 'bout you keep your racist, redneck mouth shut."

Ryan wanted a fight with this piece of shit. Not right now, but he was happy to set one up for later. He was confident he could take him, but he was also confident the fuck wouldn't fight fairly. More than likely he'd pull that knife from his thigh.

"Leave it, Brady." Bret cut his eyes back to him in the mirror.

Miles looked like he might currently be peeing his pants.

They waited in silence.

Fucking Bret. Driving like usual with all that in the back of his truck. Ryan should have told him to slow down. But he was tired of being the fucking manny today.

8:52 PM

It was decision time. Would he have the balls to go through with this or not? Or would he be a little bitch boy? The pussy he'd been called sometimes in ROTC?

He was grateful that Ryan had invited him. But the nerves in his gut were as frantic as almost they'd ever been. He wished he could have invited a friend, but Ryan didn't say a friend, he said he'd put him on the list. One. He couldn't show up with someone else, unless maybe it was a hot girl, but clearly one of the whole points of his loserdom was that he didn't have one of those.

But he had to go. He was sitting here naked and paralyzed on his bed on a Thursday night like a loser while the rest of the world was getting ready to have some wild night somewhere, and what was he gonna do? Sit here and jerk off again?

But that was the other problem, that he was really horny, and what if ...

He put his hand in between his legs and grabbed his balls and his cock. "Grow some balls," he whispered. He caressed the top of his cock a bit with his thumb. In his imagination it curved a bit to the left. And it had this slightly oversized mushroom cap, the ridge of which could drive the girls' clits crazy.

But it was only in his imagination. And what if he did get drunk tonight and hornier and someone pulled down his pants and saw his pussy? And it was the ROTC frat. Everyone would know. And then they wouldn't call him a pussy anymore. He'd no longer be one of the boys.

9:08 PM

Sara pulled out the tape for her boobs.

What would her mom think? Her mom owned a burkini, for God's sake. She could never know about Sara's life here. At least not anytime soon.

She was so glad this new boy Kyle had invited her to this party tonight to cheer her up. She needed this.

She lifted the light silk of the dress above her left boob and patted on the strip of tape with a couple fingers, then pressed the silk firmly to it. Then repeated with the right boob.

The dress was dangerously low cut. No bra could be used.

Dangerous, she thought. A dress.

She could be killed for wearing this dress in her parents' country. Her father could be the one to do it. Stone her to death like the good book says. Or like people said it says. She'd never read the thing.

God, she hoped she didn't somehow run into Tahir tonight.

9:12 PM

To trim the ging or not to trim the ging, that was the question as he looked down at his pubes.

There were definitely peeps with a ginger fetish out there, and maybe they would want his little bush. The latina girl who invited him tonight. That hot blond boy in the library showing him his cock yesterday.

But there was and probably always would be that part of him that felt "lesser than" because of his red hair. That was asked in middle school before he really even knew what it meant if the drapes matched the curtains, followed by giggles.

And if he should be lucky enough tonight to take off his pants for someone, he couldn't risk that feeling returning for even the most fleeting of seconds.

He straddled the toilet, clicked on the buzz of his trimmer, pushed his cock out of the way and got to work.

9:23 PM

Fuck. Another police car pulled up. This one in front of them. *He called for backup? Why the—? What the hell was in Bret's record?*

The officer got out and walked by the truck. He slowed as he passed them and looked at each of the boys' faces but didn't say anything. Ryan worried Fuck Face might say something. This officer was white. *Please don't speak, you fucking imbecile.*

He didn't. No one did.

The officer continued back to his colleague.

Once he was safely out of earshot, Miles made a strange long noise like a small rodent being slowly squeezed to its death. "Uuuuuuuaaaaaghhhghhhh. We're gonna be late for the party."

9:32 PM

Luke had Kristi's oven mitts on and was getting the brownies out of the oven for her. He set them down and took the knife from her and started cutting them for her.

Just a bit ago Abby said something Kristi feared way too liberal for him to keep quiet, but he did keep quiet. He listened politely and that was it. The moment blew by.

He was really trying. He'd taken the things she'd been saying for so long now to heart. He was listening.

She smiled at him as he put another fresh-cut brownie on the plate she held up for him. He smiled back.

9:35 PM

The black officer returned to the window with Bret's ticket. His words were all business and detail. Here's the box with the speed I clocked you at. Here's the box on pleading guilty. Here's your license. Your registration.

But his eye movements were disconnected from his words. They seemed to betray another agenda. As his words and his index finger pointed to the boxes they'd pointed out maybe thousands of times before, his eyes seemed to be landing on each of their faces one by one as if to remember them. And there were many glances around the cab still, floorboards, dash, searching for something.

Ryan was glad for the calmness of the officer's voice. He hoped it would help keep any voice from the back seat at bay.

9: 37 PM

He'd made it to the line and, not only that, about half way through it. His nerves were at their peak, but he just had to keep going forward, that's all. Once inside, there'd be booze, it'd be darker, people'd be drunk, it'd be easier. To make friends. *Just make one friend.* Then you'll have a buddy. Then you won't be alone at the party. Then you can relax and be yourself.

The line was moving. The beats from inside were powerful. He was glad he got there early. Figured his chances were better. This was clearly the party to be at tonight. And he had an invite. So it didn't matter that he felt so awkward in the line by himself. But was he dressed a little too cute? Did he look gay? The "Back in Business" banner across the front of the House was huge. It must of cost a ton. Frats had it all. Especially this one. Maybe he should try and join? But what if—

"Who the hell are you?"

"Max. Max Chester. I'm on the list."

He could feel the people behind him mocking him, *What's this loser think he's doing?*, as the frat guy bouncer checked a list on his phone. For sure a list of only male names, potential rushes, approved non-brothers.

"Nope. Beat it."

Fuck. No! Ryan forgot? Was he just playing with me?

"Beat it kid."

Jesus, this guy was for sure a freshman too, but he was just salivating in his sudden authority.

"No. Ryan said. Ryan ..." he was blanking ... "Sheridan. I'm in his platoon. He said for me to come tonight. I—"

It was futile. The guy's face was not playing. The line behind him, though silent about it, was screaming volumes at him from every loser moment of his stupid little life up till now. He turned to get out of there.

As he walked down the hill in front of the House, everyone looking at him, laughing at him, for sure, he willed it back with all he had but a Goddamned shit fucking tear fell.

Thanks a lot, Ryan. Thanks for making me see what a fucking fool I am.

9:41 PM

The black officer had walked back to his unmarked car, turned off his blue lights, and pulled away.

Now the white officer walked up. As he got to the windows on the passenger side he started unbuttoning the cuff of his shirtsleeve and then rolled the cloth up his arm. Then showed them his tattoo of the roman numeral "III."

He looked at the boys and motioned his head in the direction his fellow law enforcement officer had just driven off.

"He's been tailin' you since the ranch. Hopin' for somethin' more than sixteen above. Hopin' to see some reasonable cause when he pulled you.

"Neighbor to the ranch called to complain about the gunfire. She was havin' a five-year-old's birthday party."

"We were legal range at all times," Bret said.

"That's why we pulled off the property after a first look. But I figured he wouldn't let it lie there. That boy's got it in his head that blacks with guns are treated different than whites with 'em. I think he wants to even the score."

"Jesus ..." said Asshole, but the cop cut him off.

"And ... I know I at least heard somethin' more than just gun shots out there."

He let that sit in, pulled out a pad and scribbled on it, tore off the sheet and handed it across Ryan to Bret. It was a phone number.

"I'm also an Oath Keeper. You call that number you need me to keep my oath."

"Yes Sir, I will," Bret said, jammed full with respect.

"Thank you, brother," said Asswipe.

The officer headed back to his car.

Bret looked back at Asswipe for a moment.

A long moment.

10:03 PM

He just walked right through the front door. It was propped wide open by a little cement statue of an angel. Guess he didn't need the flier he was holding. This place was amazing. This was an apartment? It was huge. And beautiful. And she had a DJ booth. What? And he was dropping some seriously good beats. This guy was not cheap.

Shit. Maybe I dressed too nice. His little shorts were super cute and showed a lot of skin, but the button-down was totally too preppy for the people here. There were a lot of tank tops. *I'll unbutton it a little lower when no one's looking, show some more—*

"Yaaasssss! My little red puppy came!"

Puppy? She seemed a little drunk already, but my Gawd did she look stunning. She was in this short, sheer, low cut dress that was somehow both formal and informal and seemed to barely hang on for the ride of adorning that gorgeous body. *She kissed my cheeks.*

"I'm Jasmine, by the way, not sure I told you that."

"Jazz!" A group of girls walked in ranging from chubby to rail skinny. She headed their way for hugs and kisses.

He took in more of the space. She seemed to have … *painted?*, seriously? … right on her wall in huge letters the party's "No Way, Bro!" name. There were a couple of black-shirted guys at her kitchen island serving cocktails which looked as professional as they did. No one looked 21. Didn't she care about the cops?

He felt some pushing on his ass and turned.

"Anyway, Cutie, this is for later." She was shoving a white tank top in his ass pocket. "I want you in my pics." She slapped his back to head off again. "Hope you get laid tonight, Darling!" She stopped. "Wait. Gay or straight?"

"Both." He smiled.

"Ooooooooo. I knew I liked you. Well, either way then, I hope you get that tight little red cherry of yours popped."

She kissed his cheek again and walked away.

All right then.

10:07 PM

They were getting closer to campus. Ryan felt a growing call to acknowledge that world again. So he finally looked at his phone. A dozen texts, three missed calls, one voicemail. All party stuff. And Tracy.

He tapped on her little call symbol.

. . .

Tracy and her girls were walking up the sidewalk toward the House. Her phone buzzed. She looked at it. *Urg!* Answered.

"Uh-huh."

"We're just getting back. I gotta shower and stuff. What time you heading over?"

"I'm here now. Come or not. I don't care."

"You're the one who told me to go—" It was too late. She'd hung up.

Maybe he'd go with the second option, then.

Tracy walked past the line, girls in tow, barely acknowledging the bouncer with, "Hi Chris."

"Madam." He said. Trying to be funny or something. It wasn't. She walked in.

10:14 PM

Scotty lined up to take his shot. He was really good at this. And he knew it. And there was calm to be found in that. A good calm. A worked-for calm. Because you couldn't take it lightly. You couldn't become careless or flippant or just magically "gifted" about it. Then you'd start fucking up. You had to focus on the skill, the craft, allow yourself to feel and tap into the muscle memories.

He pulled back the cue and slid it forward through his fingers gently. The cue ball was set in motion just enough to tap the seven into motion just enough to drop into the side pocket, while letting the cue ball come to rest far enough back to leave a good line toward his next shot.

One step ahead. That's how you played when you were really on your game.

Calm.

It had been a rough day. But a good one. He was happy about the new path he'd embarked on. Happy about his new friends from BLM who surprisingly wanted to come to the party tonight and were upstairs right now as the DJ was getting the dance floor started, hopefully making some new friends of their own. And glad too to be back among his boys at the House. Back in business.

Jared had asked him to come downstairs and play a game. He told his new friends he'd be back in a bit. One had made a joke about taking out his frustrations on some white ass tonight.

Scotty put the three ball into the corner pocket.

"Damn," said Jared with approval.

It felt good to escape a bit. To put the heavy thoughts of the day aside. To just be a college kid again.

He walked around the table to line up his next shot.

This was always a good part of the night. Knowing that big-ass line was forming outside. Knowing this was your place and you could come and go as you pleased. The great expectations of what might happen in the hours to come.

Scotty took a sip of the cheap keg beer in his red solo cup. Parties like this somehow made beer like that taste good.

He bent down. Lined up his shot. Closed his non-dominant eye. And struck the ball.

Another ball in another pocket. But his next move was looking more—

"Whaaaaaat? Black guys aren't good at pool."

He looked up to see the smiling, jesting, wanting-to-be-liked face of a white pledge.

But the pledge lost his smile when he saw Scotty's reaction.

Scotty stood up perfectly straight. He knew his face showed anger. But anger held back. Leashed. The kid looked scared to death. He started apologizing. It was a joke. He was joking.

Scotty's anger was climbing up through him from a lot of different places, but most noticeably right now it was from that most nonchalantly abused place of "Goddamnit,-can't-I-just-play-a-game-of-fucking-pool-with-my-friend-without-my-fucking-skin-color-having-to-be-called-out?!"

The kid was close to him now. He was trying to put a, "We're boys, right?" hand on his arm—though Jared, thankfully, was holding him back—and was saying something about it being "post-racial," his joke, like isn't it good to laugh about racism and how stupid it is, that's all he meant, his face was red.

Scotty was going through the options of his next move.

Let his anger out the simple way? Drop the cue and beat the kid in the face? *Do that and you're the "animal," Scotty.* The lesser being. The black guy starting a fight at the party. Stereotype wins.

Calmly tell him to get the fuck out and that his pledge career is finished here? The kid looked so sincerely sorry. Did that mean anything?

Forgive him?

Tell him he had no right and never would to decide what was "post-racial" and that nothing about our current society was even remotely close to it? Did he want to say that? Did he want to argue with this little fuck who'd ruined his calming moment? Did he want to believe that argument?

Jared's face was firmly watching Scotty's. *He's waiting for my move.*

He wished for a second it was Ryan's face. Ryan and he were closest in the House, even as often as they butted heads.

About a year ago they'd been eating lunch at an off-campus restaurant and some fuck-face, who wasn't black or brown, a couple tables away said the "N" word. Ryan only glanced at Scotty long enough to know he'd heard it. Ryan dropped his burrito. Got up and in the guy's face. Maybe an inch from it. And just said, "Leave." That was it. But his face and his body said the rest. The guy looked at Scotty, then back to Ryan. And then the guy and his friend got up and left. Leaving their burritos on the table.

Scotty was grateful he didn't have to respond to it. More grateful he didn't have to pretend to ignore it. And even more grateful still that when Ryan sat back down he didn't say a word about it.

That's when he knew how close they were.

God, there were a lot of them, weren't there? So many in his "privileged" life. So many little stabs of racism. What a fool he was for dreaming.

He put his cue on the table. And walked toward the open doors to the backyard.

As he did, he heard Jared telling the kid he was out. The kid pleaded more that it had been a joke. He'd been drinking. He was just trying to befriend him with a little laugh.

Scotty didn't feel befriended.

10:21 PM

They were walking up the stairway to Jasmine's apartment.

It was like they were being brought there by some force out of their control. There was a massive party. It was a Thursday night. Their friend was throwing it. They had no choice in the matter but to go.

Kyle couldn't bring himself to tell Tristan what he did today. He wasn't sure if he ever would tell him. He wondered if somehow he might find out. And what then?

Tristan hoped Kyle might get drunk. He didn't want to talk anymore. And he most especially didn't want to talk about that commonest and most mundane of questions: What'd you do today?

Did Kyle's goodness and sweetness and innocence and hope hold him back? Keep the scared little boy alive and well and kissed and coddled?

Would Tristan ever change? Would Kyle be following him like this now up these stairs all the rest of his life to places he didn't really want to go?

He could hear Jasmine's scream over the music before he rounded the corner after Tristan. Once he did, he could see she'd jumped on him in her dress and he was holding her, her legs and arms wrapped around him.

He heard her ask about the bruises.

"Kyle's finally had enough of me."

Tristan always said all good cover stories are based on some truth.

She laughed. She was down. She was kissing Kyle hello now. He smiled back.

To play my part.

That's what we're here for, I guess. To put on face.

For some reason she was handing them tank tops.

Tristan immediately pulled off his shirt and put his on.

Above his ass it said, "... okay, stick it in."

10:33 PM

Sean was just standing there talking to some boys.

Sean was looking good. He always did. Probably smelled good too.

Sean drove a Maserati.

Sean's father drove a Lambo Huracan, black with orange seats. She'd seen it once.

Sean had always liked her.

Sean didn't believe in bros before hoes.

Mom would like Sean.

Sean would do just fine.

When Ryan finally got his un-giving-a-shit-about-her ass here and saw him dancing with her—that should give him enough of a good slap in the face to wake his stupid self up.

She got close.

"Dance with me."

The other guys looked at her like she'd lost her mind.

But it didn't take Sean that long to decide.

"Alright." He took her hand and they headed into the mob.

She lost even more respect for him.

Sean was no Ryan.

10:47 PM

Scotty had taken a couple more shots and was now holding his third. Makers. They had it behind the bar for brothers.

The tiki bar. With the big sign above it. "REMINDER: You MUST be 21 to drink!—By order of the <u>AUTHORITIES</u>." They had to be careful now. Lest privileges be taken away again.

"Are you 21?" Jared asked the 18-year-old girl as he gave her a drink and they walked away. Jared had come out to console him and be bros. And talk about it.

Scotty was looking at the waterslide now. He walked over closer to it. What an absurd mess this thing was. It was even bigger than he thought it would be. Fully blown up, it was two stories high. The air pump that kept it inflated could be heard even through the dueling music—the stuff playing out back and the vibrations coming from the DJ inside the House—if you listened for it. It was already forming a mushy spot people were avoiding in the grass where all the water came down. Scotty figured it would be a little lake by the end of the night. And no one was using it. Why would they? They were dressed for a nighttime party, not a daytime one. It made as little sense as the fact that they'd also blown up their massive float from Floatopia and had it sitting in the backyard. Although, at least with that, quite a few brothers had dreams of taking a girl back to it later for a little cushioned and somewhat private sex, what with the blow up palm trees on it and all.

It was all pretty damned ridiculous.

He remembered he was holding a shot and took it. He remembered he should go find his new friends he'd brought here. He stepped over to the keg line first though, to get one for the road.

10:54 PM

"I could stay a bit longer if you want? Finish reading you my answers."

306 | WILL KANE THOMPSON

It was sweet. Kristi was glad he'd stayed and helped her clean up. It was a big night. All in, nine people had showed. There were lots of dirty dishes. Luke stayed until her place was spotless. He really was a meticulous cleaner.

"I think I'd like to read them by myself," she said, putting a hand on his chest—his heart. And smiling. His heart was beating harder than she'd have expected. Poor thing was so nervous the whole night. "I'm exhausted."

She was. Physically. Emotionally. Everyone stayed so late. Luke had been wringing her heart dry for weeks then pumping it back up again.

"Okay." He kissed her on her cheek. She liked that. Not too much all at once.

She took him to the front door and opened it for him. He grabbed his bookbag and stepped out.

"Thank you. For filling in those blanks for me." She smiled.

He shook his head. "Thank you. For giving me the answers."

She smiled.

He smiled.

He touched her hand. Then headed home.

It took her a long time to close the door.

11:07 PM

The main floor of the House was already so packed that there was no question the brothers had succeeded in throwing the biggest party of the year, thus far. By night's end there was potential it could be the biggest party of the year, period.

Scotty knew the search for his new friends might take a bit. It seemed like it was taking ten minutes just to get across the kitchen.

People were already making such a mess. The floor was sticky beneath his feet in spots. People were rude and shoving. He had to shove back to get through. There was real cigarette smoke in the air in addition to vape fumes.

He got to the great room where the DJ was spinning. The floor was bouncing. The lights were dimmer and the strobes shot around the space like spotlights from police helicopters.

What the hell was he doing here?

He pushed into the pack. This pack he'd somehow ended up a part of. His body began involuntarily moving a bit with the beats. How could it not?—you could feel the vibrations of the speakers as much as hear them.

He looked out over this sea of people and thought he might never find his new friends.

11:20 PM

Jesus, are you kidding me? Look at these losers coming up on the line. What are they 28, 29? One of them has totally busted 30. This bouncing shit is the shit.

Oh fuck, speaking of bouncing.

"Hello, ladies." You can definitely come in. Damn, girls. Ummm. Wait is that girl even a freshman? She is totally still in high school. I definitely need to go find that later. Totally missing high school pussy already.

Okay, here we go. Jesus, look at these guys. They even tried to dress young. It's so not working. You're old. You had your chance. You obviously blew it. Get the hell—

"Hey bro."

He bro'd me.

My mouth's agape. That's perfect. Hold it there. Don't say anything. Just stare at them. Oh my God, this is great. Look how nervous they just got. Hold it. Don't laugh.

Fuck. It's too painful. I'm gonna laugh. Break this.

"You guys grad students or something?"

"No bro, we're alums. Clemson chapter."

Mistake!

"Oh yeah?" I hold out my hand. The dude goes to shake it, but curveball! "Secret handshake, bro."

Look at his face. Ahhhhhhh! Why isn't someone filming this? He has no clue whether or not we have a stupid fucking secret handshake. The 30-year-old's hand goes into his pocket and comes back out to shake mine. There's something in there, it's not …

Oh my God it is!!! It's money! It's perfectly folded into a little square too. He actually did this ahead of time. Damn it's a hundred. Keeping that.

"Yeah. You guys gotta go."

"Come on dude, we're brothers."

"No. No you're not. Get the fuck out of here before I call some actual brothers out here."

"Then give me my cash back." Now he's all hard. Shoulders raised a bit, eyebrows narrowed. Does he have any clue how fast there'll be 50 drunk guys out here to pummel his old ass into the front lawn?

"Nope. Douche tax."

He really wants to hit me.

"Hey! Everybody! I'd like to let you in the party but I can't till these old guys leave."

That did it. Insults and jeers were being hurled at will from the entire line. Finally they broke and beat it.

Huh. Kinda fun actually. And I made a hundred bucks!

Fraternity life rocks.

12:02 AM

Tracy took an opportunity while she and Sean were dancing again to run her hands down his stomach. They'd had a couple drinks, talked a bit, returned to the floor. Good. Rock solid. He'll do.

12:21 AM

Scotty had grabbed another shot from the indoor bar. He'd yet to find his new friends. Maybe they'd left. Probably they had. How could they want to hang out with so many faces thought to be white, right now?

Scotty stopped pushing through and stood there letting the ebb and pull of the mass move him with it.

Why the fuck am I here?, started to become a much bigger question. It wasn't just this party tonight. It wasn't just this fraternity, this university, ROTC.

He felt overwhelmed with the feeling that his life wasn't his own. He looked at all these different faces around him and all the thoughts from Coates's *Between the World and Me* rushed through his mind, these new friends, these words.

What the fuck are we doing here? We, all of us. The question kept growing. Someone spilt beer on his back. He thought about all the "plunder" that led to this. *Plunder.*

He thought about history. *Ours. Mine?* He needed to pee, but he didn't want to move. He wanted to stand right here and think these thoughts. Where his mind was going felt good. Felt like thoughts he finally needed to confront. The physical beating of the music on his body, beating the thoughts in more deeply.

The plunder of our bodies. The lives this country had been built upon. Lives stolen from their bodies. The labor they had given. The money they were worth. He looked at the bodies around him. Different shades. "Colors."

And with the plunder of Africa, the plunder of this country. The Native Americans we killed off. Their land we stole. The Mexicans we killed off. Their land we stole. All for what, that Manifest Destiny? What have we built here?

He got shoved harder this time. The dancers were annoyed with his immovable presence. Anger seemed to be behind the shoves now.

What, in God's name, as they said it was, was the point of America's Manifest Destiny? Why did we think we had the right to do all this? Steal all this land, commit genocide on the people who inhabited this place, the Native Americans who once lived on this very land this frat now "owns," steal all these bodies of millions of humans from halfway around the world to bring here and work its soil to bring us what? *This?*

What fools to believe this more valuable than what we replaced.

He was looking at a girl dancing by him. She was looking at him. She was so drunk her eyes seemed empty. No humanity behind them. Her body an empty shell.

He wondered how his eyes looked. He really did have to pee.

12:32 AM

Jasmine had been busy gathering evidence for a while now and continuing to act as drunk as she could around everyone. The party was a success. It was absolutely packed and mostly with randoms. There would be plenty of pictures and stories from plenty of sources to corroborate what she would send to the Florida news outlets from her new fake account.

She'd found a couple kids snorting coke in one of her bathrooms (thankfully she'd kept her bedroom suite locked). She put on her best mock sexy voice—which she knew was damn good—and encouraged one to do a line off the other's cleavage while she got a pic (no faces, don't worry! She just thought it was hot). It might feel a little cliché, but we're talking local Florida news here. To the grandma and grandpa voters of this state pics like this would be nothing short of cataclysmic. And the old men would enjoy having to keep talking about and looking at that young cleavage.

When she got back to the living room there were three lesbians (or just girls letting loose) standing on her coffee table making out. Perfect backdrop. It was time for the main event.

She went around gathering everyone for the tank top shoot. She grabbed Jenny as prearranged and gave her her phone to take the pics. She made sure to put on her drunk face.

As she got everyone gathered, Tristan and Kyle by her, she pulled up her dress over her head to get everyone in the right mood. Then pulled on her own tank. No pants. The tank was just long enough and just short enough.

And then the poses. Girls kissing on the coffee table behind them. She'd tried to get Tristan and Kyle to kiss but there was resistance for some reason. She got one guy to moon the camera for a shot.

"More, more! Keep 'em coming!" she yelled to Jenny.

She wanted lots to choose from. She needed the most raucous. The most lewd. The most ... sinful. *Ha!* The Florida preachers would have a field day. And she also needed plenty of good takes of herself to choose from, of course.

Everyone talked about what incredible children Senator Carlyle had raised. Everyone knew it because that's precisely what Daddy's press people wanted them to know. Over and over she heard news presenters and even regular people who noticed her on the street regurgitating verbatim lines the press team had cultivated, focus-grouped, marketed. Daddy gobbled up the Family Values Voters by the hundreds of thousands in part because of the Great Father image he portrayed with her help.

A senator's daughter knows when cameras come out at parties. Has developed a sixth sense for them. Turns her face just so. Tosses aside a beer cup or joint. Knows, has had drilled into her, the all-damning power of the photo.

And this with Daddy's immigration bill coming up. To be his greatest achievement thus far. Bipartisan. Massive overhaul. Ingenious compromises. Illegals gone, if only in name. And all just the first massive step toward locking in Latino and Arabic and all the new citizen votes and Daddy's ultimate path to greater things.

He'd do anything and everything to make her stop the flow of damage. She'd have him in her hands.

She'd have him create a trust for Mom so that he could never threaten her again, financially.

And, of course, she'd let him know about the bigger guns she held. She'd send him a peek. A photo of Great Grandpa Teddy near the end of his life still toiling away in the fields, his body covered in the black of the oil. And copies of some, though certainly not all, of the documents.

She'd found all of it from Grandma before she died. The myth Daddy had spun was that Great Granddaddy Teddy started as young laborer on the oil fields of Pennsylvania. Poor and hardworking. Those pictures, from his youth, were readily made available to the press. But then, the lie is added to the foundation of truth. Then Great Granddaddy mustered up enough funds for his own speck of land in the oil patch and got friends to help him dig his first well out of the kindness of their hearts and the rest, as they say, is history. That's where all the money came from, the press was told, and they ate it up. American Dream. Pick yourself up by your bootstraps. The stuff that always works.

"What a yarn!" Grandma had said. "Grandpa Teddy started out as a laborer and ended up dead as one too. He died worth less than the dried oil stuck on his skin. Should of scraped it off of him, seen what we could get for it." She laughed. That son of hers sure could tell a story. Always had been good at it. Since he was just a boy. The stories he told!

She'd found the death certificate along with other court records for failure to make payments, tax records and the like. Poor as the dirt with the oil sucked out of it. She had all the evidence she needed to puncture that foundational myth of Daddy's, the one so many others were built upon.

The one-two punch of her little black op was brilliant. The first hit, in addition to hurting Daddy just enough to seriously grab his attention, also freed her from the Good-Girl-cashmere-sweater-with-golden-cross-necklace straightjacket he'd kept her in, in front of cameras, her entire life. Yes, it was risky, since his plan was to get rid of Mom by exposing infidelity. So it was possible he could spin her new bad-girl-ness into that storyline and be rid of them both at once. But not after how often he'd spoken of her in public as his pride and joy, and most certainly not when she'd be his only remaining personal connection to the all-important Latino vote. And besides, he wouldn't risk a thing with the second punch—the one that really landed where the sun don't shine.

Stay. In. Line. Daddy.

Ha! That was the note she'd clipped to the documents of the second punch before sliding them into their classic manila bitch-you-about-to-get-blackmailed envelope.

So she knew how safe she was. That was a myth that could never be breached.

For from where, Daddy, from where oh where had all that money come?

Oh, here! She threw an arm around Tristan and Kyle both and got them each to kiss a side of her face. *That'll be a cute one.*

12:59 AM

Scotty walked up the stairs to find a bathroom on the second floor. The stairs were wet and slippery.

He went to one of the "secret" bathrooms. You had to go into one of the brother's rooms to get to it.

But when he got to it, Ryan's girlfriend had taken over the place with three topless girls and Sean and Matt, who were for some reason painting their stomachs.

"Scotty, we're busy here." Tracy said.

"I gotta pee."

"Pee out the window."

Scotty kept staring. Two of the girls had bras on. One didn't. She held eyes with Scotty as his dropped again to her boobs. She didn't seem to mind. It was like she held them there for him to look. Her nipples were hard with the open air.

"Wait, maybe you can help." Tracy held a paint jar up to the skin of his arm. Then another one. "Crap. Too dark. Never mind."

Scotty turned around and went to the window. Opened it. Unzipped. Pulled out. Checked the immediate area below. Clear enough. And finally let out his piss.

"Where's big Ry?"

"Don't give a fuck."

"Okay."

He thought someone from down below would scream at him. But no one noticed. They were all staring a few windows over. Off the little balcony the waterslide came up to. And yelling that way. As Miles, standing on the balcony was pulling off his remaining clothes and throwing them into the crowd like a rock star.

Scotty laughed, making little waves in his stream.

1:03 AM

Kyle could make out Tristan's shape standing on the balcony, his body, his hair, his presence, even through the glass with the light inside reflecting back mostly an image of himself. There were lots of people on the balcony, but Tristan wasn't with them. His back was to them. He was looking off. Toward the frat. To a place, to thoughts, Kyle knew too well.

The party had gotten to that point where it was so crowded that you could stand in the middle of it all alone. Where people were so drunk, and you were too, probably, that you no longer had to make small talk. You could just stand there and think in this altered, clearer, more messed up state.

Sara was here, he'd seen her, she was having fun, forgetting her many burdens. Some of the people from the OC were here, freshened up from the tents and the long day's sun on The Commons. The ginger boy from the library was here. Did Tristan invite him? Would he ask for a three-way as a first step in their separation? Or would he just jump straight into bed with his next fling in a long list of them yet to come that would never fulfill his soul?

Kyle laughed a little. How perfect. This. Tristan out in the dark with his dark thoughts. Kyle in the light with all the people. A room full of sexual and mind-altering distraction. *I knowing him so well, I see him even if just a dark shape through this nearly mirrored glass.*

But he is not mine.

Is he?

His back is to me too.

He is not mine.

1:06 AM

Scotty climbed out the window onto the balcony with Miles, who was now just in his boxer briefs, and a girl in a soaking wet guy's t-shirt and boxers covered in bits of grass and sand.

Scotty cheered with the rest as Miles made his grand finale and pulled off the briefs. He kicked them off his foot to the crowd like a pole dancer, but had to grab Scotty as he did as he almost slipped off the balcony. The "railing" was only a decorative one-footer.

Then Miles threw open his arms to the world he was about to conquer and sort of cannonballed himself onto the slide, shouting something about, "Back in business, bitches!" all the way down till he face-planted in the mud.

The crowd went wild.

And Scotty knew what he had to do. What he really, really wanted to do.

He started unbuttoning his shirt. The crowd cheered again. His name was yelled. The wet t-shirt and boxers girl started helping him.

Off went his shirt and into the crowd. Off the shoes. Off the pants. And then, free as maybe he'd ever felt doing anything in his life, off with the undies.

He stood there like Miles had before. Gave a little dance move. Miles yelled up something about his boy. The breeze on his cock and balls. All of campus seemingly his. The love of the crowd.

Home among these people. Love among them.

Could he pull off the other layers too and give them back?

Like Baldwin had said? "White people invented it ... your invention reveals you ... I give you your problem back."

Here you go, white people. You can have your layers back now. I don't want them anymore.

It's time you deal with the problems your people created and you've richly benefited from.

Take them back, I'm done with them. You carry their burden for a while. See how you like it.

Ha. As if they could come off so easily.

You're drunk, Scotty.

You drunk Philosopher King.

And these, my people before me.

Ha.

For some reason—just because it felt right—he turned around.

And like that trust game in elementary school where you fall back into a friend's arms, he just let himself go.

It was the biggest fall of his life because it wasn't just from standing to flat, it was even a further arc down to the plastic of the wet slide that slapped his back and the world turned upsidedown along the way and he slid and slid to cheers, his body getting soaked, and it slapped again into the squishiness of the slushy sand into which he landed.

Miles mounted him before he could protest. Both of them covered in sand and grass. Miles screaming in triumph.

Their sand-covered skin. Their naked bodies. Miles's cock and balls on his stomach.

Another crash of bodies and skin as the boxers girl landed on them too. She'd shed the shirt. She grabbed onto Miles's head to steady herself as she straddled his shoulders, her boobs resting atop his messy hair. Conquering them both. All the weight of them on Scotty's stomach, but he didn't care.

Scotty let his head fall back to the slushy sand and looked up to the night sky.

Chill the fuck out, Scotty.

Take the rest of the night off, huh?

Just fucking be.

1:11 AM

Ryan was freshly showered and dressed and looking good and standing on the sidewalk outside his fraternity house and stopped.

He was just standing there. Unsure why he'd brought himself to this point. Unsure if he should continue.

"Again!" he heard himself yell in his memory. Up the bleachers. Drop and do another set of pushups. Push yourself, push your platoon, finish the mission. The war is coming.

He thought about Bret. About Bill. About his family in the Upstate. About Tristan. About The Commons. About the division of the coming election. His mission.

His whole life.

Ever since that day on the promenade.

He has been at war.

A hidden war.

And because he'd seen it in himself, because he'd come to know it so intimately, he could see it in others too. In all the countless factions around him. Dividing and dividing more, like his equations.

He heard Professor Golding's words again. "The seeds of this war are all planted. Like a million little bombs just waiting to be lit."

And instead of preparing, we're throwing a party.

He looked at the two parties on either side of the street before him. He looked at the frat he'd given so much of his life to lately.

His girlfriend inside waiting for him with another worthless distraction.

The two Ryans were standing there at once. And they wanted to walk in such different directions that it just stopped him. He couldn't move.

The question came to him as it had so often before. The hardest question of his life. Or maybe, rather, the question that made his life so hard.

"Will Dad—"

"Don't be scared. It's just a party. They won't bite. Unless you want them too." He laughed at his own joke.

But it wasn't a joke because it wasn't funny. And it wasn't his own because people who weren't funny had said some line like that millions of times before and for some reason would keep saying it a million more.

It was Officer Chubs. He'd walked up to Ryan on the sidewalk. And Ryan couldn't bring himself to allow the man to be worthy of a response.

He just stared at him.

The man was so blind.

2:00 AM

Ryan. What was he doing right now in that house? Holding some freshman's legs up in the air for his first keg stand? Waiting, mouth open, at the base of some ridiculous ice luge for the nicely chilled vodka to make its way to his tongue? Fucking Tracy?

It looked fun down there.

It was fun here.

But that wasn't enough anymore.

Tristan thought about their drive down together. Freshman year. Ryan had sold his old car and planned to buy his truck here, cheaper than New York. So they moved down together in Tristan's Jeep, trailer attached.

So many memories of where they'd been together. And so many hopes, at least in Tristan's mind then, for the memories they'd now build together in this new adventure: college.

Where had it gone so wrong?

These years gone now. *We'll never get them back. The chance of them?*

I'm sorry.

Okay?

I'm so sorry, Ryan.

"Sometimes I think ..."

He turned around to see Kyle standing there. He hadn't noticed him step out to the balcony. He knew his own eyes betrayed his thoughts. He knew Kyle must have been watching him staring at the frat for who knows how long.

"... it's him you love."

"And no one else will ever come close."

And there it was in his big Persian eyes. The pain. The unforgivable pain. The pain Tristan had so feared causing his innocent soul.

He wanted to reach out to him. To hold him tight. To kiss the top of his head like before on their roof.

But he couldn't.

Kyle turned and walked back into the party.

2:04 AM

Luke was praying. His knees on the floor. His hands folded. His head resting on them. His elbows indenting the still perfectly made bed.

He just kept saying, "Please."

It was the only word he could think of right now. And God knew what he wanted. All that was left was to beg.

He didn't look up. Just knew it was there. Felt its presence.

The photo he'd brought to the memorial was back on his bureau. Looking at him. Listening.

Life had been taken away from Caitlyn.

But given, still, to him.

And he had to deserve that. To do something to deserve it.

322 | WILL KANE THOMPSON

Please. Please. Please. God.
Help me to grasp my Destiny.

2:09 AM

Finally, I am here.

In this place I have so long yearned to be without even knowing what it was I sought. It was just—Freedom. Freedom to be who I want to be. Who I am in my soul. Who I've always really been, but have only just begun to discover.

That's what's happening here in college. After so long living in someone else's world, being the person someone else—my parents, my high school, all the people who tell us what God wants—wanted me to be, here, away from all that, in this oasis of youth, in this center of my universe for these next few years to come, I am finally meeting myself.

And I really like who I am.

That's new. And it makes me want to cry. Both sad and happy tears. Sad for how long I didn't like the "me" I was. For how much of my life I wasted not being me. And happy. So, so happy that I've finally found *me*.

The tears do come a little. And I don't wipe them away. I let them dry there around my eyes. No one can see in the dark, right? In the sporadic strobes. And we're all too busy dancing. And maybe it's the drugs anyway.

These people around me. Their skin touching mine. The music beating through my soul.

How I wish I could grab hold of this moment and keep it forever. Not just what I, we, would look like if someone filmed us. I wouldn't even want to see that. It's what it *feels* like that I want to remember. And these thoughts in my mind right now.

And this confidence I've found. To knock my way around and thru these bodies and make it all the way in here, to the center of this dancing mass.

Us. We. All moving together to the same beats. A mass of bodies moving as if some spiritual choreographer planned all our steps, made us practice until this perfection. But it is perfect in its spontaneity. In its randomness. In its absence of any choreographer to tell us what to do.

Their skin is so beautiful in the strobe lights. Mine too, even. My love/hate affair with my skin, with these bodies we are forced to inhabit.

Tonight it's love. Because the inside parts are finally starting to feel right.

Because, Jesus, she's gorgeous. I'm moving closer. Her moves. Her confidence. The line of her collarbone is so stunning. Isn't that crazy? What is it in us that makes us think the way skin and bone have formed together can be beautiful or ugly? Jesus, this guy's abs who's dancing with her. What is that an eight-pack? How many hours a week is he in the gym?

All of these people. This other girl who just started dancing with me. Even this guy's hands I see raised in the distance. All of us together. It feels like we're one. One.

God, I wish I could capture these thoughts, these feelings, the way my body feels around my soul right now, and hold onto them forever. To know them, briefly, again as I lay dying in old age and remember that I lived.

I touch the girl's torso from behind and bring her closer. Her tummy exposed, my skin on hers. We sync our rhythm. A guy bumps into me or I into him and we don't care. I half-trip on something on the floor, but I just kick it away.

I can't remember the last time I felt this good.

I know who I am now.

I know the life I want to live.

Life.

Look at all of us. Everyone so free. Everyone themselves. Everyone one.

Living. Really, truly living.

That's what we're doing tonight.

Carpe fucking diem.

Patriots: Book Two
Sneak Peak Chapter

Friday
October, 21st

3:57 AM

He passed the lights of the 27 interchange and with them the last light in the sky from the outskirts of Miami and his eyes readjusted to the dark of the long stretch of I-75, "Alligator Alley," ahead. Terry finally took a sip of his espresso. It wasn't very good. He'd had to do this before. No time to grind new beans. Hot water over used grounds. It was in that old movie, *Kramer vs. Kramer*. Terry felt his life was more of a mess than that guy's though.

It was dark and silent now on the road. He flipped on his brights. The speedometer passed 100. The dark silence reminded him of Cho. He hadn't thought about Cho—really thought about him—in years.

Cho was why his ASAC had called this morning and wanted him out there. Terry's first significant lead in the Bureau—the Virginia Tech assist—

interviewing the students and professors who knew the shooter. Because of Tech, he had more experience with what this campus might be going through right now than probably any other agent in Florida. If the reports were accurate.

Terry first figured the likelihood high that some bullshit campus cop had called something a bomb when it wasn't, and now flying toward FSCU, like Terry, were a bomb squad, a Victims Assist. team, and local and state law enforcement from all over Southern Florida, to add to the emergency responders and campus police already there—the proverbial clusterfuck—all for no reason.

But as he made his espresso, subsequent reports came: a lot of kids hurt and at least three confirmed deaths already. This was probably the real deal. And if Terry could get the right lead, he'd soon be on the hunt for another Cho. But this one, still active.

The target was a massive college party. Hints of Columbine. Hints of Tech. Hints of the "loner," "loser" taking out his revenge on those who'd denied him socially. But Terry knew to keep his presumptions in a tightly sealed box. After all, the Columbine killers turned out to be not quite the "loner," "losers" everyone first thought they were. These things were messy. And Terry knew from his Tech interviews, more deeply even than what he'd learned at Quantico, just how messy the mind of a young killer could be. If it was a student who did this?

He looked out into the dark and thought about the secluded campus on the other side of the Everglades. The world these students knew, would be drastically changing now. Law enforcement was instituting a campus-wide lockdown. The assumption was whoever did this was still at large. There could be other devices. The killer could be armed. There could be multiple accomplices.

The news media would be descending too. Begging the kids for cell phone footage of the party. Cameras would be forced into any face looking like a student's. "Do you have any idea who would do this?" "Do you know someone who died?" "Do your parents know you're okay?" "Are you scared?" Whatever the question, always asking the same thing: *would you cry for me, right now, on camera, please?*

Has anything changed? Had FSCU implemented any of the recommendations in the aftermath of Tech? Were warning signs addressed at all or just added to another bureaucratic trash heap into which Terry would now wade, find them, and wish someone had cared to notice them before, when maybe these deaths could have been prevented?

That's how Terry's feelings about Tech ended up, and that's where they were still stuck now as he dug them up again. *Seung-Hui Cho had pointed his semiautomatic weapons and killed 32 students while we did nothing to stop him. And afterwards, I interviewed victims and wrote reports about them.*

That's what we did. Cho took himself out. He did our job for us.

But this student—if it was a student—or if it's more than one—he or they are still at large. Maybe this time we can stop them from doing more harm. Maybe this time we're coming in between Cho's first two victims in West AJ and his remaining thirty in Norris Hall and we can save these last ones.

His phone had said 1:18 to the campus. At 121 miles per hour, maybe he could cut that in half.

There shouldn't be any gators on the road with the fences. But Terry kept vigilant for the reflecting eyes of a panther. He'd hate to kill one of them. People were scared of them. But they were the endangered ones.

That seemed like most of Terry's job right there: knowing the right enemy to fear.

Thank You

Dear Reader:

Thank you for reading my crazy book. I hope you've enjoyed it.

This book has been published independently by a small team of true believers. If you enjoyed reading it—or, you know what, even if you didn't—please post your thoughts about the book online. We need all the word of mouth we can get to get this story out there.

Thank you again!

Will

 # @ .com

patriotsthenovel

Acknowledgements

Family & Friends

First and foremost, I thank my parents, Nancy and Ken, for your constant support of my crazy dreams. You don't agree with me politically, don't like the subject matter I write about, but still believe in my passion and want to help me reach my destiny. That's pretty amazing.

Patriots would not exist without Andrew Schneider. You believed enough in this story, when it was just a TV script I'd written in film school, to give countless hours of your time to co-produce and co-direct a pitch trailer with me to try to get the story some notice. After it didn't go as a series, and I decided to write it as a novel, you sat with me in that bar in Brooklyn and told me that for the first time since you'd known me, you believed I'd finally put myself into position to write the story that would launch my writing career – *my way* – *if, if, if* only I gave it everything I had. I think I have and I hope I've done you proud. You have been one of the closest friends in my life and probably the best friend my writing has ever had.

Tesha Crawford. My God, Girl. What would I do without you? You have been a steadfast supporter of my writing—even when you had some pretty harsh notes to give—and, equally important, a steadfast uplifter of my emotional state. My life is grander because you are in it and my writing is stronger for hope of impressing you.

Nicole Riegel. You said it. I think, actually, the first note you gave on the pilot was, "I think this is a novel." The note hit so hard because I knew it was true. Your words and support continue to give me the courage to keep trying.

Katie Sweeney. You poor thing. You read nearly everything in the early years of my writing. That first screenplay I ever wrote. Bits of the first rambling book. And now this rambling book. You have always been a champion and, most importantly, 100% honest.

My brother and sister-in-law, Jake and Steph; my uncle and aunt, Gary and Peggy, have given tremendous financial support to this project and your belief in me has provided an even greater value in encouragement.

My Mimi, Peggy Kane, also could not be further from me on the political spectrum, and doesn't quite understand what the heck I'm writing about, but supports me still.

My cousin, Emma Bigelow, has been a huge help in the schwag department, in addition to her and my cousin-in-law Kiwan's love for the story.

Professors

Thank you to probably the greatest professor I'll ever have, UCLA's Howard Suber. You said the best protagonists get pushed by Fate until they reach that life-defining moment in which they take up the reins of their own lives to pursue their Destinies. Dear God, Howard, I hope that's what I've done here. Thank you for sharing your lifetime of study on what makes for a good story and a good life.

Richard Walter and Hal Ackerman, thank you for bringing me into the greatest writing adventure of my life, prior to this one—the wonderful years I spent as a student in UCLA's MFA in Screenwriting program. My life is far richer because of you, and my writing is hopefully, a bit better too.

Linda Voorhees, thank you for allowing me to experiment with Patriots in your workshop and for all your great notes and encouragement. I hope President Voorhees will become a character worthy of homage to you in the coming books. I can only beg your forgiveness for the ellipses.

William Lasser, at Clemson University, thank you for helping inspire my love of politics and your recent support of the novel.

Chris Morgan, at St. Mary's High School, thank you for helping inspire my love of writing and your encouragement of this project as well.

Students

A huge thank you to all the students who participated in the focus groups I conducted on early drafts of the novel—especially those at my *alma mater* Clemson and the university that has been a part of this story from day one, Virginia Tech.

My deepest gratitude among these students is for Mary Graw and Alaina Garren at Virigina Tech, who loved the novel so much they offered to take a stab at the cover design. I, in turn, loved their design so much, I brought them aboard the team to design not only the cover, but much of the marketing campaign. I am so grateful for how organic you have made this process—college students telling other college students about their love for a novel about college students—that's pretty sweet. I am also so grateful to Caroline Rabic who's come aboard as well to draw all the illustrations for the campaign.

Early Readers & Editors

In addition to those already mentioned, I am so grateful to: Shaina Zamaitis, Daniel Hogan, Eric Malinowski, Shay Brown, James Queen, Madison Maddox, Harold Hyte, Chase Long, Allison McNeill Brown, Valerie Carullo, Melanie and Bob Graw for their feedback.

Constance Renfrow and Eliza Kirby worked on the novel as freelance editor and copyeditor, respectively. I greatly appreciate of all your superb notes and catches and all of your thoughts—even the ones I didn't go with. You were both an immense help. The book is stronger because of you.

Kickstarters

A special thanks to the major donors at the FSCU ROTC Sand Tiger Battalion, Battalion Commander level: Ken Thompson, Jake & Steph Thompson and Gary & Peggy Thompson. At the Company Commander level: Nancy Thompson, Julie Ross, and Melanie and Bob Graw. At the Platoon Leader level: Pam Beziat, Marilynne Martin Bishop, John Zois, Jeff Eklund, Emma & Kiwan Bigelow, Tesha Crawford, Scott Sullivan, Elizabeth & Ken Hageman, Josephine Green & Johnny Zhang, Annette Graw, Meredith Rothman, Chris & Kristen Venuti, and Allison McNeill Brown. Thanks also to all the other members of our battalion: Connie Smyser, Jennifer Bucholtz, Tamlin Hall, Katie Sweeney, Marette Wood, Hieu Tran, Carole Graw, Even Beziat, James Queen, Wes Smyser, Jeff Ason, Mary Cunningham, Diane Darcey, Megan Green, Jill Isherwood, Michael Bright, Shaina Zamaitis, Rob Kotecki, Jimmy Pomerantz and the anonymous donors.

Pitch Trailer

Thank you to the whole cast and crew who worked on the Trailer. It was such a blast and has definitely helped propel this story forward.

Colleges & Universities

Thank you to all the college campuses around the country where I spent time writing bits of this story and finding inspiration: UCLA, Clemson, Virginia Tech, and Florida Gulf Coast University, foremost; as well as, University of Florida, University of South Florida, University of Central Florida, UNC Chapel Hill, UVA, UMD, JHU, St. John's College, UT Knoxville, UNLV, Pepperdine, and University of Arizona.

Thank you, thank you, thank you, all.